I0819662

The Shippers

ALSO BY KATHERINE CENTER

The Love Haters

The Rom-Commers

Hello Stranger

The Bodyguard

What You Wish For

Things You Save in a Fire

How to Walk Away

Happiness for Beginners

The Lost Husband

Get Lucky

Everyone Is Beautiful

The Bright Side of Disaster

The

Shippers

KATHERINE CENTER

ST. MARTIN'S PRESS
NEW YORK

First published in the United States by St. Martin's Press, an imprint of St. Martin's Publishing Group

EU Representative: Macmillan Publishers Ireland Ltd, 1st Floor, The Liffey Trust Centre, 117–126 Sheriff Street Upper, Dublin 1, D01 YC43

www.stmartins.com

Designed by Devan Norman

Endpaper ocean illustration © Woeng Studio/Shutterstock

The Library of Congress Cataloging-in-Publication Data is available upon request.

ISBN 978-1-250-40805-1 (hardcover)
ISBN 978-1-250-40806-8 (ebook)

First Edition: 2026

10 9 8 7 6 5 4 3 2 1

This book is for anyone who
could really use a hug right now.

Our real poems are already in us
and all we can do is dig.

JONATHAN GALASSI

Author's Note

SPOILER: This book *will* end well.

People will struggle but grow. Folks will change for the better. And the two central characters, the cuties you're about to meet, will, after many shenanigans, fall madly in love.

But . . .

Is that a spoiler, though?

My big sister hates spoilers. She will throw her hands out and shout "No spoilers!" when I tell her about books I'm reading. For her, not knowing what's going to happen is the biggest part of what pulls her through the story.

But there must be different kinds of readers in the world.

I, myself, *hate* not knowing what's going to happen at the end. I hate it so much, in fact, that if I don't know how a story ends, I will google it beforehand. And I'll be honest—mostly these days, especially since the pandemic, I only want happy endings.

I only want a story that gives me something that matters to look forward to.

I can't remember the last time I voluntarily signed up to read something I knew in advance would feed my heart through a meat grinder.

I want to feel something, yes. I want to feel *all the things*, in fact—including surprise. I want the details of a story to be endlessly surprising. My greatest hope when I start reading a new story is that it will take my heart on a Tilt-A-Whirl carnival ride of every single possible emotion along the way. But—and this is essential—by the end . . . I want us all to be okay.

Better than okay, if possible.

So for me, as a reader, getting the "spoiler" that the main characters in a love story will end up together just makes me want to read the story *more*.

Maybe it's the *opposite* of a spoiler.

What would that even be called?

An *enhancer*, maybe?

I think those of us who love love stories are junkies for that joyful, blissed-out feeling of anticipating the happily ever after that's a guarantee of the genre.

All genres have their guarantees, by the way: Sleuths will solve the mystery, thriller heroes will defuse the bomb in the nick of time, superheroes will vanquish the villains at last. Part of what we like about the genres we like is the anticipation of those guarantees. We like to see the mystery solved, and the hero triumphant, and the villains vanquished. It feels good.

Nothing wrong with feeling good, right?

I suspect people who really love literary fiction have a higher tolerance for the feeling of having no idea where a story is headed. Maybe they even *like* that feeling? That's fine. That's cool. It takes all kinds of readers to make the world go round.

I'm just here to talk about love stories.

Because here, once again, is another installment in my infinite series, "Why Love Stories Are Criminally Underrated."

In an interview recently I got asked, "Why do you write love stories?"

And my answer was, "Why would I write anything else?"

What better thing is there to write about than love? Love's the best thing humans ever invented. It's our crowning achievement as a species.

What more beautiful, glorious life could I possibly create for myself than one built on studying, reading, obsessing over, and writing love stories?

My whole job is to bring more love into people's lives. And by extension into the world. A world that, to be honest, could be thriving a bit more in the love arena.

And it's hardly "a job," either. It's just my life. It's just what I do all day: think about love, and stories—and how to do justice to them both.

How sublime.

People say to find your *why*—and that's mine: I believe in every cell of my body that *love is good for you*.

I believe that helping us all, myself included, open up our battle-scarred hearts and let in more connection is the most important thing I could possibly do with my time here on this earth.

I've argued elsewhere (see my author's notes for my last four books) that love is the best kind of therapy. That love stories are good for the soul. That love stories can save the world.

All true.

But here's another great thing to add to the list: Love is good for *your health*.

For real. Google it!

Falling in love bolsters your immune system. Love soothes anxiety, prevents colds, mitigates depression, lessens pain, and promotes healing. New studies on the biochemistry of love show that experiencing loving feelings lowers stress. It counteracts the production of cortisol in the body, and it strengthens the vagus nerve—which calms and regulates mood, heart rate, digestion, and inflammation.

This isn't just some half-true nonsense that floated through my Instagram feed, by the way. I looked up the studies! This is real.

You can add "reading romance novels in the bubble bath" to your self-care list, along with yoga, and laughter, and balancing your circadian rhythm.

I'm always amazed at the number of people who come through my signing lines when I'm on book tour and tell me that they found my books during a brutally hard time in their lives: as they recovered from surgery, or while their mother was sick, or after a divorce.

Maybe they'd heard my books were funny, and they needed some laughs—or that my books were page-turning, or hopeful, or uplifting. But I can't help but think part of it—maybe the biggest part of it—is that my stories, at their cores, are love stories. And we all know, deep down, from the day we're born, that love is nourishing.

We need love to flourish—like we need air, and food, and water.

There are all kinds of ways to micro-dose love into our lives, of course—whether it's going on walks with friends, or romping around with kids, or snuggling with pets.

But why micro-dose? Let's macro-dose!

More is more when it comes to love. And that's where love stories come in. Because stories exist to make us feel things.

A really well-done story of any kind makes you believe it's real. The best stories make you forget you're reading at all—and the boundaries between you and the characters dissolve. You empathize so hard that you step into the shoes—even climb into the skin—of those people. Their story becomes your story. It's happening all around you—and *to you*.

There are studies on what happens to our bodies when we listen to stories: We synchronize with the storyteller's words. Our brainwaves start to move at the same rhythm. Our breathing and heart rates sync up. The same for when we read stories on the page: Our brains sync up with the words. We react to what's happening as if it's real. Our heart rates change. Our breathing shifts. Our brains release actual chemicals.

These are physiological changes in our bodies. *Biochemical changes.*

And if it's a love story? If it's a *romance*? Even better.

Because now you're syncing up with many kinds of emotions—but the main ones, the big ones, are *positive*. You're syncing up with joy, and kindness, and admiration—and you're experiencing genuine human connection.

Well-done love stories give you the feeling of being in love. Your brain makes it real—and shifts your biochemistry in warm, connected, healthy directions. You don't have to be a scientist to know that. You don't need a study. If you're a romance reader, this is old news.

That's not a spoiler, either. That's an enhancer.

There's a reason we love reading love stories. They're *good for us.*

Don't let anyone ridicule you away from bringing all the love into your life that you can. In every possible way.

It's funny: One of the big lessons that the main characters in love stories learn over and over, story after story, is to choose love over fear.

And that's what you're doing right now, with this book. You're your own main character, cultivating love in your own life—and by extension, the world.

Thank you for doing that.

Let's all just keep doing that.

There's a phrase that pops into my head a lot: *If anything can save us, it's love.*

I don't know all the answers. But I feel like we could use a lot more love in the world. If you're reading this, maybe you feel that way, too. And I'm so happy that you're here. And that I'm here. And that we're all here together. Standing up for love.

One

MRS. RICHMOND'S WEDDING gown was itchy, for one thing.

The kind of itchy that eclipses everything else.

And there was no way to get out of it.

And that was nobody's fault but my own.

The problem was: I was marrying her son, Pearce—my college boyfriend and fellow math major—at long last. Pearce Richmond: a certified Perfect Man. He was ungettable, and I got him. He was unstoppable, and I stopped him. He was untamable, and I rode him into the sunset.

So to speak.

And then, in a burst of postengagement irrational exuberance, I'd agreed to wear his mother's wedding dress at the ceremony. I'm sure the lace that was now strangling my neck had been the forefront of polyester technology when it was formulated thirty years ago . . . but now, after sitting so long in storage, it had disintegrated into a prickly-pear-cactus texture that would be giving me a full-body rash, guaranteed.

A rash. On my wedding day.

I could feel the microfibers boring into my skin.

And, yes—I did just say "neck." This atrocity of a wedding gown had a dog-collar-like choker of lace, which attached to a bib of more lace, which attached to a sweetheart neckline that held the whole thing up. And by "whole thing," I mean the loosest, puffiest, most sad-prom, princess-fantasy, pumpkin-skirted getup in history.

It was like a *parody* of a wedding gown.

A parody that Pearce's mom refused to have altered. Even with a whole handful of safety pins hidden in the pleats, it was still so loose that without the collar it might've slid right off. And the poofy skirt was *so very poofy* it was like I was wearing one of Maria von Trapp's curtains—as a curtain.

Light a fire under me, and I could've floated off like a hot-air balloon. For real.

But there was no getting out of it.

Literally.

Because the zipper had caught in my hair right at the neckpiece when I zipped it up, and now it was stuck. I had cut away my hair with scissors, but now the slider was cemented in place like we'd glued it. Right at the top.

I'd be noosed in this thing until Pearce—or, really, not picky at this point: *anyone at all*—ripped it off me.

Hopefully sooner rather than later.

In theory, this was the biggest day of my life. In theory, I should be savoring every second. In theory, I was smack in the bull's-eye of the pinnacle of human happiness.

In reality?

I was itching.

Not to mention stinging—from matching blisters on the backs of my heels from my new shoes.

That was the situation: A supremely bossy mother-in-law-to-be. A growing rash. Twin blisters. And a dress that made me question my human dignity.

Yeah. I was *already* ready for this day to be over.

Not to mention the venue: a church built in the sixties that they'd forgotten to add windows to, with a building-wide commitment to fluorescent bulbs instead of warm white and an odd décor obsession with beige.

Tonally off for a wedding, right? *Beige?*

I don't know what color joy is, but it sure as hell isn't beige.

But here we were.

Even my bouquet of "champagne"-colored roses could qualify as beige.

The wedding coordinator, Mrs. Allen, was seven hundred years old. As a somber volunteer for the church—where the elder Richmonds had *also* gotten married—and a fellow member of their country club, Mrs. Allen had barely tolerated me all day.

Now, as she steered me into the vestibule, her fingers pinching my elbow flesh right above the funny bone, I suddenly realized I needed to pee.

I glanced at the beige doorway leading into the beige sanctuary.

Couldn't I just hold it? Because it was sixty seconds to go-time. We had momentum here.

But even just noticing the bladder situation made it worse.

Out of nowhere, it wasn't just full—it was positively *taut*, like an overfilled water balloon.

How had I not noticed this earlier? Why did I have to wait until we were seconds out from the starting gun? I was wearing an Italian lace garter belt, for Pete's sake!

I never could make things easy for myself, could I?

Mrs. Allen was poised to shove me through the doorway when I stopped short and turned to her with a wince of apology.

"I'm sorry. I need to use the ladies' room real quick."

Mrs. Allen shook her head in horror, like this was the worst thing she'd ever heard in all her seven centuries of life. "But the organist is about to start the processional," she protested.

"Can you stall him?" I asked.

She didn't like *that* idea. She pinched her face up like I was really being a bridezilla.

But then she pressed on her little earpiece and said, "Tony, I'm going to need you to hold off on the processional. We've got a nervous bladder back here."

As I hobbled off toward the ladies' room, I wasn't sure I loved being called "a nervous bladder," like that was my whole identity. But there was no time to argue. It was going to take all the minutes I had just to contend with that lace garter.

The organ music somehow sounded louder in the bathroom, echoing around the hard surfaces.

In the stall, as I managed my undergarments and then hoisted that enormous crinoline-inflated skirt up around my waist, I decided that I really didn't love organ music. The way it was so brain-meltingly loud. The way it smeared all the notes together. Plus, it always just sounded a little sinister, didn't it?

Like someone was about to pop out of a coffin?

No offense to the organists of the world. But that was the truth of it. An organ was the last instrument I'd ever have chosen for my wedding.

Would a nice little grand piano have killed anybody?

The more I thought about it, the madder I got.

Nothing about this wedding was what I wanted. Every last detail had been determined by Mrs. Richmond. She'd picked the venue, and the color palette, and the florist, and the caterer.

Anytime I suggested anything, she shot it down with this overacted "Really?" that made me immediately follow up with, "Unless you have another idea."

Quick spoiler: She always had another idea.

What can I say?

I wanted her to like me.

Also, it was a busy time for weddings in my family. My sister, Ashley, was *also* getting married this year—six weeks after me, *on a cruise ship*, of all things—and so my mom had more than enough to worry about. She was delighted that Mrs. Richmond wanted to do it all. And whenever Mrs. Richmond chose the most expensive possible option, she'd say to my mom, "Don't worry. We'll make up the difference."

"You're getting a much fancier wedding out of the deal," my mother kept telling me. "We *never* would have sprung for that margarita drink wall."

True enough.

But now, on my long-awaited Big Day, I was kind of choking on all the terrible choices I'd agreed to.

Not that it mattered.

This was happening, like it or not.

Washing my hands at the sink, I took in the sight of myself in the mirror. The hair artist Mrs. Richmond paid for had shellacked my hair into an updo—spraying the hair equivalent of glitter into it to "brighten" my dirty-blond coloring. And don't get me started on the makeup artist, who had airbrushed my skin with foundation to cover up my freckles, used a shade of eye shadow that she guaranteed would make my eyes look "less hazel," and then spent a good five minutes enlarging and darkening my eyebrows. When she spun the chair toward the mirror, I gasped. And not in a good way.

"Can we just—fix the eyebrows?" I asked.

The makeup artist and Mrs. Richmond frowned.

"They're a little . . . Fozzie Bear?" I tried to explain.

"This is the trend," the makeup artist explained. "It makes you look younger."

Mrs. Richmond, who had recently told me I was too old to have long hair, nodded in agreement.

Was I old at twenty-six?

No matter. I wouldn't dare fight with Mrs. Richmond on her wedding day.

Sorry—*my* wedding day.

And now here I was, in a beige church bathroom with a bouffant hairdo, pausing to take in the sight of myself as a bride. And all I could see was . . . eyebrows.

Was the organ music getting louder?

Time to go. Everyone was waiting for me.

The bridesmaids were all lined up near the altar by now. My mom—who had stayed up until two in the morning assembling gift bags—was already seated in the front row with her wrist corsage on. My Grandma Dodie was wearing pearls and kitten heels. And my dad—my former-marine, workaholic dad (always an elusive get for any family event) was about to walk me down the aisle.

This was happening. Time to take my eyebrows to the sanctuary.

It's just normal, ordinary, everyday cold feet, I told myself as I hustled back along the hallway. That slight feeling of nausea? That was a *good* sign. It meant I knew what I was doing, and I was taking it seriously, and I was stepping boldly into my future.

Who doesn't feel nauseous in big life moments?

It wasn't a red flag. It was an *homage* to my upcoming best life.

And so was this itchy-ass frigging dress.

That's exactly what I was thinking as I reached the vestibule: This was a life-changing moment in every way. In twenty minutes, the whole thing would be over, and I'd be transformed—and I don't just mean covered head to toe in contact dermatitis. This single event was going to change me from JoJo Burton, serial commitmentphobe and legendary boyfriend dumper, into Josephine Richmond: happily, legally, and incontrovertibly *committed.*

Twenty minutes total to change my whole personality. Easy.

We'd timed it beforehand with the reverend.

Or, actually—maybe a few minutes more than twenty.

Because just as I was about to give the *giddyup* signal to Mrs. Allen to fire up the processional at last . . . the vestibule double doors burst open at the same time with a swoosh, blasting out the beige room with golden-hued sunlight.

And into that sunlight walked a guy.

A guy who was not in a suit, like all the others.

A guy with a rucksack on his shoulders like he was just arriving from the French Alps.

A guy with an overgrown beard and shaggy hair . . . who looked a lot, I decided, as my eyes adjusted—an uncanny amount, even—like my childhood friend Cooper Watts. Who he most certainly could not be. Because my old friend Cooper had already, most definitely, most *defiantly*, RSVPed *no* to the wedding—circling *Regrets* ten times on the return card and adding a handwritten addendum that read, and I quote:

"Don't marry that douchebag. This is a boycott."

Two

OTHER REASONS THIS person just couldn't be Cooper:

1. Cooper lived in London.
2. Cooper didn't talk to me anymore.
3. This dude was much more—um—*strapping* than any known version of Cooper.
4. Cooper knew better than to stress out my mom by crashing a wedding she was hosting.
5. Unlike this mountain man, Cooper could not grow a full beard.

At least—not the last time I'd seen him. Which, granted, was four years ago—right after college graduation. But we'd been across-the-street neighbors from ages eight to twenty-two. I was pretty sure I could pick out Cooper in any lineup anywhere.

Which is why I was so stumped to be stumped.

Was it Cooper?

Let's revisit the new physique for a second: The Cooper I knew did not have big, solid, pommel-horse-Olympian-style shoulders. He did not have the kind of muscles you could see through a T-shirt and *under a rucksack*. He didn't have forearms that seemed to be looking for something to squeeze, or a way of standing on the floor like he owned it, or a manly look that would make anybody—least of all me—stop in her tracks.

The Cooper I knew—the Cooper I'd hung out with every day for ten-plus formative years—was a *boy*. This French Alps hiker crashing my wedding was . . .

A man.

Impossible.

And yet.

My brain was saying *No, it can't be* while every other part of me was saying *Um—hello?—it definitely is*. I was like a hunting dog on point—frozen in his direction. There was something to see here. Something important. For a minute, the rest of the world blurred away and left only the two of us there.

The organ music quieted. Mrs. Allen faded. The itching stopped.

All I could see was this total stranger—who I already knew.

I stepped closer. "Cooper?" I said, peering at him.

It couldn't be.

"Hey, Joey," he said. "Happy wedding day."

Holy shit!

It *was*.

Cooper's normal greeting was to grab me around the neck and clamp me into a headlock. But he wasn't doing that now—yet.

I shook my head. "You were boycotting! You put it in writing."

Cooper shrugged. "I changed my mind."

"You're going to be in so much trouble when my mom finds out," I said, uttering our childhood catchphrase.

But Cooper shook his head. "I emailed her. She approved."

"She didn't approve *that*," I said, gesturing at his mountain-man ensemble. "You look like hell."

It's possible I was lying.

He looked like hell only if *like hell* also meant very, very . . . surprisingly sexy.

I took a deep breath to pull it together.

This was *Cooper.* He used to sit on me and fart.

But that's when Cooper lifted those dark blue eyes and looked right at me through his black lashes.

I felt a buzz in response. Like I was a doorbell, somehow, and he was . . . ringing me.

Had I just tried to convince *anyone* that Cooper looked bad?

Even Cooper didn't buy it. He gave me what can only be described as a flirty look and said, "Liar."

Now he'd gone too far.

It was one thing to crash my wedding—late—in *full Patagonia* and walk in here with all those muscles. It was quite another to give me a *flirty look.*

This was a kid I'd peeled grapes with so we could call them eyeballs. This was a kid who'd dared me to suck a spaghetti noodle up my nose. This was a kid who'd hocked Jell-O cubes out of his mouth into the air so I could catch them in mine.

We were *way* past flirting.

"What are you doing here?" I asked.

He shrugged. "My oldest friend is getting married."

"So?"

"So, I should be here."

"You RSVPed *no.* With extreme prejudice."

"I was being an ass."

"Yes. You really were."

"I'm sorry about that," Cooper said.

"No, you're not."

Somewhere, in a distant land, an ancient lady named Mrs. Allen was waiting for me to start my bridal procession.

But how could I do that when Cooper was stepping closer—and looking me over?

"You look like a bride," Cooper said next, in a tone like he couldn't believe it.

"I *am* a bride."

I guess Cooper knew enough about my whole dynamic with Pearce to ask next, "How did you get him to propose?"

I thought about lying. But this was Cooper. We were even more beyond lying than we were beyond flirting. So I confessed: "Ultimatum." Then I said, almost just to see how Cooper would react, "I told him to shit or get off the pot."

Cooper blinked and then said, deadpan, "That's romantic."

I deadpanned back, "Isn't it?"

Cooper took in the sight of me again and said, "Well. However it happened, you look beautiful."

Beautiful? I felt a funny sting in my chest.

I hadn't even been hoping for *beautiful* today. I'd just been hoping for *not covered in hives*.

Had Cooper ever said anything that nice to me before?

But there was a rasp in Cooper's voice. He meant it.

Then, before I could stop myself, I said, "You don't think I look like Fozzie Bear?"

At that, Cooper squinted at me like I was equal parts adorable and ridiculous, tilted his head, and repeated—carefully—so I could really hear the question I'd just asked reflected back:

"I do not"—a pause—"think that you look"—another pause—"like *Fozzie Bear*."

I didn't appreciate the mockery. But it did make me feel better.

"You," I said, just to get us back to normal, "look awful."

"So you've mentioned."

I reached up to tug on his beard, like it might be a vaudeville prop with an elastic strap. "What's going on here?"

"It's a beard," Cooper said.

"I see that," I said. "But why?"

A hint of a shrug. "Why not?"

"It looks like a pigeon built a nest on your face."

At that, he broke into a big grin.

"A pigeon with a bad personality," I added.

"Why do I love it when you insult me?" Cooper asked.

"Because the truth feels good."

Cooper tilted his head again. "Does it?"

"And I'm not insulting you," I said. "I'm *helping* you."

"I knew you were going to say that."

"And what's going on with *this*?" I reached up and mussed his hair next. "Is this a *man-bun*?"

"It's a ponytail," Cooper corrected.

I shook my head. "What were you thinking?"

"I grew it out."

"It's *so* bad."

"You don't think I look kind of great?"

I sidestepped the question. He *did* look kind of great. "That hair is a tragedy," I declared. "Shakespeare could've written that hair."

Cooper was still smiling. "You really hate it."

"I *one thousand percent* hate it."

"That's a lot of percentage points from a math major."

"I'm begging you to cut it," I said. "Stick your head under a lawn mower. Anything."

"Noted," Cooper said. Then he added, "You, by the way, look amazing. Just to be clear."

I didn't feel amazing. I looked down, like I'd forgotten myself. "I look like I'm wearing someone else's wedding dress."

"Are you?"

I nodded, all solemn. "Pearce's mother's, to be exact."

"Who cares?" Cooper said. "You look epic."

"The zipper's broken," I said, tugging at the collar. "So I'll never get back out. This is basically my skin now."

Cooper evaluated that idea. "Maybe that's a good thing," he said. Then, like it was a declaration: "I caught my breath when I saw you."

"Did you really?"

Despite everything—despite the job he'd taken in London without telling me, and the texts of mine he'd ignored for four solid years, and his now-famous *meanest wedding RSVP in history*—the idea of Cooper catching his breath at the sight of me made me catch my own right back.

The truth feels good.

It was maybe the best feeling I'd had all day.

But before I could savor it, Mrs. Allen cleared her throat.

I looked over.

Oh, god. I'd almost forgotten.

She gestured at the sanctuary, like *Ahem! We have a wedding to complete over here.*

I turned back to Cooper with an apologetic shrug. "I have to go get married now."

"Yeah—of course," he said, gesturing at my future. "Get after it."

"Okay," I said. "And thanks for coming after all."

Cooper gave a wry headshake. "Couldn't miss it if I tried."

"And you're not forgiven for that RSVP, by the way."

"Unforgivable," he agreed. "Hold a grudge. I support you."

"I might forgive you eventually," I said, walking backward now, holding eye contact.

"Don't even think about it," Cooper said.

Mrs. Allen was eyeing Cooper like he might be about to mug me as she came forward with my beige bouquet to usher me on. She signaled the organist, and spun me around by the shoulders to face the aisle, and was about to push me through the doors—when I heard Cooper's voice behind me one more time.

"Joey!"

I turned back. "Kinda busy here," I said as he jogged to catch up.

As he reached me, Cooper nodded, like *I get it.* Then he put his hands on my shoulders, squeezing a little, like he was steadying me.

My bare shoulders, I should note. Under his bare hands.

Next, Cooper said, "You're okay, right?"

I frowned like he'd lost his marbles. "Of course I am."

"Because you look—"

"Beautiful, right? You said. That was so weird."

"Beautiful—yes. But you also look—"

Then, before I could think better of it, I finished for him: "Like I'm about to call off the wedding?"

Cooper stilled.

I stilled, too.

Then he pulled in a breath and said, "Are you?"

"I thought that's what *you* were going to say."

"I was going to say, 'You look a little nervous.'"

"Because I'm not calling it off," I said. "Why would you even think that?"

"I *didn't* think that," Cooper said.

Now we had ourselves a standoff.

We stared into each other's eyes.

Right then, the organist began the processional—a baroque-hits favorite of the Richmonds' that launched with a howl of menacing horror-movie chords.

Wait—did I have a pebble in my shoe?

I handed Cooper my bouquet for a minute so I could grab his shoulder for balance with one hand and pull off my pump with the other.

"What are you doing?" Cooper asked.

"I've got a pebble in my shoe," I said, shaking it out.

"What is it with you and pebbles?" Cooper said.

But as I straightened up to take back my bouquet, Cooper tugged me closer by the waist and leaned in so close his breath tickled my ear. And then he said, "Don't take this the wrong way, okay?"

"What?" I asked.

"It's pretty easy," he said then, "to fake a faint."

I pushed back and glanced toward the sanctuary. "I don't see how that's relevant."

"It's not," Cooper said, lifting his hands in innocence. "Just random trivia." But then he leaned back in. "The trick is to roll as you hit the floor so you don't hit your head."

I flared my nostrils at him. Then, for my official response, I flipped him off.

Cooper feigned shock at the gesture and said, "You can't do that in a bridal gown."

"It's not my bridal gown," I pointed out.

But with a wry headshake, Cooper said, "It is now."

That's when Mrs. Allen got aggressive and tapped me on the shoulder. Hard.

I took another step back. "Time to go."

"Congrats on your wedding," Cooper said with a little salute. "And don't forget what the firefighters say."

"The firefighters?" I said, falling for it. "What do they say?"

Cooper tilted forward just a little, like *You got this*. Then, with an infuriating micro-nod, he said, "Stop, drop, and roll."

Three

WHEN I STEPPED into the sanctuary to take my dad's arm, my dad wasn't there.

Of course.

It was my Grandma Dodie instead. Standing proud for duty at five-two.

Had I been foolishly thinking that my dad would show up for the most important day of my life? That was on me.

What was I, a *beginner*? My money should've been on Dodie from the start.

She held out her elbow gallantly when she saw me—cute as a dumpling with her little white halo of hair.

I took her arm, but I had to stoop a little.

I smiled big at the whole sanctuary of guests who had turned to gaze at me as I whispered, "Where's Dad?"

"He missed his flight," Grandma Dodie whispered back, the same way.

"Of course he did," I said, brightening my smile.

"He's hoping to make the reception," she offered.

"Don't bet on it."

Now I was itchy *and* angry.

Typical. My absentee dad. He had *one job*—and now my grandma was doing it.

Per usual.

He'd already missed the rehearsal dinner. He'd missed 90 percent of the first-ever brunch with the Richmonds, too—taking a work call ten minutes in and then pacing around a side garden on his cell for the rest of the meal.

Not to mention he kept calling them the Richlands.

None of this was shocking. He was a vestigial parent, after all.

He had three children, and he could barely keep them all straight. He didn't know our birthdays. He always mixed up what schools we went to. He consistently got our ages wrong. It was a parlor game at this point: quizzing our dad on basics he should already know and then triumphing as he got every one wrong.

If you can really call moments like that "triumphs."

Anyway, it was fun, in a way. He deserved it.

Ashley once dared him to say our middle names—and he missed all three, while our mom looked on, her head tilted in wonder. For Ashley, he tried Elizabeth, Isabel, and Henrietta before my mom finally cut in with, "It's Rose, sweetheart. After your mother." I got Martha, Bonnie, and Julia before we explained that mine was Dorothy, after Grandma Dodie—my mom's mom. For our brother, Pete, he insisted on the very random name Timothy for a while before trying a whole host of others like it was a literal guessing game—"Miles? Franklin? Steven? Paul?"—until Pete finally put him out of his misery and said, "It's Raleigh, Dad. After *you*."

My father wouldn't retain this education, of course. None of it would stick.

In six months we could do it all again, no problem.

We were like the idea of a family to him—more than we were real people.

It was fine. It was funny at this point.

"Don't worry about it," my mom always said. "He's a good provider." Then she'd wink at us and say, "And you hit the jackpot with your mom."

We'd hit the jackpot with Grandma Dodie, too, who was seventy-eight years old and feistier than the whole lot of us put together. She lived with us now, and she was cultivating antique roses in the side yard, and taking an art history class on the Impressionists, and baking her own sourdough every week. She'd founded an old lady workout group called the Screaming Mimis that walked three miles every day. She had a whole crew of travel friends who had nursed their husbands through long, final illnesses and were "ready to have some fun"—and they went to see Broadway shows, and took riverboat cruises, and spent random weekends in Marfa, Texas, drinking Tito's and tonic at the hotel where they'd filmed *Giant*.

Even right now, walking the aisle, Grandma Dodie was moving faster than I was.

"We're supposed to go slow, Dodie," I whispered. "Mrs. Richmond wants the processional music to finish."

"Nonsense," Dodie said. "I'll be in a coma in the nursing home before we're halfway there."

I didn't argue. The sooner I got out of this gown, the better.

Which prompted me to notice, a little late, that the whole time I'd been talking to Cooper . . . I hadn't been itching.

Like, at all.

I'd totally forgotten to itch.

But now, as I walked the aisle like a plank, the itching was back—times ten.

By the halfway point, I had to lock my elbow and make a fist to keep from scratching my neck. You know when something itches so bad you would happily claw off all your own skin just to make it stop?

It was like that.

Down at the end, a million miles away, was Pearce. Waiting. In a tux. A tux he owned. Because he was the kind of guy who owned a tux—and the studs and cuff links to go with it.

Pearce had been a math major like me. We got together in college after a blind date where we ate sushi, talked about math all night, and then walked back to my dorm. Never underestimate the power of talking about something you love with a fellow lover of that same thing. I honestly think he seduced me by talking about differential equations.

Even though, looking back, we came at math from different angles. I liked the challenge of how to make the complexity of it more accessible. Pearce, I think, was the opposite. He liked how the complexity of it made him look smart. So much smarter than everybody else.

Our shared language was math—but we spoke different dialects.

Either way, though, it felt a lot like love.

Pearce did not kiss me when he dropped me off that first night, but he did say, and this is verbatim: "I really enjoyed our time together. Let's do this again sometime."

Who talks like that? Right?

I agree that it doesn't seem to add up. Why would a winsome young mathematician like myself embark on what turned into a *seven-year* relationship that started with such a whimper?

Because of my fraught relationship with my absentee father, obviously. Pearce turned out to be the perfect man for all my unresolved issues.

And when I say "perfect," what I mean is: He was the perfect ratio of interested to disinterested. He liked me enough to make me chase him, but not enough to let me catch him.

And that's the whole trick to dating me, it turns out: Make me want you, but don't let me have you.

As soon as you're mine, I will lose interest. Guaranteed.

It's a problem.

I'd dumped every boyfriend I'd ever had—except for Pearce. I was always the dumper, never the dumpee. But then Pearce came along. And he was so minimally interested in me that I had no choice but to get obsessed with him.

At dinner, he'd check his phone. At movies, he'd fall asleep. Texts were responded to sporadically. Invitations were deferred. Frequency was infrequent—because, for Pearce, seeing each other once a week was more than enough.

If he stayed over, he was out the door by six AM.

I hated it, but it worked. You can't argue with the results.

Not getting enough made me want more. Being with Pearce was the emotional equivalent of being ravenously hungry and then eating one Pringle.

I knew the pattern. I knew the only way to stay interested was to stay unsatisfied.

But I still wanted to get . . . satisfied.

But he wouldn't satisfy me. Or couldn't.

It was the worst relationship of my life. And the longest.

I stayed in a state of suspended dissatisfaction for three long years until finally, one day not long before we graduated, as I was bemoaning my fate to my mom on a video call—she just . . . solved it.

"I'm terrified that if he ever really gives me what I want, I'll lose interest," I said.

My mother looked at me over her readers. "Well," she said. "You know what the answer to that is."

There was an answer to that? "What?"

"Get married," she said. Like *Simple.*

I frowned. "Get married?"

My mom nodded, like *Obviously*. "Put yourself in a position where you *can't* lose interest."

"I don't think Pearce wants to get married."

"Never underestimate the value of a good threat," my mom said.

"But what if he says no?"

"Then you're no worse off than you are right now."

It was sneaky, and it was brilliant. And it worked.

One night, over dinner, I said, in the most pleasant, disinterested, robotic way possible, "Pearce, I'd like to get married. And if that's not of interest to you, we should probably break up so I can find someone else."

Pearce frowned a little, turned the idea over in his mind. And then he said, "Great idea. Let's get married."

And that was that. A week later, I had Grandmother Richmond's two-carat engagement ring on my finger.

It felt like a triumph—until we stayed that way for four years.

Engaged—but not married—for four years.

We graduated college. He went into quantitative finance, and I decided, after much soul-searching, that I wanted to become a middle school math teacher and illustrate math concepts with fun activities like origami. He decided to use his math major to make money, and I decided to use my math major to make art.

A choice that Pearce did not understand, personally or financially.

We still didn't live together. He still answered only 50 percent of my texts.

He stalled and stalled, until one night his parents sat him down and told him they would like some grandchildren.

And now here I was, walking the plank.

I mean *aisle*.

Once we set a date, I was happy at first. But the truth was, as the wedding plans became more solid, I started to feel less happy. Things that hadn't bothered me before, like how he smacked when he ate pasta, and how his earlobes were too small, and how he checked his phone every three minutes, started to loom larger.

And larger.

He never used his parking brake. He couldn't roll his *r*s. One side of his nose was a different shape from the other.

Not to mention: His favorite ice cream was Rocky Road. Maybe I was a little judgy from that high school job at Baskin-Robbins, but *Rocky Road*? That was *old people* ice cream! What was this—a retirement home?

It was as predictable as geometry. I could have written it like a proof.

Now that I had him, I didn't want him anymore.

It was like a curse.

But curses were made to be broken.

Today, in the church, I reminded myself what my mother had said: *The only way to stop running away is to stop running away.*

So here I was: *not running away.*

Heroically.

Itching like hell—but doing it anyway.

Up by the altar, Pearce looked a little itchy himself. If I'm honest.

But Grandma Dodie kept walking, and so did I.

This was happening. This was nonnegotiable. This was the best solution I could think of—and I'd be marrying Pearce Richmond tonight if it was the dumbest thing I ever did.

AT THE ALTAR, I handed my bouquet to my big sister, Ashley. My little brother, Pete, soon to graduate from college, had agreed to be Pearce's best man. When Pearce had asked him, Pete's response had been "Don't you have anybody better to ask?"

I'd elbowed Pete—hard—in the ribs and then answered for him. "That's a yes. That's a grateful and enthusiastic yes."

But now I found myself wondering, too. Why *didn't* Pearce have anybody better to ask? Cooper had never liked him the few times they'd met back in college. Was Pearce one of those guys other guys didn't like?

Pete crossed his eyes at me when I glanced his way.

I ignored him. *Stay focused.*

Grandma Dodie pulled me down to kiss me on the cheek and then handed me over to Pearce.

The itching was getting worse. Was it inside my throat now? Had I inhaled some fibers or something? My airway definitely felt tight. Wouldn't it be lucky if my throat closed up and I really fainted—for real?

Problem solved, huh?

Pearce stood next to me like a statue as the reverend, who'd encouraged us to be casual and call him "Rev," came to stand before us.

But here's the thing. I guess the rev felt like this was his moment to shine, because next, he launched into an extended-remix TED Talk about the internet, of all things, and how it was tearing us apart like nothing before in history—and how we needed to stop hating other people online and start loving them in the real world. And I didn't technically disagree. I mean: *Yes. Let's hurry up and get on that.* But my itching situation was ramping up by the second, so I really didn't have time for some big, long pontification from some old dude with yellow teeth.

Let's just say I lost focus.

My mind drifted.

Before I knew it, I was thinking about Cooper and trying to overlay the boy I remembered so well with the man who had shown up here today. That overgrown *beard.* That scraggly *hair.* What a waste of a good-looking man.

Hold on. Did I just classify *Cooper* as a "good-looking man"?

I'd actually given him a haircut once when we were kids, in our clubhouse, with some pinking shears. What were we—ten? Eleven? I remember very confidently explaining to him that the zigzags on the blades would give his hair "body." He'd been so trusting, sweet thing—and then he went home looking like he'd been electrocuted. It was so bad, my mom made me walk across the street later with a bottle of chardonnay for his mother as a peace offering.

The next time I saw Cooper, he had a buzz cut.

Which made him look like a Norman Rockwell painting.

Would Cooper wind up coming to the reception tonight? I wondered. Or was that teaser in the vestibule all the time I'd get? Because I had a question I'd been waiting to ask him. And if I'd had some warning he was coming, for god's sake—if he hadn't just crashed into this day out of nowhere—I might have had the presence of mind to ask it.

Or maybe not. I might need a bottle of chardonnay myself for that one.

Now the rev was wrapping up. He seemed pretty pleased with himself, like he'd really gotten *how love works* cleared up for everyone—and solved all of society's problems as a bonus. Were we supposed to clap or something? I looked around.

And that's when I saw Cooper, close by in a set of side pews, sitting alone with his elbow resting on his rucksack, watching me like he had X-ray vision into my thoughts. Before I could look away, he lifted his hand and touched the side of his head—and as he did it, I swear, I heard his voice as clearly as if he'd spoken out loud: *Stop, drop, and roll.*

Dammit, Cooper, I thought. *Why do you have to ruin everything?*

And then, like there was no other choice . . .

I took a deep breath.

And I let my knees buckle.

And I dropped to the floor.

Four

WAS I CONVINCING?

I have no idea.

My only plan was to keep my eyes closed—without visibly squeezing.

Trickier than it sounds.

The whole church gasped as I fell, and then it shifted into murmuring. I felt the air thicken and the sounds muffle as, I assume, my family gathered around me. I heard the rev say, "Don't worry, folks. This happens all the time. She'll be back on her feet in a jiffy."

Hell if I would.

Ashley wanted to call 911, but my mother kept insisting it was just nerves. Grandma Dodie kept asking everyone to keep back to give me some air. Pete kept declaring I was turning blue.

Which I wasn't.

After several minutes, when I still hadn't revived, the rev leaned in conspiratorially to my mom and said, "Maybe we should take her somewhere more comfortable." Pete offered to carry me—which got an instant "Not you" from my mom. Pete was protesting with "I dropped her *one* time" when I felt two arms slide under me like a forklift and hoist me up.

Good. Pearce had been suspiciously silent so far. I'd half wondered if he was checking his investment app. At least now he was doing something. Even if I *was* in the process of weaseling out of our wedding.

He didn't know that.

Yet.

And maybe I wouldn't weasel out after all. Something about being carried like that was just so . . . romantic. You couldn't escape it. You're so out of control and so vulnerable, all limp with your eyes closed, caught in swells of motion—and the arms holding you are so anchoring and safe. I felt like . . . a *damsel* or something. And Pearce, for maybe the first time ever, felt like a rescuing knight. Someone I could feel protected by.

Cherished, even.

Was that going too far? This was *Pearce.*

I was transported from the sanctuary, down the hallway, and toward the same bridal room where I'd first manacled myself into that used wedding gown.

Or, at least, I assumed that's where we went.

All I could feel was my cheek against a solid chest, the reassurance of being clutched tight, and the rhythm of walking. Plus, just . . . full-body gratitude for the rescue.

I wondered if this one little stunt might save the day.

I noticed I wasn't itching now.

Maybe the rev was right and I really would be back on my feet in a jiffy. Maybe being carried off by Pearce in this primal way would stir my emotions. Maybe we all did need to try a lot harder to be nicer to each other in this big, crazy world. I could do that, couldn't I? For a little bit, at least?

For long enough, maybe, to get back in there and get this wedding over with?

THE BRIDAL ROOM had a sofa, and Pearce laid me down on it, lifting my head to slide what had to be *his own thigh* under my head, like a throw pillow. A cool hand appeared against my forehead as someone checked me for a fever. I heard my mom asking if smelling salts were still a thing.

Here was the truth of it: I couldn't stay unconscious forever.

Pearce stayed right there, bent over me protectively, holding one of my hands as my mother took charge. You know that feeling you get when you know someone's watching you? I felt that feeling on the sofa from Pearce.

Something about that seemed impossibly sweet.

He was showing up for me in just the right way, and it surprised me so much.

I could do this. I could open my eyes, say I felt better, and get back out there.

I could marry the man holding my hand. I *could.*

And so, at that thought, I opened my eyes, planning to act dazed and lightheaded.

But the first thing I saw wasn't Pearce's clean-shaven, dimpled chin. It was an unruly pigeon beard.

"Cooper?" I said, in a tone like *Seriously?*

His name came out louder than I meant it to.

Loud enough that the whole room turned to stare at me.

The thigh I'd been resting on, and the chest I'd been cradled against, and the hand now currently *still* holding mine—the one I'd been thinking I could marry after all—had been Cooper? All along?

"Where's Pearce?" I asked, pushing myself up.

I looked around as the whole room rushed over—my mom, my grandma, my siblings, the rev, Mrs. Allen. My eyes scanned right and then left, landing at last back on Cooper.

He winked.

Meanwhile, my mother wasn't mad—yet. "Sweetheart, you fainted at the altar!" she said, like she had front-page news.

I remembered I was supposed to be woozy, so I put my hand to my head.

At that, Cooper scooted closer to me and pulled me against his shoulder as a bolster.

My mother was all concern, leaning in. "Is something hurting? Did you get lightheaded?"

"I'm fine," I said. "I'm okay."

"Ashley," my mom said, snapping her fingers at my sister, "get her a glass of water." Then my mom perched beside me while we waited. "Reverend Martin says this kind of thing happens all the time. Young brides overthink it. They forget to breathe. Next thing you know, they're passed-out unconscious." She patted my knee. "But once they reoxygenate, they're good to go."

Where was Pearce right now, exactly?

My mom stayed focused, trying to find the teachable moment. "Number-one rule for weddings—and life, too, I suppose. Just keep breathing."

Next, Ashley arrived with the water.

"Okay," my mom said, like now we were getting somewhere. "Big swig of this"—she touched the bottom of the glass as I took some gulps—"and then a little extra oxygen"—she demonstrated an in-through-the-nose breath so forceful that her nostrils moved with the suction—"and then we'll get you back out there."

I wasn't sure what to do now.

I had fallen ever so slightly back in love with Pearce while he was carrying me, but then he'd turned out to be Cooper. And I wasn't marrying *Cooper*!

"Okay, now," my mother said, still hoping the breathing would do the trick. "Sit up straight. You, too, Coop— Oh, hi, Cooper. Welcome home."

"Hi, Mrs. Burton."

"You're looking . . . burly."

His frown looked amused. "Thanks."

And then she was back to business. She tapped me on the back. "Three seconds in, and three seconds out." She counted with Mississippis out loud as she and I—and Cooper, too—took some gentle, cleansing, reoxygenating breaths, sitting side by side, three in a row.

While my mother's eyes were closed, I looked over at Cooper, like *This is all your fault.*

And he gave me a little shrug, like *You're welcome.*

Next, my mom turned to me, her face bright, and clasped my hands. "Okay, sweetheart. You ready to get back out there?"

And there was the moment of truth.

I hesitated.

I didn't say no. But apparently I couldn't say yes, either.

I guess I didn't need to say anything.

My mom read my face, the way moms do, and her shoulders sank.

"Oh, god," she said, and then she dropped to a whisper and said, "Did you fake it?"

I looked down. "I'm sorry."

"Josephine," my mother sighed—the word and the breath sailing out together. "You were two minutes from the finish line."

"It was Cooper's idea."

"Cooper," my mother scolded, like she was very disappointed.

But now it was hitting me—what I'd just done. How humiliating it would be for us to send all those guests home. How much money I had just wasted. How thoughtlessly I had just reduced all my plans for the future to rubble.

"I'm sorry," I said as tears appeared from nowhere and spilled over. "I don't know what's wrong with me."

My mom, who always had more faith in me than I had in myself, patted my back and said, "There's nothing wrong with you, sweetie. He must not have been the right one."

But honestly, if Pearce Richmond—clean-shaven, competent, tux-owning, trust-fund-wielding Pearce Richmond—wasn't the right one, then who the hell was?

I stared at my lap as the tears splatted onto Mrs. Richmond's gown—until Cooper reached over to hand me what looked like a wad of toilet paper.

I looked at it. "What's this?"

"A tissue," Cooper said.

"Is it—used?"

"Naw. It's just crumpled."

I examined it. "Where did it come from?"

"My pocket."

"What am I supposed to do with it?"

Cooper frowned at me. "I don't know if you've noticed, but you're crying."

I regarded the tissue.

"It's clean enough to blow your nose into, at least," Cooper said, giving me a look. "Don't be fussy."

I went ahead and blew—just as the rev approached my mom to say, "They're getting restless out there. What's the verdict?"

My mom gave the rev a tiny headshake, like *Not happening.*

"Got it," he said, all business. "We should make an announcement."

"I'll do it," Grandma Dodie volunteered. "You can't argue with a grandmother."

She took Pete's arm and held on to it until he got the message and escorted her out.

As they left, my mom called, "Tell them the reception's still on. They should all go."

Pete turned back. "To the reception?"

"We've already paid for everything," my mom said. "Might as well."

Pete still seemed lost. "But what are we celebrating now?"

My mom winced, like she wasn't quite sure.

"What are we celebrating?" Grandma Dodie said, like the question was preposterous. "We're celebrating life! And the courage to follow your own compass! And the freedom to make your own choices!"

Pete shrugged, like *Sure. Why not?*

"Plus, it's free food," Grandma Dodie added. "And free booze. And a DJ named Mr. Beat Feet."

"Ouch," Pete said.

My mom and I weren't taking the fall for that. "Mrs. Richmond hired him," we said at the same time.

Once they were gone, my mother turned to me. "You don't look very relieved."

"It's the dress," I said, pulling at the collar. "It's like it's made of poison ivy."

"Okay," she said. "Let's get you out of it."

"Can't," I said. "The zipper broke. There's no way out."

But that's when my mom put her hand to my jaw and looked right at me. "There's always a way out, Jo. Remember that."

Did that start a fresh wave of tears for me?

It did.

But now she was in to-do-list mode. She stood behind me and tilted my head forward to start working on the zipper. "First, we'll get you changed. Next, you'll need to have a talk with Pearce. Then I'll take you home and come back here to deal with . . . everything else."

"Thank you, Mom," I said, head tilted forward while she worked, holding still like I used to when she did my braids.

"Everybody needs a little help sometimes, sweetheart," she said.

I was nodding in agreement when the bridal room door opened and Mrs. Richmond, Mr. Richmond, Pearce Richmond, and Grandmother and Grandfather Richmond all walked in with total country club squad energy. Looking equal parts regal and outraged.

"Did you fake that faint?" Mrs. Richmond demanded. "Are you calling off the wedding?"

I stood up a little straighter. "That's something maybe Pearce and I should discuss in private."

But Mrs. Richmond wasn't interested in my suggestions. Ever, but especially now. "I heard from Mrs. Allen that a hobo told you to faint at the altar."

At that, Cooper raised his hand. "Hobo present," he said.

"He's not a *hobo*," I said, giving Cooper a look. "He's just in a fashion crisis."

Mrs. Richmond looked back and forth between us. "What is going on, Josephine?"

A fair question.

I turned to Pearce. "I'm sorry," I said. "I'm calling off the wedding."

"You can't call off the wedding!" Mrs. Richmond said, like I'd been speaking to her.

"Mom," Pearce said. "It's fine." Then he looked straight at me and said, "She can't even play tennis."

Next, the phone in his pocket buzzed. And he took it out to check it—with a significant air of *We're done here*.

But no way was Mrs. Richmond letting me off that easy. This was her only son. She'd spent months of her life planning this thing. She'd invited her entire mah-jongg group.

This was personal.

And if I was going to humiliate her, she was going to humiliate me right back.

She started talking so fast, it took us all a minute to catch up.

"I never liked you," she said. "When Pearce told me you'd strong-armed him into marrying you, I told him right then it was a mistake. I said, 'What self-respecting man wants to marry a *lady mathematician*?' He told me you work figures on a chalkboard—for *fun*. You have a favorite brand of chalk."

"All math people have a favorite brand of chalk," I said.

She was undeterred. "You don't know anything about fashion. I had to hog-wrestle you into that pair of heels. You showed up at that charity luncheon with wet hair! *Wet hair!* My friends shunned me for weeks. I begged and pleaded with Pearce. I said, 'You can't marry a woman who *drives a Honda*.' I warned him that his children would be"—she dropped her voice—"*nerds*." Then she steeled her shoulders. "But he felt so sorry for you—you'd been chasing him so long. He'd missed the chance to break up with you, and now he felt obligated. He proposed out of pity, and this is how you thank him?"

I wondered if I was supposed to answer that question.

Just as she concluded with, "*You're* not calling off the wedding—*we're* calling off the wedding!"

Ah. Guess not.

Mrs. Richmond turned to my mother. "And we won't be paying for anything related to this clown show." Then she turned back to me. "And I want my dress back."

"I'm sorry," I said. "It's stuck."

"Take it off. Right now."

"The zipper's broken," I tried to explain. "I literally can't."

I was about to offer to have it dry-cleaned and repaired and brought to her later—but I guess she was really spoiling for a fight, because the next thing she said was:

"You are not walking out of here in *my* wedding dress, you flat-footed bluestocking."

To my left, Cooper started laughing.

I frowned at him, like *Shut up*.

He clamped down into a serious face—but then he broke.

Next, before I could scold him, in what must have been a total psychotic break for a society lady, Mrs. Richmond took things to a whole different level . . . and *charged* me.

You know, like a bull.

Like she was about to wrestle me out of all that polyester lace—or die trying.

And I suddenly had a flash of fear that Mrs. Richmond might beat me to death. In a church. While Pearce stood placidly by, texting his fantasy baseball group chat.

But that's when I felt a tug on my arm—and it was Cooper turning me toward him.

And then he was bending at the waist, and moving toward me, and the next thing I knew, he'd hooked me over his shoulder and risen up to his full height, leaving me draped backward over that damned rucksack.

Then Cooper shifted into motion, stepping sideways and averting Mrs. Richmond's trajectory—just as she stampeded past the spot where I'd been standing and crashed into the sofa.

* * *

AND THAT'S HOW we escaped.

Cooper launched right into a jog after that.

He put all those new muscles to use—that rucksack and I couldn't have been *light*—and jogged all the way down the church hall, out the vestibule doors he'd burst in through, and straight to an open-top Jeep that was parked half up on a curb, like he'd screeched to the church's side entrance and just left it there.

He flipped me over, deposited me in the front seat, and tossed the rucksack into the back.

"This is your car?" I asked as he reached over to buckle me.

"This is my *rental* car."

"You rented an open-top Jeep?"

"It was all they had left."

"Is this why you showed up with a rucksack?"

"My laptop's in there."

"But why doesn't this thing have a top?"

"This seems like an odd thing to fixate on."

I gestured around. "The vibes don't suit you at all."

"Somebody took the top off at some point, okay? And I didn't have time to wait for the *one* guy at the rental counter to snap it all back on."

"Why not?"

"Because," Cooper said, pausing to look me in the eyes like we should all already know this, "my flight from Heathrow was delayed. And customs was slow. And I was running late to show up here and stop your wedding."

Five

FIRST THINGS FIRST: We got out of town.

Cooper took us south down I-45 toward Galveston—only an hour away. We didn't even try to talk. I just leaned back against the headrest, my hair breaking free of its bouffant and the puffy crinoline of the pumpkin skirt blowing everywhere, while Cooper blasted a playlist of all our favorite songs from high school.

Despite everything I knew about the gravity of what I'd just done, I felt surprisingly free.

All to say: Don't knock open-top Jeeps until you've tried 'em.

I had just firebombed my life—and left my whole family to clean up the mess. Except for my dad, of course, as usual.

Later, I'd feel bad about it all.

But for now—at least for this one drive—I was just going to *be*.

I was just going to close my eyes, and sing along, and enjoy being with my old friend, and let the wind blow all my thoughts away. We zipped down the freeway, past Texas City and its refinery flames, up over the causeway with all its roving bands of pelicans, and then down Sixty-First Street toward the Gulf of Mexico.

We'd done this a hundred times in high school. And now it felt both exactly the same and the opposite of the same.

Cooper parallel parked right there on the Seawall, overlooking the waves, and cut the engine.

We watched the breakers for a while. No talking.

Finally, he said, "What do you want to do now?"

I turned to meet his eyes, and then I said, very deliberately, "I want to get out of this insulting, ridiculous noose of a dress."

So we went to Murdochs—a hundred-year-old souvenir shop that sold everything and sat up on stilts over the waves. We must have been a sight—a French hobo and a runaway bride just hunting through the aisles.

People were definitely staring.

But I didn't care.

We found me some flip-flops, and some nylon shorts, and a T-shirt that said BEACH, PLEASE. Plus a couple of massive beach towels. Some heart sunglasses. And food—so much, we had to grab a second basket: chips, and cookies, and pints of Ben & Jerry's, and every candy bar I could find.

"We'll be eating our feelings, then?" Cooper said.

I just gave him a look, like *Try to stop me.*

On the way to check out, we passed a jewelry display. It had rings and necklaces made of shells and beads in beachy colors. Some were plastic and cheap—but a small section had pieces with sea glass inlaid in silver, made by a local artisan. I stopped to look at them—and then I remembered with sudden horror I was still wearing Grandmother Richmond's engagement ring.

I guess I had a hot-potato reaction to that.

I dropped the shopping basket with a *smack*, and then I got frantic trying to twist the ring and work it off. It had been a bit tight from the get-go, but all my yanking and tugging just made it tighter.

"What are you doing?" Cooper asked when he looked up and saw me wriggling.

"The engagement ring!" I said. "It's not coming off!"

"Slow down," Cooper said. "Don't make things worse."

But I kept pulling and twisting. "Making things worse is my whole thing."

"For real, though," Cooper said. "Just hold still."

"I can't. I'm panicking!"

"Give me your hand," Cooper said, taking it and clamping it still in his.

"Get it off! Get it off!" I said in a panicked rush, like there was a bug on me.

"Just stay calm," Cooper said. "Count some three-Mississippi breaths and oxygenate." Gently, he started trying to twist the ring. But now my finger was starting to swell. "How bad do you want this off?" Cooper asked.

"Bad!"

"Scale of one to ten?"

"A thousand!"

"Okay, then. Don't question my methods."

"Wait—what methods?"

"Just look away and don't worry about it."

But of course the minute he told me to look away, I had to do the opposite.

I watched Cooper bend over my ring finger and put his mouth on the ring—and, by default, part of my finger.

"What are you doing?" I said, reaching out the other hand to stop him.

He batted it away and kept his mouth there.

It was warm. And wet. I squeezed my eyes closed. "Please tell me that's not your tongue."

When he stood back up, the puffy part of my finger was now, shall we say, lubricated.

He started to work the ring again—and this time, it slid off.

He held it out to me.

But I didn't take it. I was busy wiping his spit off my hand onto Mrs. Richmond's wedding gown. "You just sucked my finger."

"I didn't suck it, I *moistened* it."

"That's worse."

"Stop complaining," he said, still holding it out, "and take it."

"I don't want it," I said.

"*I* don't want it," Cooper said.

But now I was studying my ruddy, still-puffy, ringless ring finger. "Can't you just stick it in that rucksack of yours?"

"Why?"

"Because I'm gonna have to give it back to her."

Cooper paused like I was crazy. "Just throw it in the ocean," he said.

I gave him a look. "I'm not a thief. That thing's worth a fortune."

Cooper sighed, acquiesced, and zipped it into a pocket.

In line to check out, I kept looking at my hand. I'd been wearing that too-tight ring for four years, and it had left an imprint. The Richmonds hadn't wanted to resize it until the deal was really sealed, which had seemed impossibly rude at the time.

I guess, in hindsight: not a bad idea.

My hand looked weirdly naked now.

It was fine, I told myself. I'd get used to it.

But I felt a wave of sadness anyway.

What was wrong with me—seriously? Why did I always have to be my own worst enemy? I was glaring down at my hand like it might answer me when Cooper jogged away for a minute, and then jogged back, stopping square in front of me.

He moved his fist into my field of vision—and then opened it.

He'd grabbed one of the sea glass rings. Pale aqua and sterling silver.

I looked up.

"For you," Cooper said. "This one's going to fit better, I think."

And when he slipped it onto my finger, it turned out he was right.

THE LADIES' ROOM at Murdochs was closed to the public for a deep clean, so even after we left, I was *still* ensnared in that miserable gown.

Back on the Seawall, I scanned for another establishment that might have a bathroom where I could change.

"Maybe the tattoo parlor?" I considered out loud.

But Cooper shook his head. "I have a faster idea," he said.

He led me down the steps to the beach, and we set down all our bags, rucksack included. Then Cooper held up the massive beach towels we'd bought, one in front of me and one behind, and clamped the corners together with his hands.

"What are you doing?" I asked.

"It's a changing tent," Cooper said.

"You want me to change right here?"

"Do you have a better idea?"

"How about *not getting naked on a public beach*?"

"You want out of that dress, don't you?"

Oh, god. I did. So bad. "Fine. But you're going to have to rip it off me."

"Happy to oblige," Cooper said.

Ultimately, the lace turtleneck really was the only thing holding everything up. It was lucky I was facing away from him. Because as soon as Cooper ripped the collar, the whole dress tried to slide right off.

I caught the bodice just in time, while Cooper blinked at me like he couldn't believe what had almost happened.

"You just came so close to being totally naked."

"Not totally naked," I corrected. "I am wearing bridal lingerie."

"Still," he said, unfairly delighted. "You were one stiff wind away from watching your dress float away like a birthday balloon."

"It's not my dress," I insisted again.

This time, Cooper agreed. "Not anymore."

"Can you just hand me my stuff, please?"

He did. And then I disappeared into the towel tent. And he waited semi-patiently as I changed, saying things like, "There are so many pranks I could be pulling on you right now."

While I changed, he listed them all—from stealing the towels to shouting "Fire!"—but he didn't do any of them. Which surprised me a little. The Cooper I remembered would've been flying that wedding dress like a kite by now.

Maybe he felt sorry for me.

Or maybe—and this was hard to conceptualize—he'd grown up.

Once I was changed, and free as a seagull in my flip-flops and BEACH, PLEASE T-shirt, I wadded the dress up and walked over to a beach trash can with a dolphin painted on it. I stuffed the dress in, but it didn't quite fit. It was so puffy, the crinoline flowed out over the top like the head on a beer.

I stepped back and put my hands on my hips, expecting to feel victorious.

"Well, that's a satisfying sight," Cooper said.

"Yeah," I said, frowning.

But he read my voice. "No?"

I thought about it. Then I walked back over to the trash can, pulled the dress back out, and shook it.

"What are you doing?" Cooper said.

I brushed the dress off. Then I started folding it up.

"That thing is not coming back in my car."

"It's not your car. It's a rental."

But Cooper couldn't fathom what I was doing.

The dress was not exactly easy to fold. It wound up in a wad. I found my pantyhose on the sand and used them to strangle it into a bundle.

"This is crazy," Cooper said. Then he pointed at the trash can. "Put it back."

But I shook my head. "No."

"It's been torturing you all day. Get rid of it."

"No."

At that, Cooper darted in and grabbed it out of my arms.

"Hey!" I said, chasing him. "Give it back!"

"Free yourself!" Cooper shouted as I swiped and missed, and swiped and missed.

We were running around in circles now.

"Give it back!" I kept shouting.

"Never!" he kept responding.

Finally, breathless, I stopped running.

Wary, Cooper stopped, too. "Why won't you do this for yourself? Just get rid of it."

"It's her *wedding dress*, Cooper."

"Were you not back there in that church? Did you not hear the vicious crap she said to you?"

I took a breath. "I just left her only son at the altar."

"Don't tell me you regret it," Cooper said. "That dude was texting the whole time."

I looked out at the ocean. "I'm not sure how I feel about it. But one thing's pretty clear. Throwing that woman's wedding dress away just now didn't make me feel better. It made me feel worse."

ANYWAY—THAT'S HOW COOPER ruined my wedding.

Classic Cooper.

As we sat on the steps of the Seawall, eating my pile of snacks and watching the whitecaps breaking on the black ocean, I assumed he'd be back home now for a few days. For a little visit, at least. That he'd see his mom, and binge eat some Tex-Mex while the getting was good, and hang out with me—as penance for dismantling my life, if nothing else.

But I was wrong.

His visit to Texas lasted less than twenty-four hours.

His flight back to London left at six AM—*that morning*.

"What were you *thinking*?" I asked, staring baldly at him when he told me that. "Everything about this is completely crazy."

Cooper nodded, like he agreed.

Then he handed me the chocolate bar I was reaching for.

Then he said, "I had something to say to you. And I wanted to say it in person."

I studied him. "What? What could you possibly have had to say that required a transatlantic voyage?"

But he scrunched his face and shook his head. "I think now's not the time."

"*What!*"

He shrugged. "I'm not ready. Or maybe you're not."

"You cannot fly all the way here *for less than twenty-four hours* to say something that major—and then just not say it!"

But he could. And he did.

No amount of begging, arguing, threatening, or guilt-tripping changed his mind.

He took off for London at six AM, as scheduled, without ever saying the thing he'd flown to Texas to say.

And all I could do was go home. And wonder what it was.

Six

THERE WERE SO—SO—MANY things to dread about my sister's wedding. The next wedding on the family agenda.

Not that I was making a list.

Did I mention that it was happening on a cruise ship?

No joke. An eight-day cruise to the Bahamas and Cozumel.

My big sister, Ashley, worked as a marketing manager for a cruise line called Escapes, and one of her many perks was discounted group fares. It was part of the reason she took the job. So when her boyfriend, Brody, popped the question, a cruise wedding was, as they both loved to say, "a no-brainer."

I wasn't much of a cruise ship person myself.

I wasn't much of a *weddings* person lately, either.

But here we were.

Six weeks to the day after I left my perfect fiancé at the altar, my whole family would set sail from Galveston, Texas, for eight endless days at sea—accompanied by eighty of our dearest friends, lifelong neighbors, and weirdest relatives.

Twice the number of takers we'd had for my wedding, by the way.

Can't beat a discount cruise.

And some—maybe not *all*, but plenty—of those people were going to be asking about, puzzling over, or teasing me about my wedding debacle for far too many of those eight days.

I should also mention that Brody, my sister's groom, was actually a guy I had dated briefly in high school—for like a week—before I'd dumped him, like all the others.

That's how he and Ashley met, in fact.

After the breakup, Brody had showed up on our front walk with flowers and stood there, *Say Anything* style, refusing to leave. So Ashley dragged him to a coffee shop—out of pity—to explain how hopeless I was. "He just seemed so lovelorn," she explained, "clutching those sad carnations." She also thought he was "kind of cute." And it wasn't his fault, she liked to say, that he was "collateral damage" from my "issues with intimacy."

She was just picking up the pieces.

In the end, he gave *her* the carnations. They became friends, and then more than friends, and now, after dating pleasantly for almost ten years, they were getting married. And it was great.

He was a perfectly nice guy.

Not to *me*, exactly—but in general.

He was good for Ashley. I was happy they were happy.

But was old Brody still a smidge bitter about me dumping him a decade ago?

Weirdly, yes.

I wasn't going to be his favorite new in-law, that was for sure.

So add *that* to the list I wasn't making of things to dread on the cruise.

How many was that now?

Trapped on a ship for eight solid days as a self-inflicted spinster while celebrating my sister's marriage to a groom who didn't like me?

Not good.

Not to mention, I had promised Ashley when we were children that I would serenade her at her wedding. Apparently she was going to hold me to that.

But that's a whole digression.

The point is: It was a lot.

I wish I could tell you that something wonderful happened in the six weeks between my aborted wedding and the start of Ashley's cruise. I wish one of the jobs I'd applied to had panned out, or I'd had a romantic dalliance, or I'd even just found a fantastic new pair of shoes. Anything, right?

Good things happen all the time.

People make new friends, and discover great little Italian restaurants, and buy fuzzy socks they wish they could never take off.

It was just, in those six weeks . . . none of those good things happened to happen to me.

Kind of the opposite, in fact—even though I was trying so hard to manifest the positive. I lost my favorite necklace. The coolest coffee shop in town closed down. My best grad school friend called to say she had to take next semester off.

Maybe I should have worked harder to find a good thing or two. I'm sure there was a sunny day in there somewhere.

But I just . . . couldn't.

Did I use those weeks to, say, come up with some insights about myself and take some wise lessons from the Pearce debacle so I could move forward with grace?

I did not.

I wallowed.

Specifically, I beat myself up with the echoing question: *What—seriously,* what—*is wrong with me?*

But it wasn't a real question. It was rhetorical.

I formatted a mental spreadsheet of all my flaws—*A record of failed relationships! A compulsive need to be the dumper! Leaving an A-list groom at the actual altar! WTF!*—like I was collecting proof that I was hopeless.

Not a growth mindset, to say the least.

Plus, I'd be paying my parents back for that margarita drink wall *forever.*

In my defense, though—how do you even begin to solve . . . *your entire personality*?

Get into therapy? Confront your absentee father? Join a fight club?

Nothing added up. For weeks and weeks, I couldn't solve the taunting, blinking question mark at the center of my life.

Until.

One night at our kitchen table, the week before we set sail, as Ashley was opening last-minute RSVP cards, and Grandma Dodie was filling welcome bags to put in guests' cabins, and my mom was working on the endless Sudoku puzzle of all the guests' cabin arrangements . . . we had an insight.

It happened right after my mom informed me that I was going to have to room with our freakiest cousin, Harmony.

Harmony, whose unofficial nickname was Grumpy Cat. Harmony, who was endlessly difficult and unlikable. Harmony, who had alienated every single member of our family so thoroughly over the years that my mom could not pick a single other person for her to room with.

My mom had gone over it, and over it, and over it, she said. Finally, she looked up over her readers and sized me up. Then she took my hand and squeezed it. Then she said somebody was going to have to take one for the team.

And that somebody was me.

"You don't mind rooming with her, do you?" she asked.

Ashley snapped her head up at that. "You *cannot* put JoJo with Harmony. She has the personality of a dung beetle."

My mom looked back down at the spreadsheet. "Our only other option is Cousin Ann. But remember when Harmony stole her wig?"

"She's still mad about that," Grandma Dodie said.

"Anybody but Harmony!" Ashley said, still aghast. "Put JoJo with Pete."

A headshake from my mom. "Pete's with Dad—to keep Pete out of bridesmaid trouble."

Ashley shrugged, like *Reasonable.*

Then Ashley said something very sweet. Something that captured just how appalling the prospect of anyone having to room with Cousin Harmony really was: "Put JoJo in with us."

My mom frowned. "With 'us' who?"

"With Brody and me. We'll get a rollaway bed."

At that, my mother put her hands on her hips and turned to face Ashley head-on. "On your *wedding cruise*?"

"Brody would frigging *love* that," I said.

Ashley sighed, like *Fine*. Then she insisted again, hollowly, "We *can't* put her with Harmony."

"I agree," my mom said, "we can't." Then she gave me a little shrug of apology. "But we have to."

Harmony it was. *Roomies.*

Here's a great life lesson: Things get worse, yes. But they also get better.

Because that's when the situation got so bad, it forced us to make a plan.

As I worked to accept my new fate, and the four of us tied bows on programs at the kitchen table in a pleasant, half-occupied rhythm, the conversation drifted pleasantly, as it often did, to the old family-favorite topic of *What's the deal with JoJo?*

I didn't mind—honestly. I'd take all the help I could get.

Ashley, after all, was studying for her master's in marriage and family therapy on top of her day job in marketing so she could go into private practice and have flexible hours in the "mom phase" of her life.

Which meant she had slowly become our family's resident psychologist.

I really didn't know what my deal was. My attempts to understand my behavior were all math-based—looking for underlying patterns—but Euclidean geometry and algebraic topology and combinatorics never seemed to get me very far when I applied them to the human heart.

Mine, in particular.

Luckily for me, the humanities had plenty of theories about what might cause intimacy issues, and Ashley had studied them all.

Her reigning theory for years—and we tweaked it and reworked it a lot in these conversations—was that I'd imprinted on our parents' unsatisfying relationship, and now I was endlessly seeking a neglectful mate to take the place of my neglectful father.

I mean: Yeah, okay.

My dad was the problem. That wasn't news.

Ashley had been a college freshman taking Psych 101 when she'd busted out this theory for the first time. "It's called *sexual imprinting*," she'd explained one night at this very same kitchen table.

"Please don't say that word," I'd said, and then I lowered my voice to a whisper for the benefit of my mother, sitting right next to me, "in front of Grandma Dodie."

"What word?" Ashley asked. Then, louder, just to mess with me: "*Sexual?*"

"Ashley!" I said, like *Hush!*

"It's a medical term," Ashley went on, totally unimpressed with my squeamishness. "Don't be weird about it."

Before I could declare my natural-born right to be weird about anything I chose, my mother took an interest in this new theory. "Is it like how ducklings imprint on their mothers?"

"Yes," Ashley said, "except that's for a maternal figure, and this is for a mate."

"You think JoJo imprinted on your disinterested father and now only wants a disinterested mate of her own?"

They both turned to regard me.

"I mean," Ashley said, "it tracks."

It didn't *not* track. I'd give her that.

Or maybe I was just cursed.

"But what about you?" I protested to Ashley. "You grew up with the same absentee dad, and you've had one nice boyfriend after another since the seventh grade."

"People are complicated," Ashley said with an apologetic shrug. "I probably imprinted on the good stuff."

All to say: This theory had gone unchallenged for so long that we all just accepted it now as a simple fact about who I was.

Even me.

But then tonight, very casually, almost as an aside, Ashley took that unchangeable fact and just . . . changed it.

"I just read a new study on imprinting, by the way," she said.

This topic needed no introduction. My mom and I looked up and waited.

"Apparently," Ashley went on, "you can imprint on a first kiss."

Well, that was news.

Ashley kept going. "It's because first kisses are so emotionally charged. In certain cases, they can become more."

"What does 'more' mean?"

"More than just memories," Ashley said. "They can become pivot points in our lives."

"Like—you never get over the person you kissed?"

Ashley nodded. "Pretty much."

My mother and Ashley both turned to study me, like this felt promising.

"Who *was* your first kiss?" Ashley asked then.

I shrugged, like *Duh*. "Finn Turner."

"What!" Ashley shrieked.

"Our Finn?" my mom asked, pointing in the direction of the Turner house down the street.

"Yeah," I said. "It was a neighborhood kids' game of truth or dare. He had to kiss me—blindfolded—out behind the sports shed at school."

"He was blindfolded?" Grandma Dodie asked.

"*I* was blindfolded," I said.

"How old were you?"

"Ten."

"And he was—"

"Thirteen, I guess."

"Bit of an age difference," Ashley said.

But I wasn't having it. "Harrison Ford has *twenty-two* years on his wife, and they're doing fine."

Ashley was already pulling out a yellow legal pad to take notes. "Was it a good kiss?"

"It was."

"Good enough to imprint on?"

I shrugged. "Good enough to spark a massive crush that lasted six years."

"*That's* how that crush of yours started?" Grandma Dodie asked.

"Yep. It started with that kiss, and it didn't fade until after he went off to college. Even that took a year."

Totally unrequited, by the way.

"Oh, my god," Ashley said. "Why didn't you tell us this sooner?"

I lifted my shoulders. "Because I didn't know it was relevant?"

"It's not *relevant*," Ashley said. "It's *everything*!"

The rest of us took that in. Then I said, "It is?"

And Ashley said, "Yes. Because we just solved all your problems."

"*All* of them?" I challenged—just as my mom, delighted, said, "We did?"

"Yes," Ashley answered us both. Then she tapped on the stack of RSVP cards she'd been sorting and said, "Because that very same Finn—that very same *newly divorced* Finn—just RSVPed *yes* to the wedding."

Seven

OKAY. THIS WAS big.

We all looked around at each other, like *Are we all thinking what we're all thinking?*

Finally, Grandma Dodie patted my hand and said, "Well, that's a nice distraction for you, sweetheart."

Boy, was it.

Finn, just so you know, grew up across the street from us—the old-est, tallest, and handsomest of three brothers—and he had been class president, the captain of the baseball team, and an actual, literal Prom King.

He was the reason I broke my arm—falling out of the tree near his bedroom while trying to spy on him. He took up 80 percent of the pages in my middle and high school diaries. And yes—he was definitely responsible for giving me a very memorable first kiss.

A first kiss I'd never forgotten.

A first kiss that every single kiss that followed had competed against—and lost.

The title of the study Ashley read was "Can Humans Imprint on a

First Kiss?" But did we need a scientific study for this? All we had to do was look at my *interminable* crush. Six formative years!

Now *that* was the longest relationship of my life.

Ashley had known all about that crush. My mom, too. *Everybody* in my house knew—even Pete. It was inescapable. I'd cut out Finn's yearbook photo and taped it to the mirror in my bedroom. I doodled his initials in little 3D lettering. I gazed mooningly at his house from our living room window for countless hours.

And now Finn was single. And coming on the cruise. We'd be trapped on the MS *Enchantment* together for eight potential-filled days.

And nights.

Ashley was on this. She flipped the legal pad to a fresh page.

"What do you remember about that moment?" she asked, leaning in like we were on *60 Minutes*.

I went with it. "Mostly sounds and sensations," I said. "Because I was blindfolded."

"And *why* were you blindfolded?" she asked.

"All the dares were blindfolded that day." I listed neighborhood kids. "Evan had to climb a tree blindfolded. Sean had to go down the slide blindfolded. Cooper had to hang from the monkey bars blindfolded."

"And you had to get kissed?"

"We were running out of ideas."

Ashley wrote something down but didn't say what. "And what do you remember about the kiss?"

"I remember waiting a long time—so long that I worried Finn wouldn't show up. Which would've been so embarrassing, right? Getting stood up for your first kiss?"

"And then he finally made it?"

"He finally made it, yeah," I said. "I heard his feet crunch on the gravel, and I was like, *Here we go.*"

"And?"

"And . . ." I thought back. "And he came close. And he put his hands on my shoulders. And then he stepped *closer.* And then he leaned in and kissed me."

"Just a peck?"

"Mostly," I said. "But there was a bit of a linger."

Ashley wrote down *peck* and then circled it. "Define *linger*."

"You know, it wasn't like how you'd kiss your grandparents. It was . . . softer. And, you know, kind of on the longer side. Duration-wise. As far as pecks go."

Ashley studied her notes.

"That was it?"

"Yeah."

Ashley sighed.

"What?"

"It's just: Aside from the whole 'blindfolded' thing, this kiss doesn't sound very special."

"I beg your pardon," I said. "It was massively special!"

Ashley studied her notes like she couldn't make the numbers add up. "Was it?"

"Very," I insisted again. "It had a kind of . . . tenderness to it." Yes. That word was right. I committed to it: "An *epic* kind of tenderness."

"Okay," Ashley said, like that might be promising.

I pushed on. "Maybe the mechanics of it, from the outside, don't seem like much. But on the inside?" I paused and pressed my palm to my chest—not sure of the right words.

"On the inside, what?"

"On the inside, it felt like an avalanche."

"Ooooh," Ashley said, like that was helping.

"I've never felt anything like it again. And the memory of that feeling has kept me company in sad times ever since."

Ashley and my mom glanced at each other like maybe that was a bit much.

"For example," I went on, trying to make my case, "on that very same afternoon, Dad was supposed to pick me up from school."

Grandma Dodie corrected: "Your dad *never* picked you up from school."

But my mom remembered.

I nodded. "It was the day Pete broke his ankle. Mom had gone to the ER, and my bike chain was broken, so I couldn't ride home with everybody else, and Dad was supposed to get me. But he didn't show up."

"He never showed up?" Grandma Dodie asked.

"I almost killed him. I really almost murdered him."

I went on. "When it started getting dark, I decided to walk home."

Our school was an okay bike-riding distance, but it was a bit far for walking. Plus, you had to go under a freeway bridge that had, as Grandma Dodie always put it, "no shortage of shady characters."

"You walked home?" Ashley said.

"I did. And just before the overpass, it started to rain. And it was cold out, and I'd forgotten my sweater, and it got dark fast—and more than one car splashed me with puddle water. I got drenched. At one point, I slipped and scraped up my knees. And even when I finally made it home, no one was there. The house key was missing from the hide-a-key rock, and so I just sat on the front steps, in the rain, with my knees and hands stinging, wet and shivering, waiting for Dad to show up."

So far, this felt like fodder for the absentee father theory.

But then I gave it a twist and said, "And that whole time, do you want to know why I didn't cry?"

I gave such a long, dramatic pause that by the time I finally said it, my mom and Ashley said it with me: "Because of that kiss."

"There's our answer," Ashley said then, circling something on her paper. "You got your first kiss on a day your father abandoned you. Was that the year you had pneumonia?" Ashley asked next, thinking back.

"Yes," I said.

"From being in the rain?"

"I don't think *rain* can give you a lung infection," I said.

"But being left out in it for hours can stress your system," Ashley pointed out.

I shrugged, like *Fair enough*.

"So Dad abandoned you and gave you pneumonia," Ashley said, making a note.

Then I said, "But that kiss . . . made things better. That kiss gave me something nice to remember in the hospital, too. I thought about it while taking my breathing treatments. And while waiting for X-rays. And when they woke me at night to take a sample of fluid from my lungs. I just kept replaying it in my head."

"Case closed," Ashley said then, slapping her hands down on the table. "That's plenty."

"Plenty of what?" I asked.

"Plenty of intense emotions to react to."

I hadn't thought about that day in so long.

Ashley went on. "You really did imprint on your first kiss. Maybe that's been your problem all along."

It was certainly a new spin on things.

"Is this good or bad?" my mother asked.

"It's always good to get to the root of your troubles," Ashley said.

"Are you saying," I said, just wanting to be clear, "that because I imprinted on one particular kiss *at the age of ten*, there is only one man on this earth I'll ever be able to love?"

Ashley winked. "Let's find out."

"Because that seems like a pretty narrow set of options," I went on. "In a world containing four billion men."

"It's just a theory," Ashley said. "But it does seem very lucky that he's coming to the wedding—single."

"Why?"

"Because now you can test the theory out."

"What are you saying?"

"I'm saying you should sleep with Finn on the cruise."

"Ashley!" I said, glancing over like she must've shocked Grandma Dodie.

But Grandma Dodie was just laughing.

I lowered my voice to a stage whisper anyway. "I'm not sleeping with my childhood crush at your wedding!"

"Fine," Ashley said. "Don't sleep with him. Just conquer him."

"*Conquer* him?"

"Just make him fall in love with you," she said with a shrug, like *Simple.*

"I have no idea how to make *anyone* do that—least of all my *appallingly unrequited* childhood crush."

"We'll figure it out. I'll help you."

"You're going to be a little busy."

"I'm never too busy for love."

"Ashley," I said. "Are we getting carried away here?"

"Think of it as an emotional reset," Ashley said, getting serious. "A chance to heal old wounds, and reevaluate emotional scripts you wrote years ago, and come to a new understanding of the story of your life." She paused. "But an epic one-night stand wouldn't kill you, either."

"Ashley!"

But Grandma Dodie started laughing again.

"This is impossible," I protested. "Finn was never, ever interested in me," I said. "Ever. At all."

"You were a kid back then," Ashley said. "Now you've grown up." She looked me over. "We're going to have to get your hair done. And your nails. And I will teach you how to walk in heels. Do you have any sexy outfits? Scratch that. We'll raid my closet." She squinted at me. "Should we do lash extensions?"

"I don't—"

"It's fine. Mascara will do."

"You can't turn your wedding cruise into some kind of Rube Goldberg love trap," I said.

I was trying to make it sound ridiculous, but Ashley nodded, like *Exactly!* "He's on the ship, and you're on the ship. He's newly divorced, and you're newly—*not married.* This is a no-brainer. You just need to show him that you're not a scrappy little pain-in-the-butt neighborhood kid spying on him from that oak tree anymore. He needs to understand that you've grown up into an irresistible, obsession-worthy love sorceress."

This felt like a high bar.

Reading my face, Ashley said, "And maybe you need to understand that, too."

"Nobody has time for any of that," my mother interrupted. "We'll be lucky to get these programs ready."

"Mom's right," I said. "Everybody's overwhelmed."

But Ashley shook her head. "This is easy. I was already working to set up half the bridesmaids. Think of all the team activities we've already planned. What if JoJo and Finn just happen to get paired up for all of them? And just happen to get seated together at every single meal? That's not more work—that's just tiny changes to a spreadsheet."

Ashley met my eyes. She knew I loved spreadsheets.

"That's just," she went on, pressing her advantage, "*holding space for destiny*."

My mom peered over her readers at Ashley like she was getting grandiose, but she let it all stand.

I let it stand, too.

And that's how, by consent agenda, we wound up launching Operation Conquest.

Ashley went back to making notes on her pad. "We should switch Finn's room, too," she went on, "and put him near Harmony's. So that JoJo has every opportunity to"—she wiggled her eyebrows a little—"upgrade roommates."

"Ashley!" I said.

But her point was valid.

Even if Finn wasn't my destiny, he was better—and I realized this could also be said of every other passenger on the ship—than rooming with Harmony.

WE WOUND UP talking so late into the night that I didn't go home to my apartment and slept over at my parents' house instead. Lying on my old bed in my old room, my personal Finn Turner wheels really did start turning. *Had* I imprinted on him? *Was* this the answer? *Could* I conquer him? He'd been quite the teenage heartthrob. The competition might be stiff. Wasn't he a fancy lawyer now?

Flipping over onto my tummy on my hydrangea-print bedspread, I googled him.

Yes. Finn was a lawyer now—a young, hotshot, *on-a-partner-track* lawyer at a fancy law firm in Chicago. And there was only one current image of him online—his professional portrait in a suit on his law firm's website. But it confirmed what was never in question: He was still handsome.

He didn't look the same, of course. He'd filled out, and solidified, and lost the wiry vibes of a teenager. His tousled high school hair was replaced with a groomed, brushed-back cut with a fade. I have no idea how much time passed as I studied that one photo, but it was long enough to notice that his eyebrows were more groomed now, and he had a new little scar on his cheek, and his jaw was more defined.

Different, but good. Different, but maybe even better?

Wait. Had Finn Turner gotten *better* looking since high school?

Of course he had.

Maybe Ashley was right.

Maybe he was the reason I'd never been able to connect to somebody else. Fair or unfair, reasonable or unreasonable, maybe my heart had just decided that Finn was the one—and would accept no substitutes.

At least it had standards.

Maybe it was lucky that I'd left Pearce at the altar. Maybe fate was keeping my options open. Maybe this was the cure for my curse, at last.

When I got tired of staring at the internet's only picture of Finn, I looked up "imprinting on a first kiss," found several more articles, read them all, and came away convinced. This explained it. People *did* sometimes imprint on one other person. And as much as I would never recommend that course of action to anyone else . . . if it had already happened, then maybe I'd just stumbled on some very good intel. A chance to change my life—and get it right at last. Maybe all I had to do was force myself onto a cruise ship, make Finn Turner fall in love with me, and let my poor, forgotten heart have what it had always wanted.

That didn't sound so hard. Did it?

Eight

ONE MORE LESS-THAN-GREAT thing happened before Ashley's wedding.

The night before the cruise began, I overheard my mother having a fight.

There was a spot by the AC vent in the hallway where you could hear everything going on in the kitchen. And here's what I heard: Apparently my dad had taken a job promotion without telling my mother. One that would require him—and by extension her—to move to Germany. And it had apparently seemed like such a no-brainer to my dad that he had said yes to it all without telling my mom.

I'd never heard her so angry.

"You didn't even *check in* with me, Raleigh," she kept saying. "You just *accepted*."

"Because you had enough on your plate already! I was trying not to add stress to your life."

"You accepted a job in another country without telling me"—my mom's voice was actually trembling—"and then you put the home that we've lived in for thirty years up for sale—also without telling me—"

I put my hand over my mouth. *Holy shit!*

"—and you thought somehow that was *not* adding stress to my life?"

My dad didn't even try to answer that question.

"I'm not going," my mother said then. "I'm staying right here. You can go if you want to, but I'm not going."

"You want to live apart?"

"We're already living apart, Raleigh. You work all the time. You missed *your own daughter's wedding.*"

"That was the airline—"

"No—you cut it too close and you missed your flight. It wasn't the airline. It was you."

"She didn't even go through with it," my dad pointed out, like that might help his case.

"And why do you think that is?" my mom snapped.

But my dad didn't answer.

"Raleigh, please listen to me. You missed. Your own. Daughter's. Wedding."

Silence.

Next, she said, "Whatever you're chasing, you're chasing it too hard."

"I'm sorry about the house," he said. "I'll make it right."

"I think it's too late to make it right."

"What does that mean?" my dad asked.

But my mom didn't answer.

"What are you saying?" my dad pressed.

"I guess I'm saying," my mother said, her voice so calm it was almost spooky, "that I want a divorce."

Wow . . .

Wow.

A *divorce*?

I mean, there were many—many—things about my parents' marriage that could be improved. But a *divorce*?

After all this time?

They just had their thirtieth wedding anniversary!

After she said the word *divorce*, my dad panicked and begged her to reconsider, but I could already call it.

My mom had made her decision.

"Don't tell me I don't love you," my dad said.

My mom sighed. "I'm just really not sure," she said, "if you even know what love is."

After a while, my parents got quiet. So quiet, for so long, I couldn't stop myself from tiptoeing down—skipping the squeaky step—and peeking into the kitchen.

My dad was in a kitchen chair, his arms clutching my mom's waist.

She was tolerating it, and absently patting his head, and staring off into the middle distance like she was still trying to absorb the conversation they'd just had.

"It's for the best, Raleigh. I really think it is."

In a thousand years, I never, ever would've imagined my parents getting a divorce. This was the life they'd built for themselves. This was what they'd agreed to. It wasn't gonna win any prizes, but they were okay. They were *fine*. They'd been fine for years.

Except, I guess, maybe they weren't.

Maybe, deep down, my mom had been seething. Or, short of that, maybe just lonely.

That was enough of a reason, wasn't it?

He really was always working. It was the only thing he liked to do. He didn't have hobbies. Or friends. Or areas of interest.

Those things were my mom's.

She maintained their social circle, and sent the Christmas cards, and made dinner, and confirmed doctor's appointments, and brought fresh flowers home from the grocery store. All the mortar that held everything together? That was her.

But I'd always thought that she liked doing that stuff.

Maybe it was more complicated than that.

My first thought was for my mom: What would the dating pool be like for a fifty-seven-year-old lady? The pickings had to be slim. She might not ever find anyone else.

But my second thought was even worse. How, exactly, would my dad even survive without my mom? He was sixty—and his own dad had lived to ninety. What on earth would he do with himself *without my mother* for the next thirty years? It was inconceivable.

A post-divorce montage for him flipped through my head: my dad in a sad, pre-furnished apartment, eating microwave dinners and drinking stale coffee, forgetting to open the curtains. All the invisible, unappreciated things my mother did that lifted up his life, *gone.*

That was bleak.

Without a man, my mom would still have Grandma Dodie, and good friends, and great food, and laughter, and her kids, and cozy mysteries to read, and her flower garden, and places to visit.

Without my mom, my dad would have . . . stale coffee.

God.

He'd wither away.

He'd forget to recycle his newspapers and become a hoarder, and stack them to the ceiling in every room—and eventually die by suffocation in his recliner when they finally avalanched down on top of him.

It was a lot to take in.

My mom concluded the talk by telling my dad not to tell anyone about this until after Ashley's wedding.

"Let's get through the wedding," my mom said, "and then we'll tell the kids."

But my dad's brain was still churning. "If I can change your mind on this cruise," he asked then, "will you change your mind?"

My mother sighed. "I wouldn't bet on it."

"One week." My dad nodded, like he was forming a plan.

"You've had thirty years so far," my mother said, "so I wouldn't get your hopes up."

I COULDN'T, OF course, tell Ashley about any of this. And I couldn't tell Pete, either, because he had no filter.

In the end, I just had to keep it to myself and wonder over and over if my mom had just made things better or worse.

Meanwhile, life was still happening, whether we liked it or not.

I still had a cruise to get through, and a childhood crush to conquer, and more than enough problems to solve.

I did go to Ashley's hairdresser, and I did get a blowout. I did pack more of Ashley's sexy clothes into my suitcase than comfortable ones of my own. I did practice walking in heels, and I did research *seduction tips for ordinary people* in the wee hours of the internet, and I did get my toenails painted hot pink.

For luck.

I worked out the exact number of hours we'd be on the ship together to try to nail down my time frame. I color-coded the activities schedule with highlighters. I even read a book called *How to Make a Man Fall in Love with You* and then made a spreadsheet from key points—with a tentative conquest schedule that included to-do items like "ask him about his job," "prioritize moonlight," and "eye contact, eye contact, eye contact."

Would it succeed? Who knew?

But by the time our whole family showed up at the wharf on embarkation day and got in line to board, all that late-night googling settled it for me. Conquering Finn—and all my intimacy issues along with him—would be my main objective on this cruise. It would give me purpose. And focus. And—*why not?*—a little bit of hope.

Not to mention, it just might work.

After all, I did get catcalled on the dock that morning by three dudes from another ship, who were all wearing T-shirts that read LET'S GET SHIP-FACED.

Which they already were, by the way. At ten in the morning. So ship-faced, in fact, that they tried to board *our* ship—the MS *Enchantment*—when *their* ship, the MS *Decadence*, was down the wharf.

Perhaps not the highest quality admirers.

But it was fine. I'd had a rough six weeks.

I'd take any encouragement I could get.

FYI: You can't just walk onto a cruise ship like you're checking into a hotel. There's a whole process. You have to wait in a long, snaking check-in line on the dock and get all your papers examined before they'll let you anywhere near the gangway.

So that's what I did that morning. I stood in line next to my family, trying to look pretty with my fancy hair, wearing a pair of shorts disguised as a miniskirt and the most painful heels known to man. Not to mention: a snug T-shirt of Ashley's with one of those gravity-defying padded bras underneath.

I didn't need padding, for the record, and the bra felt a little cartoonish, but the whole getup was Ashley's strong recommendation for the best first impression on Finn, and the stakes were too high to argue.

She was a scientist, after all.

Mostly, I just tried to stand like a pinup girl while I craned around, hoping for a glimpse of my destiny.

But my destiny turned out to be hard to spot.

Not everybody on the ship would be part of our wedding party, of course. Of the 1,600 passengers, fewer than a hundred of them were here for Ashley's wedding—and it would've been even fewer if my childhood neighborhood hadn't decided to make it into a block party reunion.

As the check-in line inched forward, I kept thinking that finding Finn shouldn't be so hard. I'd memorized his photo already. I knew what he looked like these days. But I had a confounding variable: the dominant image of Finn in my head was Finn *as a teenager*. Tall, tanned, and blessed with the metabolism of a jackrabbit. I knew *that* version of him very well. Too well. I'd carried it in my memory all these years like a photograph.

If I was twenty-six now, that made Finn—a senior when I was a freshman—twenty-nine. Which also made him, of all things, almost *thirty*. Which seemed so wrong. It was like he should have been suspended in time in the golden hues of his high school reign as class president, quiz bowl champion, and varsity captain of everything.

Could Finn be almost thirty? Would that even work?

As I stood awkwardly in line next to my secretly separated parents, trying to keep my shoulders back and wondering if I should've gone with a maxi skirt instead of a mini . . . I kept scanning the crowd for a version of Finn in a suit with a *GQ* haircut, trying to pattern-match.

And then a head-turningly cool guy decided to make a hell of an appearance on the dock.

A cool guy—in a vest.

A vest over an oxford button-down with the sleeves rolled back. Also: Ray-Bans, and perfectly faded Levi's 501s, with a short-on-the-sides-but-long-on-the-top haircut. I took it all in, along with his vintage canvas-and-leather duffel bag, like he'd just stepped out of the pages of some aspirational lifestyle magazine.

Was he Finn?

He was far away—but maybe.

I should mention that *men in vests* was my weakness. It was just a thing with me—for as long as I could remember. Any kind of man in any kind of vest: Sweater, suit, puffer. Scottish tartan. Tuxedo. Even a fishing vest might do in a pinch.

Is a vest appropriate cruise wear?

Hell no.

But did this guy somehow make all the dudes in flip-flops and sweatpants look like total amateurs?

You bet your life jacket he did.

Guessing from the crowd's reaction, I wasn't the only vest person in line to board.

Everybody stared as this guy strode past us like he was on a catwalk.

Whoever he was, he was somebody. Did he own the ship or something? Was he an actor I wasn't recognizing? Or the son of some nautical billionaire?

Or possibly all of the above?

This guy wasn't just cutting the line. He was walking right past it like it was irrelevant. He was focused on something else entirely—something up at the front—and it took a few minutes of gaping at him before I realized that the something he was focused on was . . . me.

He was walking right toward me.

As he got closer, all my visual questions started answering themselves.

And then I knew. Even before he pulled off the shades.

Dammit.

It wasn't Finn. It was *Cooper.*

Cooper. *In a vest.* Looking almost sadistically cool. Not to mention: radically different from the last time he'd showed up unannounced in my life looking like Grizzly Adams.

He smiled big when he saw me recognize him—and then, in one graceful swoop, he dropped his bag, sidled up to me, crooked his arm around my neck, and clamped me into a headlock.

"Cut it out!" I said, instantly mad, as I batted his thigh to make him let go.

He kept me clamped against him as he greeted my parents.

He was messing up my blowout. Monster!

"Cooper! Let go! Cooper!" I protested. Then, appealing to a higher power: "Mom! He's messing up my hair!"

But I guess my mom was just as mesmerized as the rest of us.

"Cooper," she said. "Were your eyes always this blue?"

"Yes, ma'am," Cooper replied.

Now I was thrashing around like a caught sailfish—but to no avail. Cooper was bigger than he used to be.

"Where's JoJo?" Cooper asked next, like he had no idea he had me in a headlock.

My parents thought this was hilarious.

"She should be around here somewhere," my dad said, playing along.

"She's not playing hooky, is she?" Cooper asked, clamping me tighter as I kicked at his leg.

"She wouldn't dare," my mother said.

Finally, I landed a good jab to the shin, and when Cooper flinched, I was able to bite him on the hip.

"Ow!" Cooper said, like I'd attacked him for no reason.

He released me, and I stood up, indignant—and then I punched him in the stomach.

"JoJo!" my mother scolded as Cooper doubled over.

But he recovered fast and stood back up straight to say, in my defense, "That's our standard greeting, Mrs. Burton."

I tried to give him a withering glare, but Cooper just started laughing.

"You look exactly like a rooster right now," he said, reaching for his phone.

"Don't take my picture," I said, well aware of how ridiculous I sounded. "And don't call me a rooster."

Cooper shrugged. "Stop looking like a rooster and I'll stop calling you a rooster."

I flipped Cooper off and turned to my mother. "How could you let him mess up my hair? This blowout cost a hundred bucks!"

"Did it?" my mom said, wincing like I'd made a bad financial choice.

"It was an *investment* in my *future*," I said, slugging at Cooper's midsection again.

He darted back, and I missed.

That's when Ashley and Brody showed up wearing matching T-shirts that read, in big scripty letters with arrows pointing at each other, I'M WITH MR. and I'M WITH MRS.

Cooper stepped forward to give the bride a civilized hug.

"Ashley doesn't get a headlock?" I demanded, finger-combing my hair back into place.

"That's *our* thing," Cooper stated. "Plus, Ashley's a grown-up."

"We're so glad you could make it," Ashley told Cooper, grown-upishly.

"Me, too," Cooper said.

Brody was older and hadn't known Cooper in high school. He squinted, trying to figure out exactly who Cooper was. "Are you"—Brody glanced my way without making eye contact—"JoJo's childhood bestie?"

"That's me," Cooper said, sounding oddly proud.

"That's a tough job," Brody said, like we could all agree I was a real pain in the ass.

But Cooper just gave me an affectionate look and said, "Yeah, but somebody had to do it."

"The word in the family," Brody went on, "is that you're the only guy she's never dumped."

Oh, god. This again. "Cooper and I never *dated*, Brody," I said, not hiding my annoyance. "So I never got a chance to dump him, did I?"

Cooper gave me a sly smile. "Missed opportunity."

I was still mad about the rooster thing. "I'll say."

Ashley leaned toward Cooper, gesturing at Brody to explain: "Brody and JoJo dated in high school. Briefly. For like a week. But they never even kissed before she dumped him."

"I remember," Cooper said. Then he looked at Brody. "Still mad about it, huh, buddy?"

God. Where was my EJECT button?

Then I had an idea. "Hey," I said to Cooper. "You aren't trying to cut the line, are you?"

Cooper looked around. "I was just saying hi."

But I was already rolling my suitcase his way. "Come on, pal," I said, tugging on his arm until he grabbed his bag and followed me. "No cutting. Let's move. All the way to the back."

Nine

AT THE BACK of the line, where I intended to stay, I couldn't stop staring at Cooper.

"What the hell did you do to yourself?" I asked, peering at him. "Last time I saw you, you were *feral*. And now you're some kind of English lord?"

Cooper smiled and looked down.

My tone was pure outrage. "And not some old, fat, snaggletoothed English lord, either! A *hot* English lord!"

Now Cooper gave me a look like I was irresistibly absurd. "My apologies."

"What's with the pectoral muscles?" I asked, poking one with my finger. "You can see them *through the vest*."

"Hey," Cooper said, covering his chest protectively.

"And who told you to roll your shirtsleeves back like this?"

"Is that a rhetorical question?"

We both looked down. You could see everything below the elbow. Specifically, Cooper's muscled, smooth, tauntingly naked forearms.

I almost lost my train of thought.

Those forearms were going to be a problem.

I pushed on: "And what's with this outfit? Is that *tweed*?"

"It's gabardine."

"It looks like tweed."

"I just flew in from London," Cooper said, like that was an excuse.

"Well, London wants its tweed back."

"What is your problem?"

"Look around you! This is hardly cruise wear. You're wearing *wool* to the Bahamas?"

"You're just mad because I look good."

"Tweed vests are my kryptonite. Did you know that?"

Cooper met my eyes. "Yes."

"Take it off," I said.

"No."

"You can't just prance around here in that thing."

Cooper looked me up and down. "If anyone's prancing, it's you."

"What's that supposed to mean?"

"It means don't give me shit for looking good when you look like that."

"I look the same as always," I declared.

But Cooper made a face like *Oh, really?* and then dropped his eyes, quite deliberately, to my cantilevered chest.

In defiance, I pushed it out further.

"And don't get me started on that miniskirt," Cooper added.

"What's wrong with it?"

"It's like they ran out of fabric and had to use a dinner napkin."

"It's not even a miniskirt," I said, resting my case on semantics. "It's shorts *disguised* as a miniskirt."

Cooper tapped his chest and then nodded at my skirt. "I'll take off *this* when you take off *that*."

I gasped. *How dare he?* But I doubled down. "Men in vests is *my* thing."

"Well, I'm a man. In a vest. So I guess it's my thing, too."

"You're not a man," I said, still trying to win. "You're *Cooper*."

"Sorry to shock you, but I am both."

It did shock me, in a weird way. Cooper had never been a man before. Who even was he now? I shifted back to my original point. "This outfit is tonally inappropriate. Do you see any other members of the *Downton Abbey* cast in this line?"

"Stop complaining."

"I haven't even *started*, pal."

But Cooper didn't accept the legitimacy of my anger. He shrugged. "It's not illegal to wear a vest," he said. Then he added, "Or get a haircut." He looked me over. "You got a haircut, too."

"Yeah. I did. Before you messed it up."

"Anyway," Cooper said. "You were so traumatized by my beard last time—"

"Your *pigeon nest*," I corrected.

"I thought I'd come back looking better."

"Yeah, but now you look *too* good."

He *did* look too good. I wondered what the math must be on that. Was it symmetry theory? The golden ratio? The exponential benefits of basic grooming?

There was no mathematical formula I could see that explained why Cooper's glow-up had made him so extra handsome. He would have to remain, on this point and many others, an unsolved mystery.

"You sure are hard to please," he said.

"I can't relax around"—I gestured with my hands at his general vibes—"*all this*." Then I squinted at him. "Didn't you bring any T-shirts that say 'Let's Get Ship-Faced'?"

"I saw those guys ogling you, by the way."

"Yeah, well. At least they didn't mess up my hair."

Why were we fighting, exactly? Seeing Cooper again at my failed wedding had been strangely lovely—despite the fact that we were, technically, *estranged* at the time. And despite my life collapsing all around me as it happened. We'd gotten along so easily—just like always. He'd been a refuge in the storm.

But today, I felt irritated with him. For not turning out to be Finn.

For showing up even better looking than last time. For claiming his right to wear a *vest*. And maybe, deep down, for being the reason that I'd be the *maid* of honor at my sister's wedding this week instead of the *matron*.

"Are you mad at me?" Cooper asked then.

"I'm not mad. I'm just wondering why you're even here."

Cooper shrugged.

"You RSVPed *no* to this wedding," I reminded him, "just like you did to mine. Though a bit more politely on Ashley's card."

"I changed my mind."

"Why?"

He squinted, watching to see if his words rang true. "Because I thought you might need me."

"What?" I demanded. "Why?"

Cooper tilted his head. "You've had a rough few weeks."

"Are you pitying me?"

"I'm definitely not—"

"Because I'm fine. I'm great."

"Okay," Cooper said, the way you acquiesce to a crazy person.

"I'm better than great, in fact. I've got a plan to fix my whole personality."

"Wow," Cooper said, like that was a tall order.

I nodded. "Better believe it."

"And can I ask what this plan might be?" Cooper asked.

"You can," I said. I was going to have to tell him at some point. Might as well be now. I took a step closer and looked around for potential eavesdroppers. Then I said, "I'm going to *fall in love* on this cruise."

In reaction, Cooper had no reaction.

His face stayed so still, in fact, that it prompted me to say, "Hello?"

Cooper shook his head, by all appearances trying to regroup. "Is that a plan?" Cooper asked. "Or . . . more like . . . a fantasy?"

"I know what words mean," I said. "It's a *plan*."

"Okay," Cooper said, lifting his hands.

"It's an Ashley-approved plan," I added, for legitimacy. "And she's a marriage and family therapist."

Almost, anyway.

Cooper didn't argue.

I went on, "And you're a central part of it now."

Cooper took that in, studying my face. "Am I the one you're going to fall in love with?"

"Oh, my god," I said, smacking his shoulder. "Cooper! Focus!"

But Cooper shrugged. "I'll do it."

"Of course not," I said.

Of course not. Cooper was the last guy in the world I could conquer. And I guess now is the moment when I have to unearth a half-forgotten moment in our friendship to explain why. Because the truth was—back in our senior year of high school, I'd allowed myself to harbor a little crush on Cooper, and I'd delusionally wondered if he might be feeling the same way about me. That is, until I had to take a shift at the kissing booth at the winter carnival. There had been a literal line for the girl on shift before me—but once I stepped into the booth? *Crickets.*

It was beyond humiliating.

I stood there like the most pathetic, unkissable person in all of human history for as long as I could bear it before I texted Cooper and told him to report to me, stat.

"I need you to kiss me," I said when he showed up with a half-eaten corn dog.

At the words, Cooper promptly coughed out the bite he'd just taken.

We both watched it hit the asphalt and roll a couple of inches.

"What?" Cooper said.

"I've got twenty minutes left on my shift, and no one is kissing me."

"So?" Cooper asked.

"So," I said, like *Duh*, "I need you to get things rolling. Start the stampede!"

But Cooper's head was shaking itself.

"I can't just stand here until the end of my shift *totally unkissed.* Gretchen Barnes had a line out the gate."

But Cooper just stared at me, his corn dog at half-mast.

"Ten seconds—that's all I need."

"I don't feel well."

"Five seconds! Three! A peck!"

"I really don't feel well."

"You were fine when you walked over here," I said, putting my hands on my hips.

"That was before you wanted a kiss."

"Cooper, this is not hard. Pretend I'm your grandmother."

"You're the *opposite* of my grandmother."

"What does that mean?"

"It means I can't."

"Are you really going to leave me here like this?"

"I'm honestly feeling sick. I'm not joking."

I let out a sigh that felt like the collapse of all my self-esteem. Then I said the only thing I could say: "Fine. I guess I can't force you."

"I'm sorry," Cooper said.

"Yeah," I said, with free-flowing bitterness. "So am I."

That could have been the end of it. It *should* have been the end of it.

But it wasn't.

Like a classic dummy, I took a bad situation—and made it worse.

What happened next resulted from a number of factors: One, I didn't believe that Cooper really wasn't feeling well. Two, my teenage ego really, desperately didn't want to come away from a shift at a kissing booth without getting even one kiss. Three, I'd been ignoring a manageable but growing secret crush on Cooper ever since Finn had left for college. And four, I kept getting the feeling that Cooper had a secret crush on me, too.

All to say, once Cooper was off the hook, he told me he was going home.

And then he spotted a trash can behind me to lob his leftover corn dog into, and as he leaned forward across the booth to toss it in . . .

I did something deeply ill-advised.

Because as he leaned closer, he was right within grabbing distance.

There was no time to think better of it. You know how reflex actions never make it to your brain? Your hand just yanks itself back from the fire without waiting for permission?

That was me right then. My body acting without my brain: reaching up, grabbing the collar of his T-shirt, and pulling his face to mine.

I know, I know.

I kissed him.

I fully ignored his very clear *no*. And did it anyway.

I don't know what my rebellious body was thinking. Maybe that he just needed a little help over the hump? That once it was happening, he'd change his mind? Decide he liked it? Bring his arms around and clasp me tight as we gave in to the bliss of shifting from friendship to love?

Yeah. Well. That's not what happened.

What did happen . . . was something Cooper and I had never talked about again—not once—since the actual moment.

It was all over in an instant: I grabbed him by the collar, planted a kiss on him, released him, saw the shock on his face . . .

And then I watched him throw up corn dog all over the kissing booth.

No need to quantify: It was *a lot* of corn dog. They had to call out the hazmat team and shut down the booth for the rest of the carnival. Come to think of it, I don't think the school ever attempted a kissing booth again.

I was mortified then, and I was still mortified now—and I had no doubt I'd continue to be mortified well into the afterlife.

Of course we never talked about it. What would there even be to say? The next time I saw Cooper, we just pretended nothing happened. Other people talked about it, of course. I became the girl who had kissed Cooper and made him throw up. Cooper, to at least a few delightful people, became Corn Dog Guy. The school newspaper even featured it as a bullet point under the main headline THE KISS-OFF in their reportage on the carnival.

So, yeah. That settled any questions I might've had about whether Cooper found me attractive. I don't think you can get more rejected than that.

Right? Case closed.

Here on the dock, all these years later, I wasn't sure how Cooper could even imagine being a candidate for Operation Conquest. If kissing a guy *makes him throw up*, he's not going to top your list of potential true loves.

Apparently, though, Cooper had not intuited this. "'Of course not'?" he asked. "Why 'of course'?"

I would not be rehashing any of this with him today. "Because you're *Cooper*."

"That's your whole reason?"

"That's the only reason I need."

"Who is it, then?"

Now we were back on track. But I suddenly felt weird about saying it. "It's someone else," I answered.

"Who?"

"Just—someone."

"Am I supposed to guess?" Cooper asked. Then, lowering his voice like it might be a secret: "Is it the captain of the ship?"

"Cut it out, Cooper. This is serious."

"I'm being serious," he said—unseriously.

"It's someone viable. It's someone who might be able to break this curse I've been living under my entire dumb life."

Cooper shook his head. "What curse is that?"

I looked him dead in the eye. Then I said, "Only loving men who don't love me back."

Once again, Cooper's reaction was no reaction.

Was he holding his breath?

Something about his face made what I'd said seem even sadder. I felt the truth of it in a way that pressed at my throat. My eyes stung with uninvited tears, but I squeezed down to get rid of them.

When I opened my eyes, after all that, we weren't really fighting anymore.

The tone of everything shifted.

Now I was saying something true to one of the only people on earth who might have a shot at understanding it. "Right?" I said, meeting his eyes, my voice softer. "It's bad. It's really bad. I called off my wedding—and even though Pearce wasn't the right person for me—"

Cooper jumped in: "Pearce was a total douchebag."

"Exactly," I said. "But I picked him. I *picked* him, and I fixated on him, and I demanded that we get married. Why did I do that, Cooper? I'm really worried something's wrong with me. I'm really scared I'm going to spend my whole life . . ." I thought back to what it had felt like to be with Pearce, and then I finished with: "lonely."

Cooper let out a long breath at that word. I had his attention now.

"This is not a joke to me," I said. "I've spent the last six weeks feeling incomprehensibly disappointed in myself. I think I might really be cursed. And I'm working like hell here to change my life. I need to get this solved. And I just really need you on my team. Can you be on my team, Cooper?"

He held my gaze for a second before saying, "I've always been on your team, Joey. Since day one."

"Great," I said. "Perfect. Because Ashley's a little busy right now, and I can't do this alone."

Cooper was looking at me like he was still on the fence. But his voice sounded like he'd given in. "So what is the plan, exactly?"

"I need to make an unsuspecting man fall in love with me before this cruise is over."

Cooper dropped his shoulders, like *Of course you do.* "You want me to help you seduce one of the other passengers."

I lifted a finger to take issue with *seduce.* "I prefer *conquer.* Or maybe even *woo.*"

"Nobody says *woo,*" Cooper said.

"*Conquer* it is, then."

Then, like he already knew he was going to hate the answer, he closed his eyes and said, "Spit it out. Who are we conquering?"

He *was* going to hate the answer. But that didn't change anything.

So I took a breath and just said it: "Finn Turner."

At the name, Cooper's head fell forward in exasperation.

And when he lifted it again, he looked right into my eyes and said, "That's the worst idea you've ever had."

Ten

OBVIOUSLY, I DISAGREED.

While we shuffled forward in the snaking check-in line, I explained all about imprinting, and how it wasn't just for ducklings, and how my problem all along was that I'd accidentally imprinted on Finn. I recounted all the information I'd gathered from both Ashley's expert testimony *and* the internet. And even though Cooper had known about my epic, endless *Thorn Birds*–style crush at the time—because everybody knew, except for Finn himself—I told Cooper something he didn't know.

That Finn had been my first kiss.

"Finn was your first kiss?" Cooper asked, seeming baffled.

"Do you want me to tell you about it?" I asked.

"Absolutely not."

I shrugged. "The point is, it happened on the same day that my dad really let me down in an epic way, and if you've read any Freud—"

"I haven't."

"—you'll recall that parental relationships are, like, a huge thing."

I hadn't read any Freud, either, to be honest.

I went on, undaunted. "And so the perfect storm of all that excitement mixed with all that abandonment on the exact same day made an emotional lightning flash that bound me to Finn Turner and Finn Turner only—forever."

Ashley had explained it much better.

But Cooper didn't buy any of it. He said, and I quote, "That's ridiculous."

"It's science," I insisted.

"It's bullshit," Cooper said.

And so we just kept arguing.

We argued about it all the way through the line.

And then we argued up the gangway.

And then we argued as we journeyed into the bowels of the ship to look for the cabin I'd be sharing with Cousin Harmony.

We argued so hard, I barely noticed the boarding process.

We argued so hard, I forgot to keep looking for Finn.

But here's what I do remember: I remember arriving at my cabin and finding a party-store flowered lei hanging on the door handle. I remember moving it aside to use my key and then pushing open the door. And then I remember my eyes getting *blasted* with the sight of Cousin Harmony and some random dude—tangled up like octopi on the tiny built-in desk in our windowless room . . . making out.

WANNA KNOW HOW my entire body reacted to that?

With a hearty *Hell, no.*

I leapt back out of the room on pure instinct—turning as I yanked the door closed behind me and landing chest-to-chest against both Cooper *and* his tweed vest.

Sorry—*gabardine.*

The impact slammed Cooper back against the hallway wall behind us—and then me into him. For a second, we were pressed against each other like that, face-to-face, while our brains tried to catch up.

"What just happened?" Cooper finally asked as I pushed myself back onto my own two feet.

"Harmony was in there," I said, still a little breathless.

"Okay," Cooper said, like *Not that shocking*.

"In there," I amended, "and hooking up with some guy."

Now that *was* a little shocking. "Already?" Cooper said, checking his watch. "We just boarded."

"Maybe they met in the check-in line."

"What do you mean by 'hooking up'?"

"What do you think I mean?"

"Were they naked?"

"I've already blocked it out, so we'll never know."

At that, the door to our cabin opened, and Harmony stepped out—her clothing ill-buttoned and a bright welt of a hickey blooming on her neck. She had dark hair, a heart-shaped face, cat-eye eyeliner, and Elizabeth Taylor vibes.

"Oh, hey," Harmony said.

There was a guy out of focus behind her, buttoning his shirt.

"Hey, Harmony," I said.

"I guess you're here," she said.

"I guess you are, too."

"Oh, I'm *definitely* here," Harmony said, glancing back at her gentleman friend. Then she looked down at the flowered lei looped over the door handle. "You didn't see the lei?"

"I saw it," I said. "I just didn't know it was yours."

"It's mine," Harmony said.

"Ah. Well." What to say? "It's very pretty?"

"I'm using it like a sock," Harmony said then.

Cooper and I glanced at each other.

"A sock?" I asked.

"You know. Like in college. If there's a sock on the doorknob . . . ?"

But I didn't know. "Why would anyone put a sock on a doorknob?"

That's when Cooper nudged me.

But too late. Harmony launched into a full explanation. "People put socks on doorknobs for their roommates if they're having sex in the room and don't want their roommate coming in and ruining everything. Like you just did."

Oh.

"Why a *sock*, though?" I asked.

"I get it," Cooper said. "It's like a doorknob condom."

I glanced sideways. "Please don't ever say *doorknob condom* again."

Cooper's shrug was almost playful. "That just makes me want to say it more."

Harmony went on: "And since pretty much everything about the cruise industry is pure evil, from the sewage they dump into the ocean, to the way they exploit their workers, to the chances of all of us getting murdered—which are like fifty percent—I am not thrilled to be here, *at all*, and I'll be putting that lei to use as much as possible to console myself."

"The chances of us all getting murdered are *fifty percent*?" Cooper asked.

Just as I asked, "Why did you RSVP yes, then?"

Between the two questions, Harmony chose mine. "For the gambling," she answered.

I nodded, like *Huh*.

"The point is," Harmony went on, "you'll be seeing this lei a lot. Get it? Because I'll be getting lei'd."

"Got it," Cooper and I said at the same time.

"You're welcome to use it, too," Harmony said.

"Thank you?" I said.

Just then, the man in the room walked up behind her.

"Who's your friend?" I asked.

"Oh," Harmony said, turning to squint at him like that was a good question. Then, going on vibes, she said, "Kevin?"

But the guy shook his head. "Kyle."

Then there was a funny silence while Harmony and Kyle turned back to stare us down—until we realized they expected us to leave now.

"Oh-*kay*!" I finally said, all singsongishly cheerful, like we'd just wrapped up a productive meeting. "I guess we'll just let you two . . . get back after it, then. And I'll circle back around on that lei situation a little bit later." I started to turn but then asked, "Can I leave my suitcase?"

Harmony wrinkled her nose. "Now's not a great time."

"Got it," I said.

Then Harmony gave me a thumbs-up.

And slammed the door.

GREAT NEWS. COOPER had a single.

But we had to go up five floors to get there. From steerage, as they would say on the *Titanic*, to accommodations much more befitting an aristocrat in a tweed vest.

Except an aristocrat would have taken the elevator . . . and we took the stairs.

At the base of the first flight, rolling my giant suitcase behind me, I stopped and looked up, like *Nope*.

But Cooper just turned back, grabbed the suitcase for me, and kept going.

And so, after standing still for a minute in protest, I followed—making sure to *vigorously* clomp the clompy platform sandals that Ashley had insisted I wear for my "silhouette."

"They invented these things called elevators," I called after Cooper as we hit the next level.

"I don't love elevators," Cooper called back, not slowing.

"Is it the ease, or the convenience?"

"This is better for your body," Cooper insisted.

"Define *better*."

By flight three, I had kicked off my shoes. By flight four, I was breathing hard. And by the time we reached Cooper's floor, as I thought about how much more fun Harmony—of all people—was having at this moment than I was? *Actively* cranky.

"So now I've met Harmony," Cooper said as we paused at his door.

I nodded. "My whole family calls her Grumpy Cat."

"She wasn't scowling today."

I bent forward and rested my hands on my knees to catch my breath.

"What does she do for a living?" Cooper asked next.

"I have no idea," I said. "All I know is nobody likes her."

"You should room with me instead," Cooper said.

Yeah—*that* wasn't happening. "Why are we even up here?" I asked. "You're not with the wedding block?"

"I need a balcony," Cooper said.

"A balcony?" My room with Harmony didn't even have a *window*.

"Yeah," Cooper said as he touched his key to his lei-less door.

He opened it and gestured me through—and I wasn't five steps in before I was overcome with envy.

I hadn't seen much in those panicked seconds when I'd entered my own cabin just now, but I'd seen enough to know it was—again: *windowless*. And also about the size of a jail cell.

This place, on the other hand, was a stateroom for dignitaries.

I positively leered at it. It had a double bed, with sconces, a patterned carpet, ambient lighting, and a full wall of sliding glass doors that opened onto a luxurious balcony overlooking the harbor.

Plus a champagne bottle chilling on ice with two glasses on the bedside table. Not even kidding.

"You 'needed' this room?" I asked, walking to open the balcony door.

"Yes," Cooper said, following me.

We stepped out onto the balcony and looked down at the harbor below.

"Define 'needed,'" I said.

"I have a condition where I need two exit points at all times."

"You mean your claustrophobia?" I asked.

"I don't have claustrophobia," Cooper said.

"Yes, you do." Our whole neighborhood knew that.

"I have *cleithro*phobia," Cooper said. "Which is not the same thing."

"What is it, then?"

"It's a fear of getting trapped."

"Yeah," I said. "Claustrophobia."

But Cooper shook his head. "Claustrophobia is a fear of small spaces."

Huh. Interesting. "Your phobia should rebrand," I said. "It sounds like a knockoff."

"I agree."

"I've never even heard of it."

"No one has," Cooper said. "It's very niche." Then he added, "My case is mild, if that's any comfort."

"Who needs comfort?" I said, glancing back toward his room. "You've got the best cabin of anyone."

Eleven

THE FIRST ORDER of cruise wedding business was a welcome gathering at noon on the sports deck up top before we even left port—a mini-golf tournament for the wedding guests with a buffet lunch afterward. Ashley put me on Finn's team, so even though I hadn't seen him yet, it was only a short matter of time.

I checked my watch. We had exactly one hour to get ready, and I'd need the whole thing.

"Can I change in your bathroom?" I asked Cooper as I unzipped my suitcase.

"You're changing for mini golf?"

"Uh-huh," I said, standing back up and holding out a tiny hot-pink cocktail dress for him to see.

"That's what you're wearing? To mini golf?"

"It's Ashley's," I said, like that explained everything.

"I've never seen you in a dress like that," Cooper said.

"That's the point. This is phase one of the plan." Then, quoting from Ashley's notes: "Change your image."

Cooper eyed the dress again. "It'll certainly be a change."

"This is *designer*, thank you," I said.

"It looks like you stole it from Baby Gap."

But I just stepped into the bathroom, deliberately unperturbed—leaving the door cracked as I peeled off my T-shirt and stepped out of my miniskirt shorts.

"I know what you're thinking," I went on as I pulled on the dress. "You're thinking it's totally asinine to wear this. You're thinking everyone else will be in sneakers and golf shirts. *This isn't cocktail hour*, you're thinking. But mock me all you want. I know what I'm doing, and I know why I'm doing it."

I wriggled the dress up into place and hooked the arms over my shoulders. Sleeveless, of all things. And snug, for sure—so snug I had to take off my bra because even just *millimeters* of padding were a deal-breaker. It was also the shortest dress I'd ever attempted to wear in public. But it was Ashley-approved. In fact, this whole plan was. And so, as strange and ridiculous and naked as I might feel, this was happening.

I reached back to work the zipper but only managed to clear my underwear elastic before it got stuck.

"Hey, Cooper," I said, stepping back out into the room. "Can you zip—"

But there, just feet away, was a sight that stopped me short.

Cooper's naked torso.

Specifically: Cooper—now changed into a pair of gray dress pants . . . and in the process of putting on a crisp white oxford shirt.

I say "in the process of" because he was midway through sliding both of his arms into the sleeves. It's hard to capture the visual, exactly. But he'd flung his shirt up and raised his arms like a great blue heron stretching its wings so the sleeves could slide down over them—and I arrived just at the apex of all this and got a sight of Cooper's fully exposed, remarkably naked torso.

Which was absolutely, utterly . . .

Like a flashbulb going off in my face.

"*What the hell?*" I heard myself say as I spun around.

I closed my eyes, too, for good measure.

Then I demanded, "What are you doing?"

Cooper was less flummoxed. "I'm getting dressed."

"But why don't you have a shirt on?"

"Because I'm *getting dressed*."

I took a second to steady myself.

"Did you need something?" Cooper asked.

Did I? I couldn't remember.

Then I nodded for a second before finding the words: "I need . . ." I said, "for you to zip me up. I'm stuck."

I stayed facing away, but I felt Cooper walk up behind me.

This seemed like a good moment for a scolding. "You can't just go around taking off your clothes like that, Cooper."

"*You* took off *your* clothes."

"In the bathroom. Like a decent person."

But that's when Cooper put his hands on my hips to assess the zipper problem.

"Where'd your bra go?" he asked, and I got a flash of what he must be seeing: a long, narrow, unzipped *V* tracing the naked length of my spine.

What was the question again?

"There's no room for it," I answered. "I am squeezed into this dress like a sausage in its casing."

"Don't say that to anybody else."

Then I felt Cooper take ahold of the zipper pull and start trying to work it up. Which took a minute. "You have bad luck with zippers," he said as he tugged.

"Bad zipper karma," I agreed.

I had just put my hair up in a bun, and so my neck was totally exposed to the brush and tickle of every breath he took.

Which somehow felt like something I should put a stop to.

Right? This was Cooper!

But I didn't.

"Is it possible this dress is too tight?" Cooper asked after a while.

"It's a full size smaller than the smallest size I ever wear," I confirmed.

"But you want me to zip it, anyway?"

"I do."

"It's really pretty snug," Cooper said doubtfully.

"Just think of it like a corset."

A funny pause, then: "You don't want me to do that."

Before I had time to process whatever energy *that* was, Cooper launched a new zipper strategy, and his hands started moving everywhere—waist, rib cage, hips—pressing and tugging as he tried to pull the two zipper sides close enough to slide them together.

Finally, I guess he decided to go down to go up.

He pulled the zipper south a few inches. But then he paused.

"What?" I prompted.

"Are you wearing cotton underpants?" he asked. "With unicorns on them?"

I glanced back. "Aren't you?"

And then we settled right back into our usual dynamic as Cooper said, "I'm so tempted to give you a wedgie right now."

I swatted at him. "Don't. For real."

He yanked up. His new strategy worked: the zipper gave in, and the pull slid up in a satisfying swoosh.

Perfect.

Success!

As long as I didn't bend. Or sit. Or breathe.

I turned around to face Cooper triumphantly, like *ta-da!*

I think—though we may never know for sure—that his eyes widened at the sight of me. In a good way. Like I was surprisingly nice to look at.

I wanted to give him a high five, but I was afraid to reach up that far.

Next, Cooper said, "That's the shortest dress I've ever seen. It looks like you forgot your pants."

I ignored him and pointed at the high heels resting on my suitcase. "Can you hand me my shoes?"

"Those?" Cooper said, sounding doubtful.

"What?"

"You can't walk in heels."

"I can now," I said.

Cooper didn't buy it. "Did you get new feet?"

I flared my nostrils. "I've been practicing for a solid week."

Cooper set the shoes down in front of me, and I held on to his shoulders for balance as I worked my feet into them. "Yes, they hurt like hell," I said, answering his unspoken question. "But guess what? There's an inverse relationship between how excruciating your heels are and how effective they are. That's just math."

Cooper looked like he was stifling a smile.

"I know what you're thinking," I said. "You're thinking I'm ridiculous."

But Cooper shook his head. "I'm not thinking that."

"You're not?"

Cooper and I both turned to check out my whole look in the door mirror.

"I get it," Cooper said, taking in the sight of me. "You need to look different today. You need to show everybody that you've grown up. You need to shock them into seeing something other than the kid who got chased by a schnauzer on the Vargases' driveway."

Well, that was surprisingly accurate. "I'd forgotten about the schnauzer."

My shoe felt weird. Did I have a pebble in it already? I turned back and grabbed Cooper's shoulder so I could pull it off.

"Another pebble?" Cooper asked.

"It's fine."

Cooper went on. "You were always—no offense—kind of a classically overlooked middle child. Ashley was always out there achieving and being perfect, and Pete was always in trouble for setting off fireworks. You flew under everybody's radar. I always wondered if you felt invisible."

What a question. I felt a funny pressure on my chest.

"You weren't invisible to me, by the way," Cooper added. "Just so you know."

I took a long breath.

Cooper went on. "So, I get it. People see what they expect to see, and Finn probably expects to see that same seventh grader who used to draw hearts on the dirty windows of his Pathfinder. But you're not that kid anymore. If he met you in a bar now, he'd ask for your number. And he'd be lucky to get it. He might not know that yet, but you do."

Why did it feel so good to hear all that?

Cooper kept going. "You need to make him see you differently. You need to make it clear that you are someone he'd be crazy not to fall in love with. And you've only got eight days."

"That's exactly what I was about to explain to you," I said, feeling something like awe. "Except you just said it way better."

"I get it," Cooper said. "I genuinely do."

Then, while I was appreciating him, Cooper turned to grab what looked like a suit jacket lying on the foot of the bed. But guess what? It was a suit jacket *with a vest*.

"Not another vest," I said.

Cooper shrugged. "It came with the suit."

He slid it on—using his same blue heron moves.

"That's just mean," I said.

"Wait till I add the tie."

I watched him pop his collar, settle a pale blue tie around his neck, and start tying a half-Windsor. I was so mesmerized by the vest, and the tie, and his words, that I didn't even notice it wasn't mini-golf wear until he slid the suit jacket on.

"Hold on!" I said then. "What are you doing?"

"Putting on the jacket," Cooper answered.

"But—are you wearing a full suit to play mini golf?"

Cooper nodded. "Of course I am."

"But why?"

"Because you're wearing that dress. And it's our whole childhood street up there. And they're going to tease the hell out of you. A lot. *So much.* And I just . . ."

Cooper lifted his gaze to meet mine, and now I found myself wondering the same thing my mother had: *Were those eyes always that blue?*

I didn't ask.

I just let him go on and say, "I just don't want you to have to do this alone."

Twelve

ALL OF COOPER'S predictions came true, by the way.

Our whole childhood street did tease me. A lot. *So much.*

I'd been hoping for a *Miss Congeniality* moment as I made my entrance—the wind blowing my hair as I strutted in slo-mo and turned every head on the deck.

Instead, nobody really noticed me one way or the other.

Finn wasn't even there yet, and the other guests were just happily gathered, enjoying each other's company, eating nibbles off a snack table. Lots of them were work friends I didn't recognize—or maybe Brody's relatives. My childhood neighbors were nowhere in sight.

Safe to say, none of these random strangers cared at all if I'd had a glow-up.

I stood there, disappointed. All that slo-mo for nothing.

Was I even at the right wedding?

Then I noticed Ashley, standing next to Brody and letting some cousins get a gander at her engagement ring. Next, I spotted Grandma Dodie, in a straw hat and drinking an enormous fruity cocktail with a dashing older gentleman I didn't recognize.

I found Pete and nodded toward the two of them. "Who's the player with Grandma Dodie?"

Pete looked over. "I just asked Mom. He's a passenger."

"Not part of the wedding."

"Nope. She picked him up at the burger bar."

"Go, Grandma Dodie." She did not come to play.

I spied my mom and dad, who were busy fighting the wind to tie up a custom-printed welcome banner that featured an engagement photo of Ashley and Brody hugging and an Audrey Hepburn quote in modern calligraphy that read *The best thing to hold onto in life is each other.*

At last, I found our neighbors—who, parents and kids alike, had gathered on the mini-golf course. Mr. and Mrs. Dunn were there, and the Vargases, and Finn's parents, the Turners. Cooper's mom was the only parent from our childhood street who had RSVPed *no*—but only because she was prone to seasickness. She'd made Ashley and Brody promise to come over for a nice dinner once we were all back.

This felt like an audience I could prove something to. I tried again for that slo-mo entrance, but there was too much Astroturf in that section to do it right.

Everybody—and I mean everybody—in that group had heard about my failed attempt at getting married and was curious to get a glimpse of the wreckage of my life. And every single person who greeted me said some jovial variation of *There's the runaway bride!* before giving me a hug.

It was fine. We all needed something to talk about. It was the only thing I'd done lately to make front-page neighborhood news. And I'd been bracing for this for a while.

They also had a few thoughts on my outfit.

I got teased for my too-formal attire, my too-fancy heels, my "new hairdo," the color of my lipstick, the length of my hem, and my hot-pink heart-shaped earrings—which were generally assessed to be too hot, too pink, and too heart-shaped.

But Cooper had a point: At least I wasn't invisible.

The teasing was no surprise.

What *was* surprising . . . was Cooper.

He stayed right by my side the whole time, like a professional hype man.

If anybody lingered too long on *what on earth happened* at my tragic non-wedding, Cooper said, "She came to her senses, that's what happened."

Over and over: When they questioned my judgment, or dismissed my choices, or not-too-subtly implied that I looked like a hooker . . . Cooper just jumped in to point out—or even exaggerate—some quality of mine that made me sound far less pathetic.

Convincingly. Enthusiastically. Like he really believed it.

Improvising lines like, "A girl like this doesn't have to settle for a guy like that."

Like he was the VP of PR for my rebranding project.

How much was I paying this guy? He needed a raise!

He boasted about me in ways that I could never boast about myself. "Did you know that JoJo graduated from college Phi Beta Kappa?" he'd demand. "In *mathematics*?"

Of course they didn't know that.

I didn't even know that *Cooper* knew that.

It didn't matter. To almost everybody who lived on our street, I was just the smallest, scrappiest kid in the neighborhood gang.

But Cooper didn't let that stop him.

"You wouldn't think a person who looks this good could be smart, too, would you?" he demanded of everyone.

Did I look good? I was too self-conscious to have a read on that.

"Brains *and* beauty," Cooper kept saying. "Amirite?"

Was he Jedi-mind-tricking us all?

Who cared? It was *working*.

"This girl," Cooper told our next-door neighbors, Mr. and Mrs. Dunn, pointing at me to drive the point home, "is the Einstein of the street." Then he turned to me and said, "Tell them your IQ."

What a question. "I have no idea," I said.

Cooper nodded at the Dunns, like *See?* Then he said, "How smart do you have to be for your own mom to hide your IQ like a state secret?"

When the Vargases said they'd heard I was left at the altar, Cooper set the record straight by telling the whole story—adding a totally fictional grand finale of Pearce bursting into tears and "crying like a donkey."

"Wow," the Vargases said.

"She's a heartbreaker," Cooper said. Then he added, like it was good advice for everyone: "Watch yourselves."

Even when people like the elderly Bishops were, in fact, just making pleasant chitchat and asking what I was up to—Cooper couldn't help but be aggressive.

"Tell them about your thesis paper for your math major," he said, elbowing me.

"They don't want to hear about that," I said.

Didn't Cooper realize that nobody wanted to talk about math? Most people on earth had either (worst-case scenario) active PTSD from terrible math teachers growing up or (best-case) a pleasant, glazed-over disinterest. Math was the last subject on earth anybody should use for small talk.

"*I* want to hear about it," Cooper said.

I glanced at the Bishops. Then I said, "Well, it was based on the mathematics of knot theory."

I checked for any sign of recognition.

Seeing none, I explained. "Knot theory, like *knots*." Then I spelled it: "*K-n-o-t-*s. Which is a mathematical exploration of how knots are shaped."

Had I lost them yet?

"So . . ." I went on. "I used knot theory to explore the loops you make with yarn in knitting"—here, I mimed knitting something—"you know, like sweaters and scarves . . ."

Their eyes still seemed focused.

"To extrapolate mathematical models," I went on, for my big finish, "that could help physicists understand how strands of DNA fold themselves."

And . . . now I'd lost them.

Their smiles had stiffened. Their eyes had glazed. As if to prove me right, they both caught sight of some other neighbors—and hurried to go greet them.

But guess who I hadn't lost?

Cooper.

He was still right there with me, wearing an expression you might call *astonished admiration*. "Holy shit," Cooper said. "*That* was your math thesis?"

Now I felt shy. "It was pretty esoteric."

"It's *incredible*," Cooper said, staring at me with new eyes. "It's the most bad-to-the-bone thing ever."

I'd never heard a regular person say *bad-to-the-bone* to describe math. But he wasn't wrong.

A smile took over my face, and I looked at Cooper with some new eyes myself.

"What?" Cooper asked as I kept smiling.

"Nothing."

"What?" he prodded.

"I've just never seen a non–math person get excited about knot theory."

"And knitting," Cooper pointed out. "And DNA. Is that why you became an art teacher? So you could teach your kids to knit strands of DNA?"

"Not exactly, but kind of," I said. I mostly became an art teacher because I felt like the world vastly underappreciated the awe-inspiring beauty of mathematics. And I wanted to get that fixed. One middle schooler at a time.

Then Cooper added, "Guess you didn't knit me that beanie in high school for nothing."

I shrugged. "Must've been destiny."

"I still wear it, by the way."

"You do?" I thought he might have thrown it away.

He nodded to confirm. "Prized possession."

The idea that he'd kept it felt important somehow.

That's when Cooper said, "Anyway. I knew it."

"Knew what?"

He put both his hands out for a furtive—and considerate—low five and leaned closer. "That you were smarter than all the rest of us put together."

COOPER AND I continued chatting for a while because Finn took forever to show up, and Ashley wasn't starting the Putt-Putt tournament without him.

This was part of the plan.

With great precision, Ashley had sorted all the young people into mini-golf teams that had the potential for love connections—and the old people were not included. They self-sorted off toward the snack table while the rest of us gathered in our teams.

I went along while wondering about Finn. Did he have a last-minute work thing? Did his plane from Chicago get delayed? Did he get back with his ex-wife?

He wouldn't mess up my plans for radical self-transformation, would he?

But just as I was thinking of checking the passenger list, Finn arrived at last. And, for better or for worse, he looked exactly like his picture on the web. Except for the golf shirt. And matching golf shorts. And . . . matching golf shoes.

A full *golf ensemble* is what I'm describing—minus the 1920s jodhpurs and argyle socks.

Like Finn was possibly taking Putt-Putt a little too seriously.

As he walked toward us, stealing my slo-mo entrance for himself, I compared this *in real life* version of Finn to my well-worn mental picture.

Yep. Still the confidence of the best-looking guy in the room.

And still just oozing alpha energy.

And—could he be taller now? Bigger, anyway. He'd definitely been working out. Professional success agreed with him. He had a new swagger: not a high-school-kid swagger, but the refined, seasoned swagger of a grown-up.

He was still—and always would be—Finn Turner. The legend himself.

Here's a random truth about crushes: They can, and do, burn out.

Even after all those crushed-out years, with no encouragement and no reason for hope, I had—genuinely—moved on. He went to college, and then I went to college, and there just wasn't enough fuel to keep that fire burning. Life shifted, and so did I. Time and distance did their work. And he became . . . just a former crush. A former crush with an asterisk and a lengthy footnote—but a former crush, all the same.

On the rare occasions when I'd see him around the street when we both happened to be home for holidays, it hardly rocked my world. I'd just think, *Oh, there's Finn. Who I used to have that insane crush on.*

But now, seeing him in person—under the influence of this highly specific new theory that *he was the only man I'd ever love* . . . It shifted things back. As Finn joined the group, all my old full-body Pavlovian high school reactions to him revved up again, and my rib cage felt like it was clamping down on my heart. Not to mention my lungs.

I forced myself to take a breath—terrified that I might audibly gasp.

But nobody would have noticed anyway. We were *all* watching Finn.

He came straight over to the neighborhood kids, and he fist-bumped everybody—which took a minute, because on our street, everyone had a signature fist bump. Ashley's was "snail," where instead of bumping your fist, she'd put up two fingers like antennae. Sean's was "squirrel," where he scampered his hand up your arm. Pete's was "stick shift," where he moved your forearm like he was shifting gears. Cooper's was "shark attack," where he made his two hands into a shark's mouth and then ate your fist. And mine was "narwhal" . . . where I just held up one finger.

Everybody had a particular fist bump.

Everybody—except Finn.

Guess what Finn's was?

Nothing. *Just a fist.*

Because Finn was our undisputed alpha. And he didn't have to go any harder than that.

He was a benevolent alpha, though. He patiently bumped everybody after he arrived, shining his star power on each of us in turn like sunshine—and he said everybody's nickname as he went.

If the person he was greeting didn't have a nickname, he just made one up.

"Coop," he'd said to Cooper, stretching out the *ooo*. His brothers, Evan and Sean, got "E-van" and "Sean-o"; Pete got "-ster" added to the end of his name to make "Pete-ster," which made Pete glow with pride; and Ashley got "Bride of the Century" and a gallant kiss on the back of her hand.

Through it all, I hung back shyly—the way you do when you come face-to-face with your future while wearing wobbly stilettos on a carpet of Astroturf—wondering what my nickname would be. I wound up the very last fist-bumper, after Finn had made eye contact with every other neighborhood kid and made each one feel like a million bucks.

And then he got to me.

At my turn, right there at the end, he looked at me blankly and then frowned around at the crowd for clues before squinting and saying, "And who's this?"

Are you kind of hoping it was the glow-up? That maybe I just looked so different in that too-tight minidress that he couldn't recognize me? That I was, in that moment, perhaps *too beautiful for my own good*?

Yeah, no.

"It's JoJo," Sean said.

But Finn just blinked, like that name didn't ring a bell.

"JoJo," Evan offered next. "From across the street."

Still nothing.

"She's the one," Evan explained, "who had a crush on you for like eight years."

Six, actually. But point taken.

"She fell out of the tree in the side yard while trying to spy on you?" Sean said.

"She used to call you all the time and hang up?" Evan offered.

"She got your school photo printed on a pillowcase?" Pete added, right behind me—before I kicked him.

Wow. I guess everybody really knew everything.

But still nothing from Finn. No recognition at all.

So brutal.

However. Like a gentleman, he didn't leave me hanging forever. At last, he nodded like he was retrieving a nebulous memory from the mists of time, and then he faked it.

"JoJo," he said, like *Of course.*

Then Finn held out his fist at last, and I did my narwhal—but I was feeling so glum by that point that I did it weakly, and its little horn was, shall we say, a bit limp.

Finn frowned and left his fist there. "What was that?"

I sighed. "A narwhal."

"It doesn't look like a narwhal," Finn said, like maybe I had my animal wrong.

And then Cooper, bless him, leaned in and hit Finn's fist with a proper version.

"A *narwhal,*" Cooper said, pointing his finger straight, like there could be no mistake about it. Then he added, I guess for posterity: "JoJo studies the mathematics of knitting."

LOOKING BACK, THIS was the point of no return.

In some other universe, there's a version of my life where I read the tea leaves of the future in that moment, left the sports deck immediately, went back to Cooper's cabin by myself, and drank his complimentary champagne straight from the bottle on his balcony until the ship left the harbor.

This is not that version.

Instead, I stayed for the Putt-Putt tournament—doggedly hoping to turn a very weak start into a strong finish.

Ashley had put me on Finn's team, after all. And I had compressed all my organs to squeeze into this outfit. Might as well make the most of it.

Cooper wasn't originally on my team. I know because Ashley had typed out all four lists and printed them on different-colored card stock for reference—adding Cooper at the last minute to the smallest team. But when my team gathered by the lighthouse to get started, Cooper was there.

"Aren't you supposed to be over by the octopus?" I asked.

"I switched with Evan."

"You didn't have to," I said. "I'm pretty good at Putt-Putt golf."

"How long has it been since you've played?"

I thought back. "Middle school?"

Cooper shrugged and said, "You might be a little rusty."

Was he being overprotective? How good could all these people possibly be at mini golf?

But that was before I noticed that Brody had also just switched cards and joined our team—risking Ashley's wrath, because he was definitely upsetting the gender balance to form a bro team. All bros, in fact, except for me.

And Brody, like Finn, turned out to be surprisingly into mini golf.

I don't need to name names, but let's just say one of them—*cough*Brody—was wearing a single leather golf glove on his nondominant hand.

To play *mini golf.*

There are people who like to compete because it's fun—and then there are other people who like to compete so they can *crush the competition.*

Brody was 100 percent *crush the competition.*

Except he seemed to think that *I* was the competition—even though we were on the same team.

Anyway—did I just say I was "pretty good" at mini golf?

Today, I was the opposite.

Did the heels have me off-balance? Was my child-sized dress cutting off circulation to the motor cortex of my brain? Or—possibly—when the biggest crush of your life *publicly does not remember you at all* . . . is that a little destabilizing?

Whatever it was, I just couldn't get those tiny little balls into any of those tiny little holes.

I just kept smacking at them with my club. To no avail.

I'll shock no one by saying that Finn most often got holes in one—or two. Three, *max*.

Brody, too.

But I was solidly, repeatedly, in the double digits.

Without ever voting, we'd all elected Finn our team captain by telepathy. And then Brody had appointed himself the scorekeeper, and—I guess in an effort to foreground that he had snagged the best of the two Burton sisters—he kept calling out loudly to ask for my score . . . and then pretending not to hear my answer.

"JoJo! What's your total?" Brody would shout, waving his putter at me.

"Twenty-three!" I'd shout back.

"Three?" he'd respond, deliberately getting it wrong.

"*Twenty*-three!" I'd have to shout again.

And then Finn would look up from his practice putt like *Twenty-three? Who could possibly get twenty-three?*

Brody did this on every round.

Twenty-three is a lot. I agree.

Even so, isn't it poor teamsmanship to leave a player behind?

But leave me behind they did. Finn, Sean, and Brody would take their shots, high-five each other, and then move on to the next anchor, or pirate ship, or mermaid.

Like I didn't even exist.

I tried to catch up, but shot after shot went too far, stopped too short, got stuck in valleys, bounced off walls, skittered off the course altogether, or got lost in the octopus's tentacles. Once, at the sandcastle, I made a shot that went into the hole, circled around, and then *popped out again* to roll back to the beginning.

And Cooper, bless him, stayed with me the whole time, offering useless advice like "Keep your wrists loose," "Find your center of gravity," and "*Be* the golf ball."

"What does that even mean?" I said, swinging my putter and missing the ball entirely.

Somewhere around shot twelve or thirteen, Cooper would start putting his hands over mine on the golf club handle, willing them to absorb his know-how. Or, perhaps, just taking my shots for me.

This helped a little.

But of course, Cooper himself was taking shots in the teens, so I'm not sure how much know-how he really had to offer.

"I'm so much worse than I thought I was," I said, when the rest of our team had rounded the sandcastle and we'd lost visual contact again.

"It's those heels," he said. "They're messing with your depth perception."

"I can't believe Finn didn't remember me," I said next.

"Big kids never remember little kids."

"He remembered everybody else."

"Maybe he was playing it cool."

"Did you see him squint at me like he'd never seen me before? I totally froze."

"You did fine," Cooper said.

"But I didn't *say* anything," I argued. "He's going to think I have no personality."

"Guess what?" Cooper said, in an effort to be kind. "In that dress, you don't *need* a personality."

* * *

THANKS TO COOPER and me, we came in last place. *Very* last place. So very last place that when Finn saw our score, he threw his club down like a golfy John McEnroe having a tantrum.

But that wasn't the worst of it.

The worst of it happened after the game. After everyone had returned their putters to the rental desk, and after Brody had removed his one weird golf glove and tucked it into his pocket, and after Finn and Brody had tried to get Cooper and me retroactively kicked off their team—as we were all walking over toward the buffet.

The irony is that I was actually getting the hang of the whole walking-in-heels thing. When I'd first started practicing, I'd mostly hobbled around on tiptoe like a kangaroo. But now, almost like a lovely little apology from the universe, as I crossed the sports deck, I could tell I had the motion down. The wind blew my hair. The sun shined affectionately. *Heel-toe. Heel-toe.*

I've got this, I thought. Could somebody hit "slo-mo"?

That short walk across the sports deck did a beautiful job of raising my spirits, in fact. I might be destined for the mini-golf Hall of Shame, but at least, as of this moment, I could officially walk in heels.

A much more valuable skill.

I decided to enjoy it. I was even considering throwing in a hip bump or two.

And then?

I hit a slick patch.

I went *heel-toe, heel-toe, heel—splat.*

My legs flew out ahead of me—just exactly like a cartoon character slipping on a banana peel—and I landed smack on my tailbone.

Which is even more painful than it is humiliating.

And it's *pretty frigging humiliating.*

I must have made a loud noise—because every single wedding guest turned to look, and for a moment, I was suspended in time in the birthing position with my unicorn underpants on full display, Sharon Stone style.

A moment that lasted a thousand years.

Next, Cooper arrived behind me and hoisted me to my feet—but as soon as I tried to turn around, he yanked me back and clamped my backside to his front.

I tried to turn again—but he clamped me tighter.

"What's going on, Cooper?"

"You are having," Cooper said then, "a wardrobe malfunction."

I squeezed my eyes closed. "Is it the dress?"

"Yes."

"Did it split?"

"Yes."

"Can everybody see my . . ."

"Unicorns. Yes."

At that, I sighed in a way that felt more like a cave-in.

"If I let go of you," Cooper said, "will you stop trying to turn around?"

Like a hostage, I nodded.

"Okay," Cooper said, slowly loosening his clamped arms. "Stay."

I stayed.

Next, I felt some air between us, and then I heard a rustle of fabric. And then, from behind, he reached for my hand, threading it into the sleeve of his suit jacket before shifting sides to do the same thing to the other.

This dress really must have been short—and Cooper must have been taller than I realized—because Cooper's jacket grazed my mid-thighs as he turned me around to button it.

"There," he said, looking pleased, like everything was fixed.

But nothing was fixed.

He read my face as it all started hitting me.

"No, no," Cooper said, clamping me into a hug.

"What are you doing?" I asked.

"I'm distracting you," Cooper said. "So you don't start crying."

"I'm not about to start—" I started. But then I realized he was right.

"And now I'm giving you a pep talk," he went on, still hugging.

"I don't need a pep talk," I said. "I just need to go back to your fancy cabin and not leave for the rest of the cruise."

"You're not doing that," Cooper said. "You're coming with me to the welcome lunch."

"Why?"

"Because it's your sister's wedding," Cooper said. "But also because you are unstoppable."

At that, my head shook itself. "I'm pretty stoppable, actually."

But Cooper disagreed. "Maybe you just took the most humiliating pratfall I've ever seen in real life. Maybe this day hasn't gone at all how you planned. Maybe Brody and his Michael Jackson glove were total douchebags all through the game. But . . . you're *JoJo.* You're the *best person here.* You look genuinely hot in that dress—and those underpants are the sexiest thing about it, by the way. You're not going to scuttle away and hide. You're going to come eat lunch, and sit with me, and I'm going to bring you all the desserts until you completely forget to be unhappy."

Forgetting to be unhappy sounded okay.

Then I asked, like this might be the deciding factor, "Do you actually think I look 'genuinely hot,' or are you just saying that to cheer me up?"

At that, Cooper pulled back to look me over and make an official assessment.

Was it my imagination, or could I feel the sweep of his eyes over my skin?

"I actually think you look genuinely hot," Cooper said.

"Even in this jacket?"

"*Especially* in that jacket."

That helped. A little. I turned to face the lunch buffet like I might start walking.

But then I hesitated.

"Today was a disaster," I said. "I'm worse off than I was before."

"Not entirely," Cooper said. "At least Finn knows who you are now."

"Not in a good way."

"All publicity is good publicity," Cooper said.

Was that true? "I didn't know it was possible to get so enraged about mini golf," I said.

Cooper shrugged. "You don't become captain of every varsity team by *liking to lose*."

"Thank you for being as bad at mini golf as I am," I said.

"You're welcome."

Everybody was still watching me. Time to do—*anything*. On instinct, I waved and smiled like we were on a parade float.

Then, before we took our first step, Cooper reached down and clasped my hand.

Then he said, "*Be* the unicorn."

And this time, I knew what he meant.

LATER—AFTER I'D CHANGED into sweatpants and flip-flops back in Cooper's luxury suite and then stalled as long as I could—it was time for me to go back to my official cabin and begin the journey of rooming with Harmony.

Cooper carried my suitcase back down the stairs for me on a trek that felt distinctly like descending into the underworld.

"Come back anytime," Cooper said as we reached my floor, like he felt guilty that his fate was better than mine. "My balcony is your balcony."

But it wasn't *his* fault I had to room in a sex dungeon.

I decided to focus on the positive. "Thank you for the pep talk, by the way. And for all the nice things you said about me—to everyone. And for hoarding all the Oreo cupcakes off the dessert tray."

"My pleasure," Cooper said. Then, as we peered down the hallway in the direction of Harmony's lair, he added, "You don't have to do this, by the way."

I sighed and started walking the final hundred feet toward the cabin. What choice did I have?

Cooper followed and kept talking. "You can just stay with me."

"I can't stay with you," I said.

"Because there's only one bed in my room?"

"Among many other reasons."

"We slept in the same bed sometimes as kids."

"Yeah. *As kids.*"

"It wouldn't be that weird, is all I'm saying."

"It would be weird enough."

But as we pulled up to the door of Harmony's room, we got a new comparison point for *weird*.

Because Harmony's lei was on the doorknob, and she was . . . putting it to good use.

Loudly. Gymnastically. To be clear: Anyone walking by would know with certainty that Harmony's lei was not, in any way, going to waste.

We stood there a second, averting our eyes from *everything*, before Cooper finally said, "Sounds like it might be a while."

I closed my eyes, fully defeated.

Then Cooper asked, earnestly, "Would you like to . . . wait here?"

I kept my eyes closed and shook my head.

"Come on, then," Cooper said, like that was that.

He grabbed my suitcase and walked it back the way we'd just come.

And as I watched him go down the hall, I saw the future clearly.

The immediate future, anyway.

Maybe Cooper had mysteriously stopped talking to me for four years and never told me why. And maybe he'd RSVPed *no* to my wedding *and* to this one before showing up last minute to both. And maybe teaming up with him felt exactly like old times—but better. And maybe he was being far too nice to me. And maybe this whole day with Cooper had made me miss him *worse*, somehow, now that we were together again. And maybe he'd brought a whole steamer trunk of gabardine vests.

And maybe I had more questions about Cooper now than answers.

But one thing was clear.

He was rescuing me from the underworld right now.

He was rescuing me, and taking me back to his room—and we were going to share his balcony, and his *one* bed, and all the contents of his mini-fridge, until he kicked me out. And I really didn't have any other options.

And it was actually okay.

Because after this long, mortifying, soul-crushing day . . . Cooper's cabin turned out to be the only place I wanted to go.

And so when he turned, saw I hadn't moved, and said, "Hey! Let's rock! Those stairs aren't going to climb themselves!"—what happened next was easy.

I just did exactly what I wanted, and I followed him home.

Thirteen

THAT'S HOW COOPER and I became roommates.

I got sexiled by Harmony—and had nowhere else to turn.

"This is really not that bad," Cooper kept saying on the walk back to his cabin, making it sound worse.

"Let's just not tell anyone, okay?"

I'd eaten nothing but desserts at the welcome lunch, so Cooper's first order of business was to get us club sandwiches from room service. Then we sat on his balcony and ate them as the ship started at last to move away from the dock.

It was oddly thrilling to set out to sea.

We watched the harbor slide by, and the flying fish skittering over the water's surface in zigzags, and we drank Cooper's champagne, and he tried to steal my fries, and before I knew it, we'd left the Port of Galveston behind and were surrounded by the wide blue Gulf . . . and I was feeling better.

Like maybe rooming with Cooper wouldn't be so weird after all.

Until it was time for bed.

I showered, and put on my PJs, and brushed my teeth, and flossed . . .

and then, when the only logical thing left to do was claim a side of the bed and pull back the covers, I hesitated.

Cooper, for his part, had done all the same things and then stood next to me in a gray T-shirt and navy sweatpants—and watched me hesitate.

"What's the problem?" he asked.

"I think we should build a barrier," I said, turning to check the closet for spare pillows and triumphantly returning with two. With mathematical precision, I arranged them down the middle to bisect the surface, and then I measured with my arm to make sure both sides were even.

"Better," I said.

"Is it?" Cooper asked.

"It's nice and even," I said.

"But there's no room left for us."

"Sure, there is," I said. "It's all mental."

Cooper frowned at the setup.

"Now we won't bother each other," I said.

"If I wanted to bother you," Cooper said, "those pillows wouldn't stop me."

I gave him a look. "But you're *not* going to bother me, right? Because you know that today was the most humiliating day of my life, and all I really want to do is go to sleep and stay that way until this cruise is over."

Cooper gave in. "I'm not going to bother you."

And then carefully, deliberately, we each pulled back the comforter on our respective sides, and got ourselves settled, and clicked off our sconces.

And then, of course, I couldn't sleep.

And neither could Cooper.

We just lay there, arms at our sides, looking up at the reflected moonlight on the ceiling—occasionally shifting position and rustling the sheets.

Finally, after what felt like at least an hour, I heard Cooper's rustling get louder.

"What are you doing?" I said in a half whisper.

"I'm getting up to pee," Cooper said. And then, at the bathroom door, he paused. "I'm not closing the door all the way."

"Why?"

"Because of my cleithrophobia. I'm leaving it cracked."

"I thought you said it was mild."

"If it bothers you so much, go out on the balcony."

"Nothing bothers me," I said. "You can't be worse than Pete."

When Cooper came out, he said he'd forgotten to do his push-ups. So he dropped to the floor at the foot of the bed and did a bunch. So many, I lost count.

Not that I was counting.

I crawled down and watched him. After a while, I asked, "Why are you doing so many?"

"I'm just doing a normal number," he said.

"It seems like more than normal."

"How many push-ups do *you* normally do before bed?"

"Zero."

"Well, that explains it."

Cooper drank some water after that. And then he remembered to plug in his phone. And then he dug around in his suitcase for a while.

"Would you be asleep right now if I weren't in your bed?" I asked.

"It's three in the morning in London right now, so—*yes*."

"I forgot you were jet-lagged."

"I'm running on adrenaline."

"I really appreciate you taking me in."

"Well, we couldn't leave you in Harmony's sex dungeon."

Cooper came back to bed and got in . . . and then we both lay there like a matching set again.

After a while, I said, "I have a fear, too. It might not be a *phobia*, exactly. But it's something."

"You do?"

"Yes."

"What of?" Cooper asked.

I sighed. "Singing."

"*Singing?*" Cooper said. "That can't be right. You love to sing. You sing all the time!"

"Used to," I corrected. "I *used to* love to sing. And only ever with you, by the way."

"Only ever with me?"

"Did I never mention this? I never sang as a kid—not even in groups. And when I was forced to, like, say, the national anthem or 'Happy Birthday,' I'd just mouth the words and pretend. And if anyone ever asked me to sing—which fortunately doesn't happen often in life—I'd make some excuse and get the hell out of there. It wasn't until you brought your mom's old record collection over that I ever sang at all."

All true. In ninth grade, Cooper's mom—who had wanted more than anything in life to be a singer but had never made it—set her entire vinyl collection out on the street for garbage collection. Cooper found stacks and stacks of records all piled up, along with her record player, just in time—and he rescued everything and brought it to my room for safekeeping.

After that, he had full permission to climb through my window anytime and play her records. And so he did. All the greats: Dean Martin, Ella Fitzgerald, Johnny Mercer, Anita O'Day, Frank Sinatra. If it could be sung in a lounge, Cooper's mom had collected it.

"But you and I—we sang all through high school. All the time. Every day."

"Yes," I said. "I sang all the time with you. But you were the only person I ever sang with," I said.

Cooper stared in disbelief. "Is that why you used to be so quiet?"

"Yeah," I said. "Until I got the hang of it."

Singing with Cooper had been the exception in my life, not the rule.

Next, Cooper asked, "Why did you stop?"

Did he really need to ask this question? I thought about saying, *Because you broke my heart when you left.* But that felt a little on the nose. Instead, I just stated a fact. "You weren't there to sing with," I said.

"You don't need me to sing."

I sighed. "Yes, I do."

After Cooper left for London without telling me, I never sang again. Even thinking about it now, I couldn't imagine anything more lonely than singing by myself in my room, Cooper-less.

"Hearing that makes me want you to sing something," Cooper said.

"Nope."

"Why not?"

"I told you. I don't sing anymore."

This really wasn't computing. "But we used to sing *all the time*. We'd harmonize and everything. Your face would light up."

"I remember."

"You seemed like you were having fun."

"I was having fun."

"I just don't see how you shifted from memorizing every lyric in my mom's old vinyl collection to never singing at all."

The answer was right there. But if he couldn't see it, I wasn't going to show him.

Moving on: "You're missing the point, anyway."

"What's the point?"

I took a breath and said, "The point is, it gets worse. Because despite it all, I have to sing *at this wedding*."

"This wedding? This week?"

"Ashley wants me to serenade her at the reception in lieu of a toast."

"Why?"

"Because when we were little kids, we promised each other we would do serenades at our future weddings. And back when *I* was the one getting married, Ashley signed up for actual voice lessons so she could totally crush it at mine. But when I finked out, she was off the hook."

"Why would you make a promise like that with Ashley if you had a fear of singing?"

"I didn't know the contract was binding."

"She can't hold you to a promise you made *as a child*."

"It's Ashley. She can do what she wants."

"Just tell her you can't do it."

"I did," I said.

"And?"

"It didn't work."

"What do you mean, 'It didn't work'?"

"She thought I was lying so I could surprise her."

No response from Cooper, like he was trying to imagine how that could happen.

I explained. "I told her, 'Look, I'm not going to serenade you at your wedding after all. I'm just going to do a normal maid of honor speech.' And then she said, 'Okay,' and then she winked at me."

"She winked at you?"

"Yeah. So I said, 'I mean it, though. For real. I'm really not going to sing.' And she winked again and said, 'I got it.' So I said, 'Ashley, I'm serious.' And then she gave me a look like *You adorable rascal* and then said, 'I know.'"

"She thought you were lying to her so she'd be expecting a speech but get a song instead?"

"Exactly. I just kept saying, 'I mean it. For real. I'm serious,' and she just kept agreeing with me—and winking."

"So now, if you don't sing, she'll be disappointed."

"As usual," I said, "with Ashley, there's no way to win."

Cooper didn't disagree.

Then I pointed out, "In a way, this is all your fault."

"*My* fault?"

"If you hadn't made me sing with you every day in high school," I said, "Ashley wouldn't think of me as a person who loves to sing, and I wouldn't be in this mess."

"I was only singing because you were singing," Cooper said.

"Well, I was only singing because you were."

We both sighed.

Then I went on. "And now I'm doomed. Because Ashley can't imagine a version of me that doesn't walk around the house singing nonstop."

More than doomed, really. Because now it was worse than it had been before high school. I was still shy about singing in public, like always, but now I was also out of practice—*four years* out—on top of it. And! Singing in general now—even the idea of it—seemed to turn the whole world gray.

"I can't imagine a version of you like that, either, honestly," Cooper said.

"Well, that's how it is."

"Can't you just seriously explain it all to her—like you just did for me?"

"I can. I should. But the thing is, a few weeks ago, she told my mom that the number-one thing she's most excited for on this cruise—besides the getting married part, I guess—is that serenade. She's been looking forward to it for weeks. Or decades, depending on how you count."

Cooper rolled back on his pillow to contemplate all this.

Cooper knew about music. He was a composition major in college. He could play the piano, the drums, and the mini banjo. Oh, and he had perfect pitch, too.

I'm sure this was hard for him to relate to.

"The thing I can't get past," Cooper said then, "is that you're great at singing. It's not like you're tone-deaf. Or you don't have rhythm. Or you lack tonal memory. You have—really—a good voice."

"Thank you," I said, like you do when a compliment doesn't penetrate.

"You don't believe me?"

I thought for a second. "I guess it doesn't really change anything. I've just always been . . . afraid to sing in public."

"But why?"

"Does everything have to have a reason?"

"Probably."

We were doing therapy now? Fine. "I had a mean music teacher."

"Define *mean*."

"She used to single me out and tell me I sounded like a yowling cat—*in first grade!*—and make me stand at the head of the class, repeating sections of songs in front of everybody until I got them right. But I never could get them right. It got so bad, I started faking stomachaches before class. Then she decided I was a troublemaker—and started doing it more."

"Wow," Cooper said.

"It kind of snowballed."

"It sure did."

"I'll state for the record that I had many wonderful teachers in my life—most of them math teachers, by the way—which was lucky. But she was the only music teacher at our elementary school for years. So I had her three years, first grade through third, before she quit."

"The year I moved to our street," Cooper said, putting it together.

"By fourth grade, we had Mrs. Cantorna—who was, as I'm sure you remember, the epitome of loveliness."

"But by then it was too late for you."

I nodded. "By then it was too late for me."

Cooper was quiet for a minute after that. Then he asked, "Are duets allowed?"

"Where?" I asked.

"At Ashley's reception."

I pulled in a breath. Was he asking what it sounded like he was asking?

Cooper went on. "What if I serenaded Ashley with you? What if we did it together?"

At those words, a rolling wave of relief cascaded over my body. I turned onto my side, ripping the pillow barrier away so I could check his face in the moonlight. "Really?"

He met my eyes. "That could work, maybe—right?"

I nodded. That could work, maybe.

"But do you think she'd mind an extra person?" Cooper asked.

"Not if it's you."

"We're going to have to practice, okay?" he said. "And it has to be a song that's easy for you. One you know really well."

"Like what?" I asked.

Cooper shrugged, like *What else?* "'Tonight, You Belong to Me.'"

What else, indeed.

That was our song.

Or, at least—if we'd *had* a song, it would've been that one.

Of all those songs—from "I'll Be Seeing You" to "All of Me"—that one was our favorite. We spent the whole summer after junior year up on the roof of my house, singing it over and over. I took the melody, and Cooper took the harmony, the accompaniment, and the whistle solo. It was just one of those songs that never got old.

"You could sing that song in your *sleep*," Cooper said.

"You're not wrong about that," I said. I probably had.

"We'll just pretend we're in your bedroom," Cooper said. "Easy."

I was nodding now, liking this idea more and more. "If you're going to do something terrifying, it should be something you already know by heart."

"You should get that as a tattoo," Cooper said.

"Maybe I will."

Could it be that simple? Had we just solved it?

I rolled back to study the ceiling again.

It was like that glorious feeling—my favorite feeling in the world—with a problem set in math where you'd spent days, and weeks, and study sessions, trying to fit the pieces together . . . and then they clicked into place.

And then Cooper started singing, like we'd done so many times: the sweetest, saddest song, written to a love who now belonged to somebody else, leading up to his favorite line:

But tonight,
You belong to me.

He hadn't even hit the word *tonight* before I jumped in, too, and by *you belong to me,* we were fully harmonizing like we'd never stopped.

He'd started with my part, the melody, so I just did his harmony—as easy as breathing.

I guess it really was that simple.

And that's how we finally drifted off to sleep, at last.

We lay in Cooper's bed, divided by a wall of pillows, as we churned across the moonlit surface of a deep ocean . . . and we sang ourselves to sleep.

Fourteen

BREAKFAST THE NEXT morning wasn't just breakfast, by the way. It was a matchmaking event with its own subsection on the spreadsheet.

That was my whole reason for going to breakfast: to get back on track and right my course with Finn.

But breakfast somehow wound up being about anybody—and everybody—*but* Finn.

Ashley had reserved a group of dining tables for the wedding guests, but she'd put place cards at only one: the hookup table for all the bridesmaids, the groomsmen, and the *one sister* who needed love connections.

Should I have been seated next to Finn at breakfast?

One hundred percent.

Ashley had drawn a seating chart: with me flanked by Finn on one side and my wingman, Cooper, on the other. This was the backbone of Operation Conquest: proximity and charm. Ashley's job was to make sure that Finn was seated next to me at everything, and my job was to be relentlessly delightful.

Foolproof, Ashley insisted.

Except that Finn decided to be late, leaving an opportunity for Grandma Dodie to show up in a turquoise pashmina, fully ignore all the place cards, and plunk right down in his seat.

Cooper looked at me, like *What now?*

And I looked at him back, like *This lady can sit anywhere she wants.*

At that, Cooper moved to Grandma Dodie's other side, leaving his seat open for Finn, and charmed her so aggressively that, at one point, I heard her say, "I just don't remember you being this handsome."

To which Cooper replied, "Well, I've been working on it."

Meanwhile, I restored order by switching Finn's and Cooper's place cards and draping a napkin over Finn's new chairback—trying to emphasize how *very taken* that seat was.

As Cooper asked Grandma Dodie all about her Spanish lessons, and the pastry-making class she was taking, and her upcoming trip to Barcelona, I kept the hostess podium in my sights, waiting for Finn to appear.

But no luck.

Instead, our table filled up, and every time someone tried to sit next to me, I'd hover my hand over Finn's seat, like *Sorry, taken.*

I must have turned away ten people.

Ashley's place cards idea was a bit of a fudge. There weren't really assigned seats in the dining room. And once Grandma Dodie had joined us, that gave license to other grown-ups to join. Before long, our neighbors the Vargases and the Dunns had also ignored the place cards and taken up spots once reserved for love connections.

Ashley saw what was happening and sent Brody over, trying to stem the tide. He added a bridesmaid to the table, a friend of Ashley's from grad school whose name I could never remember—a person I just thought of as Bridesmaid Two.

Ugh. Bridesmaid Two. The worst of all the bridesmaids—and the one Ashley had just suggested setting up with Cooper.

"You can't set up Cooper," I'd protested. "He's got his hands *fully* full with Operation Conquest."

"After that's *over,*" Ashley explained. "Once you're happily together with Finn, and all that is mission accomplished. *Then* I'll set them up."

"Don't you have somebody better?"

"What's wrong with her?"

"I don't like her," I said with a shrug. "Women that pretty never had to develop a personality."

"Her personality is fine," Ashley insisted.

But I disagreed. "She's an interrupter. And whatever she interrupts you with is never as good as what you were saying."

"You won't care, anyway," Ashley said. "You'll be off on the Smooching Deck with Finn."

God willing.

But the situation wasn't good.

Bridesmaid Two settled in at our table like she belonged there, acting like the cruise director–hostess of the breakfast table—warmly chatting with the neighbors and even prodding Grandma Dodie about the gentleman friend she'd been canoodling with.

"What's his name, Grandma Dodie?" Bridesmaid Two teased.

Hey! That was *my* grandmother. *I* was supposed to be doing the teasing!

Grandma Dodie made an innocent face. "Edward?" she asked.

"Is he your boyfriend?"

"Not yet," Grandma Dodie said, looking mischievous.

"You've got this, Grandma Dodie," Bridesmaid Two said, making a hand heart. "I'm shipping you."

Grandma Dodie frowned. "Shipping me?"

"Both of you," Bridesmaid Two explained, like that should clear things up.

Grandma Dodie looked around the table like that didn't compute.

"She's rooting for your relationship," Cooper explained. "*Ship* comes from *relationship.*"

Cooper glanced over at Bridesmaid Two. What were they now—a team?

"Are you sure that's a real word?" Grandma Dodie asked, pulling a tiny pencil and pad of paper from her purse to write down this newfangled term.

"Don't worry about it, Grandma Dodie," I said.

But Grandma Dodie kept writing, forming the word *ship* in her careful, slanted cursive, and then writing *verb* in parentheses before writing the definition. As she wrote, she said, "If people are doing it to me, I want to know what it is."

Can't argue with that.

Bridesmaid Two. Already causing trouble. I glared at Brody, like he'd saddled us with her on purpose.

At this point, the table was almost full—and Finn's empty seat was still in demand.

Even Harmony tried for it. She just walked right up and started pulling out his chair.

My hand flew out. "I'm sorry," I said, looking up. "This seat's—"

And there Harmony was, in a scoop-neck shirt, covered—positively *wallpapered*, shoulders to jaw—in purple hickeys.

I was so shocked that I hesitated for a microsecond, and then, by the time I finished with ". . . taken," Harmony had already planted herself firmly in Finn's seat—the last empty one at the table—and shaken out her napkin, and smoothed it over her lap.

With that, Finn's reserved seat was gone.

Gone, but not forgotten. I stared at his place card mournfully.

"Sweetheart," Mrs. Vargas asked as Harmony settled in. "What happened?" She touched her own neck to indicate she was asking about Harmony's.

Was that a real question? Did Mrs. Vargas not know what those were? Was this appropriate breakfast talk?

"Oh, these?" Harmony said proudly. "These are love bites."

Silence from the table—as everybody just stared.

"Good lord," Mrs. Dunn said after a while. "I haven't seen one of those in years."

"I thought she'd been strangled," Mr. Vargas said to the rest of the table, like this was a big relief, as Mr. Dunn chimed in with, "Or had a clotting disorder."

"Good for you," Grandma Dodie said, raising her orange juice. "Life is short." Then she flipped another page in her notepad and wrote, *Love bites—(noun)—hickeys.*

Another long pause from the table as Harmony poured herself some coffee from the carafe.

Then, awkwardly, Mrs. Dunn tried to calibrate us back toward pleasantries. "And what do you do, Harmony?" she asked.

"I work in marketing," Harmony said pleasantly. "But my academic background is in semiotics."

Cooper and I looked at each other, like *Well,* that *was unexpected.*

"Is in *what*-iotics?" Mr. Vargas asked.

"Semiotics," Harmony repeated. "It's the study of signs and signaling in communications—and how to create meaning without words."

Everybody just blinked.

"Like," Harmony went on, sensing we needed help, "you know how you can look at a book cover and just know at a glance whether it's a thriller or a romantic comedy? Just by the font and the colors? Like a thriller's going to have a black cover with caution-tape-yellow block text, and a rom-com's going to be hot pink with script?"

We all nodded.

"That's semiotics."

"People study that?"

"Oh, yeah," Harmony said. "It's a massive field. The research is exploding. We're all reading signs in the environment—and each other—all the time. Picking up on nonverbal cues and information. Words really seem so pitiful in comparison. That's how these happened, actually." Harmony brushed her hand over her neck to indicate her love bites.

"Semiotics gave you *love bites*?" Grandma Dodie asked, trying out her new vocab.

Harmony leaned in, like she'd been waiting for just this question. "I've been doing a little reading on *bio*semiotics—which is how living systems signal to each other. Just dabbling. Just for fun."

Cooper and I looked at each other again, amazed. Harmony—*Harmony*—spent her free time "dabbling in biosemiotics."

She went on, "Like flocks of birds, for example—how they signal their formations to each other. And of course humans use biosemiotics all the time in social signaling. What we wear, how we carry ourselves, what facial expressions we use—it's all signaling, all the time. And I've had a problem in my life with seeming a bit . . . aloof. Like I guess I have a resting shrew face."

Cooper and I tilted our heads at each other, like *Does she know that's not the phrase?*

Grandma Dodie wrote that down, too.

Harmony went on, "I'd just started a new job in a new city, and I was having trouble making friends. As usual. And so I started taking a deep dive into human social signaling, and comparing it to my own behavior, and trying to take some lessons from it—you know, like how smiling a lot will make people more likely to approach you."

Not sure we needed *the science of semiotics* to know that, but okay.

"And that's when a crazy thing happened to me," Harmony finished.

She had our attention now. We all leaned in.

"I randomly hooked up with this guy from Brazil," Harmony began.

Oh, god. Where was this going? There were elderly people at the table!

"And he was a very enthusiastic person, if you know what I mean."

I looked around the table. All the older women were nodding.

"Long story short: I woke up at his place late for work, had to do a sprint of shame back to the office, and I didn't even notice until I got home after work that I'd had a massive bruise on my neck the whole time."

"At work?" Mrs. Dunn asked, in a tone like *Oh, dear.*

Harmony nodded. "But guess what? I'm not always good at what they call 'playing well with others.' It's never been easy for me to make friends . . ."

"What about your Brazilian?" Grandma Dodie countered.

Harmony winked. "I don't have trouble making *those* kinds of friends. But real friends? That's harder for me. Lots of days, I just go into the office, do my thing, and accidentally never talk to anybody. But on that day? *Everybody* talked to me. In the halls. At the water cooler. Stopping by my doorway. I was the belle of the office park. And I thought: Maybe it was the signaling. Maybe everybody had a certain idea about me, and who I was, and then this unexpected sign broke that idea—and let them see me differently."

"*Very* differently," Mr. Dunn agreed.

"Sometimes," Harmony said, "*anything* different is good."

The table couldn't argue with that.

"The thing is," Harmony went on, "it worked. I got invited to happy hours after that. Someone asked me to join the softball team, and then a cooking class, and then an axe-throwing night. It absolutely changed my life."

The adults were baffled. "It really worked?" Mrs. Dunn asked.

"Like a charm," Harmony said with a wink. "It's working right now."

At that, Harmony's pancakes arrived. She poured syrup all over them in a spiral while the adults just stared at her. Finally, just before stabbing a pie-slice-sized bite with her fork, Harmony looked around the table, smiled, shrugged, and said, "Don't knock it 'til you've tried it."

I WASN'T HAPPY. Things were going off the rails. We were losing focus. This breakfast was supposed to be about Finn Turner—and Finn Turner only.

Next, in a bad-to-worse move that felt almost like deliberate sabotage, Brody announced broadly to the table, "I hear JoJo was a real rascal as a kid."

And then the grown-ups were off to the races.

Wasn't Brody supposed to be *helping*? Not sure why Ashley assumed he would do that.

And *was* I a rascal?

No!

Not on purpose, anyway.

But the adults all had stories. And they told *every damn one.*

Breakfast turned into a litany of testimonials. The time I fell off Old Man Pipkin's roof. The time I built a fire in the Pesikoffs' driveway. The time I ran my bike into a parked car in front of the Turners' house.

Not to mention all the math-based businesses I'd tried to start in the summers: Algebra Tutoring for Dummies, Master Your Times Tables at Last, and (Fun) Math Camp. No takers for that one. We also reminisced at length about the time I set up a lemonade stand, but instead of selling lemonade, I tried to sell *financial advice.* I was like Lucy from *Peanuts,* but my hand-lettered sign read BECOME A MILLIONAIRE!

I'd garnered one client, and it was Grandma Dodie.

But everybody's favorite story, of course, was the time I was selling Girl Scout cookies, and Mr. Dunn answered his front door while brushing his teeth, and I saw the foam at his mouth, thought he had rabies—and ran away screaming. That really cracked the table up. My *fear of rabies.* Hilarious.

I endured all these stories with the scowl of a wet cat.

"Why does everybody only remember *my* shenanigans?" I asked, after far too long. "Cooper was involved in ninety percent of these incidents. *Masterminded* most of them!" Then I pointed at Cooper like *J'accuse!* and said, "I only built that fire because Cooper wanted to make s'mores! And Cooper was the Director of Putting Up Flyers for the math camp! And Cooper was the one who shouted 'Rabies!' at Mr. Dunn before we *both* ran away screaming."

"Cooper just had such a sweet face," Mrs. Vargas said, like he could never be a troublemaker.

We all turned to regard Cooper's face.

And that's when Bridesmaid Two, ever the interrupter, decided to ask, "What do you do for a living, Cooper?"

"He's in a band," I said.

Just as Cooper answered, "I work for the BBC in London. I'm a Foley sound artist."

I turned to him. "You're a *what*?"

He wasn't in a band? How did I not know this? I mean, yes—he'd been gone for four years, so he'd had plenty of time for a secret career change. But I'd seen him a lot lately.

Hell, we'd just *slept together*!

But, now that I thought about it, had I asked Cooper even *one* question about himself since he got here? I felt a punch of guilt for having been so very *all about me* for the past twenty-four hours.

"What's a Foley artist, Cooper?" Mrs. Dunn asked.

"We make the sounds for movies."

"Like the soundtrack?" Bridesmaid Two asked.

But Cooper shook his head. "The sounds, not the music."

Brody liked this. "Like explosions and stuff?"

"Yes, that. But—everything. Movies mostly just record the actors' dialogue, and everything else gets added in later. Glasses clinking. Grocery bags rustling. Footsteps."

"Footsteps?" Mr. Vargas asked.

Cooper nodded. "You can create every possible human emotion with footsteps. We have a whole closet of prop shoes."

Now *this* was a good topic. Why hadn't we spent all of breakfast talking about this?

"So if you need to make the sound of thunder, would you go out and record some thunder?" Mr. Dunn asked.

"For thunder," Cooper said, "I like to use a piece of aluminum sheet metal. You punch it and then ripple it."

"Is that better than the real thing?" Mrs. Dunn wanted to know.

Cooper nodded. "The sound has to fit the visuals just right—plus, the pacing of the scene. So you watch the screen as you record the sound."

We all nodded.

"That's *such* a cool job," Bridesmaid Two said, looking decidedly starry-eyed.

Okay, Bridesmaid Two. Settle down.

Though . . . it *was* a cool job. I couldn't resist one-upping her. "That," I corrected, "is *the coolest job in the world*."

Cooper nodded at me. "It really is."

"And you're in London?" Mrs. Dunn asked.

Cooper looked at me. "I just got an offer to move back, actually."

"To Los Angeles?" Mrs. Dunn inquired, like Cooper was still talking to her.

But he kept his eyes on me. "To Austin," he answered. "They make a lot of movies there."

Mrs. Vargas again: "But you couldn't possibly leave London?"

Cooper's gaze stayed fixed on mine. "I could be talked into coming home."

It was really bothering me that I hadn't known about Cooper's job all this time. But that's what his mom had told my mom after he left: that he'd gone to London to play in a band.

That's what he'd been doing in my head for four years.

"Your mom said you were in a band," I said accusingly.

"I was—at first," Cooper said. "We still play sometimes."

"In clubs?" Bridesmaid Two interrupted.

Cooper shook his head. "Mostly busking for money on the Tube."

"There's no Tube in Austin," Mrs. Vargas cautioned.

"No," Cooper agreed. "But there are lots of tacos."

I processed it all.

Maybe I really hadn't wanted to ask him about what he'd been up to all this time. Maybe I'd wanted to just act like those four years had never happened.

But I guess they had happened, after all. Days after we graduated college, after we'd returned home and formulated a plan to get summer jobs at the same bookstore together, Cooper ghosted me. Left without a word. One minute, I was showing him my new engagement ring, and telling him Pearce had an internship in DC, and making Cooper promise that we'd make the most of my last summer as an unmarried woman . . . and the next minute, Cooper was just—gone. Hardcore gone. Like not answering calls or texts gone.

His mom was always so apologetic when she saw me. "Maybe his phone doesn't work over there," she'd say. Like that might make me feel better.

It didn't.

I'd been so absolutely wrecked by the way he left—and the question of how my oldest friend could do that to me—that the fact of it stayed centered in my mind like a wound that refused to heal.

But I guess Cooper had been doing fine.

Doing fine, and living his life. His *cool* life. Working for the BBC and busking in Tube stations. Without me.

At some point, I'd have to ask what the hell, exactly, had happened.

But the problem was, I wanted to know precisely as badly as I *never* wanted to know.

And, at least for now, that would have to be that.

I WAS RESENTING Bridesmaid Two for churning up all my emotions when my parents came up to our table to check on how everyone was doing.

"Is everyone settled in?" my dad asked the group, in full host mode.

Oh, yes, everyone confirmed.

"Today's an 'at-sea' day," my dad said, making air quotes like he might be starting a vocab lesson, "but there are activities planned from morning till midnight." Then, and I'm not even kidding, he started handing out printed schedule pages to everyone at the table.

I squinted at him, like *Where's my real dad?*

My real dad never knew anything about *any* family schedule.

My real dad wouldn't even *be* here. He'd be stuck in a work meeting somewhere.

But this must have been part of trying to win my mom back. He must be trying to prove that he had at least the potential to participate. I looked him over as he worked the table with that big trying-too-hard smile—giving thumbs-ups to Mr. Dunn and slapping Brody on the back.

It had a real whiff of desperation about it.

And then it hit me.

My dad wanted us all to see him differently. He was attempting to rebrand, too.

And I got that. I *so* got that.

Too bad he missed Harmony's TED Talk on the semiotics of love bites.

For maybe the first time in my life, I felt sympathy for my dad.

It's not easy, is it, buddy? my heart wanted to say.

But that heart of mine was about to have bigger concerns.

Because, next . . . the guy I'd been waiting for all this time showed up at last.

"Finn!" Mr. Dunn said warmly, spotting him first. "There you are!" Then he gestured toward me. "JoJo's been pining for you all morning."

How could *Mr. Dunn* have intuited that? Just how obvious was I being?

I felt an urge to say, "No, I wasn't!" But of course that would've been worse.

"We've been reminiscing about the old neighborhood," Mr. Dunn continued. "And that time JoJo got diarrhea on the Fourth of July."

Seriously, Mr. Dunn?

"That's not—" I started. I was going to say "fair," but I decided, instead, to finish with "appetizing." As if the only person Mr. Dunn had just harmed was Finn.

Then I gave Finn an apologetic look.

But Finn just shook his head, and shrugged, and frowned—all at once. Like none of it mattered, and he was completely unbothered by everything. And definitely like he didn't need me to stand up for him. And, frankly, like he had no idea—again—who this "JoJo" person with digestive issues might even be.

Fifteen

"WHAT IS *WRONG* with people?" I demanded after breakfast as I dragged Cooper in circles around the promenade deck, not even noticing the lovely and vast ocean view all around us. "What exactly was the point of spending *three hours* telling humiliating stories about me at the table?"

Breakfast had lasted thirty minutes.

"Of all the available items," I went on, "on the infinite menu of topics for human breakfast conversation, why *me*? Why my life? Why weren't we talking about *you*? I could watch a whole ten-part documentary about your off-the-charts amazing life! Why does my diarrhea from fifteen years ago outrank your daily use of *thunder metal*?"

"I thought the stories were cute," Cooper said.

"Diarrhea?" I challenged. "You think *diarrhea* is cute?"

Cooper shrugged like he knew better than to answer.

"It's like they want me to fail," I said.

"They don't even know you're trying," Cooper said.

"Are you defending them?"

"I'm just saying it's not malicious."

"You don't know that," I said.

"Mr. Dunn wasn't sabotaging you. He's just clueless."

"That's the point. Everybody's clueless. This isn't working."

"It's only day two," Cooper pointed out.

But I was shaking my head. "Something has to change. These old neighbors need to stop seeing me as a nose-picking little kid with poopy pants." My brain scanned its options frantically, and then, in a eureka moment of pure brilliance, it landed on something.

I stopped sprint-walking and turned to face Cooper—the wind whipping my loose hair all around.

"What?" Cooper asked warily.

"I've got it," I said.

Why was Cooper so good at predicting my shenanigans? "I don't like that look on your face," he said.

"Yes," I conceded. "It *will* require a small favor from you. But it's absolutely no biggie in the grand scheme of things."

Cooper narrowed his eyes. "What's the favor?"

I pinched my fingers together to give him a visual of something tinier than tiny. "I just need sixty seconds of your time."

"Sixty seconds of my time," Cooper repeated, "doing what?"

But now I wasn't sure how to frame it.

"Doing . . . something that'll help me change my image."

Cooper was already shaking his head.

I pushed on. "Something that'll make it clear to the whole ship that I am a grown-ass adult."

He closed his eyes and kept shaking.

"Something that could turn Operation Conquest around."

At that, Cooper let out a long sigh, like he knew he was already doomed.

"What is it?" he asked, opening those ocean-blue eyes. "What do I have to do?"

I took both of his hands and clasped them in mine, stepping closer and angling underneath him so I could look pleading and puppyish.

And then I said, "I'm gonna need you . . . to give me one of Harmony's love bites."

AT THE TERM *Harmony's love bites,* Cooper froze—like he could not have heard what he thought he'd just heard.

Then he just said, "No."

I pressed up on my tiptoes. "Just hear me out."

But he pulled his hands out of my grip. "I'm not giving you a hickey."

"Love bite," I corrected.

"Either one," Cooper declared.

"I would do it for you," I said. "I would do it for you *in a heartbeat.*"

"Bad idea," Cooper said next.

"Genius idea," I corrected. "Didn't you hear Harmony saying how this one little change transformed her life?"

"You want *Harmony's* advice on transforming your life?"

But I was liking this idea. "No wonder mini golf was a total fail. Slutty dresses are a dime a dozen! We need the semiotics of social signaling to make me a Person of Interest."

"This is a terrible idea," Cooper said.

"Maybe. But what if it *works*? Operation Conquest is already tanking. I can't get any traction with this guy. He's forgotten me *twice* in two days! I think Harmony's onto something. Nobody's forgetting her!"

"Yeah, but not in a good way."

"I need to level up! The clock is ticking! I've only got seven days left."

At that, I turned my head, leaned in, and pulled my collar aside, saying, "Just do it. Real quick."

Cooper stared at my neck in horror.

"No," he said again—and then he turned and strode away.

I chased after him. "Hey!"

But his legs were longer than mine. I had to jog.

"Cooper! I need you!" I called after him.

"Not for this, you don't," he called back.

"Hey!" I said again. "That's all? Just a flat no? Are you refusing to help me right now?"

Cooper kept striding.

But I kept bobbing along behind him.

The wind was loud in my ears, and before I knew it, I was yelling.

"You said you were on my team, Cooper! You said, and I quote, 'I've been on your team since day one.' Is *this* the kind of team player you want to be? Is this the kind of one-handed-golf-glove energy you want to cultivate in your life? I'm telling you I need you—for real. My mom is totally preoccupied, and Ashley's marrying the douchiest guy on the planet, and Pete's an idiot—a sweet idiot, but still—and my dad has never, not once, given a shit about me. So you're it, Cooper. You're all I've got. I'm sorry, but that's how it is! You're not just *on* the team—you *are* the team. You're the whole thing."

Never mind that *zero* of those people were viable alternatives for this task. Saying all of this out loud—shouting it, really—forced me to feel it. The more I chased him, and the more I begged, and the more he didn't turn around or even slow down . . . the more heartbreaking it all started to feel.

I heard my voice waver, but I kept going. "I don't have anybody else I can turn to, Cooper! You promised to help me—and I trusted you! Are you really going to make me chase you like this? Are you really going to just walk off and leave me here?"

I know I'd been trying to pretend like the last four years of Cooper ignoring me hadn't happened. I know I'd been insisting to myself that our newly reactivated friendship was as solid and dependable and safe as ever. But it wasn't. It couldn't be. And pretending was harder than I thought. I'd been talking about my family being disappointing—but I was also talking about Cooper.

My friend who had moved away without telling me. My friend who had gone radio silent for years. My friend who might just have been the worst heartbreak of my life.

I probably should have stopped shouting when I felt all those emotions seep into my lungs. But I had some rhetorical momentum, you know? So I tried for one last zinger. "Are you really going to walk out of my life and forget all about me—again?"

At the end of that question, my voice broke.

And I just stopped walking.

Stopped chasing, stopped begging.

It was all too much.

He didn't want to help me? Fine. I'd find somebody else. There were plenty of other people on this ship with—with—*mouths.* If this was such an offensive chore for Cooper, if that's how utterly dismissive he wanted to be about getting anywhere near me for any reason—even a really, really good one . . . Fine.

Half the men on this boat would be drunk by lunchtime, anyway.

But underneath all that defiance, there was genuine heartache.

He'd thrown up at the touch of my lips back in high school—and now he was fleeing at the sight of my neck? Just exactly how repulsive did this guy think I was?

Maybe he wasn't on my team after all—and maybe he never had been.

Cooper had always been my person. But I guess I just . . . wasn't his.

My breath got shaky at that idea. And then there were tears on my face.

I'd never known why Cooper left, but I'd always held on to hope that he had some kind of really good explanation.

But maybe there was no good explanation.

Maybe he just didn't really care.

And I'd learned a lesson from my dad a long time ago: You can't force people to care about you. If you didn't matter to someone, you didn't matter.

Maybe I didn't matter to Cooper.

Maybe I should let him go.

Or—actually—maybe I should've let him go four years ago. Instead of holding out all that stupid, embarrassing hope.

That's where I was landing with it all . . . when Cooper stopped walking, too.

I wiped the tears off my cheeks fast with my shirtsleeve.

Then Cooper turned around, and he took a breath like he was gathering his strength, and then, step after step, he walked back until he reached me.

"Have you been crying?" he asked, leaning in to look.

"No," I said defiantly.

I clearly had.

Then Cooper looked all around my blotchy face, from my eyes to my mouth and back again, with that signature affectionate look of his. I'd always felt, from that look alone, like I was special to him. But maybe that was just his face. Maybe that was how he looked at everyone.

But that's when Cooper sighed and said, "Where do you want it?"

"Want what?"

He gave me a look. "The hickey."

But believe it or not, I had a shred of pride to salvage.

"I *don't* want it," I said. "Anymore."

NOW IT WAS Cooper's turn to beg. Which helped me recover my moxie.

"I'm fine with it," he said. "I am."

"You didn't seem fine when you were sprinting away from me."

"That was before I made you cry."

"I don't need a pity hickey, thanks."

"You know, I just—" Cooper looked around and then rubbed his neck. "I wasn't expecting that request. And I panicked."

"I'll say."

"But I've had a minute to regroup," he said. "And it's fine."

But I shook my head. "I'll ask someone else."

"Who?"

"I don't know." I shrugged, like it didn't matter. "I'll go to the casino after dinner."

"You are *not* going to the casino to solicit hickeys from random cruise dudes."

"That's not really up to you."

"I said I'll do it. It's fine."

"But it's not fine. You *hated* this idea. You were *horrified*."

"I was just—taken aback for a second. I'm good now."

"Don't worry about it," I said, turning and starting to walk back the way we'd come.

Maybe he didn't want to be a poor team player. Or maybe it was my heartfelt admission of how alone I was. Or maybe he just felt bad for making me cry.

But now *Cooper* was following *me*.

"Slow down!" Cooper called.

Wow. The dynamic had really done a one-eighty.

"No!" I called back.

"I said I'd help you!" Cooper said.

"Too late!"

Cooper caught my wrist and stopped me. "JoJo! Cut it out!"

Why was I resisting him? He was giving me what I wanted! But he'd just rejected me, and I couldn't seem to do anything but reject him right back.

I met his eyes with defiance.

"It'll take sixty seconds," he said—quoting me back to me.

"It'll take sixty seconds," I agreed, "but the cooties will last forever."

At that, he broke into a *You're adorable* smile that went all the way to his eyes.

Then he reached down, grabbed my hand, and started tugging me along behind him toward the rear of the ship.

"Hey! What are you doing?"

"I'm taking you someplace private," Cooper said, "so I can suck on your neck."

BY THE TIME we reached the railing at the stern, we were both a little breathless.

I looked around. "I thought you said someplace private."

Cooper gestured at the empty deck and the ocean beyond it. "Who's going to see us? A whale?"

"Okay, then," I said, covering my own sudden hitch of hesitation by pretending to study the churning wake trailing behind us. "Let's get it over with."

"Right," Cooper said. Then he turned my shoulders to face him. Then he stepped closer, looked down, and frowned.

"You look worried," I said.

"I'm just concentrating."

I pressed two fingers to a spot near the jugular and said, "Somewhere around here. Nice and visible, you know? And don't hold back. Really get in there. Go big!"

Cooper nodded, studying the area like a topographical map.

I dropped my hand, tilted my head back, and waited.

But Cooper just stood there.

"What?" I asked, like *Hurry up*.

"I'm just—formulating a plan."

"Don't overthink it," I said.

"I've just . . . never done this before."

"You've never—?"

"Given someone a hickey. That I know of."

I let out a little laugh and said, "You haven't?"

"Have you?" Cooper asked.

"I'm not the issue here."

"You are *one hundred percent* the issue here."

"Fine," I said. "I haven't, either."

Cooper was still hesitating. I watched his dark hair blow in the wind. At breakfast, it had been so neat—swooped forward and up. But now, after all this upper-deck drama, it was scattered all messy over his forehead.

He'd started out the day so coiffed. And this was what I'd done to him.

Though I couldn't decide which way looked better.

"How hard can it be?" I finally said. "Just pretend I'm a water bottle and you're really thirsty."

"Why is that not helping?"

"My point is, if cavemen could do this, so can you."

Cooper sighed, like all this talking was just making it worse.

"Okay," he said, dead serious now, his eyes on the target.

"Okay." I gave a thumbs-up.

He clutched my shoulders again and started to lower his head down—and as much as I had been insisting all along that everything about this was *the opposite* of a big deal, as it actually started to really happen . . . as Cooper actually leaned down closer and closer . . . I felt the anticipation of it like electrical sparks in my body.

Cooper must have felt it, too, because he got about two inches from making contact, and then he just stopped and hovered there.

"What?" I asked.

"Nothing," Cooper said, pulling back a bit.

"Look, if you hate this so much—"

"I don't hate it."

"So what's the problem?"

"I just—want to do a good job."

"Any kind of job will do," I said. "Seriously. I'm not picky."

"Okay, okay. Got it," Cooper said.

Then something occurred to me. "You're not going to throw up again, are you?"

Cooper's eyes snapped to mine. "You remember that?"

I looked at him like he was totally bananas. "Of course I remember it. It's one of the top five most humiliating moments of my life. I think about it once a week, at least. Sometimes I remember it out of a dead sleep and wake up screaming."

Cooper squinted. "You're joking, right?"

"I am fifty percent joking."

"I'm really sorry about that day. I was—"

"I tell myself you had food poisoning. I tell myself you couldn't possibly have been so repulsed by the touch of my lips that you had to barf up a corn dog. If I'm wrong, don't tell me."

Now Cooper looked right into my eyes. "I didn't have food poisoning. And I wasn't repulsed."

I looked out at the ship's wake again. What other option was there?

Cooper took a breath. Then he said, "I was nervous."

"Nervous?" I frowned. Could being nervous make you throw up?

Cooper nodded.

"Are you nervous now?" I asked.

His eyes were steady. "Yes."

I stepped back. "Do not barf on me, man."

"Hold still. Not that kind of nervous."

I stepped closer again, but cautiously. "Can you do this?" I asked, suddenly not so sure.

"Of course," Cooper said.

He regrouped and went in for another landing. This time, though, when he got close enough, his breath tickled the peach fuzz on my neck—and before I knew it, I was pushing away.

"What?" Cooper demanded, backing off again.

"It tickles," I said, squeezing my eyes closed.

"Got it," Cooper said, all serious—though now all that anticipation had me in full tickle mode, and he'd barely launched again before I was squealing and wriggling away.

But guess what?

This time, he was ready.

This time, as soon as I started to pull back, he used both of his arms to catch me, clamp me tight against him, and hold me there. And then he totally stuck the landing—cradling me close, draping himself over me, pressing his mouth purposefully to my throat, and going absolutely all in.

And that, my friends, put an end to the giggling.

I don't know if you've asked anyone to give you a hickey lately, but may I just recommend it? I'm as shocked as anyone, but Harmony, of all people, was right: If you know a nice person with a mouth—friend or foe—who might be willing to put it on you . . . just go for it. Submit your request.

Because *holy hell.*

We should have a national holiday for this.

What was happening?

The first thing I realized was that Cooper hadn't had time to shave this morning—as we scrambled out, late, to breakfast. The minute he made contact, I felt his stubble scratching and prickling my skin like the most erotic sandpaper in the world.

Instant, full-immersion chills—just rolling up and down that whole side of my body.

I closed my eyes and leaned back.

Cooper clutched tighter and kept working. I guess he really took that water bottle advice to heart, because he was positively drinking me down. I could feel his jaw shifting and his lips pressing and pulling, and his tongue doing . . . something.

Something good.

And my whole body just . . .

Just sank into the moment like time itself was a hot, sultry bath.

And I don't know what the etiquette is for exactly where to place your hands when a childhood friend is giving you a pity hickey after making you cry . . . but my hands decided to make their own rules. They just floated their way up over his shoulders and combed themselves into his hair without my consent.

He wasn't *kissing* me, of course.

He was—just performing a necessary service.

Not unlike if I'd been bitten by a snake, for example—and he had to suck out the venom.

That's not a *kiss.* That's medical care!

And yet.

And yet . . .

It wasn't a kiss. It was *not* a kiss.

But it was the best kiss I'd ever had—in adult life, anyway.

I got positively submerged in it. It was like every single nerve in my body decided to take a sip—or maybe a gulp—of Cooper's complimentary cabin champagne. I started to float and churn and glow like a phosphorescent tide. My breaths got deeper and slower, overflowing the edges of my lungs and seeping out into the rest of my body—swirling at the toes, and the fingers, and everywhere.

Had he really never done this before?

Liar.

He had to know what he was doing.

He was a musician, after all, and I was like a musical instrument that was being played *just exactly right* in every possible way.

And what do musical instruments do when you play them like that?

They . . . *sigh erotically*.

Wait—

Hold on—

But, yeah. That's what happened.

I didn't even realize at first the person sighing was me.

It could have been—anybody, I guess. Out in the world. Anybody who was having a very, very unexpectedly nice morning.

But then—it had to be me. Cooper must have realized it, too.

Next, everything stopped.

Cooper ceased all hickey-making, released me, and took a step away.

I stumbled back a little but grabbed on to the railing.

For a moment, the ship's motor just kept humming, and the wind just kept whipping, and the wake behind us just kept churning.

I took one of those three-second breaths that are supposed to be so good for you.

Cooper regrouped first. He coughed, and nodded, and looked around.

And then—decisively—he dusted off his hands. "Well," he said. "I hope that worked." Then he checked his watch and said, "You wanted sixty seconds, but that was actually closer to two minutes. Hope that's okay."

That felt like too much math. And there was no such thing as too much math.

I kept clutching the railing and nodded.

Cooper peered in at my throat, all business, to check his work. "Looks good. Red and blotchy, for sure. That'll bruise up great."

I was still too melted to speak.

Then Cooper shoved his hands into his pockets and said, "Okay. Great teamwork. Got it done."

I nodded liquidly.

Next, the hands came out of the pockets so Cooper could gesture over his shoulder at the staircase with his thumb. "Well, I've got—some things to do back at the—somewhere. So I'm just gonna—go—make that happen."

Then he held out that same hand to me so we could shake.

Like business partners or something.

I draped my hand over his like a silk scarf, and he pumped it up and down for a while. Then he looked down at his shoes before nodding a couple of times, like he'd decided to say something.

Then he said, to his shoes, "I'm sorry I made you cry."

Then he added, to the deck, "I hope this hickey solves all your problems."

And then he looked up to say one last thing. "And just for the record?" He met my eyes. "I *never* forgot about you. And I never will. Even if you *fucking marry* Finn Turner."

Sixteen

THE HICKEY DIDN'T work. Is that a spoiler?

I mean—it *worked.* Whatever Cooper had just done to me left a bruise on my neck that lasted for the rest of the cruise and beyond.

It's just that nobody thought it was a hickey.

Even though it was *so clearly* a hickey.

And yet, as I spent the rest of that day at sea fully avoiding Cooper and staying out of our shared luxury cabin, people noticed my neck, and remarked on it, and asked about it . . . but all with comments like: "You've got a smear of strawberry jam on your neck."

Really? *Jam?* People thought I could wander around smeared with jam and just *not notice*—like some kind of truffle pig?

Blackberry jelly was also suggested, for the record.

But it didn't stop at condiments.

Pete wanted to know if I'd been punched in the throat. My mother worried I was breaking out in hives. Ashley thought it might be a smear of Tabasco. And Mrs. Vargas—who herself had just seen Harmony's *baker's dozen of hickeys*—thought I'd been stung by a bee.

A *bee*! On a cruise ship!

I also got asked if it was paint, ink, a rash, contact dermatitis, chocolate ice cream, sorbet, shampoo, hair gel, ketchup, or a very rare bruising disorder called Henoch-Schonlein purpura, which the Bishops' grandson had recently recovered from. They showed me pictures.

The point is, nobody—not one person—thought it was a hickey.

Cooper and I went through all that for nothing.

Nothing, that is, unless you count the full-body intrusive reveries that kept washing over me all day afterward in waves of sudden 3D flashbacks: Cooper's arms clamping me tight. His mouth just consuming my neck. Not to mention . . . the symphony of reactions he'd conducted in my body with that one mouth of his alone.

You know how they say the color black isn't just one color, but all the colors put together?

The memory of Cooper doing *whatever he'd just done to me* wasn't just one emotion. It was all of them at once. It was . . . a lot. It was so much that when a memory overtook me as I was helping my mom put up decorations in the cocktail lounge, I had to turn and put my head down on the bar until it passed.

If just thinking about Cooper could do all that to me, I wasn't sure what seeing him in real life might do.

Nor was I in any hurry to find out.

But the total fail of the hickey solution was going to force a reckoning—sooner rather than later. We were going to need a new plan.

And when Bridesmaid Two dared to ask me if it was a *tattoo of a hickey*?

That was it. Time to go find Cooper.

But Cooper wasn't in the room when I got there, and so, even though I was supposed to be folding flower decorations for my mother, I went looking for him instead. I checked the promenade deck, and then the sports deck, and then the library—and I was on my way to the snack bar when I passed the empty side ballroom that would hold the wedding reception in a few nights' time . . . And there he was.

With his mini banjo.

"What are you doing?" I called to him as I walked in.

He jumped a little at the sound of my voice like maybe he'd had a few intrusive reveries of his own. But then he recovered.

"I'm checking out the performance space," he said.

I'd taken the virtual tour of this room with Ashley last week. "She's putting the head table by the windows." I pointed. "And the mic for toasts right next to it."

"Are you busy now?" he asked.

"I'm supposed to be helping my mom decorate the bar for happy hour," I said. "But I was looking for you instead."

I walked to meet him.

As soon as I got close enough, Cooper leaned in to appraise my neck. "Nice," he said, nodding. "No mistaking that."

"Are you kidding me?" I said. "Nobody—not one person—has guessed what it is."

Cooper frowned.

I started counting on my fingers. "I've gotten blueberry juice, and fruit smoothie, and food coloring. I've gotten poison ivy, and 'allergic to shellfish,' and bedbugs. Grandma Dodie insisted it was a mosquito bite. But a total of *zero* people have asked if it's a hickey."

"A *mosquito bite*?" Cooper demanded, like that affronted his masculinity.

I shook my head. "We went through all that for nothing."

And then, like the memories of "all that" were playing in his head, Cooper said, "Yeah."

"So that's why I'm here," I said, back to business. "The hickey thing was a total fail."

"Did Finn see it?"

I flared my nostrils. "He thought it was eczema."

Cooper scratched the back of his neck. "That *is* a total fail."

"We need a new plan," I said. "And before you storm off again and make me chase you around the boat, I want to make it clear that I am *not* about to propose that we fake date each other."

"Didn't know that was a possibility, but okay—"

I cut him off. "Just that we fake *flirt*."

A pause. "Fake flirt?"

"Yes."

"With who?"

I gave him a look. "With *each other*."

But Cooper shook his head.

"What's with all this negativity?" I demanded.

Cooper just kept shaking.

"Fake *dating* doesn't help either of us, see? Because then we're not available to other people."

Cooper sighed.

"But fake *flirting*," I went on, "has all of the upsides and none of the downsides."

Cooper squinted. "Does it?"

I stood firm. "*Social signaling!* It shows the world that we are fun, and playful, and attractive—right? Because if we pretend to be attracted to each other, then we are both attractive by definition. And! It ramps everything up because nothing fans the flames of longing like a little competition."

Cooper just frowned.

I shrugged. "I read that on the internet."

Cooper didn't fight me.

"And don't think this plan is all for me, by the way. Ashley has a plan to set you up with Bridesmaid Two after we get the Finn thing done. So this is a win-win all around."

"Bridesmaid Two?"

"That's the girl who asked you about your cool job at breakfast. Which is a lot more than I've done for you on this trip, by the way."

"That's debatable."

"The point is, Bridesmaid Two can be yours. And fake flirting with me is a surefire way to make that happen."

But Cooper was wrinkling his nose. "I don't like her."

"I don't like her, either," I said. "But it's already on Ashley's spreadsheet, so I'm not sure either of us has much say in the matter."

Cooper was still trying to catch up. "So, by 'fake flirting,' you mean—?"

"I mean, we hang out all the time, and goof around, and laugh at each other's jokes."

"We already do that."

"Yes. But we ramp it way up. Make it loud and public. Get noticed."

"And then what happens?"

"Then other people get interested in us. And then they're ensnared in our love trap."

"Don't say *love trap*."

"But you'll do it, right?" I pressed. "Out of guilt, if nothing else? Since Finn thought your weak-ass hickey was eczema?"

There were those blue eyes again. "I'll think about it," Cooper said. Then he added, "If you do something for me."

"What's that?"

Cooper said, "Let's practice our song."

I DIDN'T WANT to. Of course.

It was one thing to sing again for the first time in years quietly, in Cooper's private cabin, in bed, in the dark, with rustling insomnia as the only other option.

It was another thing to sing in a ballroom.

Even if it was empty.

"Is there anything *else* I could do for you?" I asked.

Cooper shook his head.

I eyed the stage area.

"The fact that you don't want to is the exact reason why you should," Cooper said.

I looked around the small ballroom. Had it gotten bigger?

"You agreed to practice," Cooper urged.

"Fine. Yes. Okay," I said. "I agreed to practice."

And so we got arranged on an imaginary stage and stood in front of an imaginary mic stand—but then Cooper started strumming real music on that mini banjo, and after the intro, when he nodded a cue at me to jump in and start, I looked around at the cavernous room, and I felt a little squeeze in my chest, and I just . . . stood there.

Cooper stopped strumming. "That was your cue."

"I know."

"Try again," Cooper said, and started over.

But the squeeze happened again.

"You know what?" Cooper said. "Let's just do the melody together. No harmony."

This time, Cooper jumped in at the cue, too—but instead of joining him, I just listened.

He did two verses, hoping he might get me in the mood, but then he petered out.

I looked over at him. "I think it's the ballroom," I said. "It's so . . . big."

"How about you close your eyes," he suggested, "and pretend it's ten years ago—and we're up on your roof?"

I looked at him doubtfully.

"Just for now. Just until you get comfortable."

So I did it. I closed my eyes, and I imagined that we were still in high school, that Cooper and I had never given up on each other, and that we were up on the roof just like we had been the night before, and the night before that . . . and that I was still a person who could stand under the moonlight with her best friend and just belt out a song without any hesitation.

And guess what? It worked pretty well.

Once I closed my eyes, there was nothing but imaginary moonlight, and Cooper's familiar voice, and the mini banjo I'd heard him play a million times . . . and that lovely little song that I knew so well by heart.

I just fell into it.

We sang it three times, in the end, and it was easy.

"Next time, we'll do it with your eyes open," Cooper said as he walked me back to find my mother before I got in too much trouble. But as we passed the gift shop, Cooper stopped to examine something on a spinning rack.

When I turned back to look, Cooper had put on a pair of red heart-shaped sunglasses.

"What do you think?" he asked.

"I think those look weirdly great on you."

"Not for me," he said. "For you. To wear onstage."

"At the reception?"

He nodded. "So you can close your eyes if you need to."

But I shook my head. "I'll be okay."

And then he nodded and said, "Yeah. You will."

Seventeen

COOPER TURNED OUT to be phenomenally good at fake flirting.

For a guy who'd never even imagined such a thing until today, he caught up fast.

By dinner, he had tickled me, rested his chin on his hands to gaze at me, stolen my hat and made me chase him all around the lido deck to get it back, and laughed uproariously at more jokes than I had actually told. He also grabbed me while I was walking by and made me sit on his lap, threw me over his shoulder like some pillaging Viking, and gave me three new Josephine-based nicknames, including JJ, Jo-burg, and Pheenie.

"You are *really* good at this," I told him as we changed for dinner back at our cabin—me, as always, in the bathroom with the door cracked, and him out in the room.

"I researched *flirting* on my phone," he said.

"You've got a knack for it, buddy."

"I do, don't I?"

"I'm going to write you a kick-ass recommendation," I declared, "for your next fake flirting job."

We were supposed to dress up for dinner tonight. Sneakers and tank tops were banned, and jackets and ties were required. I was wearing another dress of Ashley's, this one loose and silky and flowing—with spaghetti straps. It slipped on easily—no zipper required. I bent down to put on my most ridiculous pair of heels yet, and I heard Cooper say, "It physically hurts me to see you mutilating yourself in all these shoes."

I'm sure I was about to say something deliciously witty, but when I lifted my head and saw him—it went blank.

Whoa. His hair was coiffed in that swooped-forward way he liked, and his tie was tied, and he looked neat and ironed and . . . truly handsome.

Ugh. I said it.

"What happened to you?" I demanded, looking him up and down.

Cooper eyed me. "What do you mean?"

"How did you turn into a Disney prince?"

"You think I look like a Disney prince?"

"I really do."

"You think I look like a cartoon?"

"Not a cartoon like SpongeBob. A *sexy* cartoon."

"Pretty sure there's no such thing."

"Of course there is. It's like when you watch *Lady and the Tramp*, and you're kind of attracted to the Tramp—"

Cooper squinted at me, like *Please be kidding*.

"—and you're like, 'Nothing about this is right, but the heart wants what it wants'?" I pushed on. "You're *that* kind of cartoon."

"I didn't know you were attracted to cartoon dogs."

His eyes were mocking, so I dug in harder. "Cartoon foxes, too. Remember *Robin Hood*?"

"That's why you had that poster in your room?"

"Yep."

"Of all the Robin Hoods, that's your choice? Not Sean Connery, or Kevin Costner, or Russell Crowe?"

"I think I'm in the majority on this."

He frowned doubtfully. "Live human men are losing out to cartoon dogs and foxes?"

"This has been going on for decades," I said, like *Try to catch up.* "But that's not a problem for you."

"Because?"

"Because you're in the same category. A cartoon prince ranks just as high."

"As a dog?"

I gave him a look. "Count your blessings."

"So. Which prince am I?"

"All of them," I said.

"*All* of them?"

"If I had to pick, I'd say Prince Eric from *The Little Mermaid*."

This was so clearly not a touchpoint for Cooper.

So I googled it for him. "It's the hair. Look! It's kind of the same. And the blue eyes. And the—I don't know . . . *general dreaminess*."

Cooper looked back and forth between the image on my phone and the mirror, like he wasn't quite sure if he wanted to agree.

"The resemblance really is uncanny," I said.

"Maybe we're related."

I gave him a look. "This is a huge compliment," I said. "Do you know how they draw those princes?"

Cooper shook his head.

"They do like thirty different versions, and then they invite focus groups of women to come in and choose the most attractive parts of all of them—and then they combine everything into one man."

Cooper looked baffled. "Huh."

"See?" I said, pointing at Cooper's swoopy hair. "Hair shouldn't look this good in real life. How do you get it to do that?"

"I dated a girl who worked as a barber."

"And those shoulders," I went on, like he was being unreasonable. "And those relentless blue eyes. And you have a nose that doesn't even look real. It's like an illustrator drew it."

Cooper listened closely while I gestured at everything.

"I don't know how I never saw it before," I said.

"In your defense," Cooper said, "back in high school . . . I was more like Shaggy from *Scooby-Doo*."

He wasn't wrong.

"But then you moved across the ocean," I said, finishing out the story of his life, "and did some push-ups, and dated a barber—and *boom*! You got handsome."

"You really think I'm handsome?"

"Haven't you been listening? I think you could've been *designed by a focus group*. That's the kind of handsome you are. You could have any woman on this ship. Just select one at your leisure."

"Any woman?" he asked.

"Of course," I said. But then I had to backtrack: "Though—you don't actually get to pick. Ashley has preselected a mate for you."

Cooper frowned. "Can Ashley be overruled?"

"Not usually," I said. "Why? Did you have someone else in mind?"

"No."

"Because I support you," I went on. "Fight back! Bridesmaid Two is the worst."

Then I turned him back toward the mirror and gestured at his—everything. "All this," I said, "should not be wasted on a basic bridesmaid."

Cooper considered his new cartoon-based handsomeness.

I considered it, too. "You need to know this about yourself, Cooper," I said. "Time has been good to you."

"You really think I look like a Disney prince?"

"I don't *think* it. It's just a fact."

"Except I'm better than a Disney prince," Cooper said then.

"Wow. Bold statement. Okay. Why is that?"

Cooper shrugged. "Because I'm real."

ON THE WALK to dinner, we ran into Finn, of all people, in the hallway.

Finn greeted Cooper with "Coooop!" and a loud slap on the shoulder. Then he turned to me and said, "Josephine, right?"

"JoJo," I corrected while nodding, like *Exactly right.*

Then Finn went on like he was practicing for a quiz. "Maid of honor. Math genius. The girl who fell out of our oak tree."

"Yes!" I said, raising my hand for a high five. "Nice job!"

May I just point out that we had lived across the street from each other *since birth*?

Why was I high-fiving him? These were basic details!

God, my bar was low.

On the other hand, these were basic details that Finn definitely hadn't known yesterday. Nothing wrong with progress.

Next, the three of us stood there for an awkward second.

Then Finn said, "So. Who gave you that hickey?"

My eyes went wide.

Cooper and I glanced at each other, like *What!*

I lifted my hand to the place on my neck. Then I said, "I thought you thought it was eczema."

"I was joking."

"You were?" Then—because he'd apparently made a joke earlier that I hadn't laughed at—I giggled as an apology.

"Was it this guy?" Finn asked, nodding toward Cooper.

"No," Cooper and I said in unison, guilty as crows.

Next, I started panic-yammering: "No, no. We're just—childhood friends. We would never, ya know, *hickey each other.* We just goof around and do friend stuff. This hickey came from another person. Who I met on the boat. Since I'm supersingle and open to adventure."

Supersingle? Seriously?

Finn looked back and forth between us like he wasn't sure he bought it. "Are you *sure* you're just friends?" he asked me. "Because he seems genuinely into you."

I was so flustered that Finn Turner was even talking to me, I almost—*almost*—answered, *Oh, that? He was just faking.*

But Cooper jumped in and saved me from myself. "I've had a thing for her since we were kids," he said. "But she doesn't like me back."

Quick thinking, Cooper!

Finn nodded at that, like now it all worked. "So you guys aren't—dating?"

"Us?" I asked in falsetto, like he was crazy. "No! No, no, no."

I expected Cooper to join in, but he was examining something on his shoe.

And then, with that settled, we recommenced walking to dinner—now as a group of three, with me in the middle, flanked by the boys. Cooper—presumably to give me space to make a love connection—got quiet and put his hands in his pockets to stroll along beside us.

Finn leaned close and pulled me into conversation.

"I was hoping to run into you," Finn said as we walked.

"You were?"

He bumped his shoulder against mine. "We arrive at Nassau tomorrow," he said.

I nodded like that was interesting news.

He went on. "And I see there's a kayaking excursion."

I nodded some more.

"And I'm wondering," Finn said as we reached the dining room, "if you might like to go with me."

"Go . . . kayaking?" I asked.

Finn nodded. "On a date."

I so badly wanted to take a moment to react to that. Not just react, but savor. *Finn Turner was asking me on a date.* I would've given anything to call up my teenage self right then and give her the news.

But, instead, just as we arrived at the dining room, I caught sight of my parents presiding over the block of wedding party tables. My mom was proudly gazing at Ashley and Brody, and my dad was proudly gazing at . . . my mom.

We never really know what other people are thinking, right? It's all just guesswork, based on our own best interpretations of facial expressions, and body language, and tone of voice. Especially if we're talking about people like my dad—who are, to put it mildly, deeply stoic.

But there was no doubt about this moment.

Whatever else you might say about my dad, and I'd probably said it all . . . there was no doubt that he loved my mom.

He just loved her.

And he wanted to be with her.

Maybe he wasn't great at love. But something in his eyes right then made me think that he wanted to get better.

And that was all I needed. Right in that one second, I signed up for Team Dad.

I had always been on my mom's team by default—as all of us kids were. And my dad had always been all by himself. I guess I'd thought that was where he preferred to be. But looking at him right then reminded me of this morning—of how lonely it had felt to tell Cooper that he was the only person on my entire tragic team of *one*.

And then I realized that my dad didn't even have that many.

He was just endlessly on his own.

So I joined him—even if only in my head. If he wanted my mother back? If he wanted to change her mind? He was going to need some serious help. It might already be too late. It might take an actual miracle. But in case you missed it, the undisputed alpha of my childhood pack had just asked me out—on a date. And if that didn't qualify as a miracle, I wasn't sure what would.

If I could make *that* happen, I could do anything.

I looked at my dad with compassion.

Poor guy. He'd screwed up the best thing in his life—and he seemed to have no idea how it happened. From my new vantage point of success, I decided to help him.

It was a heck of a role reversal—from him being the neglectful father who had created all my neuroses to me being the love savant who could share some of my wisdom with the less fortunate.

I'm not sure if this is how compassion always works, but something about that moment gave me strength.

My dad seemed to sense me watching him. He looked over, and I gave him a little salute, like he'd taught us when we were kids.

Finn was still waiting for my response to his invitation.

So I turned to Finn—not as the ten-year-old me he'd kissed, or the fourteen-year-old me who'd memorized his license plate number, or even the yesterday me who was so nervous she got a score of *three hundred seventy-nine* in mini golf.

Just as regular old me.

Regular me who was ready to take a good, hard look at her destiny, at last.

I met his eyes. Then I smiled with every tooth I had. Then I said, "Finn Turner! I thought you'd never ask."

DID COOPER AVOID looking at me all through dinner?

I don't know. Maybe.

Or maybe he had indigestion.

We were, of course, seated together at the same table with Finn. And we did, of course, sit three in a row—me in the middle again. This was all decreed on Ashley's spreadsheet.

What wasn't part of the spreadsheet—certainly not on our second night—was the sudden addition of Bridesmaid Two on Cooper's other side.

What a fourth wheel.

The fact is, Cooper and I should've been celebrating.

His failed hickey hadn't failed at all. In fact, it might be the most accomplished hickey in all of human history. Not to mention the lady he'd given it to might still have been experiencing a few aftershocks of delighted shivers, even all this time later.

I'd have to add that to my letter of recommendation.

But instead of getting to savor this triumph with my wingman, I had to spend all of dinner watching Bridesmaid Two leaning against Cooper's shoulder and squeezing her boobs together to create a type of cleavage that felt aggressive, to say the least.

I had to actively look away to preserve my appetite.

Seriously.

She was leaning over so far, she had to bring her fork over from her plate at a 45-degree angle with every bite.

I think at one point she dropped a pea down there.

All to say: Maybe Cooper wasn't avoiding me after all. Maybe Bridesmaid Two was just making him nauseous.

Finn, on my other side, kept getting texts that he had to respond to. "I'm so sorry. I have to take this," he kept saying, getting up to step away from the table. But during those times, I couldn't talk to Cooper because Bridesmaid Two was relentlessly hogging his attention, asking all about his life: What was the best thing about London ("the pubs"), could he do a British accent ("sometimes"), and what did he miss about Texas ("the sky").

Bridesmaid Two was mostly asking Cooper all about his job like she was the first person to ever make vocational chitchat. It bugged me for many reasons, but I guess the biggest one was that she was getting answers even I didn't have. And I'd always had all the answers about Cooper.

Yet somehow here I was, eavesdropping.

She forced Cooper to describe the studio where he worked, and list movies he'd done, and explain how he created all kinds of sounds. And dammit, it was fascinating. He snapped stalks of celery, for example, to make the sound of breaking bones. He recorded bacon frying to make the sound of rain. He whooshed a stalk of bamboo past the mic to make the sound of an arrow.

"What about kissing?" Bridesmaid Two dared to ask.

"That's easy," Cooper said, "you just kiss your forearm."

I side-glanced over to see him roll back his shirtsleeve to reveal his naked forearm underneath—and then lean forward to *demonstrate what he meant.*

I meant to look away. I really did. But my eyes got stuck.

At the sight of him bending down, parting his lips, and then pressing them against his own skin . . . things seemed to shift into slo-mo for a second.

Was Cooper Watts *Frenching his own forearm* at the dinner table?

Whatever was going on, I'll be honest: My hickey might've tingled a bit at the sight of it.

That is, until Finn returned to his seat, patted me on the hand, and said, "Where were we?"

Ripped back to reality, I turned and said, "You were telling me about how you review contracts."

Was I jealous that I was listening to Finn use legal terms like *mutual covenants and agreements* while Bridesmaid Two got to watch Cooper passionately smooching his own arm?

Yes. Yes, I was.

Bridesmaid Two was having so much fun, she wasn't even interrupting.

Which felt massively unfair.

Even though, technically, I was getting what I wanted.

I forced myself to notice that Operation Conquest was starting to work.

Wasn't that what I was here for, after all?

I needed to refocus!

Whenever Finn was at the table, I doubled down on my *How to Make a Man Fall in Love with You* research and asked him all about himself. My plan was to launch endless searching questions about his interests and talents. According to the book, asking people about themselves makes them think that *you* are fascinating.

But now, inspired in part by Bridesmaid Two's cleavage, I added some physicality to my conversation with Finn. When I asked him about his class ring, I made sure to reach out and brush his fingers with mine. When I laughed, I touched him on the shoulder. And once, when I stood up to go to the ladies' room, I pretended to lose my balance so I could fall sideways onto his lap and let him catch me.

I won't confirm or deny if I tried to use my own cleavage as a weapon, but let's just say Bridesmaid Two wasn't the only person in the dining room who could lean toward a man at a 45-degree angle.

I might have lost a pea or two myself.

I'd started out the meal intending to laugh uproariously at every funny thing Finn said. But then it turned out that Finn didn't say funny things. Instead, he seriously told me about his life as a litigator. He seriously explained how golf had become a "real passion" for him. And then he seriously described his new BMW to me like he was doing a Consumer Reports performance review, including in-depth assessments of its turbo, torque, and thrust.

I listened intently, like we were discussing world affairs.

Like nothing on earth could be more fascinating.

Like my oldest friend wasn't eighteen inches away, *making out with his own arm.*

I was just visualizing my soul-sucking boredom as a pinhole leak in a pool float, and I was feeling quite deflated, when Cooper rescued me again.

He interrupted a soliloquy of Finn's on the perils of tax law to turn all attention to me and ask, "Tell us about your amazing job, JoJo."

Everyone stopped talking. Even Finn.

"My amazing job?" I asked, like I'd forgotten all about it.

"JoJo teaches art to middle schoolers," Cooper said. "But that's not the coolest part."

I frowned at him, like *What's the coolest part?*

"It's not just any old art," Cooper said. "It's math art."

"What's math art?" Bridesmaid Two wanted to know.

I narrowed my eyes at Cooper, like he had once again forgotten how supremely uninterested most of the world was in math. But then I said, "Well, it's mostly trying to find ways to bring mathematical principles to life using art. So the kids can see and feel how these patterns exist in the world all around us. So, like, I have them draw seashells using Fibonacci numbers, so they can see how that sequence works in nature. And I help them visualize hyperbolic geometry by showing them crochet patterns that follow the geometric formulas of nonlinear shapes. One of my favorite activities is to blow their minds by having them make Möbius strips."

"What's a Möbius strip?" the ever-eager Bridesmaid Two asked.

"It's a non-orientable, non-Euclidean infinite loop," I said.

I admit it was a bit of a flex to lose her for a second. "You make it with a strip of paper," I explained next, "like you would if you were making a paper chain. But instead of taping the two ends directly together, you twist the strip once before connecting the ends. Doing that one thing—twisting the strip—changes it from a shape with two sides, an inside and an outside, to a shape that has only one side. If you run a pencil along it, it will draw on both sides before you ever get back to where you started."

I wasn't sure Bridesmaid Two was following—or Finn for that matter. But Cooper was leaning back in his chair, enjoying every sentence I uttered, like he was responsible for sparking the best conversation topic of the night.

But I'm not sure anyone but me agreed.

Before long, Bridesmaid Two had Cooper talking about London again, and Finn was sharing his thoughts on the municipal court system—but I appreciated Cooper's attempt.

As time wore on, to be brutally honest, I did find myself absently touching the little hickey that had made all this triumphing possible. And yes—my mind kept trying to drift back to the moment it had happened.

That was Cooper's fault. A random bridesmaid asks you about kissing and then you just volunteer to demonstrate—for hours? *Set some boundaries, Cooper!*

But I stayed focused on my goals.

Through it all, I kept wanting to get a minute alone with Cooper to celebrate our massive victory and thank him for his service—a moment that never came. But I took comfort in the fact that as stuck as I was with Finn . . . Cooper was equally stuck with Bridesmaid Two.

Eighteen

FINN WOULD TURN out to be a gear guy.

Remember how decked out he was for mini golf?

Double it for kayaking.

He brought a helmet. A *helmet.*

Plus a wet suit, neoprene shoes, and—rather on-theme—gloves.

I'd googled *kayaking* after he asked me, trying to get a sense of what I'd just signed up for, and I'd watched more than one extreme sports video of dudes kayaking down waterfalls, slamming into rocks, and basically murdering themselves.

Those guys needed helmets.

But as far as I could tell, the Escapes Cruise Line version of kayaking was just . . . paddling peacefully around a lagoon.

Maybe we'd see a turtle. Or something.

Anyway—my gear amounted to a swimsuit, some shorts, and a pair of water shoes I borrowed from Ashley. She'd handed them over at the door of her bridal suite that morning in a robe, looking quite, um, tousled.

"I can't believe how hard you are crushing Operation Conquest," she said. "It's *working*!"

I nodded. “Right?”

Next, she noticed my neck. “Is that a hickey?”

“Yesterday, you thought it was Tabasco sauce.”

She covered her mouth. “Who gave it to you?”

But I shook my head. “It’s a whole saga,” I said.

She would normally know all the details already. But it’s a lot of work being a bride, and there had been no crannies of time when I could grab her and share. And it certainly wasn’t happening now, with Brody clanking around in the room behind her. I wasn’t even sure whose side he was on.

“Did you take my sunscreen?” he asked Ashley right then, and she turned back to answer.

Sunscreen. I’d be needing that today.

When Ashley turned back to me, she took one more look at my neck and then gave me a sly smile. “You should tell Finn it *is* Tabasco sauce,” she said. “And then dare him to lick it off.”

“Ashley!” I scolded, looking both ways down the hall.

But nobody would overhear. The bridal suite was above the waterline. Definitely not with the wedding block.

“How is it rooming with Harmony?” Ashley asked then, wrinkling her nose.

“That’s—another whole saga,” I said, implying I’d have to tell her later.

Would I tell her later? I had never withheld anything from Ashley. But things were already different now. Seeing Ashley and Brody framed through the doorway in their matching robes? They really looked like a married couple.

Did husbands and wives tell each other everything? Could I trust Ashley now to keep anything between just us two? By the end of this week, she and Brody would be married. She was going to take his last name—and leave “Ashley Burton” behind for the very unfortunate “Ashley Cockburn.”

And even though Brody’s last name was technically pronounced *Coh-burn*, that didn’t make it any better. Once you saw it written out—on a name tag, or a wedding invitation, or, maybe worst of all, the back of a sports jersey—you couldn't unsee it.

As Pete liked to say: *Ouch*.

But there was no reasoning with Ashley. This was happening.

They'd already put a down payment on a house and merged all their bank accounts and everything.

Before we knew it, they'd be making little Cockburn babies.

Soon, she'd belong to him.

Which meant, I realized with a sting of loss, that she wouldn't belong to me anymore.

That's when Brody called, "Ash? I need you."

Ashley glanced back, very pleased to be needed, and then blew me a goodbye kiss.

As I walked down the hallway, she popped her head out to call after me, "I want all the details the minute you're back!"

I turned around to say, "You got it!"—not even sure if that was true.

But she'd already closed the door.

In the elevator, I ran into my dad. His arms were full of bags of paper flowers.

I took a couple from him to be helpful.

"Hey, sweetheart," he said.

"Dad," I said then. "Are you busy?"

He obviously was.

"Not at all," he said.

"Could I talk to you for a minute?"

"Sure. Of course."

He was headed to give those bags to my mom, but we paused at a little outdoor seating spot along the way and set the bags on a table.

"I need to tell you something," I said.

"Okay," my dad said. "Shoot."

"I know about you and Mom."

My dad's eyes widened. He looked—*caught*. "You know—?"

"About all of it," I said. And then, in a move that felt like revealing a state secret, I said, "I heard you. Through the vent on the stairs."

"You heard . . . ?" He waited for me to clarify, like he was hoping we had different definitions of *all of it*.

"I heard everything." Then I leaned in to whisper, "About Mom wanting a divorce."

My dad frowned, like he wasn't sure how to feel about me knowing. Then he glanced around and said, "Please don't tell your sister."

"Of course I won't," I said. "I wasn't even going to tell *you*."

"Why *are* you telling me?"

"I heard you say you were going to try to change Mom's mind."

My dad nodded.

"How's that going?"

My dad shook his head.

"Because I decided something last night, and you need to know about it."

My dad nodded, like *Tell me*.

"I decided to help you."

"Help me?"

"Help you change Mom's mind."

At that, he lifted his hand to rub his eyes. "Sweetie, I'm not sure you *can* help me. I'm not even sure I can help myself."

"It's not too late," I said.

My dad looked away, like he was studying something in the ocean. Then he said, "I think it might be."

"I love that you're trying," I said. "I can tell that you are."

"I am," he said.

"You're doing all the right things," I said.

My dad nodded, like that was good feedback.

And I cannot describe to you the shock I felt at what my dad did next, because such a thing had never, to my recollection, happened before.

He spoke in a *whole paragraph*.

A long one.

I'm telling you, the man must have been holding in an emotional Mount Vesuvius, because once he started talking, he couldn't seem to stop.

There might have been more words in this one moment than all the words he'd ever spoken to me before that.

"You know," he said, watching the ocean, "my parents never got along. They fought all the time. They barely tolerated each other their entire marriage. I never remember them laughing, or having fun, or even touching. And the thing they fought about was money. Every day, they fought about money. I grew up poor. Paycheck-to-paycheck poor. We were always struggling. So it seemed pretty clear to me that being poor was the problem. And when I met your mom . . . I just fell so hard for her. I wanted us to be happy. I always thought my number-one job was to work hard so that you kids and your mom could have a nice life. What if we lost the house? What if one of you got really sick? What if I became expendable at work? So I said yes to every opportunity, and I took overtime, and I gave it all I had. But everything's a trade-off, JoJo. You can't be everywhere at once. Being at work meant that I wasn't at home. I told myself it was better that way. That the best gift I could give you kids was time with your mother. I thought if I could just do that, we'd have nothing to be unhappy about."

My dad pressed his hands down on the ship's railing. Then he took a deep breath. "Maybe I took your mom for granted. Or our family. But that was because, for me, there was never any question. You all belonged to me, and I belonged to you, and that's just how it was."

My dad looked down at the water, then up at the sky. "But I guess that wasn't how it was. I worked too hard. I was gone too much. Your mom was unhappy. I thought I was the only one who was lonely."

And then, I swear to god, my ex-marine dad's eyes filled with tears.

"Have you said all that to her?" I asked.

"I'm just trying to get through this wedding," my dad said.

"Yes," I agreed. "But you're also—at the same time—trying to save your marriage."

"I'm not sure I can."

"It's not over 'til it's over," I said. "You should say all of that to Mom—exactly the way you just said it to me."

My dad looked down at the water skimming the edge of the boat below. He nodded, like he was really considering it.

I felt an impulse to hug him.

But we really didn't know each other that well.

Instead, I just stepped closer. "Dad," I said. "I believe you. And I want you to know something: I am on your team."

My dad frowned, like he hadn't realized there were teams.

So I said, "You're not alone."

And then my dad sighed, like those were words he hadn't realized he needed to hear.

As if she sensed us talking about her, my mom appeared on the deck, saw us, and started walking in our direction. I could tell, even from a hundred feet away, that she needed those flowers and she wasn't too pleased with our dawdling.

My dad could tell, too.

"Talk to her," I urged.

"She's busy," my dad said. "I don't want to add to her stress."

"It's not stress to find out that your husband loves you madly."

My dad blinked, like that was really a new way of framing it.

"Tell her," I said. "Tell her you love her! Tell her you were gone all the time *because* you love her. Tell her that it wasn't neglect—it was the opposite. Tell her how hard you were trying. She thinks you weren't around because you didn't care. Don't let her leave you for the wrong reasons!"

My dad's face was tight with worry. "Can you write all that down?"

"What?"

"What you just said."

"I was just summing up what *you* just said."

"But you're saying it with a better vocabulary."

"It's not about vocabulary. It's about speaking from the heart. And also setting the record straight. Have a real conversation with her, Dad. She might still leave you, but at least you'll both know why."

"I don't want to seem like a whiner."

"Wanna know what you seem like to me?" I asked.

My dad met my eyes.

"You seem like a man who loves his family very much. And who's trying like hell to get it right."

My dad was fidgeting. Vulnerability was not his favorite emotion.

"That's your homework," I said then. "Pull her aside. Tell her everything you just told me. Tell her you can change. And ask her to take you back on a trial basis."

"A trial basis?"

I nodded. "Once that's done, we'll move on to phase two."

"What's phase two?"

"I don't know yet, but we'll figure it out."

My mother was almost within earshot.

"More to come on this," I said, giving him a little salute.

And then, I guess because he also wanted a hug but *also* had no idea how to make that happen . . . my dad just nodded and saluted me back.

Nineteen

LET'S JUST SKIP the kayaking, okay?

Did I go?

Yes.

Did Finn wear his helmet?

No. But he was clearly disappointed about that.

And was I so nervous all morning before going that I fully forgot to put on any sunscreen—at all—and came back from that five-hour excursion broiled like a lobster?

I'm sorry to say: *Yes.*

But sunburns can take a while to set in. I didn't really notice what I'd done to myself until I got back to the room and Cooper, who was practicing his mini banjo, looked up and said, "That's a hell of a sunburn."

"Is it?" I asked, suddenly getting the shivers.

"Didn't you put on sunscreen?"

I shook my head. "I was so nervous, I forgot."

Cooper came closer to look me over. "No hat? Nothing?" he asked, hoping for a different answer.

"Nothing," I said.

I turned toward the mirror. I did look a little pink. And, now that we were noticing it, I felt a little pink, too.

Then Cooper nodded like a doctor with a diagnosis. "First," he said, "Tylenol. Then take a lukewarm shower to get the salt water off before it starts stinging too bad. Did you bring aloe?"

I shook my head.

"I'll check the gift shop. And I'll get water bottles. You have to hydrate like crazy."

"Sounds like you've had a few sunburns yourself."

"A few," he said.

This was the real result of my date with Finn. Not a post-excursion glass of champagne with the man I was trying to turn into my destiny . . . but conking out afterward for twelve hours in Cooper's bed.

Before I fell asleep, though, Cooper made me drink a full bottle of water while he covered me with aloe—as I wore only a bra and a pair of short shorts.

My most sensible bra, though, if that helps. Cotton—not lacy. It could almost have been a bikini top.

"Sorry not to have a shirt on," I said to Cooper.

"We're in a medical situation," he said, like *It's fine.*

"Pretend it's a bikini," I said.

And then, I guess for a comedy callback, he said, "You don't want me to do that."

It had been a long time since I'd had a sunburn. Childhood, maybe?

But Cooper insisted the aloe would solve everything.

All he had to do was apply it all over every burned inch of my body.

But as I sat on my side of the bed, looking at the glob of gel in his hand, I shook my head. "I think I'm fine," I said.

"I'm not going to argue with you," Cooper said. "But you're not."

"I just—don't want to be touched. Even fingertips seem like sandpaper."

"That's why you put the aloe on really thick," Cooper explained.

My worst areas were my shoulders and the tops of my thighs. Cooper took a scoop of the gel on his fingers and moved toward my knee. "Let's do one square inch," he said, "and if you hate it, we'll stop."

One square inch. I didn't stop him.

And it actually felt fine. Cool and smooth and soothing.

"How's that?" Cooper asked.

"It's good, actually."

"Permission to do the rest?"

I nodded.

And so Cooper spent the next half hour slathering my back side with half the bottle—though he had to pause a few minutes in to put my hair up in a ponytail. He did my shoulders first—gliding cool strokes down to my bathing suit line and up to my hair. Then he blew on my back for a while to dry it before sending me to the bathroom for one last pee and then helping me lie back on the bed.

"You're going to stick to the sheets a little," he said, "but there's no way around it."

Once I was positioned, it was time to do my front side.

Cooper pulled up a chair to get to work.

I closed my eyes and said, "Tell me about the worst sunburn you ever got."

But Cooper just sucked air through his teeth like nobody would benefit from that. "How about I sing to you instead?"

"That works."

And that's how we spent the evening. Cooper took requests—"Rocky Raccoon," and "I Heard It Through the Grapevine," and the Kermit the Frog classic "Rainbow Connection"—while covering me, face to feet, in goo.

Despite everything, it was fun.

The aloe was so smooth and cool. Favorite areas included my cheeks, my collarbones, my knees, and the tops of my feet. "You're good at this," I said, when Cooper was midway through "American Pie."

In response, he switched out one of the *bye-bye*s with *thank you.*

Anyway: I had no trouble falling asleep that night.

Apparently, all I needed to get comfortable in bed with Cooper was a pampering serenade and a touch of sun poisoning.

But it worked. No fidgeting tonight. I conked out effortlessly and slept four hours straight—only waking later and peeling myself off the sheets to go pee. It's a bit of a blur, but I know at some point, Cooper made me take more Tylenol and drink more water. And he did at least two reapplications of aloe in the middle of the night.

After the second bathroom run, though—maybe around four in the morning?—I couldn't get back to sleep.

I lay in the bed with my skin hot and irritated, wide awake, unable to get comfortable and endlessly adjusting positions—as quietly as possible, hoping not to wake Cooper.

After about twenty minutes, Cooper said, "You probably need more aloe."

"I'm fine," I whispered. "Just go back to sleep."

"Too late," Cooper said, sitting up.

He came around to my side of the bed. Then we went through all the same sunburn-care steps again, silently, sleepily—until the final section, when he was sitting on a chair next to the bed and working the gel all over the front half of my body.

"Cooper?" I asked, my eyes closed in the dark as he slid the pads of his fingers across my collarbones.

"What?"

"I've been wanting to ask you a question for a long time."

"Oh, yeah?"

"But I keep not asking."

The question I wanted to ask, of course, was why he had disappeared four years ago.

But once I knew, I couldn't unknow.

And what if the answer ruined everything?

I'd chickened out of asking him about it on the night of my non-wedding. And tonight, with nothing else to do and nothing else to talk about . . . I would chicken out again.

"What's the question?" Cooper asked.

It was right there—just sitting in my mouth like a butterscotch candy: Why did you disappear?

But at the very last second, I shifted.

I reached up instead and touched the scar on his upper lip. "How did you get this?" I asked.

The gel stopped. But then it started again.

I breathed in and out.

"It's kind of a long story," Cooper said, coating a thick layer of aloe down into an area that in any nonmedical situation we would call *cleavage*.

"I've got time," I said.

"Shouldn't you be going back to sleep?"

"Shouldn't you?"

Cooper sighed. Then he said, "You remember when my mom and I moved to our street, yes?"

"Of course," I said.

I fully remembered. Our gang of kids were all out riding bikes in the street . . . and I suddenly noticed this new kid in a red T-shirt with a cut on his lip and a cast on his arm, standing in the Hickses' old driveway, watching us.

I rode over to him. "What happened to your face?"

"A fencing accident," Cooper had said.

Looking back, it was such an odd thing to say. But I never questioned it. I just assumed that this brand-new child in my life had been brandishing a sword a little too roughly.

"Do you want to ride bikes with us?" I asked him next.

"I don't have a bike," Cooper had said. "We had to leave it at my old house."

At that, I climbed off my bike and pushed the handlebars toward him. "Take mine," I said.

"What about you?" he asked.

"I'll go get my brother's skateboard."

Inside, as I hunted in Pete's messy room for the skateboard, I saw a pack of markers, and I grabbed it and brought it outside with me. Back in the street, I called all the kids over, and then I pointed at Cooper. "What's your name, new kid?"

"Cooper Watts," Cooper announced, quite formally.

"Can we sign your cast, Cooper Watts?" I asked.

At that, all the kids noticed the pristine white cast on his forearm and dropped their bikes right there in the street to run over and grab markers. I'm still not sure what was so enrapturing about signing a cast, but by the time we were done with him, there was no expanse of white left. I myself signed it, in my prettiest cursive: *Welcome to the neighborhood! Your friend, JoJo.* And I dotted the *i* in *friend* with a flower.

Cooper had thanked me many times for that welcome, as if my declaring him to be our friend had made it happen. I'd tried to explain that it would've happened no matter what—but he persisted with the idea that I had somehow done something vital and life-changing for him that day.

Now, all these years later, as he applied aloe along my collarbones, he thanked me again. "When we moved onto our street," Cooper said, "I was recovering from—a thing that had happened."

He was? "What was the thing?"

"That's why I had the cast, and the cut lip. It was the reason my mom and I moved, actually," Cooper said.

I waited.

"Wow," Cooper said then. "I guess I don't talk about this much."

"What happened?" I prompted.

"So . . ." Cooper said. "In our old town, while my parents were in the middle of getting divorced . . . there was an incident where my dad came by after school one day before my mom was home from work . . . and he took me to his apartment for a sleepover—without actually telling her."

"Wait—what?"

"Yeah. So that was rough. She got home, and I wasn't there, and she couldn't find me anywhere . . . and then she called the police."

"Why didn't your dad tell her he'd picked you up?" I asked, hoping maybe he'd just forgotten.

"Apparently," Cooper said, "he was trying to scare her."

"Hold on," I said, sitting up straighter—sunburn forgotten. "Are you saying your dad kidnapped you?"

"I wouldn't say 'kidnapped.' He just . . . took me. Without asking. And didn't tell my mom."

"Cooper," I said. "That's *kidnapping*."

"Not if it's your dad."

But I couldn't let that stand. "Even if it's your dad."

Cooper shrugged. "I guess, technically—fine. You could call it kidnapping."

"Technically?"

"I didn't feel kidnapped, if that makes it better."

"Not sure it does."

"Yeah. So. My dad wasn't the nicest guy. Or—sometimes he was okay, I guess. But he was very controlling. Like, he never let my mom do anything by herself or make any decisions. She told me not long ago that he wouldn't let her have a credit card. She had to do everything with cash that he gave her. And he told her what to do all the time—like what to have for dinner, and where she could and couldn't go, and what to wear. Crazy stuff. Stuff that didn't matter—like which earrings she could buy. And I guess, after a while, she really didn't like that. Finally, she decided to leave him . . . and he didn't take too kindly to that news."

"Like—how?"

"She won't give me specifics. But I know she had to get a restraining order."

"Oh," I said.

"I'm not like that, by the way," Cooper said, like I might think less of him now.

"Of course you're not!" I said.

"I've spent my whole life working very hard to not be anything like my dad."

"Have you?"

"And I'm a great boyfriend, by the way. Ask anyone."

"Cooper," I said. "That's a given."

"All I have to do is think *what would my dad do* in any situation—and then just do the opposite."

I was still taking it in. "That's how you wound up moving to our street? You were on the run from your dad?"

"Not 'on the run,' exactly. Maybe just more like in hiding. A little bit. My mom worked really hard to make things feel normal after that. But yeah—when we moved, she changed our last name to Watts, after her favorite music teacher in high school. And she started calling me by my middle name."

"So your dad wouldn't find you?"

"That was the idea."

"So the situation was . . . really bad."

Cooper thought about it. "The situation had the *potential* to be really bad. If he'd come after us, it could've been really bad. But he never did. Either he couldn't find us or he didn't try. I never saw him again after that."

"So your real name isn't Cooper?"

"It's my real middle name," Cooper said.

"What's your first name?"

"Teddy."

Teddy? In no way did Cooper look like a Teddy. "Teddy what?"

"Teddy Franklin. Theodore Cooper Franklin."

"Your original name was Teddy Franklin?"

"Sounds weird, doesn't it?"

"You don't look *at all* like either of those things!"

"I'm not. Anymore. I got rid of the Theodore officially when I got rid of the Franklin."

"Why?"

"Because Teddy was also my dad's name."

I thought about that little kid in the red T-shirt and how much he'd been through, and I felt so glad that I'd pulled him right into our gang. "Cooper," I said. "This breaks my heart."

"You know what, though?" Cooper said. "It's a story with a happy ending. My mom took her life back. We moved to a better town—with a better school, and a better street. My mom got all the moms in the neighborhood, and I got you—all of you. My mom got a new job working at a foundation that gave out grants to artists—and she loved that job. So, yes . . . my parents' marriage was bad, and leaving my dad was no doubt a nightmare for my mom, but once she got free, everything got better."

"Is that why your mom gave up her dream of being a singer? Is that why she threw away all her records?"

Cooper nodded. "Yeah. You can't be famous when you're hiding."

We both took a second to appreciate what a bummer that was.

Then Cooper said, "If I could go back and rewrite her life, I'd make it so she never even met my dad."

"But then you wouldn't exist."

"That's fine. I wouldn't know."

"I can't support that idea."

"But given how bad things got . . . things turned out better in the end than she ever hoped for. Her words, not mine."

"Does she still worry he might come after her?"

Cooper shook his head. "He died a few years ago."

"Oh," I said. "How was that for you?"

I expected Cooper to tell me he either felt sad about that or didn't. But Cooper just shrugged. "I kind of hoped it might cure my cleithrophobia, but it didn't."

"Why would your father dying cure your cleithrophobia?"

"Oh," Cooper said, like he'd almost forgotten. "Because during the whole kidnapping thing, he made me stay in a closet."

"He *made you stay* in a closet?"

"I guess, more accurately," Cooper said, "he *locked me* in a closet."

"What! He *what*? For how long?!"

"I think it was four days?"

"Four days?!"

"He put a TV in there, though. And blankets and pillows. And he let me have all the Froot Loops I wanted."

"Cooper! Are you defending him?"

"I'm just saying—it wasn't that bad."

"Yes, it was!"

"It was a long time ago. I'm fine now."

"You're not fine! You have cleithrophobia."

"It's mild."

But I was so outraged on his behalf. "I can't believe you went through all that! I can't believe that happened to you—and all this time I never knew about it!"

Cooper gave a little *what-can-you-do* shrug.

I said, "I want to give you a hug right now—but I can't touch anything or *be touched*."

"It's fine," Cooper said. "You're in your underwear, so that's probably best."

I looked down. I'd almost forgotten. "This bra is practically a bathing suit."

"We can go with that."

Fine. No hug. Instead, I looked into his eyes. "Cooper . . . I'm so sorry."

He shook his head. "We all go through things."

"But we don't all *get kidnapped*."

"It brings me back to your question, though," Cooper said.

I couldn't even remember the question at this point.

"About this," he said, touching his scar.

"Your fencing scar," I said.

I lifted my hand and ran the pad of my pointer finger over the spot. I could feel a little indentation that cut all the way down through the rim of his lip. "That's deeper than it looks," I said.

"It happened when I escaped. From my dad's."

"You escaped?"

Cooper nodded.

"I was hoping he'd just come to his senses and taken you home."

Cooper shook his head, like *Nope*. "He forgot to lock the closet handle one day when he went out, so I climbed out the second-story window."

"That was brave."

"I missed my mom."

I peered in to look closer at the scar. "Your dad didn't catch you, did he?"

"No. He wasn't even there. I just—lost my balance and fell, and hit a chain-link fence on the way down."

I winced and sucked in a big breath. "Oh, my god."

Cooper nodded. "I came home completely covered in blood with a broken arm, and I scared the hell out of my mom. Next thing I knew, we were moving across the country to Texas."

"How have you never told me any of this?"

"I guess because I've never told anyone."

"I thought I knew everything about you."

"You know more than anybody else."

And then, even though it was a terrible idea, and even though I was technically in my underwear, and even though it really did hurt, I pulled Cooper into a hug, and I didn't let him go.

Twenty

I WOKE UP the next morning to the shocking sight of Cooper—texting.

With *Bridesmaid Two*!

"What on earth are you doing?" I asked.

"I'm canceling."

"Canceling what?"

"My plans with Bridesmaid Two."

Why was this information so appalling? "You had plans with *Bridesmaid Two*?"

"*You* had plans with Finn," Cooper said in his own defense.

"That's different," I said. "I don't have a choice about that."

"It's weird that you don't know this," Cooper said, "but you have all the choice in the world."

But not today. Because at the end of our kayaking day yesterday, in Nassau, Finn had asked me to go out with him again today, once we docked at Freeport. This time, to go snorkeling.

I'd been too sunburned yesterday to celebrate that win.

In fact, I forgot all about it—until I woke up. Docked. In Freeport.

According to the spreadsheet, it was time to snorkel.

"You can't be thinking of going?" Cooper demanded, reading my face.

"I'm feeling much better this morning."

"Guess what?" Cooper said. "There is no shade in the ocean."

"I'll put sunscreen on this time," I said with a shrug. "I'll bring a hat."

"No," Cooper said.

"No?"

"You're no stranger to dumb things. You've done some Guinness Book–level dumb things. But you're not doing this."

This really was a first. In my whole life, Cooper had never, ever, tried to tell me what I could or couldn't do.

"Look," he said. "I told you all about my dad last night."

"I remember," I said.

"So you know for sure that I make it a policy not to tell other people what to do."

"That sounds like a great policy."

"So it really takes a lot for me to say this to you . . ."

I waited.

Cooper crossed his arms over his chest. "But you're not going anywhere."

Wow.

"You need to stay here and drink water and rest. I did not stay up all night taking care of you just to watch you give yourself sun poisoning again today."

"Did you stay up all night taking care of me?"

"Yes," he said, his face grumpy. "I did."

"Thank you," I said—and I meant it.

It wasn't a hard sell. If I had to stay in Cooper's luxury cabin all day for health reasons, then I had to. And if Cooper had to stay, too, as my primary caregiver? Fine.

He opened his sliding glass doors to let the fresh breeze in. He kept me hydrated and slathered me with more aloe. We ordered room service grilled cheeses. We watched bad TV. We practiced our song. We talked about old times.

By midday, I felt better enough to slip on a light cotton cover-up and sit out on Cooper's balcony in the shade.

The big excitement of the day was when we realized the cruise ship parked in the slip next to ours was the MS *Decadence*—the ship we'd been docked next to back in Galveston. And as we stood on our balcony, looking at all the other folks across the way who were looking at us from *their* balconies, we spotted the cruise dudes from before.

The ones who had ogled me on the wharf.

"Look," I said to Cooper. "It's the ship-faced guys."

"It can't be," Cooper said.

But then we read their T-shirts. One of them read BEER MODE ACTIVATED, another read POWERED BY BEER, and the third one kept it simple and just said BEER LIFE.

"Those guys really love beer," I said.

"Uh-huh," Cooper agreed as we openly stared at them.

And then, I guess in that way that you can sometimes just sense when people are looking at you, the guys noticed us—and started elbowing each other. And just as Cooper and I were about to wave hello like we were friendly acquaintances from across the Gulf, all three men turned around at once, pulled down their pants, and pressed their butts up against the glass of their balcony railing.

I TEXTED ASHLEY—WITH a selfie for proof—about my sunburn, and she gave me a pass for the day to recover, but she also replied that she fully expected me to be in attendance at tonight's variety-show-slash-dance-contest, looking, and I quote, "gorgeous."

She even sent Pete down with a baby-blue sundress she wanted me to wear to offset the "broiled neon" color of my skin.

"Bruh," Pete said when he saw me. "You really messed yourself up."

"I'm better now," I said. And I was. Mostly.

But that evening, as I did my hair, and put on mascara, and stepped gingerly into the dress, Cooper paced around, refusing to get dressed.

"I'm not sure this is a great idea," Cooper said, while I was putting on my lipstick.

"What?"

"I kind of think maybe you need to take one more night to recover."

"Are you kidding?" I said. "Ashley would never stand for that."

"You still look pretty pink," Cooper said.

"It's fine," I said. "The lights'll be dimmed."

"I'm not worried about what other people will see. I'm worried about how you'll feel."

I stepped out of the bathroom to frown at myself in the mirror.

"I'm serious," Cooper said then.

"About what?" I asked, rotating to get a look at my profile.

"About how you should stay in tonight."

I looked over. "I'm not staying in, Cooper. I wasted too much time today already."

But I guess he was a little touchy. "You think today was a waste of time?"

"No," I said. "But you have to admit I didn't make any progress."

Cooper was studying me. "I don't know if you know this about yourself, but sometimes you get so focused on a goal that you kind of lose perspective on everything else."

I did know that—but I hadn't known that *Cooper* knew that.

"Like the time," Cooper went on, "that you decided to paint your high school car hot pink—but you had the wrong kind of paint, and it wasn't sticking, and it kept peeling off as it dried, but you just kept painting and painting and stayed up all night and then slept through your geometry test the next day?"

"Yeah, that . . . wasn't great."

"It was a disaster. And it was a disaster from five minutes in, by the way. But you just kept painting. It was like you'd decided you were painting *that* car *that* night with *that* paint, and so you were locked in."

He wasn't wrong. This was kind of a thing with me.

"You have to be able to shift direction sometimes. It's okay to change your mind."

"Okay," I said, trying to work in one of my earrings. "Great life advice. Thank you."

"Are you listening?" Cooper asked.

"Of course," I answered. I wasn't, really.

"Then what am I saying?" Cooper asked.

"You're saying," I repeated back, "that if I'm too sunburned, I don't have to go to this thing tonight."

"Okay," Cooper said.

"And also that it's okay to change direction in life. And I don't disagree."

"Exactly," Cooper said.

"But I'm fine," I said.

"You don't look fine," Cooper said.

But I held out my pink arm and touched my fingers to it several times. "See? I'm fine. It looks way worse than it is. I'm ninety-five percent normal."

"I think you should stay here."

"What are you talking about?" I asked.

"I'm talking about this whole plan."

I shook my head. "What whole plan?"

"Operation Conquest."

But I still refused to take his meaning. "What about it?"

"You're trying so hard to get Finn interested in you," Cooper said. "But what'll you do if it *works*?"

"Um, I'll live happily ever after, thanks."

"You can't possibly think that."

"I absolutely think that," I said.

"JoJo," Cooper said then. "Finn is absolutely one hundred percent wrong for you."

What a hell of a thing to say.

I stared at Cooper in disbelief for a second before I said, "Well, I disagree."

"Why?" Cooper demanded.

"What?"

"Name one thing about him that *isn't* wrong for you."

But I was so flummoxed. Weren't we on the same team? Didn't we have the same goals? Like a dummy, I tried to answer. "I can name plenty of things! He's successful, he's . . . tall, he's got a very fancy car . . ."

"None of that counts. You don't care about any of that. What about him is right for *you*?"

My brain seemed to freeze up. "Look," I said. "Right or wrong isn't the point."

"It's exactly the point."

"No. I came here with a plan. And you agreed to help me execute the plan. And we're doing great. We're crushing it! Why would you start questioning everything when we're almost there? Ashley has rigged a whole fake slow-dance contest tonight, and whatever couple wins the slow dance has to kiss! Each other! And no matter what, Finn and I will be winning—and therefore kissing. Which means tonight is a very big night for me—a poetic opportunity for me to confront some highly unresolved issues in my heart—and I'm not just going to stay in this cabin with you and order soft serve and watch reruns of *Friends* on your iPad. Okay? I'm going to this lunatic parade that my sister has spent months planning, and I'm wearing this dress, and I'm doing whatever she tells me—sunburn or no. And then I'm finally going to break this curse and start living my best damned life. Starting with kissing Finn."

I felt like that was a pretty great explanation. But here was Cooper's takeaway: "Why—*why*—would you want to kiss that guy?"

"Haven't you ever read a fairy tale? That's how all curses get broken."

"But this is real life—not a fairy tale. And that dude is not a prince. He's a frog."

"Says you," I said.

"Says anyone," Cooper said. Then he started counting off on his fingers. "He's prematurely middle-aged. He only cares about status and cars. He's weirdly competitive about mini golf, he doesn't care about you, he's not funny, and he's boring as hell!"

But that was enough. I was done arguing.

I didn't need Cooper's permission to get this done.

I looked through my suitcase for my strappy heels, and instead of holding on to Cooper's shoulder while I pushed my feet into them, I held on to the wall.

Cooper watched me. "Those shoes look like torture devices."

"That's your guy privilege talking."

"You will one hundred percent have blisters, a sprained ankle, or a missing toe by the end of the night."

"But high heels are all about *beginnings*."

"Isn't doing the same thing over and over hoping for a different result the definition of insanity? Why do you keep doing this to yourself?"

I gave Cooper a look. "We'd need a semester-long college seminar to answer that question."

"I'm begging you to wear sneakers."

"And that," I said, "is why you'd flunk my seminar."

I stood up and admired my look in the mirror.

Maybe shoes like these were the definition of insanity. But I just didn't care.

For a second, I hoped we were done with the Finn conversation.

But Cooper wasn't. He revved back up. "Look," he said. "I see your eyes glazing over when he talks to you. I see the boredom rising off you like steam. You're so focused on what you think you're supposed to want that you can't feel what's real. Is that how you want to spend the rest of your life—bored into a coma by a man who can't appreciate you? Stop selling yourself short, JoJo. Raise your standards!"

But that just made me mad. "My standards were just fine when I was about to marry Pearce Richmond. But you had to fly across an ocean to shut that down, didn't you?"

"Pearce Richmond was a total wanker," Cooper said. "Not one cell in his body was good enough for you."

"But that's true of everybody, Cooper. According to you! Nobody's ever good enough for me! Have you ever liked even one person that I've dated?" Asking the question made me realize how true the answer was. "No. You've hated them all. You've mocked them and you've picked on them and you've fixated on what was wrong with them until *I* fixated on what was wrong with them."

"Only because—" Cooper started. Then he regrouped: "Only because you *were* too good for any of those guys. You need to be with somebody who gets you, and who admires you, and who makes you laugh, and who looks after you. That's what you deserve, JoJo—and you shouldn't ever settle for anything less."

But I'd just made a really good point. Cooper had torn down every guy I'd ever tried to date. I might have spent my life as a *dumper*, and maybe that was on me, but Cooper certainly hadn't been helping. I felt a surge of indignation as a flash montage of all the men I'd rejected churned through my head.

Next, I leaned toward Cooper until we were eye to eye, and I lifted my brows like a challenge, and I said, "Got any suggestions?"

Cooper looked away.

"I'm serious. Name one person—*anybody*—who fits your standards. I'll marry him right now. I'll marry him tonight."

Cooper turned to meet my eyes, and there was a funny pause where I had the weirdest feeling like Cooper might nominate . . . himself.

But he didn't.

Instead, he just said, in a much quieter voice, "Don't go tonight. Stay here."

But I walked toward the door. "I'm going."

"Why?" Cooper asked as I pulled the door open.

And then I suddenly had this feeling like I needed to give Cooper a real reason.

I wanted him to understand.

And so I took a breath, and, standing right there in the half-open doorway, I turned back to him and said, "One afternoon, when we were kids, we were playing truth or dare after school on the playground. And Finn got dared to go kiss me while I was blindfolded. And so I went off behind the shed, and I dutifully tied on my blindfold, and then I waited for Finn to show up. I waited so long, I thought he might not show up at all. But then he did. And I was so relieved. Because I'd been thinking that whole time that I might get stood up for the first kiss of my life. Minutes went by that felt like hours. The playground got quieter and quieter as kids got picked up for car pool and went home. But I kept waiting. I refused to lose hope. And then . . . he showed up. I heard his sneakers on the gravel, and I felt like my whole body was just filling up with gratitude. And then he put his hands on my shoulders, and he leaned down, and he gave me—honestly—the sweetest kiss in the history of kisses."

I had Cooper's attention now.

"There are lots of reasons why that particular day was important in my life—and Ashley and I have used her psychology training to examine every one of them. But the main reason is just—the kiss. The kiss itself. I can still remember it like it just happened. I can feel the pressure of his hands on my shoulders, and hear the sound of his breathing. I could tell you every detail. I could go all night. It's like that one moment cast a spell over my life that I've lived under ever since. It's like the sweetness of that kiss set the standard that no other kiss could ever meet." My voice felt shaky, and I hoped like hell Cooper couldn't hear it as I went on. "I have no idea what's going to happen tonight—but I know I need to go and find out. I need to go and confront that kiss, and everything it's come to mean, and the guy who gave it to me."

I don't know what I was hoping for from Cooper. A nod of sympathy, maybe? A little validation that what I was trying to do wasn't ridiculous?

But instead, I got . . . clarifying questions.

"*That* was your first kiss you've been talking about all this time?" Cooper asked. "During that game of truth or dare?"

I nodded.

"*That* was the kiss you imprinted on so hard that it ruined you for all other kisses?"

I nodded again.

"That's the kiss you think is your destiny?"

"Yes, okay? Yes. So I'm going. And you don't have to help me—you really don't. But kindly do me a favor—and don't try to stop me, either."

With that, I stepped out into the hallway.

And I slammed Cooper's door behind me.

Twenty-One

ASHLEY REALLY WAS a force of nature.

She should be running a Fortune 500 company. But instead, she was organizing a variety show to pair up all of her single friends before her wedding cruise was over.

Arguably a more noble pursuit.

She zipped over to me as soon as I walked into the little side theater. "Finn's not here yet," she said, "but we've got time. The slow-dance contest isn't until the very end." She looked me up and down. "Are you okay?"

"I'm okay enough," I said, looking around. "I'm wearing two full layers of aloe."

"I had you signed up for the piggyback race and the wheelbarrow," Ashley said, "but I found a replacement."

"Thank you."

"So that really just leaves the slow dancing for you," she said, checking her clipboard. "Unless you'd like to do the beach ball pass, or the cancan line, or the group pyramid?"

All of these elements were scientifically engineered—by Ashley—to create love connections between the participants. But I wasn't sure how much participating I could handle.

"I think the slow-dance contest is plenty," I said.

"Got it," Ashley said, giving me a wink. "I hope you win."

THE VARIETY SHOW was pure torture.

Ashley had decided to go hard on the Cooper/Bridesmaid Two pairing. So even though Cooper did show up in the side theater a little after I did—now in proper attire—almost as soon as he found me, and took the seat beside me, and leaned right up against my ear to say, "I need to talk to you," Ashley showed up and snapped her fingers at him.

"I need Cooper on the stage. Right now," she said, holding her clipboard like a threat.

Things could have gone differently, of course. Another person—one who hadn't been conditioned into obedience by a lifetime of Ashley being the bossy mom of our little street gang—might have politely declined.

But Cooper just gave me a strangled look and then rose to follow her—turning back to me as he went and saying, again, "I really need to talk to you."

I guess we both thought that he'd be back at some point.

But he never was.

Ashley included him in almost every scene of the show.

Him—and Bridesmaid Two.

Hadn't Ashley and I talked about this? She wasn't supposed to matchmake them until the Finn thing was settled!

But she must've thought it was as good as settled, because she made Cooper and Bridesmaid Two do it all.

And I had to sit there and watch.

Eventually, Finn showed up and took the empty seat next to me—which Ashley had reserved for him by writing his name in thick black marker on a five-by-seven card.

"How's the sunburn?" he asked as he sat down.

"Much better, thanks," I said.

And then we ran out of things to say.

Which means the next two hours were just Finn and me sitting silently side by side, with Cooper's declaration that Finn was *a frog* bobbing around in my brain. In fact, in the wake of all the mean things Cooper had just said about Finn, I found myself looking at him differently. Was he prematurely middle-aged? Did he care only about status? Was he boring as hell?

The more I glanced at him in the light of the stage, the more I wondered if Cooper was right. He did seem more like a man in his fifties than a guy our age. I wouldn't say he was balding, exactly—but that hairline wasn't gonna win any awards, either. He'd added a little doughiness around the jawline, too. And were those long hours reviewing legal briefs preventing him from getting enough sun? Because maybe it was just the stage lights, but I'm not going to lie: He looked a little pasty.

Fine. You want me to say it? I'll say it.

Cooper had called out the lens I'd been seeing Finn through—and made it disappear.

And now I found myself considering the very possible possibility that I'd been seeing the Finn Turner I wanted to see all this time. That I'd amplified all the good and erased all the bad. That Finn wasn't a living legend, after all . . . but just an ordinary person. One who, perhaps, if I was truly honest with myself, might, indeed, have *peaked in high school.*

At that thought, I put my hand over my mouth. Who was Finn if he wasn't a total stud? Did he even exist? Once the thought came into my head, it sat down and refused to leave. Finn Turner: Not a god. Just an ordinary guy whose hairline wasn't what it used to be. Ultimately, though, it didn't matter. I didn't need *peak* Finn Turner to break this curse. I just needed *any* Finn Turner. If he was the person I'd imprinted on, then he was the person I'd imprinted on.

I'd made my choice long ago.

Besides, I was hardly in danger of getting talent-spotted as a supermodel myself. Maybe we were better matched now. And it could never have been easy to just *force a man to fall in love with me.* Maybe that hairline was my new best friend.

It should be a *relief* that he was past his prime, I thought as we watched all the single people—but especially Cooper and Bridesmaid Two—run the highly abnormal obstacle course of variety-show activities that Ashley had constructed for them down on the stage.

What's a *normal* variety show, you ask? It's talented people doing talent-based things. Singing. Juggling. Tap dancing.

This was none of that.

This was more like a field day.

Ashley made them do egg tosses, and piggyback races, and trust falls.

And despite the fact that none of it made any sense at all, everybody in the audience loved it.

Everybody except one.

As I watched Cooper and Bridesmaid Two pair up over and over—him carrying her and her climbing on him, and the two of them back-to-backing each other—I got crankier and crankier.

Had I just been insisting my sunburn was all better?

Maybe I was relapsing.

My skin felt raw and hot. The silky material of Ashley's dress felt rough and burlap-y. I spent the whole handstand contest looking so thoroughly through my purse for some painkillers that I didn't even notice that Cooper and Bridesmaid Two had won.

What *was* it about her that was so irritating to watch?

I left to "go to the bathroom" not once or twice, but three separate times, though really I was just popping out to the ship's deck to gaze out at the ocean and wonder what I was doing with my life.

The last time was just before the slow-dance contest, and Finn was already on the stage waiting for me by the time I made it back. Ashley emceed at the mic, explaining that this was the grand finale of the evening, a slow-dance contest that would be judged by a panel of experts. Contestants would be evaluated on their moves, their musicality, and their ability to embody romantic essence.

"Teams," Ashley said, gesturing at the stage like we were at the Indy 500. "Start your engines."

"I don't understand what we're supposed to do," Finn said as I stood in front of him.

I was looking around for Cooper and Bridesmaid Two. And—yep: Ashley was making them do this one together, too. "We're supposed to slow dance," I answered, like *Weren't you listening?*

"But—that's it?" Finn said. "We just sway like we're in seventh grade?"

And then I got it. Finn wanted to win.

He wanted to win this like he wanted to win everything—but he wasn't clear on *how*. Plus, he didn't know it was rigged.

"She just gave us the criteria," I said, trying to sound helpful. "Moves, musicality, and romantic essence."

Finn put his arms around my waist—a little stiffly, if I'm honest—as he thought about it.

And then Ashley fired up the music—the Ed Sheeran classic "Thinking Out Loud." And it was time to do this. I reached my arms up around Finn's neck as we started to sway back and forth.

"How is this a contest?" Finn kept complaining. "There's nothing to do."

"Don't worry about it," I said.

But I'll tell you something. It's a good thing this contest was rigged—because as much as I knew I should look up into Finn's face and gaze at him, just oozing romantic essence, instead, my gaze just kept wandering over to settle on Cooper and Bridesmaid Two.

God, she was just *attached* to him like Velcro.

Were they gazing into each other's eyes?

As Finn and I rocked stiffly back and forth with plenty of air between our bodies, I felt overtaken by an appalling idea. Could Cooper have actually become interested in Bridesmaid Two?

Impossible.

But then, as I watched her tug his shoulders down a little closer to her mouth so she could whisper something in his ear, and as I watched the way his forearms were draped over her hips, it seemed . . . less impossible.

And I felt myself wanting to march right over and cut in. And then spend the rest of the dance trying to talk Cooper out of falling for Bridesmaid Two in exactly the same way he'd just tried to talk me out of falling for Finn.

I wouldn't do it, of course. I'd stick to the plan. Like always.

I was just recommitting, in fact, to sticking to the plan when I felt something buzz under my forearm. And it turned out to be Finn's cell phone—in his breast pocket.

"Sorry," he said, fully stopping moving to reach in and pull it out.

I watched him read the screen.

"Do you need to check that right now?" I asked.

"It's for work," Finn said, continuing to check it.

"Could it wait five minutes?" I asked.

But Finn wasn't listening. "I'm sorry," he said next. "I have to take this."

And then, with that, he *walked off the stage* with his phone and *left me standing there.*

Alone.

For a second, I stood frozen, like *What just happened?*

Then I turned to make eye contact with Ashley, like *Did you see that?*

But all she could do was stare back at me, baffled, with the same question.

Finn just left the dance floor?

He couldn't do that, could he?

I mean, let's just set aside for a minute the nonzero amount of humiliation you get from being abandoned in the middle of a slow dance . . .

The real problem was: Finn walking out meant that we couldn't win.

Right? I mean, no matter how rigged a rigged contest might be, there was no winning a couples' dance contest if there was no couple.

Which meant that someone else would be getting *my* kiss tonight.

And it also meant, I realized with horror, that the actual best slow dancers would win. And there could be no doubt about who the real winners would be.

Cooper and Bridesmaid Two.

As all those realizations came avalanching down into my head, I felt a funny panic. I actually didn't know what to do. I found myself just standing there, alone, surrounded by swaying, happy, romance-tipsy couples.

The obvious next step was to follow Finn's lead: pull out my own phone like I also had some critical business and stride off the stage, too.

But—like in a nightmare—I couldn't seem to move. And then I understood with certainty that if something didn't change somehow, I would—guaranteed—start to cry any minute.

I could feel the tears crawling up my throat.

What was Cooper's formula for faking a faint again? Stop, drop, and roll?

I willed my legs to crumple beneath me.

But I couldn't even make *that* happen.

And then, just as my eyes started to sting, someone grabbed me around the waist and pulled me close.

Cooper.

"I've got you," he said into my ear. "Just reach up and hold on."

So I did. And then I leaned my forehead against his chest. My throat had been feeling so thick, but somehow, at the rescue, it cleared. I took a deep breath and said, "What about Bridesmaid Two?"

I couldn't stomach anyone getting left mid-dance at this point. Even her.

"She's fine," Cooper said. "Pete cut in."

"Pete's not allowed near the bridesmaids."

"Emergency protocol."

I didn't have to feel bad for Bridesmaid Two, did I? She'd had Cooper to herself all night, after all. She could let someone else have a turn, right?

Cooper grasped one of my hands in his—and crooked the other around my waist. Then he clamped me tighter to him and spun us around a little.

I pulled back to smile up at him. "I was about to start bawling."

"I could tell."

"But you rescued me. Again. You keep doing that."

"It's always an honor."

"Thank you, though," I said. "Seriously."

"You're okay, JoJo," Cooper said.

"Am I?"

"You really are."

And then, as if to prove the point, he pushed me out for a spin and then pulled me back in. Which made me laugh a little.

"See?" Cooper said. "That didn't hurt, did it?"

"Nothing hurts right now," I said. And it was true.

I wasn't alone on a stage. That was a win.

And my sunburn was better.

And I wasn't—I suddenly noticed—miserable. For the first time all evening.

Was it my fault if he had a way of making everything seem like it would be okay?

As we danced, I couldn't help but contrast everything Cooper was doing now with what Finn had done before. Finn had held me at a distance, but Cooper nestled me close. Finn had swayed stiffly, but Cooper pulled us into the waves of the music. Finn seemed to be concentrating hard to hear the rhythm, but Cooper seemed to just feel it. Finn wanted to win, but Cooper didn't care about winning.

He just wanted to make me feel better.

As all the other couples swayed around us, Cooper pushed me out and pulled me back in. He spun me and dipped me. He dropped his head to whisper teasing things into my ear. And by the time the song started to wind down, I was having actual fun.

Of all things.

But then, as the music faded, Cooper said, "I still need to talk to you."

"Sure," I said. "Talk."

"Not here. In private."

"Okay."

"Outside, okay? After this?"

"Sure."

As the slow dancers all let go of each other and stepped back to clap, I looked around and realized that the other couples seemed to be clapping *for Cooper and me.*

Like we'd accidentally become the winners of this contest.

And I didn't even have time to register that before Finn—suddenly done with his phone business—showed up between us and tapped Cooper's shoulder, like he was cutting in, even though the song was over.

"I'll take my partner back now," Finn said.

Cooper just looked at me, like *Are you gonna let that happen?*

But that's when Ashley fired up the mic and started thanking everybody for an epic night of fun and frivolity. "I'm about to announce the winners of the slow-dance contest," Ashley said, "and the rule is that they have to go find a lovely patch of moonlight somewhere and kiss each other. But let me just remind you that smooching is for everyone. You don't have to win this dance to go find your own patch of moonlight."

It seemed pretty clear now that Cooper and I were going to be the winners.

We'd just received a standing ovation. Sort of.

Before I had time to think any of that through, though, Ashley announced the winners. And the names weren't JoJo and Cooper. They were JoJo and Finn.

"Yes!" Finn shouted, throwing his arms up in a victory V—as if he'd gotten exactly what he deserved.

Cooper and I just frowned at each other, like *What the hell?*

But only for a second.

Because the next thing I knew, Finn had grabbed my hand and dragged me off the stage—presumably to kiss me. Again. For the second time in my life.

Twenty-Two

ON THE UPPER deck—not far from the noted historical site of Cooper and JoJo's Epic Hickey—Finn pulled us to a stop beside a section of railing. The ship's wake stretched out beyond us, lit by the moon. The wind flapped all around. It should have been romantic.

But it wasn't.

"What the hell was that back there?" I demanded. "You left me all alone on the dance floor!"

Finn frowned like he couldn't understand the question. "I got a work message."

"An *urgent* work message?" I asked, trying to help him answer the question better.

"No," he said. "Just a regular one."

"You walked out ten seconds into the song. I had to stand there by myself like a lost puppy!"

Finn couldn't fathom the melodrama. "Why are you complaining? We won."

"That's not a surprise. It was *rigged* so we'd win."

"Who cares? Winning is winning."

"I'm not sure that's right."

But now Finn was thinking about it. "Why would it be rigged so we'd win?"

He wanted to know? Fine. He could know. "Because Ashley wants you to kiss me."

Finn didn't understand that, but he liked it. "Okay," he said, stepping closer.

"Aren't you curious about why?"

Finn frowned, like it hadn't occurred to him to be curious. Then he said, "Why?"

"Because I had a crush on you for six long years when we were kids. And now you're single, and so am I. And we're both on this ship. And apparently I have some unresolved issues about men, and love, and abandonment. And Ashley thinks I might have imprinted on you, so you might be my destiny. Or not. But either way, she thinks I need to find out."

"Okay," Finn said, shrugging like none of that made any sense to him but he didn't care.

"Okay?"

"Okay, sure. Twist my arm. I'll kiss you. We can do more than kiss, if you want." He shrugged again.

I'd never noticed how unromantic shrugging was until just this moment.

Or maybe it depended on who was doing the shrugging. A montage suddenly flashed through my head of Cooper shrugging. Shrugging a jacket over his shoulders, shrugging into a vest, shrugging his answer to my question of why the hell he was crashing my wedding. Why was it sexy when Cooper did it?

Finn reached up to smooth his hair with his hands.

I'd spent years longing for a kiss from Finn, and now here we were.

But now that I had one for the taking, I wanted it to be . . . better than this. In my endless, persistent fantasies about getting a real kiss from him, the moment was always dreamy and swoony. It was always breathtaking and life-changing. It was always adrenaline-infused joy sprinkled with magic.

It was never like it was now: *annoying*.

Now Finn cleared his throat.

This was happening, I guess.

But why didn't I feel anything good? Why did this feel like a chore I had to perform?

Maybe I was stalling—but next thing I knew, I was explaining it all to Finn like he might care. "You see," I said, "you were my first kiss." Before I lost my nerve, I kept going. "That truth-or-dare kiss on the playground that day was a big deal for me. My sister thinks that—for personal reasons of my own—I imprinted on that kiss. And that it's become a kind of curse for me where no other kiss can compare. And so the theory goes that if I can get you to kiss me again, I can break the curse."

"Huh," Finn said.

"Yeah," I said, thinking he was interested by the theory.

But then Finn said, "What truth-or-dare kiss on the playground?"

I looked at him, like *Seriously?* "At school?" I prompted. Then, waiting for something to ring a bell: "On the playground? I was ten and you were thirteen? All the dares that day were blindfolded ones—do a handstand blindfolded, climb the pear tree blindfolded? That kind of thing?"

"I was blindfolded?" Finn asked.

"No, *I* was blindfolded."

"Huh," he said, factoring that in.

"Nothing?" I asked.

More headshaking. "It's not ringing any bells."

"Think," I demanded.

"I'm thinking," Finn said. "But I really don't remember kissing you."

"How many people have you kissed in life for this to *not even register*?"

Finn gave a little shrug of apology. "Lots," he confessed.

I looked around. Just exactly how forgettable was I? This was wildly insulting.

"Maybe," Finn suggested next, "if we kiss now, it'll jog my memory."

Great. Now I wanted to kiss him even less. Did I want a second kiss from a guy who couldn't remember the first one?

But maybe it wasn't a bad idea.

I should probably do it. I should get closure, if nothing else. I should see if Ashley's theory was right.

"What else is there to do, anyway?" Finn pressed.

I cannot stress enough how surreal this was. I was right here, on a moonlit deck, about to get exactly what I'd been working so hard for this whole time from Finn. My life's biggest crush—the guy I'd longed for, fantasized about, and lightly stalked for so long—was standing in front of me on a moonlit ship's deck, Cary Grant style, leaning in.

It was a personal triumph beyond description.

My inner teenager needed a fainting couch.

But as Finn's face came at me like a fish-eye lens, his lips already puckered in a way that seemed premature, I realized something: I didn't really want that kiss.

I was curious about it. I still thought it might turn out to be the closure I needed to fix my whole life. I was still determined to do it . . .

But those were all *head* decisions.

My *heart*? Wasn't interested.

I didn't stop him. I watched his face come in for a landing, and then I felt those puckered lips collide with mine. And then I stood very still and endured it.

I can't say he was a bad kisser. *I* was the bad kisser.

But as he mopped my face with his mouth, slurping me like I was a plate of spaghetti, all I could do was wait for it to be over.

When he was finished at last, he pulled back with a self-satisfied expression.

"There," he said. "How was that?"

I wiped my mouth with the hem of my dress and then gave him a thumbs-up. "I think we can check *closure* off the list."

He took it like a compliment. "Did I just solve all your problems?"

"Maybe. I'll report back."

Then Finn said, "Want to go back to my cabin?"

I squinted. "Not really, no."

Another unromantic shrug from him. "I should go find someone else, then."

Another thumbs-up from me.

"And *you*," Finn said, "should probably go find Cooper."

"I should?"

"Yep."

"Why?"

"Because I think he really does have a thing for you," Finn said. Then he gestured toward the staircase. "And he followed us here. And he just saw me kiss you."

I TOOK OFF running toward the stairs—in my dumb heels: no easy feat.

But it felt impossibly important to set Cooper straight right this instant.

Finn had gestured like Cooper might still be there, but when I got to the stairway, he was gone. Would he have gone back to the afterparty in the side theater? Or one of the many bars? Or the casino?

Of course not.

He'd have gone back to our room.

I hobbled down the two flights to our floor as fast as I could, and then, defeated, I took my shoes off.

Cooper really wasn't wrong about my footwear choices.

I resolved to start listening to him more often.

Barefoot, I doubled my speed. I wasn't sprinting, exactly—but close. I passed a bar, and then a casino—all while slaloming through crowded passageways and around random passengers without slowing. Even when I passed a second bar and, out of the side of my eye, I spotted my dad, alone, perched on a stool under a tiki-style thatched bar hut—with a bourbon in one hand and his head in the other—I didn't break stride.

At first.

Right? I mean, yes—that was my father looking like the dictionary definition of *despair*.

But I couldn't *stop*! Right?! I was smack in the middle of the mad dash of a lifetime!

But then, my dad decided to get up from his barstool. And I guess that wasn't his first bourbon of the night. I saw him rise, take a step—and then lose his balance and collapse to the floor.

Gah. Couldn't not stop for that.

It's a big thing when a large man falls to the floor. A collapsing human makes a *thud* sound that's really unlike anything else. Despite the bar music and human chatter and ambient noise, the sound of the impact cut through it all.

"Dad!" I called out, stopping for just a second before rerouting over to him.

I kneeled over him as I arrived—expecting him to be choking, or unconscious, or mid–heart attack, at least. But as he rolled onto his back and I got a look at his face, he was laughing.

"You're laughing?" I demanded.

"Mostly out of humiliation," my dad said.

"Are you hurt?"

"Just drunk, I think."

"Did you break anything?" I asked. "Did you hit your head?"

"I think my body broke my fall," he said.

"Let's get you up," I said as the bartender came around to help.

We each took an arm and maneuvered my dad toward a captain's chair at a low table nearby. Once we had him positioned, the bartender and I watched him for a minute, like he might tumble back out, but he didn't.

"I've never seen you drunk before," I said next, taking the chair across from him.

My dad met my eyes with a little wince before pulling it together enough to say, "She said no."

"Mom?" I don't know who else *she* would've been.

My dad nodded.

"To what? To taking you back?"

He nodded again.

"But . . ." I was so flabbergasted. "Did you tell her all that stuff you told me?"

The bartender showed up with some water in a pint glass, and my dad waited until he was gone.

"I tried to," he said. "But I panicked."

"What does that mean?" I asked.

"You know that I'm a man of few words, right?"

"Yes," I said. If there was one thing any of us knew about him, it was that.

"Well," he said. "In that moment, I was a man of *fewer* words."

"Did you panic?" I asked. "Or did you choke?"

My dad considered that and then said, "Both."

Then he took a sip from the pint glass, realized it was water, and tried to order another bourbon. "Bartender!" he called, like a man who really didn't spend a lot of time in bars. "Another bourbon, please!"

The bartender and I met eyes and then shook our heads at each other, like *Nope*.

My dad patted the table where my drink should be and said, "What are you drinking?"

"Nobody's drinking anything," I said, pulling out my phone. "Especially not you."

"What are you doing?" my dad asked, watching my phone as I typed.

"I'm texting Mom."

"Don't text Mom," my dad said. "She hates me."

"She doesn't hate you," I corrected. "She's *given up on you*. That's different."

"I don't want her to see me like this."

"Too bad," I said. "I'm in the middle of my own personal crisis."

To my mom, I typed: Dad is drunk at the tiki bar and just collapsed. Please get here ASAP. He needs to see the ship's doc!

Was I allowing the situation to sound a bit more dire than it was? Of course. I wasn't leaving my dad here alone. Not until I had a replacement. Which would've been nice like *five minutes ago*.

Next, I texted Cooper.

I need to talk to you, I typed—and hit Send.

Then I added, ASAP !!!

Then I sent one more: Come find me. I'm in the tiki bar with my drunk dad.

Then I set my phone on the table, face up, as I set about giving my dad some top-notch relationship advice while I waited for reinforcements. "Okay," I said, like I'd had just about enough of this nonsense. "You need to pull it together. Mom didn't reject you."

"She definitely did. She said, and I quote, 'I don't think that's a good idea.'"

"I reject her rejection," I said.

"Is that allowed?"

"You didn't make your case for yourself!" I said. "She's making the same decision as before because she only has the same information as before. You haven't *talked* to her."

"I can't talk to her," my dad said.

"Sure you can," I said. "You've been married thirty years."

"That's exactly the problem," my dad said. "It's because we've been married thirty years."

I was just about to gently explain to him that he was making zero sense when he went on.

"I've built my whole life around her. She's the reason I do everything. She's the reason I get up in the morning. She's the reason I go to work. I don't know who I am without your mom—or *why* I am. But there's no way to explain that to her. There aren't words in the world that can capture it."

"Dad!" I said, totally making heart eyes. "You're a complete romantic!"

"I know what you're thinking," my dad said. "You're thinking how can she mean that much to me when I was never around?"

"I mean, I wasn't thinking that. But it's a good question."

"She's my Penelope."

"She's your who?"

My dad blinked at me, like *How are you not getting it?* "Penelope. From the *Odyssey*."

"Are you explaining your love life to me through the works of Homer?"

"Odysseus's whole purpose in life is to get home to Penelope," my dad said. "That's your mom for me."

Okay, that was actually unbelievably sweet.

Was I going to have to rethink all my theories about my dad? Or worse—go read Homer?

"So," I said, "what I'm hearing is, the pressure of that conversation is making you clam up."

My dad nodded, like it was hopeless. "Give me a Cyclops any day of the week. But a *conversation*? With your mother? I'm doomed."

I looked down to check my phone. Cooper still hadn't texted me back, but my mother had.

Sigh, she typed. On my way.

"Dad," I said, "Mom's on her way, and I've gotta get going."

"Don't leave me," my dad said.

"Maybe this is an opportunity for you," I said. "Maybe being a little drunk will make it easier to talk to Mom."

"You think so?"

"I mean, I wouldn't recommend it on a daily basis. But given the situation . . . it's worth a shot."

He sighed like it was hopeless.

"Talk to her. You're a marine. You're great at physical courage. This is emotional courage. It's the same thing—only harder."

My dad frowned.

"But that's what the bourbon is for!" I tried to sound encouraging. "Your inhibitions are down, and she's on her way. Let all that alcohol fuel you to excellence! Haven't you read Brené Brown? It's our vulnerabilities that connect us! Don't be a tough guy. Be tender! Be desperate! Cry a little if you have to!"

My dad gave me a look like now I'd really gone too far.

I sighed. "Just tell her how you feel, okay?"

My dad didn't argue with that. He nodded like life had defeated him. "Okay."

I stood up and grabbed my shoes to go. "You've got this!" I said, putting out my fist for a bump. "What Would Odysseus Do?"

My dad didn't seem to follow my meaning. "Poke out the eye of the Cyclops?"

"No," I said. "He'd *keep going*! He wouldn't give up. He'd be the hero of his own story, and he'd take Penelope in his arms, and he'd tell her the truth about how much he always loved her."

"I don't think the *Odyssey* is a love story."

"Maybe that depends," I said, "on how you read it."

BY THE TIME I finally made it to Cooper's hallway, a full half hour had elapsed—and still no reply text from Cooper. And it wasn't until I got close to our room that—with a plummet in my chest—I realized why.

Because when I got to our door . . . there was a sock on the doorknob.

At the sight, I stopped walking.

Then I put my hand over my mouth.

Then I double-checked the cabin number.

Then I tiptoed a little closer to peer at it.

Yep. That was one of Cooper's socks. One of Cooper's dirty socks, to be specific. Straight outta the laundry pile.

Holy shit. *A sock on the doorknob?!* Was it a sex sock? Was Cooper in there doing unspeakable things with Bridesmaid Two?

Focusing on the bright side, there were no . . . *sock noises* emanating from the room.

That was a blessing, at least.

Could it be a joke? Should I knock?

But the second I had that thought, I wanted to snatch it back out of my mind. You couldn't pay me a thousand dollars to even touch that door right now, much less knock on it.

Honestly, I really didn't know what to do.

As the astonishment wore off, I felt my whole body just *saturate* with disappointment.

Never mind that I wouldn't be setting the record straight anytime soon. And never mind that I'd have to find another place to sleep tonight.

More than anything, I just . . . couldn't believe it.

Because I'll tell you something true. The reason that I hadn't wanted to kiss Finn Turner tonight was because the person I really wanted to kiss . . .

Was Cooper.

And I guess, after all that lovely slow dancing, I'd been thinking Cooper wanted that, too.

This was the second time in my life I'd let myself like Cooper Watts—and the second time I'd thought he liked me back.

And—apparently—the second time I was wrong.

Really wrong. About as wrong as you can be.

I turned away and started making my way back down the hall the way that I'd come, and my reaction was physical. My breaths were shallow. I got lightheaded. I had to stop near the elevator bank, lean against the wall for balance, and remind myself how breathing worked.

Three seconds in, three seconds out. Where was my mom when I needed her?

Cooper . . . had put a *sock* . . . on our cabin doorknob.

Cooper was in our room right now doing some kind of sock thing . . . with a sock person . . . who wasn't me.

And whether this was fair or unfair, right or wrong, justified or not . . . it felt like the biggest betrayal of my life.

It felt like something I'd never recover from.

That's what I was thinking as I walked back to the theater to find Ashley and ask if I could stay in her room. And then, after finding the theater emptied out, as I walked to Ashley's cabin. And then, after hearing a few possible sock noises outside *that* door, as I walked down to Harmony's room—which did not have a lei on its knob yet but was emanating sexy music like it was about to.

Was this whole boat just *fornicating*?

Maybe I'd just have to sleep outside on a deck chair.

I was making my way back down our hallway—toward the outdoor lounge—when I ran into Finn. Of all people.

"Is this your floor?" I asked.

"I never sleep below the waterline," Finn replied, tilting his head at his cabin door.

Huh. He'd been three doors down from Cooper this whole time.

"What are you doing up here?" Finn asked.

I decided to go with a partial truth. "My roommate kicked me out."

"Who's your roommate?"

"Our cousin Harmony," I said, and when he showed no recognition, I added, "The girl with all the hickeys."

"Ah," Finn said, like *Of course*. Then, putting it all together: "Sounds like you need a place to sleep."

How astute. "That's true."

"You can use my room, if you like."

I hesitated. "How do you mean 'use' it?"

"Sleep there," Finn said, like *Duh*.

"With you?" I finally had to specify.

"Oh!" he said. "No. I'll be joining a new friend I made at the bar. Just as soon as I pick up some—toiletries."

Yes. The whole ship *was* fornicating.

But I got to the point: "You're not using your room tonight?" I asked.

"Not unless my luck takes a nosedive."

I can't say it was a good idea to sleep over at Finn's, given the whole context. But I also wasn't sure that I saw another choice.

So that's how I wound up sleeping in Finn's cabin.

I spent the night in my dress, on top of his covers, studying my blistered feet and cursing the man who'd invented high heels. It was not exactly relaxing, but it was better, I kept telling myself, than sleeping outside.

Small blessings.

When I finally conked out, I slept until Finn showed back up in the morning.

He knocked politely with a knuckle, and we greeted each other pleasantly with big-brother, little-sister energy. He somehow seemed a lot more likable now that I wasn't trying to force myself to fall in love with him.

And maybe he felt the same way about me.

He even let me use a spare travel toothbrush and invited me to breakfast. Which I was more than happy to agree to. Since if I never went back to Cooper's cabin, it would be too soon.

Did I want to strap my terrible sandals back on and go to breakfast in my dress from the night before with an unshaven, bed-rumpled Finn?

Why not, right?

Cooper was probably ordering room service right now with Sock Girl.

Like a gentleman, Finn opened his door for me, and I stepped out into the hallway.

And there, just three doors down, standing at our cabin door, alone . . . was Cooper.

Staring right at us.

Twenty-Three

"OH, HEY," FINN said, giving a wave.

My heart clenched at the sight of Cooper: wearing his suit from last night, too, wrinkled and disheveled like the rest of us, his ice-blue tie hanging open against his chest.

We all took in the unmistakable morning-after vibes.

Just as I, in my walk-of-shame dress, said to Cooper, "It's not what it looks like."

Cooper shook his head. "I don't care."

I felt a flash of guilt. But I pushed back. If anyone should be guilty, it was Cooper. For his disloyalty, if nothing else! And his bad taste in women! And his *sock*.

"We're headed to breakfast," Finn said then, pleasantly, "if you'd like to join us."

But Cooper didn't respond. He just turned, all high-and-mighty, to walk the other way down the hall.

Read the room, Finn.

"Hey," I said, launching into a high-heeled jog after Cooper. "You never texted me back!"

Cooper just kept walking.

"I needed to talk to you!" I went on, gaining on him. He didn't just get to make a wrong assumption about me and then walk away.

"I was busy," Cooper said, not slowing.

Finn didn't follow us. "Does this mean you're not having breakfast?" he called.

But he was already forgotten.

Cooper kept walking, and I kept following.

Where were we even going? This direction didn't lead anywhere but out to a deck.

Next, I said, "You needed to talk to me, too, by the way."

"Not really," Cooper said.

"Yes," I insisted. "You said that twice at the variety show."

Cooper paused to push open the doors that led outside, slowing to look my way and then glance back at Finn—who was now walking off to breakfast on his own. "It's not relevant," Cooper said. "Anymore."

"What was it, though?" I asked, as he resumed his pace. "What did you need to say?"

"Doesn't matter."

"Maybe it does."

"Why are you even here?" Cooper said. "You should be having a postcoital breakfast with Gear Guy."

"That's what I was texting you about!"

"Don't text me about that," Cooper said. Then he added, "Or anything."

We emerged into the full sunshine of the deck now. And when Cooper realized it, he stopped abruptly, let out a dropped-shoulders sigh, and then did a one-eighty to come back toward me.

"What are you doing?" I demanded as he grabbed me by the waist and rotated me around, too.

"There's no shade out here," he said, steering me back toward the interior hallway.

Even mid-fight, he was protecting my sunburn.

But he wasn't softening. As soon as we were back inside, he was striding ahead again, and I was trotting after him.

"I'm trying to talk to you, Cooper," I said, in a tone like *Slow down.*

"I don't feel like talking."

"What is your problem?"

"Maybe it's 'cause I didn't sleep last night. At all. Even for one minute."

Didn't sleep at all—with *Bridesmaid Two*? My body clamped down at the thought.

"And it's your fault," Cooper added.

"Pretty sure that was all you, dude," I said. How dare he?

But Cooper just kept walking.

"I don't get what we're fighting about," I said.

"We're not fighting about anything," Cooper declared.

We reached our cabin door.

"I also don't get why you're so mad about seeing me with Finn just now"—I gestured at the knob where the sock had been—"when you clearly had quite an evening yourself!"

For the first time all morning, Cooper met my eyes.

But he wasn't *looking* at me. He was glaring.

Not fair. "How," I demanded, "can you possibly be mad at me for anything right now, when you clearly spent the night in our cabin with the shallowest, ickiest bridesmaid on this ship?"

But Cooper didn't respond. Just unlocked the door and pushed his way into the cabin.

I followed.

"No response to that, huh?" I prodded. "Too embarrassed to reply?"

"I'm not embarrassed about anything," he said, charging toward the balcony doors—like now that he'd entered our cabin he wanted nothing more than to get back out.

"*I'm* not embarrassed about anything," I countered.

But again—no response. Now Cooper was working the latch on the sliding doors—which shouldn't have been that challenging—flipping it up and down, pushing and pulling, throwing every single shoulder muscle into it, all to no avail.

"If anyone should be embarrassed," I went on, pressing my advantage, "it's the person who spent all night desecrating our beloved cabin with Sock Girl!"

"Don't call her *Sock Girl*," Cooper said as the latch gave way and the door slid open. "Her *name* is Bridesmaid Two!"

We both paused at that as the wind rushed in.

"What *is* her name?" I asked then.

But Cooper just growled like I was driving him insane and escaped out onto the balcony.

And so, of course, I followed.

I've been over the memory of this moment so many times. How could things have gone so far off the rails? How could we have been right there together, just the two of us, surrounded by all the real facts of the situation—and not managed to clear up even one meaningful thing with each other?

Maybe it was sleep deprivation. Or too many emotions all at once. Or the way time can shift into fast-forward without permission. We hurtled through that moment at warp speed, and I never could get my bearings. It was too much too fast to even start.

Maybe if I hadn't been wearing yesterday's clothes, and maybe if Cooper weren't so shockingly, nothing-like-I'd-ever-imagined angry, and maybe if I hadn't stayed up half the night desperately *not thinking* about what appalling things Cooper might be up to . . . maybe I could have navigated this moment better.

If I'd been thinking even a tiny bit more clearly, maybe things could've sorted themselves out.

But I *couldn't* think clearly. My brain was wobbling off its axis. Things were all out of order. I hadn't even sorted out *yesterday*, much less gotten clear on this morning.

What I should have done was calmly explain to him the most important thing: I had *not* just slept with Finn. I'd only let him kiss me.

It wouldn't be news to Cooper, of course, if he'd watched it happen.

But what might be news to Cooper—what might be really vital information right now—was that enduring a kiss that I did not want from Finn only clarified to me what, and who, I did want.

Looking back: It was so obviously crucial to say that—ASAP.

That was just basic triage.

But that's not what I did in the blur of it all.

I guess I was trying to start at the beginning? Trying to create order by going chronologically? Without considering that I might never make it to the end?

"Look," I said, "I need you to understand that we should have won that dance contest last night. It was totally unfair for Finn to just strut in at the end and take a prize he hadn't even competed for."

Cooper just turned and leaned out over the balcony like he was longing to take flight. "You think I care about winning a fake dance contest?"

"And I never should have let him drag me out of there like that," I went on, talking to Cooper's profile. "He just—did it. And, true—I didn't stop him. I didn't *want* to go with him, but I also didn't fight him. But"—*how to explain?*—"I have unfinished business with that guy! You have to understand how big that first kiss was in my life. It meant much more to me than it should have, yes—but I can't change that. I mean, I could replay the whole thing for you second-by-second in slo-mo and include every detail—from the ambulance siren in the distance to the sound of girls jump-roping twenty feet away. That whole three-minute segment of my life is indelibly tattooed on my brain. I remember the exact weight of his hands on my shoulders. The precise rhythm of his breathing. The scent of his grape-flavored bubble gum. Not to mention the tragic spasms of joy that my heart lapsed into as soon as he got close. I could pick that kiss out of a lineup. I'd know that kiss anywhere."

"Really?" Cooper said, now turning to face me. "You'd know that kiss *anywhere*?"

Why was this making Cooper madder?

His chest rose and fell. His neck pulsed. His shoulders rounded, like an ape or something. And he was, I think any witness would agree, positively glowering.

"What?" I said. "I'm just trying to explain to you that the kiss he gave me was a huge, massive big deal in my life. I know I haven't been making the best decisions, and maybe I've been giving Finn more benefits of more doubts than he ever deserved, but I wasn't just being stubborn—or stupid. I wasn't just being a pain in the ass for no reason. We're talking about life-defining stuff here."

Cooper took a step closer.

I reread his face. *Was* it anger? Or just—intensity?

"That," Cooper said, "is what I wanted to tell you yesterday."

"What?" I asked.

"That kiss? That life-defining kiss?" he said.

"Yeah?"

"That kiss that you can't let go of—or forget?"

"Yeah?"

"The kiss that ruined your life? The one that's had us trailing around after that dumb douchebag this whole week? The one you imprinted on so hard that you'll never be able to love anybody in your whole life other than *the one guy who gave it to you*?"

This felt like a lot of buildup. I waved my hands, like *Hurry up*. "*Yeah?*"

Cooper looked straight into my eyes. "That was me."

Twenty-Four

I FORGOT TO breathe for a second. The wind on our cabin balcony thrashed all around me.

But then I shook my head. “No. It was Finn.”

“It was me.”

What was Cooper doing right now? “It wasn’t.”

“How do you know?” Cooper demanded. “You had a blindfold on.”

“Because,” I said, digging in, “*Finn* was the one who got the dare.”

Cooper squinted. “Why does that prove he’s the one who did it?”

“Because!” I said, like that was a legitimate answer.

Because this was a bedrock, unchangeable fact of my life. This was a basic cornerstone of my personality. This was what I’d believed for almost twenty years. Cooper couldn’t just go around changing facts! It was like he’d said my parents weren’t my parents. Or the sun rose in the west. Or the sky was made of water. Some things just were what they were—and you couldn’t alter them without altering everything else.

I like to think of myself as somewhat mentally nimble.

But in this moment, under these circumstances? I just wasn’t.

"Look," I said. "You can't tell me I've been wrong about that kiss my whole life."

"Yes, I can," Cooper said. "Because it's true."

"No, it isn't."

"Yes, it is."

"Cooper, this isn't funny."

"JoJo, I'm not kidding."

Cooper was leaning in, studying my eyes, waiting for me to believe him.

But I couldn't just rewrite my life story in twenty seconds like that.

"You don't believe me?" he said then.

I frowned. I didn't know what to believe.

The wind was relentless. Without breaking eye contact, Cooper brought his hand to one end of the open tie draped against his shirt and yanked until it slithered free from his collar.

Then he gathered the tie up in his hands and said, "Do I have to prove it to you?"

"What are you doing?"

"You said you'd know that kiss *anywhere*. You said you could pick that kiss out of a lineup."

"Cooper—"

"Let's see you do it."

He took a step closer, so I took a step back—and we kept going like that until I'd backed up against the separation wall between us and the next balcony.

Who was cornered now?

Then Cooper said, "You're not the only person who could pick that kiss out of a lineup."

"Cooper," I asked. "What are you doing?"

He lifted the tie up, like he wanted to see if I'd object. "I'm changing the story of your life."

"Are you *blindfolding* me right now?"

"I'm letting you see for yourself."

"This isn't going to work."

"This *is* going to work."

"You're not the right person."

"I'm exactly the right person."

"You can't do this!" I said.

"If you really want me to stop," he said, meeting my eyes, "say so right now."

He waited for my answer. He gave me a good several seconds.

But I guess I didn't really want him to stop.

I could tell Cooper to stop *in my sleep* if I wanted to.

But I didn't.

Finally, he said, "That's a yes—yes?"

But saying yes felt like too much. So instead, I just said, "This is so dumb."

"Hold still," Cooper said next, placing the tie across my eyes. I felt the weight of his arms over my shoulders as he reached behind my head, and then his hands pushing my hair out of the way, and then the tug of the silk as he pulled everything taut.

"This isn't going to work," I said.

"Only one way to find out."

Next, he started talking—his voice softer now, like he was telling me a secret. "Pretend it's that day. It's after school, and our whole street gang is goofing around on the playground. It's spring, but it's still cool out, and you've got a pink-and-purple argyle sweater on. You've been playing so hard on the monkey bars that your flower barrette has slipped all the way down beneath your ear, and it's just dangling there. You're waiting for the boy who was dared to kiss you to show up. But he's not showing up. Because he's not going to show up. He rode off on his bike with some other kids and ditched you.

"Luckily, you've got a friend—a really good friend, a *devoted* friend—who saw it all happen. And he runs to find you and explain, so you won't just sit there waiting until sundown. But when he arrives, he sees how nervous you are in that blindfold, and how you're fidgeting and biting your lips. He sees how hopeful you are—like this moment might turn out to be something good in your life. Then he sees you tuck your hair behind your ear and knock that barrette to the ground without even noticing.

"And he just can't tell you. He can't disappoint you. So he kisses you instead. Problem solved. Just a peck—it's over as soon as it starts. And then, before he runs away, he picks up that barrette of yours off the ground and sticks it in his pocket."

At that, I felt Cooper put one hand and then the other on my shoulders, just the way Finn had that day. And then I felt him step close. And then I could just sense his warmth, or his breathing, or his *presence*, push through that force field we all wear around our bodies all the time that keeps us, so often, from ever getting close.

Was he really going to do this? Did he think he could re-create that kiss with any kind of historical accuracy? Did he think he could prove anything?

The real kiss on the real day all those years ago had been an age-appropriate ten-year-old peck.

But I guess Cooper had no interest in historical accuracy.

That's not what he did.

Not at all. Not even remotely.

And we certainly weren't ten anymore.

Cooper hovered close to my mouth for a good, long buildup of anticipation until I felt like a hot-air balloon—floating and drifting at the mercy of the wind.

Then he lifted one of his hands from my shoulder and cupped it behind my neck.

"That never happened," I said.

"I know," Cooper said.

Then he slid his other hand behind my waist.

"That never happened, either," I protested. But weakly.

"I know that, too," Cooper said.

I was practically lightheaded from all the waiting.

"Here's another thing that never happened," he said.

True, I couldn't see right then. But, maybe because I couldn't see, I could sense him. More than usual. More than ever before. I could hear his breath. I could sense his warmth. His hands on me shone like bright things in the universe—something to navigate by, like stars.

I couldn't *see* what happened next, but I could feel it. I could anticipate his movements the way you sense the rhythm of a song. I could read my senses like sheet music, giving in to the crescendo of it all as Cooper—my lifelong friend Cooper—pressed his mouth to mine and kissed me.

Kissed me like . . .

Like . . .

Like his life depended on it.

He kissed me like nothing else existed. He kissed me out of time and space. He kissed me like this one kiss was the answer to everything. He brought us there and then he kept us there, pressing and kneading and cajoling me to soften and open and kiss him back. Which—with no resistance at all—I did. And that's when he shifted closer and brought the rest of his body into the project, pressing me into place against the wall.

It was *insistent*. And *urging*. Like an argument he had to win.

It might have given me a glimpse of eternity.

I can't be sure.

At the minimum, it was very, very convincing.

Convincing of *what*? I don't know.

Maybe of how everything can be totally wrong and exactly right at the same time?

One thing was certain: I didn't need to know. Or maybe I'd known all along.

I just let that kiss have its way.

Cooper pressed and brushed and savored—and I did all those same things right back to him. It was as good as the hickey—all the shivers and the waves and the astonishment—but it was also better. Because this time, I got to kiss him back.

Had we just been *fighting*? I couldn't for the life of me think why. I was melting, and flowing, and getting so lost—in ways that felt exactly like being found.

And then, abruptly, Cooper stopped.

And stepped back.

And then I was alone, chilled by the breeze. I put my hands back against the balcony partition to steady myself.

I waited for a second, still blindfolded—thinking for sure this couldn't be the end. Why on earth would anyone ever stop doing something so lovely?

But we didn't start up again.

I reached up in slo-mo to pull the tie down from my eyes like I was lost in a dream, and I saw Cooper right there, looking right at me like he was waiting for my answer—though any chance of clearing anything up with Cooper from my end was now completely gone.

My brain was fully scrambled.

"The same, right?" he said, searching my eyes, expecting me to agree. "Exactly the same."

I'm surprised I could even corral enough breath to respond. "Not even close," I said.

But I guess he didn't realize I meant that *in a good way.*

At my answer, his expression hardened like a slammed door. He remembered he was angry, and I remembered he was, too.

I guess he must have thought I was sticking to my story. I was choosing Finn.

Finn, who, looking back, Cooper thought I'd just spent the night with.

A thought that seemed so laughable now.

But it was like I'd been *drugged.*

I just couldn't break my daze. I stayed slumped against the wall and watched as Cooper turned away. He moved back inside and shoved the sliding door closed behind him.

For a minute or two, all I could do was stay braced and still—just me and the wind, chaotic and alone.

What just happened?

Had Cooper actually, truly just changed the story of my life?

I turned to watch him through the glass door, but the reflection of the sky blocked my view. I stepped closer and leaned my forehead against the glass, looking through my own shadow. He was moving around the room, opening and closing cabinets and drawers, and it was Cooper, of course . . . but it was like I'd never seen him before. The way his shoulder muscles flexed under his shirt. The press and release of his calves with each step. And his forearms—good god, *his forearms*—as he packed up his things.

Wait—as he *what*?

I slid the door open and stepped inside. "What are you doing?" I asked, alarm sobering me up.

"I'm done," Cooper said. "I'm out."

"Out? Out of what?"

"I can't stay here," Cooper said. "I'm losing my mind."

"I'm losing my mind, too," I said. "I'll come with you."

"You're not coming with me," Cooper said.

"But we still need to talk!" The daze was burning off now.

"I'm done talking," Cooper said then. "I'm done with everything. I quit."

"You quit? What is this—a job?"

"Worst job I ever had."

"Are you—*packing*?"

"I'm leaving."

"Leaving?" I couldn't wrap my head around it. Was he getting off the ship—permanently? "Are you just going to live here? In the Bahamas?"

"I'll find a prop plane or something."

"A prop plane—back to London?"

"I can't watch it anymore," Cooper said.

"Watch what?"

"You making the worst possible choices for yourself *every single time.*"

"I don't!"

But at that, Cooper dragged his eyes deliberately down my body to settle his gaze on my tragic, mangled, blistered feet, still in those ridiculous heels—and he stared at them until I looked down, too.

I mean, he wasn't wrong. "Not *every* single time."

But Cooper just shook his head. "I'm going."

"Don't go! I need to talk to you!"

"I'm done talking. Make your awful choices. Live your worst life. I'm done looking after you. Look after yourself for once." He hoisted his bags onto his shoulder, and then he said, "And for god's sake, put some better damned shoes on."

Then he grabbed my hand and pressed something into it like he was tipping me.

And then he was out the door so fast, it was closed before I looked down to see what he'd handed me.

I unfurled my hand.

It was my flower barrette.

The one I'd lost on the playground when we were ten.

Twenty-Five

I WENT AFTER him, of course.

But I had to change into sneakers first.

Not because he told me to.

But because, at the sight of the barrette, it hit me at last.

No more resisting. No more refusing to comprehend.

It had been Cooper all along.

Cooper was the person I'd imprinted on. Cooper was the reason I couldn't make anything work with anyone else. Cooper was the one who'd ruined my life.

Everything was Cooper.

And if I was going to chase after him right, I'd need some shoes I could run like hell in.

Dammit.

How long does it take to put on a pair of sneakers? Whatever it is, I halved it—and then I flew out the door in the sundress I'd slept in, and I sprinted down the hall.

But Cooper, I may have mentioned, is a pretty fast walker.

He was almost to the elevators before I even made it to the hallway.

"Cooper! Wait!" I called—but he didn't.

He wouldn't get on the elevator, of course. I could catch him on the stairs.

But guess how badly that guy wanted to get away from me?

At the elevator bank, he glanced back and saw me running—and then, against his entire personality *and his lifelong cleithrophobia*, he slipped through the elevator doors just as they were closing, and he disappeared.

I TOOK THE stairs two at a time. I told myself to stay focused. I had to catch him before he disembarked. Cooper *could not leave this ship* before I explained that I hadn't slept with Finn.

I mean, what right did Cooper have to be mad at me for anything I had or hadn't done with anyone?

Yes, I was swooning over all the realizations, and yes, he had just kissed me senseless—but let's not forget that he "didn't sleep—at all—even for one minute" last night with my least favorite person on the planet.

Nothing he could be imagining about me was worse than that.

Of course, if he'd slept with Sock Girl only because he thought I was off canoodling with Finn . . . maybe that made it better?

Or maybe that made it *so much worse.*

I mean, at least tell me the truth about my destiny before you give up on me forever!

Right?!

If that was even what was going on.

Because I had no idea what was going on.

All I knew was I had to catch him. Everything rested on setting the record straight—about Finn first. And then about this: When I'd said that kiss Cooper gave me just now was "not even close" to the same, I meant that in a *let's-get-married* way.

Though maybe I wouldn't put it like that.

Look. Did that smoking-hot-to-the-melting-point, blindfolded, deeply *adult* kiss Cooper had just bestowed upon me resemble in any way the chaste little peck I'd received on the playground as a kid?

No. Obviously—no.

But I didn't need a replica kiss for proof. I didn't need proof at all.

I believed Cooper.

I could always tell when he was lying, for one thing. But—more important—he would never lie about something like this. Something that mattered.

It was true because he said it was true. And that was it.

More than that, I wanted it to be true.

Did it mean the entire story of my life had been built on a lie?

Maybe. There was a lot to unpack there.

But I had my whole life to process that. Right now, I just had to stop Cooper.

WHEN I MADE it to the gangway, Cooper was nowhere in sight, but I didn't slow down. In fact, I upped my speed.

But just as I launched into a full sprint, my dad intercepted me. Physically. He hooked his arm around my waist as I was running past him—restraining me like a seat belt before letting me drop to a full stop beside him.

"Whoa, whoa—slow down!" my dad said.

I turned to face him. "Dad!" I said, breathless. "I can't stop!"

But my dad pointed at me. "Stay right there."

Was it not obvious that I was mid mad dash? "I'm in the middle of something here."

"Well," my dad said, "your sister's in tears. So she's in the middle of something, too."

That got my attention.

Ashley was *never* in tears. Tears were not Ashley's thing.

This was serious—whatever it was.

"What's going on?" I asked, regaining my breath.

My dad pulled me off to the side like he had something truly top secret. Then he lowered his voice to a whisper I could barely hear, and he said, "There's an issue with the bridal gown."

An "issue"? Had she forgotten to bring it? Spilled coffee on it? Ripped the train?

"What's the issue?" I asked.

"You know she got it a year ago on sale at that bridal expo."

"Yes," I said. It had been half off—which, in the world of wedding expenses, was practically *making* money.

"Well, apparently, it's been a while since she tried it on . . ." my dad said.

"And?"

He looked around like we were spies. "And it no longer fits."

"That can't be right," I said, shaking my head. "She must've checked before we left."

"She didn't."

"This is *Ashley*," I kept protesting. "She would never have left her bridal gown to chance."

"Do *not* say that to her," my dad cautioned. "She will tear you limb from limb."

"But . . ."

"Look, she and Mom already went over this. It's been a busy year. It fit perfectly when she bought it. She meant to double-check, but she wasn't worried. And then, with everything else she was doing, much of it for *you*, apparently, she just—never got around to trying it on."

I sighed. "And now?"

"Now she's having a little trouble squeezing in."

"How much trouble?" I asked.

At that, my dad looked torn—like he couldn't decide between being kind and being accurate. Finally, he said, "She looks like somebody stuffed a Honey Baked Ham into a tube sock."

"Dad!" I scolded.

But he just shrugged. "Hence, the emergency."

"So—what's the plan?"

"Your mom worked it all out," he said, crooking his arm behind me to start leading me toward their cabin. "We're docked at Bishop's Cay today."

"Yeah?"

"And, lucky for us, there's a tailor on the island who can let the dress out before we set sail again this afternoon—if we can get it there by ten in the morning."

"Wow," I said, checking the time. "That's tight."

"Yes, it is," my dad agreed. "And that's where you come in."

"Me?" I glanced again at the Cooper-less gangway.

I really don't want to sound like I wasn't a team player—but given the whole urgency of the Cooper situation, I was just about to ask my dad if *he* could take the dress to the tailor . . . when he put his arm around my shoulder and started walking us back toward the elevators.

As soon as the doors closed, my dad lowered his voice and said, "She took me back."

My brain was still a little addled. "Who?"

My dad looked at me, like *Who the hell else?* "Your mother."

Wait—this was huge! "She did?"

He nodded. "On a trial basis."

I held out my hand for a high five. "Did you go full Odysseus on her?"

"Does 'going full Odysseus' mean bursting into drunken tears and begging? Because that's what I did."

We stepped out onto my parents' floor. "Hey," I said. "It worked, didn't it?"

"It worked. For now. As long as I, and I'm quoting here, 'prove to her that I can change.'"

"What does that mean?"

"Well, for one thing, it means *you* have to take the dress to town, and *I* have to stay here and tape up wedding decorations."

Nothing about that was right. "But you don't have any manual dexterity," I said.

"She needs to see me trying," my dad said.

"You've been trying this whole time."

"But now she's looking. And I have to make sure she likes what she sees."

I gave my dad an appreciative nod. "Dad! That's very emotionally astute!"

"I was quoting your mother."

Ah.

As we reached my mom's cabin, I got it. My dad going ashore—and being gone again, as usual—wouldn't help his rebrand at all.

My dad knocked, and my mom threw open the door. "Oh, thank god!" she burst out. "You found her."

"Caught her escaping," my dad said, like he was the world's best bounty hunter.

Ever frugal, my mother had assigned herself to a Harmony-like cabin: also below the waterline with no window. But she'd zhuzhed it up with some paper flowers and a piña colada–scented room spritz.

"Were you headed somewhere, JoJo?" my mom asked.

In the background, Grandma Dodie and Ashley sat on the foot of the bed. Ashley was slumped and defeated, her post-sobbing face still puffy, while Grandma Dodie patted her knee.

This really was a family emergency.

"I just—need to catch Cooper, and he went ashore."

At that, Ashley started crying again.

"But I've got this," I declared, meeting my dad's eyes and giving him a nod. "I'm on it."

"Great," my mom said, ripping all her notes out of their pad and handing them to me. "The address is here. The seamstress is Yolanda." She glanced over at Ashley. "Sweetheart, toss me that sunscreen." Ashley tossed it, and my mom caught it one-handed without missing a beat, flipped open the cap, and started applying it to my shoulders. "You know," my mom went on, "you don't have to stay at the tailor's. You could drop the dress off and *then* go find Cooper."

Sure. If he wasn't already prop-planing his way across the Atlantic by now.

"Just as long as you make it back to the ship by four o'clock," my mom said. "That's when we shove off, and they won't wait for you."

"They won't wait for you?" I asked.

She shook her head like she'd heard some horror stories. "They set sail when they set sail, and if you're not here, they leave you behind. They're very tough-love about it."

"They really leave without people?" I asked.

My mom nodded.

"What if you're literally running down the dock waving?"

But my mom just gave me a firm headshake, like we mustn't even speak those words. Then she said, "Let's not find out."

Twenty-Six

I WAS HOPING I might see Cooper once I made it ashore.

But I didn't.

I did, however, see the three cruise dudes from the MS *Decadence* while waiting in line at the taxi stand. They were all, once again, wearing beer shirts: BEER ME, IT'S BEER O'CLOCK, and JUST HERE FOR THE BEER.

I stood behind them in the taxi line, holding Ashley's dress—on its hanger, gently encased in a dry cleaner's thin plastic bag—with the greatest respect. I can't say for certain how many sheets to the wind the cruise dudes were at nine in the morning on this fine Wednesday, but I can tell you that they all three decided at one point to pee on the same clump of sidewalk weeds at the same time.

That's not a visual you can unsee.

Near them, but not with them, was another guy in an island shirt and a straw pork-pie hat.

Bold choice.

I've never seen anyone pull off a pork-pie hat in real life. Have you? That's a tough look.

I tried very hard to not particularly notice any of them and just enjoy the island breeze.

Especially when Pork Pie started trying to flirt with a woman who was both wearing noise-canceling headphones and clearly had no interest in talking to him. At all.

Read the room, Pork Pie!

It all started when he sidled up to her and asked, "Where are you headed?"

She didn't reply. *Because she was wearing noise-canceling headphones.*

But rather than just put the pieces together and move on to some other activity, like crushing ants with his shoe, Pork Pie decided to act offended.

"Hello?" he said, waving his hand in her face until she saw him.

She gave what I think anyone would describe as an I-have-no-interest-in-talking-to-you faint smile, and then looked back down at her phone.

Dismissed.

Another opportunity for Pork Pie to find, ya know, *anything else* to do.

And yet he kept waving. "Hello! Hello? I asked you a question!"

Finally, she looked up and pulled the headphones away from one of her ears.

"I *asked*," Pork Pie said, now stroking his goatee, "where you were headed."

She frowned at *why on earth he'd think she'd answer that question*, and then she shook her head. "I'm just busy here," she said, holding up her phone to indicate where "here" was.

A reasonable decline, I thought.

But Pork Pie disagreed, and so did his face, which seemed to be getting pinker. "What's your deal? Did your mom tell you not to talk to strangers?"

At that, she frowned, pressed the headphone back against her ear, and turned back to her phone.

Was she friendly? No. Was she afraid of strangers? Possibly—who knew? Did she have any interest in talking to that dude? Absolutely not.

All of this had to be clear, right? It's hard to imagine anyone could have people skills low enough to *not* read these signs. Her signals were clear as glass.

And yet, he couldn't let it go.

I watched it all, aghast. I would never want to talk to a person who had no interest in talking to me. Conversations aren't fun unless they're mutual, right? Like everything else in life?

But Pork Pie? The more disinterested the woman was in talking to him, the more he needed to make her do it. Maybe he was embarrassed to be so flatly rejected. Maybe he liked a challenge. Maybe he had the tragically misplaced overconfidence to genuinely think he could charm her, if she'd just give him a chance.

Or maybe he really thought that the choice wasn't hers.

Whatever it was, he kept at it so long that I felt like somebody had to do something. I glanced at the cruise dudes, who were scuffling around on the sidewalk, trying to wedgie each other.

I sighed.

When he tried to grab her phone, I had to act. "Hey," I called to Pork Pie. "She doesn't want to talk to you."

At that, he turned and saw me. Still wearing Ashley's morning-after dress, I'll add. The one I'd slept in.

As he turned to confront me, the cruise dudes looked up and noticed. "Hey," Beer Me called out, waving like we were old friends. "It's Short-Shorts."

I gestured toward Pork Pie like *What the hell?* and then said to Beer Me, "Are you just going to let him harass her like that?"

Beer Me looked nervous. "Isn't he just . . . flirting?"

"That is not flirting," I said. I looked over. "Right, Beer O'Clock?"

Beer O'Clock shrugged uncomfortably.

"Flirting," I explained, "is enjoyed by both parties."

The cruise dudes nodded, like they hadn't thought of it like that.

But Pork Pie wasn't in a personal growth mood. He took a few menacing steps toward me. "Why are you butting in?"

"Because she doesn't want to talk to you."

"How do you know what she wants?"

"Everyone at this taxi stand knows what she wants—except for you."

He tilted his head to crack his neck, and I heard it. "It's not your business, though, is it?"

"It's the business of the Sisterhood," I heard myself say, as if it were some real organization I might report him to.

But Pork Pie didn't find the Sisterhood intimidating in the least.

"Just leave her alone," I said. "Take a snorkel lesson or something."

He squared his shoulders and stepped closer to me. "I don't remember asking your advice."

"It's free. You're welcome."

In the background, slightly out of focus, I could see the woman giving up on her cab and walking away.

I'd had her back—but now who would have mine?

Because the madder Pork Pie got, the more menacing he seemed.

It's a crucial life skill for women, learning how to read men. You have to tune your radar to distinguish between harmless idiots and harmful ones. You need to be able to tell the difference.

The cruise dudes who'd mooned me? Harmless.

But Pork Pie?

With him, my danger radar went off.

And as soon as I felt it, without ever deciding to, my first instinct was to look around—for Cooper.

Who wasn't there. Of course.

What was there instead was a cab pulling up. And now that he'd driven away the headphones girl, Pork Pie was next in line.

But did he really deserve to go next, after his poor behavior?

As the cab came to a stop, I slipped past them all, opened the back door, and slid in.

Saved by the cab.

I waved to the dudes through the window, extra glad to be escaping, as I mouthed a not-sorry "sorry," and Pork Pie squinted at me like I was his new prey.

THE TAILOR WAS easy to find, and I dropped Ashley's dress off, no problem. I texted the family group chat that Yolanda the seamstress said it would be "an easy fix" and she'd have it back in plenty of time—and Ashley texted back a GIF of a cartoon rabbit hugging another rabbit so hard that they both fell down.

So—crisis *de-escalated.*

Ashley was better.

And my dad, now embarking on his second chance with my mom, was better.

But I was pretty sure I . . . was worse.

Things with Cooper were worse, at least.

As I walked the streets of town, passing restaurants, and shops, and open markets with vendors selling everything from straw hats to beaded cover-ups to woven beach blankets, I had the feeling like I'd missed my chance to catch Cooper.

I sent a text but got no answer. I tried calling but got voicemail.

Even still, my eyes scanned endlessly for him while my brain churned through all its new input. Was it really possible for him to kiss me like that and then just *leave*? Had he finally given up on me? And could I even blame him?

It was so much to process.

Cooper had been my first kiss.

Not only that, he'd been rescuing me—again, as always—from disaster.

Of course Finn didn't remember our kiss. He hadn't been there!

He'd ditched me.

That kiss wasn't Finn's. It was Cooper's. And it always had been.

I guess Cooper hadn't told me the truth about that day at first because he thought I'd be embarrassed. And even when I kept going on and on about imprinting on my first kiss, Cooper didn't know it was *that* kiss I'd been talking about.

No wonder he'd been so shocked when he found out. And then Finn showed up after the talent show and dragged me off as Cooper tried to stop us and tell me—but I chose Finn over him? And then Cooper thought I slept with Finn under the influence of false information?

Cooper had every right to be horrified by it all.

Technically, the person I should have been chasing all this time was Cooper.

Not that he would have wanted me to chase him, necessarily—but he was definitely robbed of some proper credit.

And what a near miss on Finn! Good thing he had a terrible personality and a texting addiction, or I might have slept with him for no reason. *Whew!*

Though, it had been an honest mistake on my part.

I'd been blindfolded, after all. And *ten years old.*

And Cooper wasn't exactly perfect, either. I got that he might've been frustrated by the way everything unfolded, but was it really worth leaving the ship over? Quitting the wedding? Abandoning his post as my duet partner? Didn't *giving up on me forever* seem a little extreme? Couldn't he give me, like, a *moment* of grace to absorb this huge new twist in my life story before ditching me?

And don't get me started on Cooper's deeming Bridesmaid Two sock-worthy.

I mean, *come on.* Unforgivable.

There was no excuse for Bridesmaid Two—in any situation.

I WALKED THE streets of Bishop's Cay for two hours that morning, scanning for Cooper and trying to clear my head.

The town was the epitome of beachy charm. Quaint buildings in bright colors, a little marina full of painted boats, and lush flowering plants everywhere you cared to rest your gaze: vinca, and parakeet flower, and bougainvillea.

It had lots of good things. Just not Cooper.

Was he gone already? Or might he have booked a hotel room to grab a quick nap after staying up all night with the worst person in the world? Or was he, perhaps, doing a little sightseeing to kill some time? Hadn't there been an abandoned lighthouse on Bishop's Cay that he'd wanted to go explore?

Anybody's guess, I guess. Since he wouldn't answer his phone.

I'd walked most of the streets, and I'd bought a straw hat and some extra sunscreen, and I'd paused at a sidewalk café near the edge of town for some conch fritters, before I saw a wooden sign pointing toward a trail that read BISHOP'S LIGHTHOUSE 1 MILE.

Could Cooper be there?

I tried to call him but: straight to voicemail. Again.

I decided to walk the trail. Maybe he'd be there, or maybe not. Either way, I'd get to see an abandoned lighthouse. And it was the best lead on Cooper I had.

The path was a hiking trail down the center of a peninsula—a sandy ribbon worn down by many visitors. There were tall palm trees above, rustling in the wind. As I walked, I had this rising feeling like something was about to happen. And I went ahead and let myself hope that it might be something good.

SOMETHING WAS ABOUT to happen. I read that right.

But it wasn't something good.

As I walked, I started noticing the sound of feet on the path behind me. For a while, I thought it must be another friendly sightseer, like me. But then . . . that sightseer threw a pebble at the back of my head.

I felt a sting out of nowhere, and I put my hand to my head and turned around.

And it turned out to be Pork Pie.

With a look on his face like he might be out for revenge.

I turned back to the path, and picked up my pace, and straightened my shoulders, and shifted into the kind of purposeful walking women do when they refuse to be scared.

If I could just make it to the lighthouse, I figured, there'd be someone there. Right? A docent, maybe? A volunteer? A salty old lighthouse keeper? Cooper?

But Pork Pie caught up to me before I could get there.

He strode up alongside me and matched his pace to mine. And then, appallingly, draped his arm over my still-sandpapery sunburn.

"What's up, pussycat?" he said.

I shrugged out from under him and kept walking. For a second, I let myself hope that the much more good-natured cruise dudes might also be nearby.

"Where are your buddies?" I asked.

"I don't have buddies," he said.

Okay. This wasn't good.

Was there any possibility he was just a lighthouse enthusiast? "Why are you here?"

"Oh," Pork Pie said, "I spotted you in town, and I followed you."

"Why would you follow me?"

"Well," Pork Pie said, falsely friendly, "so we could finish our conversation—from before you stole my cab."

"I wouldn't call that a conversation," I said.

"Have it your way," Pork Pie said. "The point is, I missed you. And I bet you missed me, too."

He had a beer in his hand and one tucked into his cargo shorts pocket, and he had that sour smell people get when they've had so much to drink that alcohol is not just on their breath, but off-gassing from their skin, as well.

He offered me a sip.

"No, thank you," I said.

I sped up my pace, but he stayed alongside me, bumping into me over and over and knocking me off the path.

Lighthouse. Maybe there'd be a tour group up ahead when we got there. Or an armed guard. Or a bus full of nuns.

But when the lighthouse came into view, it was heartily deserted. I slowed down with disappointment, and Pork Pie draped his arm over my shoulders again.

"I'm sunburned," I said, shrugging away, like this might remind Pork Pie of our shared humanity.

It didn't.

Ashley's sundress had spaghetti straps that tied in little bows at the shoulders, and Pork Pie shifted his attention to them, alternating shoulders—untying one bow and then, while I was retying it, untying the other.

"Cut it out," I said—refusing to be intimidated, and summoning dismissive irritation like I was talking to Pete.

"Where'd you get that hickey?" Pork Pie asked next.

Ugh. Why couldn't *this guy* think it was eczema? It felt like the most appalling invasion of privacy. True, I was wearing a spaghetti-strap sundress that left it on full display . . .

But this hickey was supposed to be used only *for good*.

I assessed my situation.

Disadvantages: I was all alone at the end of a peninsula on a cay in a wide ocean with no other humans around—and Pork Pie was definitely harboring some malice.

Advantages?

I was a good swimmer, so I might be able to fling myself into the ocean. He was not sober—so I had more wits about me. My cell phone battery was charged. I wasn't wearing ridiculous footwear, for once. This was a tourist site, so other people might come along. The lighthouse might provide refuge for me, if I could run that way and get there first. And I had a cross-body purse with a leather strap that, if it came down to it, I could use to strangle him.

Was it hard to strangle someone?

I'd never tried it before.

Pork Pie seemed larger now than he had this morning.

Was that possible? Maybe the beer had bloated him.

I recommenced walking, holding the lighthouse in my line of sight.

I'd taken a self-defense class back in high school, and the one thing I could remember from that class was our instructor telling us that our best bet against a male attacker was to kick him in the "you-know-where."

And so that's what I wound up doing.

The more Pork Pie messed with me, the clearer it became that he had no intention of just, say, losing interest and going back. I put up with him and put up with him—until, with the lighthouse still a good two hundred feet away, he decided to try to shove his hand up under my sundress.

That was it. No more polite deflection.

It was you-know-where time.

"Cut it out!" I shouted at a murder-level volume—and then I launched my foot at his crotch with every bit of high school soccer muscle memory I had. I hit the target, and then, as he dropped to the ground, I took off running in the only direction there was to go.

To the lighthouse. As they say.

It wasn't much of a head start. And Pork Pie didn't stay down for long. I could feel him gaining on me as I pumped my arms and legs with everything I had, grateful to my sneakers as I hurled myself toward the door of the lighthouse.

I'm honestly not sure what I would have done if it had been locked.

But it wasn't.

I reached the door, turned the cast-iron ring handle, and scrambled in. I threw my full weight against it to slam it behind me—then found a bolt on the inside and shoved it into the locked position.

For a second, as I leaned back against the door, breathing, I felt a wash of relief.

But that's when Pork Pie made it to the door—and I guess the pain had given way to rage because he started beating on it. And kicking it. And throwing things at it.

It was a metal door—iron, maybe?—and everything he hurled against it made thunder sounds. And while I didn't really think he could break down the iron door . . . I also wasn't gonna stick around to find out.

I sprinted for the spiral stairs that wound around the interior walls of the lighthouse, Fibonacci style. The steps were also made of iron, and I clanked up them in double time. That lighthouse was four stories tall—how many steps is that?—but I don't remember pausing, or resting, or even slowing. I hauled myself to the top on pure adrenaline, entering the light chamber through a trapdoor.

And then I lowered the trapdoor behind me, and I sat on it. For good measure.

NEXT, THERE WAS nothing else to do but call for help.

Only when I pulled my phone out and saw it trembling in my hands did I realize how scared I actually was.

I should call Cooper, I thought, commanding my hands to stop shaking and behave.

This time, he answered, and I said, all business, "Cooper, I'm in trouble."

"What's going on?" Cooper said, instantly on it.

How to sum it up? "I came ashore looking for you and headed to the lighthouse, but a drunk dude followed me. He tried to get handsy, and so I kicked him in the you-know-where."

Cooper knew that catchphrase. "Did it work?"

"It worked. I got away. But now I've locked myself inside the lighthouse, and he's losing his mind with rage outside the door."

I held the phone toward the trapdoor so Cooper could hear. It sounded like Pork Pie might be beating at the lock with a crowbar.

Over the sound of the banging, Cooper said, "You're inside the lighthouse?"

"At the top," I confirmed. Like he might climb with a toprope up to get me.

Which he actually might. This was Cooper, after all.

Then Cooper said, "I'll be right there," and he hung up.

But then twenty minutes went by, and nothing. Then another twenty.

After an endless hour or so, I noticed that the banging had stopped. Had Pork Pie lost interest? Wandered back to his ship? Found someone else to menace?

The railing around the light chamber made it hard to peer down below. I decided to go down and put my ear to the door.

I lost my balance a little as I started down the stairs—enough, in fact, that I got that dropped-stomach feeling as I looked down. I caught myself—which was good. But in the process, I dropped my cell phone through the hatch, and it went tumbling down the staircase instead of me.

I watched it go in horror. It hit a stair, and then bounced up and hit the wall, and then hit another stair, and then another wall, and zigzagged on and on like that before plummeting, at last, to its death on the cold stone floor below.

I gave the moment a chance to change its mind.

When it didn't, I slowly, carefully, tiptoed down to go examine the body of my phone.

Case gone, screen shattered. Pieces of phone everywhere. Beyond dead.

I gathered all the pieces up tenderly, like we might go to the hospital and have them surgically reattached, and cradled them in my palms.

At that point, I was still thinking Cooper would be there any minute.

With no phone, I had no clock. A thousand hours went by—or maybe that was just boredom bending time—and when the bright midday sunlight started to shift into the muted light of afternoon and Cooper still hadn't shown up, I started to worry that I might miss the boat. Literally.

I finally decided to undo the bolt, look around outside, and, if the coast seemed clear, haul ass back to town. I still had to pick up Ashley's dress, after all. And get back to the ship before four o'clock sharp.

But guess what?

When I finally worked up the nerve to open that door . . . it was locked. This time, from the outside.

I had locked Pork Pie out—but I guess he had locked me in.

When the door didn't open, I slapped it, and kicked it, and threw myself against it over and over.

But nothing. Not even a budge.

And that's when I sat down on the stairs and started to panic.

This was bad.

I was locked in the lighthouse, and I had no way to call for help, and no way to get out.

I wasn't just going to miss the boat, and my sister's wedding, and any chance at ever making up with Cooper . . .

I was going to *die*.

Twenty-Seven

YEAH, THAT'S RIGHT. Cooper never showed up.

But guess who did?

My dad.

Of all people!

I was weeping with abandon, crumpled on the bottom steps—going whole hog with full-body sobs after losing all hope—when there was a knock at the door. And then I heard my dad's voice, muffled through the metal. "JoJo? Are you in there?"

I stood up. "Dad?"

"It's me, honey. Open up."

"How did you find me?"

"I tracked your phone's GPS."

"But my phone died," I said.

"Last known location," my dad said.

"You can do that?"

"It's easier than it should be," my dad said.

"Dad," I said, starting to cry again. "I'm so glad you're here."

"Let's go, sweetheart," my dad said. "We need to get back to the boat."

"I can't," I said. "I'm stuck."

"Define 'stuck,'" my dad said.

"Somebody locked me in," I said. "I might have to die in here."

It tells you a lot about my state of mind that it did not occur to me that my dad could let me out until he did. I heard a *clank* and then a *chunk* and then my dad swung the iron door wide open.

"Dad!" I shouted, so overjoyed at the sight of him standing there holding Ashley's dress that I hurled myself over the threshold and into his arms—with so much force that my dad tumped right over, and we both hit the ground.

It was the first hug I could remember giving him since I was a kid.

And it was nothing short of a doozy.

WE MADE IT back to the boat, but just barely.

We cut it so close, my dad asked the cab driver taking us back to the dock to "step on it" three different times. We cut it so close, my mother called to say they were paging us over the ship's loudspeaker to report to the purser's desk and account for our whereabouts. We cut it so close, we ran—actually *ran*—up the gangway, the dry-cleaner plastic of Ashley's dress fluttering over my dad's shoulder like a kite.

Technically, we were late. There's an all-aboard time for a ship about to disembark, and then, forty-five minutes later, there's an actual pulling-away-from-the-dock time.

We made it with two minutes to spare on the second one.

They were paging us again as we arrived.

Guess who else they were paging?

Cooper.

"Passenger Cooper Watts, please report to the purser's desk to confirm your return."

Cooper wasn't on board?

I looked around, like maybe I could locate him, just as my mom and Ashley showed up, demanding to know what had taken us so long.

"We ran into some traffic," my dad said, giving me a little wink, like that was all they needed to know.

Ashley took her dress and cradled it. "Thanks, Dad," she said.

"You got it, squirt," my dad said, like a guy who'd just saved the day.

Which he really had, I realized. He'd grabbed the dress, saved my life, and gotten us both back to the ship—all in record time. But here was another thing I was noticing about my dad: He wasn't a guy who liked to take credit for things.

My mom was squinting at my dad like she could tell there was more to the story, and then, as we all started to make our way back to the main deck, she noticed him limping a little.

"What happened to your leg?" she asked then.

My dad glanced at me. I'd maimed him a bit with that hug earlier, that's what happened.

I gave him a little nod, like *Tell her!*

But he just gave me a tiny headshake, like *Not necessary.*

But it *was* necessary—right?

It's one thing to not be show-offy about things—it's quite another thing to not even mention them. How exactly was my mother supposed to appreciate him if she didn't know what there was to appreciate?

This guy needed a PR team!

"Dad is being modest," I said. "He didn't just pick me up back in town . . . he rescued me. He *saved* me."

That got everyone's attention.

"Rescued you?" my mom said.

Just as Ashley said, "Saved you?"

Did we need to get into the whole *menaced by Pork Pie* situation? No. Those vibes were too creepy to make the conversation-topic cut for the best week of my sister's life. Pork Pie was not worthy of our attention today. We could process all that later—if ever.

But the topic of *how great my dad was*?

That, we needed to process right now.

"I got myself locked into a lighthouse," I explained.

My mother sighed, like this was really not the week for shenanigans of that nature.

"An *abandoned* lighthouse," I added, trying to capture my desperation, "out at the end of a peninsula, with nobody around." I was trying to cherry-pick my details without actually lying about anything, and I decided it was fair to classify Pork Pie as "nobody." I glanced at my dad to see if he caught the Homeric reference, but he was studying the ground, like he really, truly was uncomfortable getting any credit for anything.

Huh. Had he always been this way?

I went on. "I was locked in, and then I accidentally shattered my phone, and I really, really thought nobody would ever find me and I would just have to die there. Right? How would anyone ever even think to find me? I thought I would just slowly starve to death, like a lizard in a sunroom."

I took a step closer to my dad, and then I put my arm around his shoulders like we were BFFs.

"But this guy figured it out," I continued, "like a total hero—and he came to my rescue."

I wasn't even exaggerating.

"He noticed I wasn't back yet, and he couldn't get in touch with me, so he went ashore to check in with the tailor, learned that she'd texted me the dress was ready but never heard back, did some stalking on his phone to figure out my last known location, showed up there, got me out—and then brought me and the wedding dress back here just in the nick of time. All without a wrinkle!"

It occurred to me as I said it that it might not technically be true. That dress had hit the ground pretty hard when I knocked my dad over. And I was feeling a little wrinkled myself, to be honest.

But the point remained.

My mom was taking it all in, frowning. "And the limp?" she asked.

"I was so overjoyed to be rescued," I said, "that I tackled Dad with a hug—and knocked him right over."

My mother looked back and forth between us. "You hugged your dad?"

I nodded.

"So hard that you knocked him over?"

I shrugged and said, "Yeah," like *Of course*. Like we all tackled Dad with hugs all the time.

My mom looked at my dad.

He shrugged, too.

But she was impressed. I could tell.

That's when Cooper got paged again, and we all paused at the sound of his name. "Is Cooper not back yet?" my mom asked.

"Sounds like maybe not?" I said.

"Well, where is he?" my mom demanded of me, like he was being naughty and I had to account for it.

"I really don't know."

"You always know everything about Cooper," my mother said.

Not everything. Not always. "He might not be coming back to the ship," I said, thinking my mom probably didn't need to be actively worrying about Cooper on top of everything else. Then I said, "He might have missed the boat on purpose."

"On purpose?" my mother asked.

I sighed. Time to say it. "This morning, he said he was quitting."

"'Quitting'? Quitting what?"

Quitting me, I supposed? The idea squeezed my heart. "Leaving the ship," I clarified. "And going back to London. Today. That was the last thing he said to me."

"How's he going to get there?" my mom demanded. "Swim?"

"He said he'd figure it out."

My mom was so baffled, but as she turned it all over in her mind, she started to suspect it was my fault. "Okay," she said, putting a hand on her hip. "What did you do to him?"

"Nothing!" I said. "We just had a—misunderstanding."

Sheesh. If *that* wasn't the understatement of the year.

My mother tilted her head. "A 'misunderstanding' that made him want to *leave the ship*?"

"I guess, technically," I said, "it was more like a fight."

"What were you fighting about?"

Where to begin? "I don't know. Just—the usual."

Just then, the ship blew its horn, and we all looked around to notice we were moving. The dock was sliding away past us.

I ran to the railing. "Are we setting sail?"

We clearly were. Without Cooper.

I searched the dock in vain, willing Cooper to appear, running after us on the wharf and waving his arms.

But nothing. Just dockworkers. People milling about. Seagulls.

"Looks like he really did quit," my dad said.

We watched Bishop's Cay drift away from us for a few minutes—nobody talking—and I had that time-lag feeling where I just couldn't seem to grasp that what was happening was really happening.

Had we truly just left Cooper behind? Had I really never set him straight about anything that mattered? Had I genuinely called him for life-and-death help—and then he actually didn't show up?

Most important: Was there nothing at all I could do to rewind time, do this day over, and get it right?

I kept flashing back to that moment just before Cooper had stepped onto the elevator—and rewriting it in my mind. What if, propriety be damned, I'd shouted all the way down the hall, "I didn't sleep with Finn!" Could I have bought enough time to explain?

I guess we'd never know.

When we were fully, undeniably, irreversibly at sea, my dad announced to the group, "I'm going to walk JoJo to her room now."

More befuddlement from my mom: "You are?"

My dad assessed me. "She needs to rest before dinner."

I nodded, glad to be rescued. Then I nodded at Ashley. "I'm okay. You should go try on the dress."

"Let's hope it fits," my mother said, shifting back to the original crisis of the day.

And so we went our separate ways—my mom in charge of Ashley, and my dad in charge of me.

But here was the problem: I really didn't want to go back to the room.

The room was the last place I wanted to go, in fact. Even the thought of it, all empty, with every trace of Cooper gone, felt bleak beyond words.

Had he really just . . . *left*?

Even when he'd declared out loud that he was done—I didn't really think he was *done*. I didn't think he could possibly give up on me so easily. Sure, I was frustrating—but that wasn't news! I'd been frustrating my whole life!

It had never bothered him before.

As my dad walked me back, I decided it was the last place on this ship I was willing to go. "Dad?" I asked then.

"Yeah, sweetheart?"

"Let's stop for a drink."

MY DAD WASN'T drinking, so he got a water "on the rocks," but I went ahead and ordered the hardest liquor I could think of: a tequila shot.

But then I didn't drink it—because when I started to lift the shot glass, I realized my hands were still shaking. And I didn't want my dad to see. So I sat on them instead.

All he knew, really, was that I'd gotten trapped in an abandoned lighthouse.

Maybe that was all he ever needed to know.

We sat in the shade beside the deck railing for the sake of my lingering sunburn, and I watched Bishop's Cay float away behind us.

What happened next was the longest conversation I'd ever had with my father in my entire life. Possibly longer than all our other conversations put together.

And it happened mostly because I was stalling.

Because I couldn't face Cooper's empty room.

So I opened with a real headline-grabber. "I always worry," I said, "that I'm too much like you."

"Too much like me?" my dad asked.

"You know," I explained. "Not good with people."

"I'm good with people," my dad protested.

I gave him a look.

"*You're* good with people, anyway," my dad corrected. "You're joined at the hip with Ashley and Pete. And your mom, too, by the way. Not to mention that kid Christopher."

"Christopher?" I asked.

"The kid with the scar."

"Dad, that's *Cooper.* How are you so bad with names?"

My dad shrugged, but now he was thinking about Cooper and me. "In my whole life," my dad said then, "I've never had a friend like that."

He hadn't?

My dad went on. "I remember that first summer he moved to our block. You were both so scrawny. And completely inseparable, by the way. The two of you fell asleep playing board games in your room almost every night. He wasn't even supposed to be there! He must've climbed in through the window. And I'd be going through the house, turning off lights and checking on everybody, and I'd find the two of you curled up like lambs. So I'd scoop him up and carry him home to his mom."

"You did?" I asked. "I don't remember any of that."

"Well," my dad said. "You were asleep."

"What were you doing checking on me?"

"What do you mean?" my dad asked. "I checked on everybody every night. And I made sure the doors were locked—and the cars, too."

"But why?"

"Why?" my dad asked, looking at me like I was crazy. "Because I'm the dad."

Wow. "Does Mom know about this?"

My dad thought about it. "I don't know. I guess she was usually asleep by then."

"You should tell her."

"Why?" my dad asked.

"Because you've really got to start taking more credit for things."

My dad shook his head, like that really wasn't his way.

To make my point, I asked, "How's your second chance going?"

My dad sighed. "I don't know. When your mom first fell for me, I was younger and better looking. Not sure why she'd want to hang on to this craggy old face now."

"You don't have to make her fall in love with you," I said. "You just have to remind her that she already did."

My dad considered that.

"Once you love somebody," I said, "once you've decided to let yourself love somebody . . . it's hard to turn that off."

My dad nodded, but then he said, "She's just been so unhappy for so long."

"Doesn't matter," I said.

"No?"

"Cooper didn't talk to me for four years, did you know that?"

"I didn't."

"We both came home after college graduation, and I thought we were going to spend the whole summer hanging out. But Cooper went radio silent for a few days, and then, when I went to find him at his house, his mom told me he'd moved to London to play in a band. And when I asked her when he was coming back, she said, 'He's not.'"

My dad frowned.

"He just disappeared. He didn't return my calls or my texts. He completely ghosted me—*for four years*."

My dad said, "I *thought* I hadn't seen that kid around for a while."

"Yeah. And then he showed up at my wedding out of nowhere. And then he showed up at *this* wedding out of nowhere. And he never explained to me anything about why he disappeared from my life. But—you know what?"

"What?"

"It didn't matter."

"What didn't matter?"

"Any of it! His disappearing. His lack of apologies—or explanations, or RSVPs. He just showed up at the front door of my life like he had his own key—and let himself back in."

"Are you saying that once you love people, it's hard to unlove them?"

"I'm saying you still have Mom's key. And if you really want her back, you'd better hurry up and use it."

Then I demanded he give me his phone and made him take a selfie with me so we could send it to the family group chat with the message Greatest dad in the world.

When my dad saw it, he got all bashful. "Who's gonna believe that?" he wondered aloud.

But I just raised my hand like I was volunteering. "I do."

At that, my dad reached over and ruffled my hair—and it felt exactly like we were close, and, more than that, like we always had been. And then, before I even realized what I was doing, I was crying. My throat was thick, and my breaths were shaky, and my face was wet.

"Sweetheart," my dad said, frowning and scooting closer. "What is it?"

And then everything came tumbling out. All of it. Operation Conquest, and sharing Cooper's cabin, and my wild hatred for Bridesmaid Two, and Finn Turner turning out not to be the one. Even the whole first-kiss situation.

And I guess I got so caught up in the telling of the story, and trying to connect all the pieces together just right, that I kind of shared some of Ashley's theories about my father issues without thinking. "And Ashley says," I concluded, not even fighting the tears now, "that because you never made it to school to pick me up that day, and then I had to walk home in the rain, and then I got pneumonia, that that whole first-kiss thing is melded in with all my abandonment issues, and it'll haunt me for the rest of my life—but now it's even worse because it's not some random dude on our street I'm forever bonded to, it's *Cooper*. Who just quit. And left the ship. I never got to explain the truth. I never got to clear anything up. And now he's given up on me for good."

My dad looked totally baffled.

"It's a lot of details, I know," I said, blowing my nose with a cocktail napkin.

But my dad shook his head. "What was the part about me not showing up to get you at school?"

Kind of a side detail, but okay. "You know," I said, wiping my face with a fresh napkin. "That day you forgot to get me at school? So I tried to walk home under the freeway? And then the scraped knees . . . the rain . . . the pneumonia . . . blah-blah-blah?"

But he was still shaking his head. "I didn't forget to pick you up that day."

"Yeah, you did. It's fine."

"No," my dad said. "I was there. I was fifteen minutes early, in fact. I parked in that big driveway out front, and I waited until four thirty—and when you never showed up, I got out and started looking for you. I went through every classroom. I asked the cleaning staff. I combed the entire playground. In the rain. I was about to call the police when your mom called me home."

"You were out front?" I said. "The whole time?"

My dad nodded.

"But car pool," I explained, realizing he was getting this detail a bit late, "was on the back driveway. Near the gyms."

"Guess I missed that memo."

"Did you tell Mom? That you were there—that you hadn't forgotten?"

"You know, I'm not sure. The whole house was in chaos by the time I got back—and then you got so sick."

"You didn't tell her."

"I didn't *not* tell her. Not on purpose. We were just—a little busy."

"Dad!" I said. "She's been mad at you about that for *two decades*."

"She has?"

"We all have! We developed a whole theory around it—that you abandoning me that day is the seed of all my intimacy issues."

My dad looked affronted. "But I *didn't* abandon you."

"Well—it would have been nice if you'd mentioned that to literally anybody."

My dad was taking it all in. "*Do* you have intimacy issues?"

I burst out with a "Ha!" Then I added, "I faked a faint to get out of my own wedding . . . so. Yeah. Pretty sure I do."

"I never liked that guy."

I nodded, like *Good call.* Then my dad and I just looked at each other for a minute, taking it all in. How could we all have had it so wrong all this time?

"Dad," I said after a while. "You have to tell Mom that you came to school that day, okay? She really needs to know that about you."

"Okay," he said solemnly. Then he reached out and squeezed my hand. "I'll tell Mom that about me if you'll tell Cooper something about you."

"Tell Cooper what about me?"

My dad made his voice very gentle, like he might be giving me news I hadn't heard. "That he's the one who has your key."

"He does?"

My dad nodded. "Even I can see that."

My eyes filled up again. "You can?"

"And I'll bet you something else, sweetheart."

"What?"

"You've got his, too."

Twenty-Eight

THAT NIGHT, ALONE in Cooper's cabin, I couldn't sleep.

As hard as it had been to fall asleep with Cooper in the bed, it was a hundred times harder without him. The room was too quiet. The pillow was too lumpy. People in the hallway were too raucous. The moon was too bright. Also—was I itching?

He'd left. He'd really left. He'd kissed me like that, and ruined my life . . . and then just *left*.

And then I'd asked him for help—in a real moment when I actually thought I was going to truly die, or get mauled by Pork Pie, which, arguably, would've been *worse than death*—and Cooper never showed up.

It's one thing to be mad. It's quite another to abandon your dearest friend in her moment of darkest need.

Anyway, that was it, I decided.

Keys or no keys—if he was done, I was done, too.

Cooper wasn't the only person in this friendship who could quit!

"I quit!" I declared out loud over and over before thrashing my legs out from under the covers because I was too hot—and then shoving them back under when I got too cold.

As I shuffled through all my regrets, one in particular just kept coming back. I should have asked Cooper about why he went to London after college without telling me. I'd wanted to ask him for so long, and now I'd missed my chance.

But it was too late now. Who cared?

He was done, and I was done *even harder.*

Or, at least, I was trying to be.

NIGHT WAS BAD, but day was even worse.

We had two at-sea days as we crossed the Gulf to our final stop in Cozumel.

Two at-sea days where every person I ran into could not fathom the sight of me without Cooper. "Where's Cooper?" the whole boat asked—endlessly.

"He missed the boat," I said, letting people reach their own conclusion about whether he'd *wanted to* or not.

"Oh, that's too bad," Mrs. Vargas said.

"It really is."

"Seriously, though," she prodded. "How did that happen?"

"I don't know," I said. "Traffic? Work call? Flat tire?"

"I mean," Mrs. Vargas went on, "the rules are just so clear. They really will leave you behind!"

"Guess he knows that now."

Grandma Dodie remained convinced that Cooper would find a way back to the boat, and I didn't have the heart to set her straight.

I don't know how many of these conversations I'd had by the time Ashley asked me. Infinity?

"Are you okay?" she said, steering me away.

"Not really," I said.

She patted me on the shoulder. "You lost your wingman."

I shrugged. "It's okay. Operation Conquest is over."

"Wait—it is?"

She'd really missed everything, hadn't she? "Yeah. Terminated."

Ashley put her hand over her mouth. "Did Finn reject you?"

I straightened my shoulders. "I rejected *him*, actually."

Ashley frowned, like that idea was really doubtful.

"Is that so hard to believe?" I said, my throat feeling tight.

"No, I—just thought it was going so well."

"It *was*. And then it wasn't. And then everything fell apart." At those words, my eyes filled with tears, and Ashley steered me by the shoulders outside to the deck.

"JoJo," Ashley said, "what is going on?"

I shook my head, but the tears spilled over.

"Talk to me!" Ashley said. "Why won't you talk to me?"

I *wanted* to talk to her. Ashley was my number-one person for processing anything. But that was before the confounding variable of her, ya know, merging her life with Brody. Finally, I sighed. "If I tell you—you have to promise me you won't tell Brody, okay?"

She shook her head like she couldn't fathom why that would be a condition.

"Because this is very personal," I said, "and very private. And it's the kind of information you share with your beloved sister—but it's not exactly something you'd share with a guy you dumped in high school who's still irritated about it."

"You guys are going to have to get past this," Ashley said, like we were both equally at fault.

"I agree," I said. "And I'm sure we will. But we're not there yet. So if you could just keep all this to yourself, that'd be perfect."

Ashley sighed and said, "Okay."

But then, with the coast clear to share, I wasn't sure how to begin. I let out a long breath and then said, "The thing with Finn is off because it turns out he wasn't my first kiss after all."

Ashley's eyes went wide. "The playground kiss wasn't Finn?"

I shook my head.

"Who was it?"

"It was Cooper."

"Cooper!" Ashley shouted.

"Shhh!"

She shifted to a whisper. "The person you imprinted on was *Cooper*?"

"Apparently."

"How did you find this out?"

"Cooper told me."

"But Finn was supposed to do it!" Ashley said.

"He ditched me. And then Cooper came to find me and explain—but I guess then he felt sorry for me, and so he took Finn's place instead."

Ashley took it in. "All along . . . it was Cooper."

"All along, it was Cooper," I confirmed.

"But isn't that a good thing?" Ashley asked. "You guys are fantastic together."

"Yes," I said. "Except."

"Except what?"

"Except when he told me, I didn't believe him."

"You didn't believe him?"

"I guess I just couldn't shift my thinking that fast."

"Did you fight?"

I nodded. "We fought. And then he kissed me to prove it. And then he stormed off the boat."

"Hold on. Back up. He *kissed* you?"

I nodded.

"How was it?"

I tried to answer, but the words were half tears. "It was so good, I might never actually recover."

"Ohhh, JoJo," Ashley cooed like I was adorable as she pulled me against her shoulder and hugged me.

And then it all came tumbling out—everything I'd been wanting to tell her all along. Harmony's lei, moving in with Cooper, sharing a bed, the hickey, the sunburn, the slow-dance contest—all of it.

"But this is awesome!" Ashley said. "You're perfect together. Everybody agrees. The whole ship has been shipping you this entire time."

"The whole ship has been shipping us?"

Ashley nodded—but then amended, "Except for Finn. And Mia Macall, of course."

I frowned. "Who is Mia Macall?"

Ashley frowned back, with a slight air of *What's wrong with you?* "My bridesmaid. The one I've been trying to matchmake with Cooper."

Bridesmaid Two had a real name? "Huh," I said.

"What?"

"I never knew her name."

"The point is," Ashley went on, "everybody *else* agrees. I was only Team Finn when I thought he was the first kiss. If Cooper is the first kiss, then I'm Team Cooper."

I thought about it. "But guess who doesn't agree?"

Ashley waited.

"Cooper."

"He'll get over it," Ashley said. "He always does."

But I shook my head. "I don't think so. Not this time. I think he really hates me this time."

"He doesn't hate you. He couldn't hate you."

"Ashley," I said, "I didn't just accidentally get locked in a lighthouse back on Bishop's Cay."

"What does that mean?"

"I got menaced," I said, "by a drunk dude. And I had to rack him and run to hide in the lighthouse. And then he locked me in."

Ashley took that in.

"And I called Cooper and begged for help—while this guy was beating on the door, trying to get in," I said, "and Cooper didn't come."

"That doesn't sound like Cooper."

I nodded. "I think he might be really done with me."

"Maybe he couldn't find a ride," Ashley said, brainstorming. "Maybe he got lost. There's absolutely no way that Cooper just *left you there.*"

"But there's one other thing," I said.

And I was just about to spill all the beans about the Sock Girl situation to Ashley when I looked up and saw the Sock Girl herself, with our brother, Pete, strolling toward us.

As I watched her approach, I relived the way my heart had collapsed in on itself when I saw that sock on Cooper's cabin doorknob, and I found myself deciding that just because she *had a name* didn't mean I had to use it. She'd always just be Bridesmaid Two to me.

Of course, her first question was about Cooper.

"How could he possibly miss the boat?" she asked us all, shaking her head.

How, indeed. "I hope you're not too upset," I said to her, not meaning it at all.

"Me?" Bridesmaid Two asked, frowning.

"Yeah," I said, like *Of course*. "You two had such a very nice night together—and then the next day he was just gone."

Pete looked down at Bridesmaid Two. "Did you have a 'very nice night' with Cooper?"

"No," Bridesmaid Two said.

"You don't remember spending the night in Cooper's cabin?" I asked, calling her bluff.

Once again, Pete: "You spent the night in Cooper's cabin?"

"No!" Bridesmaid Two protested again.

"Two nights ago?" I prompted, like *You can't remember two nights ago?*

"Two nights ago," Bridesmaid Two said, leveling her gaze at Pete, "I spent the night in *your* cabin."

"Ah," Pete said, looking up in reverie like a flood of heavenly memories was pouring into his brain. "That's right. Yes, you did."

"False," I said, all *gotcha*, pointing at Pete. "You're rooming with Dad."

But Pete shook his head. "Dad moved in with Mom."

Well, that was a development.

Now it was Ashley's turn to point at Pete. "You were supposed to stay away from the bridesmaids," she said then, like everybody had misbehaved. "That's the whole reason we put Dad in there with you to start with."

"Look," Pete said. "This doesn't have to be a thing. No bridesmaids were harmed."

"So the person you liked," I said to Bridesmaid Two, "was Pete? All along?"

Bridesmaid Two looked up at Pete all smitten and nodded.

And then the weirdest thing happened: I suddenly liked her.

"Mia Macall," I said, considering it. "I love that name."

She smiled. "You do?"

"I really do," I said, riding a surge of affection. "It's like a movie star name."

"Too bad I'm an accountant, then," she said.

A math person, too! Her stock was going up by the minute.

"You make it glamorous," I said, and I meant it.

I FELT BETTER for a little while after that. But of course, if Mia wasn't Sock Girl, then who was? Some other bridesmaid? Some random stranger? Good god—please don't let it be Harmony.

I guess I'd never know.

Didn't matter anyway.

Cooper had given up on me. And so I had no choice but to give up on him back.

Which I would totally be doing. Very soon.

Just as soon as I stopped longing for him to miraculously show up on the ship.

Here's what I was up against: Nothing was fun without Cooper.

The ship seemed grayer, the people seemed duller. Even the ocean seemed . . . wetter. I didn't want to be alone in the cabin, but I didn't want to be out with the passengers, either. Every conversation I had to endure was interminable. Cooper had ruined me for everything—and everyone—else.

Two days at sea. Two days where I pretended to laugh, and pretended to be interested, and pretended to taste my food.

On the second night, we adjourned after dinner to the little theater where the slow-dance contest had been—this time to watch slideshows about the bride and groom. Brody's slideshow, put together by his mother, consisted mostly of school, team, and mall portraits of the same kid with the exact same smile and the exact same haircut.

Yawn. No wonder I'd dumped him.

But Pete had been tasked with putting Ashley's slideshow together, and he'd taken the project next-level seriously. He'd gone through every photo my mom had in every shoebox in the attic and pulled out all the sweetest, goofiest ones—of angelic Ashley, but also of our neighborhood gang: climbing the Vargases' magnolia tree, handwashing the Hamels' cars, forming a human pyramid. The show had plenty of other photos, too, of course—but at least a third of them were the neighborhood kids.

And Cooper was in every single one of those.

Usually right next to me.

That's what I saw as the photos flashed by—in every picture, Cooper and I were together. He had me in a headlock, or I was sitting on his shoulders, or we were upside down together on the jungle gym while everyone else was right side up. In picture after picture, Cooper was sitting on me, or holding my ankles for a handstand, or giving me rabbit ears.

And guess what else? In half the pictures Cooper was in, he was wearing—wait for it: *a vest*.

That's right.

Now that I saw the photos, I remembered. Cooper's mom used to dress him in vests for anything even halfway fancy. And there it was: I liked guys in vests because they reminded me of Cooper. And now Cooper wore vests because I liked them. So we were basically a puppy chasing its own tail.

Of course we were.

Everybody agreed. The whole ship was shipping us, after all.

The whole ship—except for Cooper . . . who had finally had enough of me, in the end, to do the opposite.

It was fun to see the old photos at first—I laughed and squealed with everybody else—but the more images that flashed by, the more bittersweet it all started to feel. I missed those kids. I missed *being* a kid. I missed the momentum of childhood—that feeling like you were working toward something that mattered. Growing up, if nothing else. The comforting notion I used to carry that one day not far off, I'd have it all figured out.

Watching Pete's slideshow, I missed it all.

But that was just a fact about the past. You had no choice but to let it go.

Even if you didn't want to.

Even if you would remember exactly the way it had kissed you senseless on a windblown balcony for the rest of your miserable life.

THE MORNING OF Ashley's wedding, she came and found me at breakfast with some front-page gossip. "You are about to be so glad you gave up on Finn," she said, steering me off into a corner.

"Why?"

"Because I just ran into Harmony in the elevator, and she was rattling off her list of conquests—literally counting on her fingers. And guess who is on her list—twice?"

"Just from context," I said, "I'm gonna guess Finn?"

Ashley nodded, wrinkling her nose at having to deliver such unsavory news.

"Ugh!" I said, clamping my eyes closed and waving my hand at Ashley, like *Stop!*

"Apparently," Ashley went on, "he's been on quite the sex bender since his divorce. Harmony estimates he's in the double digits already—on this cruise alone."

I shifted my hand down from my eyes to my mouth—and stared at Ashley.

"I'm sorry," Ashley said then. "Is this upsetting to hear?"

I considered the question. "Actually? No."

"No? You're not heartbroken?"

I held still to see if I could detect any unhappiness rattling around in my body. Then I answered, "Nope. Nothing."

"I know you had decided against him, but still—"

But I just shook my head. "Maybe he's on a healing journey."

Ashley snorted. "*Sexual* healing."

"The traumatizing part is being one degree of separation from Harmony," I said.

"That *is* way too close for comfort," Ashley agreed. "Although, apparently, she's become friends with Grandma Dodie."

"She—what?" Grandma Dodie was the best person in the family. How could she be consorting with the worst?

But Ashley nodded to confirm. "Grandma Dodie thinks she's 'very bright.' She's become a fan. They've been knitting together on the lido deck."

"*Knitting* together?" Knitting was my thing!

Ashley shrugged. "She's making a vest."

"A vest?!" Now this was going too far.

"Anyway," Ashley said, "Grandma Dodie says she's not all bad. And we should all be more open-minded about each other."

Huh.

Ashley watched me think about that, and then said, "You're not jealous, are you?"

At the word *jealous*, I burst out with a laugh. "I'm fine."

"But she got what you wanted."

"Yeah," I said. "Except I don't want it anymore."

I took a refreshing breath at how true those words were. The Finn journey was complete. The only man on—or off—this ship who could break my heart now, apparently . . . was Cooper.

* * *

THE GUESTS WENT ashore for a relaxing tropical day while our family stayed on the boat, frantically managing final details—including organizing tip envelopes, wrapping gifts for the wedding party (earrings for the ladies, cuff links for the guys), and checking in (again) with the photographer. My mother had also printed off a totally ridiculous Day-of on the Big Day checklist that included both "keep hydrated" and "drink a mimosa to calm your nerves."

My mother took the list very literally. "I guess I need a mimosa."

"That's for the bride, Mom."

All to say, my mother put us all to work, and I was glad, honestly, to have something to do.

Because yet another of the infinite downsides of Cooper quitting the wedding was that he'd left me to serenade Ashley at the reception alone.

Alone—as in *utterly*.

I didn't have any idea how I'd manage to do it—but I had no idea how to get out of it, either. If I'm honest, a tiny, tragic, ridiculous part of me kept hoping that Grandma Dodie was right and Cooper would show up—like magic. I knew it was impossible. I knew I was just manufacturing fantasies to offset my dread.

But that's how I coped.

As well as by keeping wildly, frantically busy every single minute.

Still, though—nightmare singing scenarios came at me all day like I was being dive-bombed by pelicans. What if I croaked like a frog? What if I burst into tears? What if *Ashley* burst into tears? What if somebody filmed it all and put it up on YouTube? *Tone-deaf maid of honor destroys family with worst toast ever—and you'll never believe what happened next!*

What happened next?

I so badly wanted *never* to know.

But there was no way out. I'd be living through this day, and this wedding, and this reception, and this serenade, whether I wanted to or not.

Alone.

I wished over and over that I'd never agreed to let Cooper help me.

It was bad facing this alone. But thinking for a while that I *didn't have to*—before reverting back, again, to facing it alone?

A hundred thousand times worse.

I comforted myself with the idea that time doesn't play favorites. It tromps along at its own pace no matter what. Moments you wished could last forever moved at the exact same tempo as moments you wished were already over. All you had to do was just not die.

I pep-talked myself. I could do that, right? *Not perish* for the length of one song?

Guess we were about to find out.

Twenty-Nine

THE WEDDING ITSELF was undeniably lovely, held out on the aft deck on our final night at sea after we set sail for Texas—with a ribbon of wake in the water behind us and an orange-and-purple sunset as a backdrop.

I tried to focus on my sister's happiness and not my own misery, I swear.

I tried to stand up there in my genuinely lovely pink organza strapless bridesmaid dress and feel insistently grateful that Ashley's newly altered gown draped perfectly now and made her look like an absolute goddess. I tried to focus on that blazing sunset, and the thrill of the breeze, and how Grandma Dodie had brought her new gentleman friend, Edward, as her plus-one, and how my parents were now sitting side by side in the front row—holding hands.

There really was so much to feel lucky about.

But the dread of the serenade pierced through everything.

And fine. I'll say it. It wasn't just dread.

It was dread plus heartbreak.

Thanks a lot, Cooper.

Name any emotion that *it sucks to feel*, and I was feeling it.

So, yeah. It was hard to just *decide to be happy.*

But I sure did fake it.

Once the deed was done, we took a thousand photos before we lost the light. And then we went inside to the ballroom, and I stared at—but could not bring myself to eat—a pale white chicken cutlet with capers on top . . . while sitting next to Cooper's empty seat.

I cut the meat and rearranged the pieces, covering my plate with a hundred tiny cubes like mosaic tiles.

That's when Ashley raised her glass and clinked it, and as we all got quiet, she thanked us for being here, declared earnestly that it had been the best week of her life, and announced that her sister, JoJo, was going to kick things off.

And so here we were. We'd arrived at my moment of not dying.

I rose and walked toward the microphone. I wasn't sure I could feel my legs. And was that a rushing sound in my ears, or just the ocean outside being noisy? We'd set the A/C in this room too low, that much was certain, at least. What was it in here? *Forty degrees?* I had actual goose bumps on my arms.

I picked up the microphone with cold hands and turned around to face the room.

What was I supposed to do again? *Not die?*

I didn't like my chances.

The sight of all those faces turned toward me prompted an icy crackle of fear in my chest—and I remembered the tragic feedback loop of how *being afraid* can make *being afraid* worse.

But I ignored it. I brought the mic closer to my mouth, and I clutched it tight.

So tight, my hands felt like the metal claws in those claw machines.

And then I just stood there.

I couldn't sing. But I also couldn't *not* sing.

I couldn't do the thing Ashley wanted—but I also, apparently, couldn't let her down and *not do the thing she wanted*, either.

And so I just . . . froze.

I froze with a miserable smile on my face, and I listened as the pleasant ambient sound of forks on plates and cups on saucers shifted into a building murmur of concern.

But that's when, as I was really just about to change my bet on the dying thing, I saw a figure moving through the room and coming toward me.

Cooper.

FOR REAL: COOPER.

The same Cooper who had missed the boat. The same Cooper who had quit the wedding. The same Cooper who had—in no uncertain terms—*left*.

Here he was. Magically returned, somehow.

Ashley's tropical vision for her wedding involved linen and pastels. To my horror, on her "Ashley & Brody Forever" home page, she'd encouraged the men to wear linen suits to the ceremony with their own choice of solid tie. Tropical, three-piece, beige linen suits.

"Beige?" I'd demanded, when I saw the look.

But Ashley held up a hand, like *Stop*. "Not *beige*. *Natural*."

Needless to say, most of the wedding guests were *not* pulling off this look.

Even Brody, ostensibly the most important man there, looked a bit wrinkled.

But then Cooper walked in, mini banjo in hand.

His beige suit was too hip to be beige. Maybe it was *flax*. Or *biscuit*. Or *stone*.

Whatever it was, it was *working*. Cooper looked absolutely lethal: rocking his linen suit—vest and all—and wearing the very same ice-blue tie he'd blindfolded me with.

I stared at it in horror as he strode closer.

"What are you doing here?" I asked, ventriloquist style, when he got close enough.

Cooper shrugged, like nothing was weird. "Rescuing you."

I turned to face away from the audience so I could speak to him normally—remembering to cover the mic. "I don't need to be rescued, thanks very much."

But Cooper wasn't there to fight. He just said, "Okay. You don't need to be rescued. But would you *like* to be rescued?"

I didn't want to give him the victory. I didn't want to give him anything.

How dare he show up here and be nice?

Dammit!

But I was too desperate for principles.

"Fine," I said.

"Fine, what?" Cooper said, a smile peeking through.

"Fine, you can rescue me this time. But don't do it again."

"You got it," Cooper said with a little nod. "Never again."

Then he turned around to face away from the audience, too, lining up next to me. And then, out of the breast pocket on his suit jacket, he pulled out a pair of heart sunglasses and slipped them to me like we were passing notes in class. Then he pulled out a second pair for himself.

He gave me a sideways look and a nod, like *This is what we're doing.*

Reading his movements in sync, I slipped my glasses on just as he did his, and then I turned around when he did—Blues Brothers style—to face the room.

Like this had been the plan all along.

The room burst into cheers.

Okay, maybe I had needed to be rescued—a little bit.

With Cooper beside me, and the safety blanket of my new heart glasses, I closed my eyes and did what I was best at: I pretended Cooper and I were in my bedroom.

Next to me, Cooper started strumming our opening chords. And then I gave myself over to Cooper, and his mini banjo, and the soul-deep pleasure of singing a perfect harmony with another person. And then I just *knew*, in a way that I never, ever knew anything, that I was going to be okay.

Thirty

IN THE END, we got a standing ovation.

Ashley jumped to her feet, pumping her arm and whooping wildly as soon as we were done, and the whole room followed her lead and stood up. Even Brody.

Okay, this was superior to just *not dying*.

I couldn't help but feel a little good. Just try to feel bad when a full ballroom of wedding guests is cheering for an encore—I dare you.

It was Pete's turn next, and as he took the mic, he said, "Well, that's gonna be a tough act to follow."

As all eyes shifted to Pete, I took Cooper's hand and dragged him out to the hallway.

Out of earshot, I spun around, grabbed Cooper by the tie, pulled him in close, and said, "Where have you been?"

"Careful," he said, disengaging from my grip.

"You literally missed the boat! Who does that? Even Pete didn't miss the boat!"

Cooper nodded. "Yeah. It's a long story."

"Did you miss it by accident—or on purpose?"

Cooper looked up to think. "Little bit of both?"

"Don't be infuriating," I warned. "You quit! You left! You declared you were 'done.' What are you doing back?"

Cooper took a breath. "I changed my mind."

"About what?"

"About quitting."

Was that how it worked? He got to quit and then un-quit at random—and never experience any consequences? Were those the rules for Cooper? He could disappear from my life whenever he wanted and then just show back up like it was all fine?

No. He couldn't say he was coming to rescue me—and then leave me to be murdered. He couldn't offer to sing with me and then just disembark. He couldn't move to London and never, ever explain why.

Not today.

"No," I said then, turning and walking away.

"No what?" Cooper demanded, following me.

"No, you can't change your mind. You can't show up here with your mini banjo and your forearms and act like nothing happened. You left me. You said terrible things and walked off! You wouldn't even let me explain!"

"Yeah," Cooper said, nodding like he fully agreed. "I'm sorry about that."

But I wasn't done. The anger felt good.

I walked faster—but Cooper paced himself a half step behind me.

"And then I begged you for help," I went on, "even knowing that you had *quit our friendship*. Do you have any idea how desperate I must have been to do that? But I thought you were my person. I thought if anything ever really went down, you'd be there—no matter what. And something was really going down. I had faith in you like I don't have faith in anyone else. And then you abandoned me."

"I didn't abandon you."

"What part of 'I quit, I'm done' and then *leaving the ship* isn't abandoning me?"

"I was just—having a moment."

"Weren't we all?"

"I never *meant it*, I mean."

"I'm not sure if that's better or worse."

"Seeing you with Finn that morning—kind of put me in a mood."

"A 'mood'?" I glanced back. "More like a blind rage."

"Fine. Yes. A blind rage."

"I've never seen you in a blind rage."

"Me neither."

"Which seems kind of unfair, right?" I went on. "Nothing about that moment should have made you so mad."

"Seeing you kiss Finn made me mad."

"I was *supposed* to kiss Finn! That was the whole point of this whole plan."

"I know."

"So I don't see why I'm suddenly in trouble for achieving our joint goal."

"It was your goal, JoJo. It was never mine."

"Clearly!" I said, speeding up.

"Can you slow down?" Cooper said. "We really need to talk."

"I agree. That's what I was trying to do the other morning *when you jumped ship*."

"I wasn't ready to talk then," Cooper said.

"Are you ready now?"

"No. But I'm doing it anyway."

Wait—hold on. What did he want to talk about? Did he want to tell me his version of Sock Night?

Because wow—holy cow—did I *not* want to know about that.

I felt a hiss of fear in my body. What if he told me something I couldn't bear to know—and then I had to know it for the rest of my life?

At that thought, I didn't just start walking faster. I started *fleeing*.

"Hey," Cooper said, following me. "Where are you going?"

"You know what?" I said. "We don't have to talk."

"JoJo. We do."

"I'm good," I said, turning down a utility hallway.

"JoJo," Cooper said, still on my heels. "What are you doing?"

"We don't have to talk about anything, Cooper," I said, now desperate to escape.

But Cooper had no intention of letting me do that. "Hey," he said, reaching out and grabbing my arm, pulling us both to a stop in front of a door to some utility stairs.

I looked up into his face—that face I'd adored for so long.

I shook my head.

I didn't want to know.

And so when Cooper took a breath and said, "JoJo, I need to confess something to you," I did the first thing I could think of to stop him.

I said, "I didn't sleep with Finn!"

And with that, I was out.

Before Cooper could respond, I pushed open the door to the utility stairs with a *kachoonk*, and I launched myself through—right past a sign that read AUTHORIZED PERSONNEL ONLY. Conversation over. If I never found out about the real Sock Girl, it would be too soon.

Just inside, though, I stopped short and looked down. No wonder they didn't want passengers in that stairwell. These were the steepest stairs I'd ever seen—like if a staircase and a ladder had a baby.

But they were also the perfect escape, I thought as I pattered down them full speed anyway: They were in an enclosed space.

Which meant Cooper definitely wouldn't follow me.

But then Cooper followed me.

I hadn't even reached the first landing before I heard the stairwell door *kachoonk* open again. And then feet tapping the steps behind me—catching up.

"This stairwell is authorized personnel only!" Cooper shouted.

Was he trying to get me on a technicality? "I authorized myself!"

"We can't be in here!"

"So get out!"

"I can't get out until you get out," Cooper declared.

"How are you even following me?" I asked. "Isn't this an enclosed space?"

"It's not *that* enclosed," Cooper said.

"What about your cleithrophobia?" I insisted, like I had a technicality of my own.

"It's mild!"

"You always say that."

"If I have a distraction, I'm okay."

"What distraction do you have?"

"Uh—" Cooper said, like this should be obvious. "You just saying you didn't sleep with Finn!"

At that, I slowed a bit. These stairs were scarily steep, anyway. I reached the landing on the next floor down and slowed to a stop.

Out of politeness, I suspect, Cooper stopped, too—and left about a half staircase between us.

"I didn't just *say* I didn't sleep with Finn," I said, looking up at him on the stairs behind me, "I actually didn't sleep with Finn."

"If that's true," Cooper said next, watching me carefully, "why did you come out of his cabin together in the morning?"

"I slept in Finn's cabin," I said, "but *alone*."

"Why would you sleep in Finn's cabin?"

Was Cooper really asking me that? How dare he?

"Why did I sleep in Finn's cabin?" I demanded. "Because ours was taken! Because I came back to our room looking for you—only to find a sock *on our doorknob*. A dirty sock, too. You asshole!"

A beat. Then, like he was getting a vivid flash memory of me calling Bridesmaid Two "Sock Girl" in our hallway that morning we fought, Cooper said, "That's right. You saw that."

"And then," I went on, letting my voice calibrate to full bitterness, "I had to go around, *cabinless*, looking for someone to take me in. And just when I thought I'd have to sleep outside on one of the deck chairs, Finn came along, and felt sorry for me, and offered me his room. And since he was on his way to a last-minute booty call, I took it."

Cooper closed his eyes. "I can't believe you saw that sock."

I started down the stairs again, calling back, "Wasn't I supposed to see it? Wasn't that the whole point? You don't put a sock on a doorknob for your roommate unless you want your roommate to know exactly what's going on inside. And don't even think about telling me who you were in there with. I don't ever want to know."

"JoJo—slow the hell down."

"No."

"JoJo, I need to tell you something."

"Nope."

"JoJo—I wasn't in there with anybody."

At that, I stopped.

Cooper stopped on his step, too, but he'd been catching up. Now he was just a few steps behind me.

"I saw Finn kiss you," Cooper said then, his voice quieter. "On the deck. *Our* deck. And I was so jealous—you have no idea. Plus angry. And miserable. For a minute there, I wanted you to be miserable, too. So I went back to the room and did the sock thing—thinking if you could go off and mess around with people, I could do the same. I *wasn't* doing the same. But I figured you'd come back at some point and see it there and, if nothing else, leave me alone. I wanted to lock you out. I wanted to make us even. Or maybe make you jealous. Even though, of course, if you were off madly in love with Finn, you wouldn't even care. I wasn't thinking things through. My mind was just—short-circuiting.

"But as soon as I closed the door, I thought about how you'd feel if you saw it. Maybe you wouldn't care. But this would be the first time in my life I'd ever lied to you on purpose. Or tried to hurt you on purpose. And I got very clear very fast that I just didn't want to ever do that. Period. For any reason. Not if I could help it."

I took that in.

"So I went back out—and took it off."

He went back out. And took it off . . .

Cooper went on. "Your timing's incredible, by the way. It couldn't have been there longer than five minutes."

I turned back to meet his eyes. "You were there alone—all night?"

"I was there alone all night," Cooper confirmed, "waiting for you to come back."

"And you thought I was with Finn that whole time?"

Cooper nodded.

"And so when you said you didn't sleep at all . . . ?"

"I was just—pacing the room."

"And so by the time you saw us in the morning . . . ?"

He shook his head at himself. "I was not well."

I took a couple of calming breaths. There was no Sock Girl.

Which meant I didn't have to run away anymore.

I turned back to meet Cooper's eyes. "I didn't kiss Finn," I said.

"Pretty sure you did."

"It wasn't what it looked like, is what I'm saying."

"It looked like you and Finn smooching."

But I shook my head. "He kissed me, but I didn't kiss him back."

"That feels like semantics."

"But it's really not."

"What were you doing, if not kissing him back?"

"I was standing there, tolerating it, waiting for it to be over."

Cooper considered that.

"I allowed myself *to be kissed by* Finn," I specified. "But I knew I didn't want that kiss even before it happened."

"So why did you let it happen?" Cooper asked.

I shrugged. "I thought I needed closure."

"And did you get it?"

How to explain it? "Even before I knew the truth about that kiss on the playground, even when I still thought everything had started because of Finn, that kiss he"—how to phrase it?—"*conducted* on me made one thing very clear."

"What?"

"Finn doesn't matter to me anymore."

Cooper waited.

"I thought Finn was my unresolved issue," I said. "But it turns out—it's you."

At that, Cooper closed the distance between us on the stairs. "JoJo, I need to tell you something."

He was poised to say something big. That much was clear. The look on his face had that much intensity. He was about to say something that would change our lives.

But then I didn't get a chance to hear it.

As soon as he reached me, we heard an impossibly loud, ship-clattering *BOOM*—like an explosion that seemed to rattle everything.

And then all the light in the stairwell disappeared.

By *disappeared*, I mean the stairwell turned so dark that I couldn't see Cooper right in front of me. As the light went, so went the sound. That comforting, constant 24–7 hum and churn of the ship's engines just went . . . quiet.

The world became dark and still.

Not good.

"Did we just blow an engine or something?" I asked.

"We just lost power," Cooper said. "That's pretty clear."

"Shouldn't some emergency lighting be kicking on right about now?" I asked.

"That would be nice," Cooper said.

Other questions I could've asked: Was the ship about to sink? Did we have enough lifeboats? Were these the last remaining minutes of our lives?

Also: Was Cooper about to have a cleithrophobia problem?

First things first. We needed to get out of this stairwell.

I found myself really hoping that all the times Cooper had said "it's mild," he'd meant it.

"What's wrong?" he asked, sensing my worry.

"Nothing," I said, making my voice bright and smiley.

"Do you think the door we came in through is open?"

"It has to be open," I declared. "Legally." I had no idea.

Next, wishing for even the tiniest sliver of light, I said, "You don't happen to have your phone, do you?"

"I left it in my banjo case."

"We'll just have to echolocate, then," I said, overly cheery. "Grab the railing."

I set an example by starting to climb.

I'd made it up exactly five steps when I sensed that Cooper wasn't following.

"Cooper?" I asked, reversing steps until I was close to him again. "Are you okay?" I turned to feel for him, and my palm landed on his chest.

Some darkness gets brighter as your eyes adjust. But this was not that kind of darkness. He might as well have been invisible.

He was breathing a little fast. "I'm fine," he said—voice tight.

"Are you having a cleithrophobia attack?" I asked, moving my hand up to his face—to what? Read him like braille?

"I'm not sure," he said.

"Because this wouldn't be great timing for that."

"I agree."

"Could you postpone it," I suggested, "until after we get out of here?"

"I'm not sure that's how that works," Cooper said.

We were basically nose to nose.

And then I had an idea. "Cooper," I said. "Do you need a distraction?"

"What?"

"You said it helps to have a distraction."

He wasn't quite sure where I was headed with this. "Sometimes, yeah."

"Do you want me to distract you?"

"Not if you're going to slap me across the face or something."

But that wasn't what I had in mind.

Instead, I said, "Don't take this the wrong way. This is medicinal."

And then I leaned into the darkness, pulled him toward me, found his mouth—and kissed him.

I went all in, too. My mouth led the way, but my body followed.

The second Cooper registered what I was doing, he kissed me right back.

His arms came up and tightened around me, and before I knew it, we were twined around each other like passionflower vines. I couldn't see him, true—but I could definitely feel him. In every possible way.

Was this a good idea?

I had no clue.

But if distracting Cooper would help me get us both out of this stairwell, it seemed worth a shot. More important, if we all were about to die—maybe this wasn't a bad way to spend a minute or two before the end.

But that's when a loudspeaker crackled to life, and a voice filled the stairway and put an end to the smooching. "Passengers, this is your captain speaking."

Cooper and I broke apart to listen.

The captain went on. "I'm sure you all just heard a rather loud noise and have no doubt noticed our sudden lack of power. Please be assured the problem is a simple blown electrical transformer. The ship is fine, and our backup generators should be up and running momentarily. We appreciate your patience. Full power should be restored within the next hour."

"Do you think that's true?" I asked.

"I think," Cooper said, "that if there were a real problem, he'd have told us to go to lifeboat stations."

I let out a sigh. "That makes sense."

Next, the emergency stairwell lights flickered on at last—low and greenish, but *on* all the same.

Cooper and I took in the sight of each other for a second.

At that, it was time to go—before the distraction wore off. "Come on," I said, turning and not just *climbing*, but—now that we had some light, in an effort to hurry up and get us out of there—more like *jogging* up the stairs.

The very steep stairs.

And Cooper followed.

"Sorry for kissing you just now," I called back as we went.

"You're sorry?" Cooper called up.

"I didn't give you much warning."

"I thought you were going to tell me to take a three-second breath."

"No," I said.

"I guess you had a different idea," Cooper said.

"Very different," I agreed. And then, out of curiosity: "Did it work?"

There was a nice long pause with just the sound of our feet clanking up the steps before Cooper said, "Like magic."

"Well, then," I said, "you're welcome."

We kept up our pace, turned on a landing, and started the next flight. We were almost home free. I could see the AUTHORIZED PERSONNEL door waiting for us up ahead. Getting out of here wouldn't fix everything, but it would definitely take *cleithrophobia problem* off the list.

But that's when Cooper decided to say something else.

We were still jogging up those tight stairs. He was right behind me. We were making good time.

And then, in what must have been the weirdest timing for a statement like this in all of human history, Cooper just said, behind me, mid–stair flight, "You don't ever have to apologize for kissing me, JoJo."

"No?" I said, just kind of making idle chitchat until we reached the door. "Why not?"

"Because . . ." Cooper said then, "I think I'm in love with you."

WORDS ARE MORE powerful than they seem. Right?

They don't have any weight or mass or heft. They're just sounds in the air.

And yet.

The sound of those words stopped me short. My whole body just stopped moving—froze, right there, halfway up the ladder.

I stopped so fast that Cooper ran into me from behind.

At the impact, he lost his balance and missed his footing—and I heard an *oof*, then some clattering as Cooper half slid, half tumbled back down the stairs we'd just climbed and landed at the bottom.

The only sound I heard as I turned around was a string of curse words.

Down below, Cooper was clutching the stair rail like that was how he'd caught himself.

"Cooper!" I called. "I'm sorry!"

"I'm good," he said, holding up a hand to wave me off like he didn't need help.

"Are you okay?" I asked.

"Yes," he said, but he kept himself crouched like maybe he was still deciding.

"Can I help you up?" I said, moving back down toward him.

"I've got it," Cooper said. Then: "I do think we might need to find the infirmary, though."

"The infirmary?" I asked. "Did you get hurt?"

"I'm fine . . ." Cooper insisted.

But as he got his feet under him and stood to start climbing again, I sucked in an involuntary gasp at the sight of his torso. His stone-colored linen vest was now blooming crimson with blood.

"You're bleeding!" I announced—like he might not know.

Cooper looked down. "I'm fine," he insisted again. Then he added, "But it looks like I just popped my stitches."

Thirty-One

THE INFIRMARY HAD its own generator. They had lights and everything.

Quite the contrast from all the prehistoric darkness we'd had to fumble through to find it—and also so bright that it took our eyes a minute to adjust to the room.

When the doctor on call arrived, he wasn't half as freaked out by Cooper's blood-soaked shirt as I was.

"Hey, it's the hero," he joked when he saw Cooper. Then, leading us back to an exam room: "Back so soon?"

"*Back*?" I asked Cooper. "Have you been here before?"

Cooper was looking down at the blood on his shirt. "They changed my dressing earlier today."

Changed his dressing? "Cooper," I said as he leaned against an exam table and started unbuttoning his shirt. "What's going on?"

I guess you could say Cooper answered me with his naked torso. Because once that shirt came off, I could see a ten-inch-long diagonal of sterile gauze taped to his abdomen—the bottom half of which was soaked with blood.

I put both hands over my mouth. "What happened?"

"You haven't heard the story?" the doctor asked, helping Cooper lie back on the table.

"No," I said. "What's the story?"

The doctor peeled off the gauze to reveal a line of black sutures running diagonally down Cooper's torso—holding together a long gash. A gash that was neatly reassembled until your eyes landed at the popped part. There, it was bright red and bleeding.

"Cooper?!" I demanded.

Cooper looked down. "It looks worse than it is."

The doc took one look and said, "We're going to need to re-suture."

"How did you get this gash?" I asked Cooper.

"It's not a big deal," Cooper said.

I redirected my question to the doctor. "How did he get this gash?"

"I could tell you," the doctor said, "but it probably violates about ten doctor-patient privileges."

"It's going to be one or the other of you," I said, trying to sound authoritative. "So who's it going to be?"

"You should tell her," the doctor said to Cooper. "She'll be impressed."

"You can take this one, Doc," Cooper said, closing his eyes like he was less fine than he claimed. "I won't sue."

The doctor found some vials of local anesthetic and then got washed up.

"And make me sound good," Cooper added from the table, keeping his eyes closed. "I'm always trying to impress this girl."

"You got it," the doctor said, planting himself on the rolling stool and getting to work.

I stood behind the doctor, peeking over his shoulder while he worked.

"Apparently," the doctor began, "Mr. Watts here has a lady friend who got into some trouble back on Bishop's Cay."

My eyes widened.

"She called him for help as she was hiding in a—a lighthouse, was it?"

"A lighthouse," we both confirmed.

"Anyway," the doc went on, wanting to stay on track, "when Mr. Watts showed up, there was an angry drunk man loitering outside, guarding the door."

Pork Pie.

"Mr. Watts tried to encourage the loiterer to leave the area," the doctor went on. "But he really didn't like that idea, and things escalated."

I pointed at Cooper's stomach. "Escalated—to *this*?"

"Please explain to the lady," Cooper said then, eyes still closed, "that Mr. Watts is totally manly and could easily have taken this guy, no problem. Except that one of them—and not Mr. Watts—had a weapon."

The doctor nodded. He was having fun. "Mr. Watts could easily have bested this gentleman, given how very pickled he appeared to be, but then the man put his hands up in surrender and pretended he was going to leave peacefully before suddenly smashing his beer bottle against the side of the lighthouse and then slashing at Mr. Watts with the broken edge, cutting open Mr. Watts's T-shirt—"

"His *favorite* T-shirt," Cooper added.

"—and creating a superficial laceration of approximately ten inches down his torso."

"That drunk dude got lucky," Cooper said poutily, like the ending of the story insulted his pride.

"*You* got lucky," the doctor corrected Cooper. "The bottle didn't cut through the fascia. It's just a surface laceration. But it could have been bad. No swimming this week, and no limbo contests. Just keep it clean, follow instructions, and stop rescuing women in lighthouses—and you should be fine."

I stepped forward and took Cooper's hand—careful not to get in the doctor's way. "You came to the lighthouse?" I asked.

Cooper opened his eyes at that, met mine, and nodded.

"And that drunk dude *slashed* you?"

Cooper nodded again. "He looked totally shocked when it happened," he said, "like he never thought it would work. And then suddenly I was bleeding like mad. And when he saw the blood, he pushed me in the chest and took off running."

"He pushed you?"

Cooper nodded. "I fell back. I guess I hit my head. The next thing I remember, I was waking up in the Bishop's Cay hospital with twenty stitches."

I sighed. "So you probably have a concussion, too."

"He definitely does," the doc chimed in, not realizing he was no longer a part of the conversation.

Cooper gave me a shrug. "They said it was mild."

"Everything's always mild with you."

"At least I don't get pebbles in my shoes."

I was still putting the pieces together. "The police came to the lighthouse?" How had I missed all this? Those stone walls must have been thick.

"I called them on my way to you, but I guess I wasn't too clear about the situation because when they got there and found me unconscious and bleeding, they thought I was the person they came for. By the time I told them about you, hours had gone by—and they said you were gone."

"My dad rescued me," I said.

"You weren't hurt, were you? That guy didn't hurt you?"

I refused to let Pork Pie register as a trauma in my life. "I'm more insulted than hurt," I said.

Cooper closed his eyes. "I'm sorry all that happened to you."

"I'm sorry all that happened to *you*."

A pause while the doc finished up the sutures and taped a fresh dressing back over them. He wanted Cooper to rest on the exam table for a few minutes after that.

I took the rolling stool after the doc left the room, and I slid it up next to Cooper to stroke his forehead.

"That's why you missed the ship in the Bahamas?"

Cooper closed his eyes. "Uh-huh."

"But how did you get from being in a hospital in the Bahamas to reboarding a cruise ship in Cozumel?"

"I took a puddle jumper to Key West and then a 737 here."

"When? Today?"

"This morning."

"Had they—discharged you?"

"I kind of discharged myself."

I frowned at him like he'd really been naughty. "*Cooper.*"

"I wasn't leaving you to do that duet alone. I would have *swum* here if I had to."

"I thought you didn't show up," I said. "I thought you were *that* mad at me."

Cooper kept his eyes closed. "I could never be that mad at you, Joey."

"I thought you gave up on me," I said.

"Sadly for me," Cooper said, "I don't seem to be able to do that. No matter how hard I try."

But now it was hitting me. My breath got shaky, and my eyes got teary. "I'm sorry I was mad at you," I said. "I should have been thanking you. You came to the lighthouse. And you tried to save me. And then you almost died."

"More like a few stitches and a tetanus booster. But 'almost died' also works."

"Thank you," I whispered.

At that, Cooper opened his eyes and saw my teary face. Then he took my hand and squeezed it. Then he said, "Listen really close now, JoJo—because I need you to understand something."

"Okay," I said, leaning in.

Then Cooper looked straight into my eyes and said, "There is no universe where you call me for help and I don't come running."

Thirty-Two

ONCE WE HAD the medical all clear, the doctor let us go. Cooper's shirt was too bloody to put back on, so the doctor offered a T-shirt from a stash in the cupboard, one that said NO CRUISE CONTROL. It was a little tight on him, to be honest—but in a good way.

He slid his suit jacket back on to dress up the T-shirt, Don Johnson style, and then stuffed the bloody tie into his pants pocket on the way out.

"Pretty sure that tie is trashed," I said.

Cooper shrugged. "Keepsake," he said.

We headed back toward the wedding reception to check on everybody, but I wasn't sure that was a great idea for him medically.

"I'm fine," Cooper said.

"Your twenty stitches say otherwise."

The ship was still dark. Cooper and I walked along an outside deck so we'd have the moonlight to see by.

"Do you have any other secrets you're withholding?" I asked.

"Lots," Cooper said.

"Like?"

He thought about it. "Like I'm actually really good at mini golf."

I gave him a look. "Of course you are."

Cooper thought he remembered a set of side doors from the deck to the ballroom, and sure enough, as we reached them, we found they were not just unlocked but propped open.

We could see straight into the ballroom—all the guests sitting at their candlelit tables, decidedly not panicking, just chatting and waiting good-naturedly for the lights to come back on. Very different vibes from the stairwell.

Ashley would be worried about where I'd gotten off to, though. My mom and dad, too.

We should go in.

But just short of the threshold, as we were about to leave the deck and the moonlight behind, Cooper asked me a question that stopped me in my tracks.

"Can I ask you something?" he asked.

"Sure."

"Did you ever wonder why I moved to London?"

I stopped walking.

Hey—that was my *question!*

"Is that a real question?"

Cooper shrugged. "Yeah."

I couldn't believe he was asking me this. The question I'd been chickening out from asking him since the day he showed up to ruin my wedding—and now Cooper was just *casually asking it like we were making chitchat*?

I tilted my head. "You're asking me if I ever wondered why you disappeared to London without a word and never contacted me again?"

Cooper nodded, like this might be a trap.

"You're asking if," I continued, "when my best friend for over ten years—the person I'd spent the most time with in my life, the only person who really got me and the only person I could truly say anything to—abruptly moved to another continent without telling me and then completely ghosted me in every possible way . . . if I ever wondered why that happened?"

"Okay. I see your point there."

I wasn't sure how to continue. Should I shrug it off? Act jokey and cool? Or should I just . . . be honest?

In a minute, we'd step back into the ballroom and back into the current of life. But right now, here, just outside the doors, on the quiet deck in the moonlight, it felt like we were just outside of our lives somehow. Like this was a little pause we shouldn't take for granted.

And so I took a breath, looked up at Cooper, and said, with no pretense, "I've been wanting to ask you what happened every day for the past four years." Then I said, "Hence, all the texts asking you what happened."

Cooper nodded, like *Of course*, and looked down.

Then I added, just to be clear: "You disappearing was the worst heartbreak of my life."

Cooper met my eyes. "I'm sorry," he said.

I shrugged.

"I know I owe you an explanation," Cooper said.

I waited.

"But I keep chickening out."

Of note: Chickening out was *also* my thing.

"Are you going to chicken out now?" I asked.

Cooper shook his head. "This is what I've been trying to talk to you about."

"Okay, so tell me. Why did you leave like that?"

"It was because I had to end things."

"You had to end things?"

Cooper nodded. "With you."

With me? "But—why?"

"Because," Cooper said, "you got engaged to Pearce."

"So?"

"And I just . . . couldn't take it. I had to stop."

"Stop what?"

"Stop being in love with you."

Oh.

Wait—what? "*Were* you in love with me?" I asked.

Cooper nodded. "I just told you that. In the stairwell."

"I thought you were joking."

Cooper gave me a look. "No you didn't."

"But—" It still wasn't computing. "When?"

"Always."

Always?

Cooper took a breath and shoved his hands into his pockets. "After you told me you and Pearce got engaged, I made the decision. I couldn't stay. I couldn't be part of your life anymore. You were like a drug that I had to give up. I thought, *Just let her be happy*. Right? You'd made your choice. I didn't have to fight with you about it."

"Fight with me about it?" I said. "I didn't even know there was a choice."

Cooper nodded. "Looking back, maybe I should've said something."

I gave him a look, like *Ya think?* "I didn't pick Pearce over you. I didn't know you were an option."

"I thought I shouldn't tell you what to do. That's what my dad always did to my mom. Told her what to wear, and who to be friends with. I didn't want to be like him. I wanted to be the opposite of him. I trained myself not to ask for things. I had a lot of regret after I thought I'd let you marry Pearce without ever telling you how I felt. I reevaluated how I'd been living my whole life—but too late."

"You didn't just not tell me how you felt," I said. "You didn't even tell me you were leaving."

"I was afraid even one objection from you would stop me. And so I just—left. It was the only solution I could come up with. I didn't even have a plan. I just figured I'd figure it out . . . but it didn't work. I left, moved far away, started over, made new friends, and dated people, too—thinking if I waited long enough, I'd forget all about you. But I didn't. I couldn't. I just . . . missed you. Even when I wasn't missing you, I was missing you. It was like grief—but it didn't get easier the way grief is supposed to. It was like there was a hole blown open in my chest that I could never close back up.

"But as bad as it was, I figured it had to be better than the alternative—which was watching you marry Pearce and build a life with him. Watching him get everything I wanted and take it all for granted. I told my mom not to tell me anything about your life, and for a while that worked. But I guess she didn't fully get the importance of that rule, because she forwarded me your wedding invitation—and that's how I found out you weren't already married."

"Cooper—*seriously*?"

"I was so enraged to see it—the real thing in my hands—that I went to a pub and drank and stared at it . . . and then stumbled to a postbox and drunk RSVPed."

"Hence, the boycott."

"Hence, the boycott. Humiliating—but I told myself *that settled that*, at least. But then . . . when I woke up the next day hungover, I had this terrible idea in my head. Maybe this was my chance for a do-over. And the more I thought about it, the more I thought about it—until suddenly I was on a plane. Crossing the ocean. Heading home to stop you. It was foolish and hopeless and way too late—but I did it anyway."

"I thought you were kidding about that, too."

"I have never been more dead serious in my life."

I took a slow breath.

Cooper went on. "When I saw you again in that church—it was all I could do not to throw you over my shoulder and carry you off like a Viking."

"You did wind up doing that," I pointed out.

"But after you'd made your choice."

"How gentlemanly."

Cooper continued, "My plan was actually to stand up and object. And then to make a speech about how I couldn't let you marry the wrong man—when I knew that I was the right one. I had a whole argument written out on an airsickness bag."

"That's romantic," I deadpanned.

"Isn't it?" Cooper deadpanned back.

"I can't believe you wrote a speech," I said.

"I can't believe you faked a faint," Cooper said.

"It was good to see you that day," I said.

"It was agony," Cooper said, "to see you."

"So you stopped my wedding—and then you went back to London."

"Sure, I mean—I'd called in sick to work and left the country."

"And then you came to Ashley's wedding, too."

"Yeah. I went back, regrouped, got a job offer in Austin, got a haircut, bought a few extra vests, and came here planning to do the exact same thing to you that you've been trying to do to Finn."

"Hold on. Have you been a double agent this whole time?"

Cooper shrugged. "Why do you think I asked your mom to make you room with Harmony?"

"My *mom* was in on this?"

Cooper nodded. "So was Ashley."

"No, no," I said. "Ashley was the architect of the whole thing with Finn."

"She was playing both sides of the field," Cooper said.

I shook my head. "Ashley was trying to set you up with Bridesmaid Two!"

But Cooper just raised his eyebrows, like *Why do you think she was doing that?*

I gasped. "Was *everybody* in on it?"

"Just the important folks."

"This is appalling!" I said then, feeling like I should be outraged. "How dare you!"

"It's no worse than what you were doing."

Fine. He had a point there.

I frowned. "Were you actively working against me? Was there *sabotage* involved?"

Cooper shook his head. "I just wanted to change your mind."

"About Finn?"

"About me."

"Cooper . . ." I said. "Why didn't you tell me?"

"I'm telling you right now."

"Why didn't you tell me *earlier*?"

"I guess," Cooper said, "it just took me a couple of decades to work up the courage."

But then I wasn't sure. "What is it that you're telling me right now, exactly?"

Cooper squared his shoulders and went on. "I'm telling you you're my favorite person on this overcrowded earth. I'm telling you that I've loved you my whole life long. I'm telling you I've had my own Operation Conquest going this whole time. And the person I was trying to conquer . . . was you."

WHAT ELSE COULD I possibly have done?

I grabbed him by the neck of that NO CRUISE CONTROL T-shirt and pulled him down into a kiss. And he kissed me right back. Like crazy.

Of course, minutes later, when we'd had just enough time to get thoroughly entangled in each other's arms . . . that's when the power came back, and the ballroom lights blared on—and lit up the two of us through the open doors like a spotlight.

And before we realized what was happening, the whole room full of wedding guests had turned to notice us snogging like teenagers—and erupted into cheers.

Cooper and I turned, still a little dazed, and took in the sight of them all: Ashley jumping up and down with her arms up in a victory V and Brody beside her, shaking his head. My mom and dad smiling and clapping, shoulder to shoulder. Pete and Bridesmaid Two . . . *nowhere to be found*. Plus the whole wedding party, and all our childhood neighbors and long-lost friends, together again, at least for a little while.

Somebody uncorked a bottle of champagne. The DJ fired up the turntables. The disco ball started spinning, sprinkling little stars of light all over the room.

And then Cooper pulled me out of the spotlight and into a moonlit corner at the ship's railing. Where we could have some privacy.

And then we kissed again like mad—breathless, and blissed-out, and lost in it all.

Like we'd been waiting all our lives to belong to each other.

It really did feel like destiny. And I guess Cooper must have felt it, too. Because right about the time I thought he might be about to suggest we make our way back home to our cabin to dispense, at last, with that useless pillow wall . . . Cooper tightened his arms around me, rested his forehead against mine, closed his eyes, and said, "Why don't you put us both out of our misery and just marry me?"

And . . . the moment screeched to a halt.

I froze.

And I coughed out a "What?!"

And then I stepped back.

His hair was all mussed, and his eyes were glassy, and his mouth was flushed. And he looked—let's face it—even more devastating than usual.

Heartbreaking, even.

"Did you just ask me to *marry* you?"

Cooper nodded.

"Cooper, we've been together for *five minutes*."

He nodded, like *Oh*. "Too soon?"

"Way too soon, man!"

He nodded. "That's fair. I retract that."

But now reality had broken through the fantasy, and reality was crashing back in.

What was I doing? What was I thinking? There was no way this could work. This was *me* we were talking about. I'd dumped every guy who'd ever tried to be with me. Just look at what I'd done to Brody! Not to mention the humiliation Pearce's mother had to face with her mah-jongg group. I was a fountain of misery! A love ruiner! A chronic dumper! I couldn't just *fall in love and be happy*. Who the hell did I think I was?

"We can't do this," I said, taking another step back.

"Can't do what?" Cooper asked, glancing around.

"I can't kiss you! What was I thinking? We can't kiss!"

"Too late."

"I take it back. Erase it from your mind."

I started to turn.

But Cooper stopped me. "Erase it? I'm not erasing it. How could I?"

"Figure it out."

"I don't want to! What are you talking about?"

"We can't—be together."

"Why the hell not?"

"Because—" How to sum it all up? "Because I'm terrible at love."

Now Cooper gave me a look like I was being adorable. "That's not news."

"This is not a joke, Cooper. Haven't you been paying attention? This"—I gestured between us—"is doomed. My entire love life is a catch-22. If you like me back, I won't want you anymore."

But Cooper shook his head and said, "Nah. We're good."

"Cooper—for real. I'm cursed."

"Are you being serious?"

I knocked on Cooper's forehead. "Haven't you been listening? We've been talking about this all week."

"But we were joking."

"*I* wasn't."

"You can't really think you are actually cursed."

"Sure, I can. Why not?"

"You're saying you can't kiss me because of *black magic*?"

"I'm saying I can't kiss you because I've dumped every guy I've ever dated!"

"But that was different. All those guys were different."

I shook my head. "Why?"

Cooper looked straight into my eyes. "Because none of those guys were me."

At those words, I could feel myself starting to lose this argument.

I mean, *come on*—right?

But I still had momentum. "You know what that is?" I demanded. "That's wishful thinking! Let's be practical."

"I am being practical."

"Not unless *practical* and *wrong* are the same thing."

I didn't want him to be wrong. I wanted him to be right.

But I'd known myself too long.

Cooper looked into my eyes, like *You've got this*. Then he said, "When Finn kissed you after all these years—and then you didn't like it, even though you thought he was your destiny . . . Why was that?"

Easy. Simple. "Because the only person I wanted to kiss was you."

"Guess what? The only person I want to do *anything* with is you."

"I don't want to break your heart," I said.

"I'm not scared of that," Cooper said. "You break my heart all the time."

But now I had tears in my eyes.

Cooper cupped his hand against my jaw. "Did you forget? I was your first kiss. I'm the guy you imprinted on. You're good to go."

"That's just a theory."

"Yeah," he said, his voice soft with affection. "A theory you planned a whole cockamamie scheme around."

"Okay—but I never really thought it would work!"

"This is going to work," Cooper said.

"Nothing has ever worked before. Not for me."

"This time it's different."

"Why?"

"Because . . ." Cooper said. "I'm your loophole."

I paused at that.

"Look," Cooper said, "I lied to you before when I said, 'I think I'm in love with you.'"

"You lied about that?"

"I don't think I'm in love with you. I *know*."

I took that in.

"I know," Cooper went on. "And I've always known."

He took a step closer.

"I'm your loophole," Cooper said, "because I've loved you all along."

I frowned.

Cooper had loved me all along.

"And the reason nothing ever worked for you with anybody else," Cooper said, "is because you've loved me all along, too."

I scanned back over all my Cooper memories. Cooper making me a tiny snowman. Cooper trying to teach me to drive stick shift. Cooper sleeping out in the backyard in a tent just because I wanted to. The two of us—over and over, my whole life long. Climbing up on the roof. Conking out on my bedroom floor. Sending each other new favorite songs.

"You've always known I loved you," Cooper said then, like he'd already won. "And you've always loved me back anyway."

I stared at him in astonishment.

Then he gave me a little wry smile, like he knew this terminology was wrong but he didn't care. "It's just algebraic topography," he said with a shrug. "Can't argue with math."

I thought about the duet we'd just sung at the reception—how I'd loved that song since I first heard it. Something about the harmonies, and the shape of the notes, and the twists and turns, and the way it made me feel . . . the way everything about it came together just *never got old.*

Maybe Cooper was like that song.

I could've tried a hundred more counterarguments. I could've explained that wanting a thing doesn't mean you can handle it. I could've quoted statistics and dire predictions. I could've insisted that humans are always our own worst enemies.

Not to mention: If we messed up this friendship, we'd never get another one this good as long as we lived.

But I didn't.

I didn't argue.

What can I say? I didn't want to.

I didn't argue when Cooper kissed me again. And I didn't argue when he took my hand to lead me back to our cabin. And I didn't argue when he threw all the pillows across the room and declared, "No walls allowed."

The only time I argued, in fact, was after he'd kissed me down onto the bed, when he reached back with one hand to grab his T-shirt by the collar and start working it off over his head, and I stopped him and told him we would definitely not be doing anything that might pop his stitches.

"I don't care about my stitches," Cooper said.

"I do."

"I'm fine."

"You're definitely not."

"The doc said I should stay off my feet."

"That is not what he meant."

"Are you saying we're going to finally tear down this ridiculous wall—and then we're just going to cuddle?"

I nodded.

"I feel like if I try hard enough, I can talk you into it," Cooper said.

"Knock yourself out, buddy," I said.

Nothing wrong with trying.

And that's how our friendship ended—and how the *everything else* it would turn into began. Except even then I had a feeling like there had never been two sides to us at all—like maybe the way we loved each other was an emotional Möbius strip. And we'd been endless all along.

Maybe I was wrong, and maybe I'd regret it.

Maybe I really was cursed.

But there was only one way to find out.

Because if anyone on earth could break a love curse for me, it was Cooper.

And maybe if you're going to take the biggest chance of your life—it should be with someone you already know by heart.

Epilogue

PETE AND BRIDESMAID Two didn't last, by the way. Let's get that out of the way right now. A force of nature like Pete can't be contained.

But guess who did last?

Grandma Dodie and her new friend, Edward. They've already signed up for another cruise. Together.

My parents lasted, too. Thank god. For my dad's sake, if no one else's.

My dad didn't take the promotion—in fact, he scaled back his hours—and he never talked about selling our house ever again. My mother took to showing him all her household bookkeeping, just to help him stop worrying, and it became a little joint hobby for them. They were never going to be Rockefellers, my mom loved to say, but they were just fine. I think my dad found it soothing. And my mom liked the way he gained a whole new appreciation for the household systems she'd been running all these years.

It was the most affectionate I'd ever seen them.

They weren't, like, chasing each other around the living room sofa like twenty-year-olds or anything.

They were just . . . content. Just peaceful. They signed up for a beginner Spanish class so they could plan a trip to Mexico City and see the pyramids. They built a raised vegetable garden and started researching heirloom varieties. They got matching pedometers and started taking walks in the evenings after supper.

I took on the job of trying to help my dad grow as a person—forcing him loudly at family dinners to take credit for sweet things he'd secretly done, and outing him over and over. "Dad filled up Mom's gas tank today," I'd announce to everybody. "Isn't that romantic?"

"What's romantic about gas?" Pete would ask.

"If I have to explain it to you," I'd say, "you don't deserve to know."

It embarrassed my dad beyond words to be praised like that, but I didn't stop.

"This is good for you," I'd say, slapping him on the shoulder. "It's only making you stronger."

The one thing I couldn't square with my new sense of my dad was his problem with names. It was really bothering me. It didn't fit. How could *anyone*—honestly—be so bad with names?

Guess what?

I googled it, and there's a real condition called nominal aphasia . . . where you can't remember names. My dad's not the kind of guy who'll ever go in for official testing on that. But just knowing that condition exists, and knowing that he fits all the diagnostic criteria—that's plenty for me. And I made sure this was front-page family news. It wasn't that our dad didn't care enough to remember our names. It was that he had a genuine, diagnosed-off-the-internet neurodivergence.

My dad thought it was all hooey, by the way.

But I thought it explained everything.

I regret how we saw him before. The working too much, the never taking credit, the forgetting names . . . we used it against him. We never questioned it. We never looked deeper for underlying patterns—or tried to understand why.

I'm sorry for all the time we wasted. I'm sorry we misjudged him. But I know that sometimes you can't solve the problem until you solve the problem.

* * *

MY PARENTS WEREN'T the only happily married couple in the family. The newlywed Cockburns were also doing well—and I'm happy to report that becoming literal relatives with me did help Brody work through his bitterness about me dumping him in high school.

Eventually.

Ashley and Brody bought a fixer-upper and decided to renovate it all by themselves—despite the fact that neither of them was particularly handy. The family got a betting pool going on how long it would take. My mother, ever the optimist, predicted three years, and my dad predicted five—but my money was on ten. Still, despite a brief mold problem from a plumbing leak, a possum infestation under the pier-and-beam living room, and a moment when they worried a door in the attic that kept slamming by itself might be a ghost, my sister and newest brother were moving forward on All Things Married with verve.

"You and Cooper should get engaged," Ashley kept pulling me aside to say. "Lock Cooper down before he comes to his senses."

"Noted," I'd say.

"How can you be so chill about this?" Ashley would demand.

"There's no rush to get engaged," I'd say.

And there really wasn't.

Because we were already engaged.

It turned out Cooper really hadn't been kidding about wanting to get married. One of the things he'd been doing on Bishop's Cay while I was wandering around looking for him was buying us rings. Not fancy rings, of course—tourist rings carved out of conch shells. Twenty-dollar rings. You might barely notice we have them on.

But we do have them on.

The night we got together, we stayed up until sunrise. And sometime around three AM we found ourselves sitting on Cooper's balcony, watching the moon over the ocean.

"Remember when you wanted to get married earlier?" I said.

"Of course."

"I might have overreacted a bit on that."

"Might have?"

"Says the man who once threw up a corn dog when he had to kiss me."

"I blame the corn dog."

"But," I went on, "I actually think it's a good idea."

"What is?"

"Getting married."

"You do?"

I met his eyes. "I do."

And at that, he was out of his deck chair and down on his knees in front of mine. "If I propose to you right now, will you say yes?"

I took in the sight of him like that, with the moon and the ocean behind him.

"Because if you're not joking," Cooper went on, "it's happening."

I could tell he was serious, and I could have backed off right then. I could have waved him away and laughed. I knew just from his expression that he was going to do it unless I stopped him.

So I didn't stop him.

Instead, very deliberately, looking into his eyes, I said, "I'm not joking."

And so he took the seaglass ring he'd once given me off my hand. And then we put new rings on each other. And then we got engaged—and started dating.

WHATEVER HAPPENED TO Pork Pie? Was he brought to justice?

Yeah—*no.*

We reported him . . . and nothing else ever came of it.

I hate to say it, and I'm sorry if this is news, but we live in a world where villains pull off a lot of villainry.

I wish it were different, but I don't know how to change it. All I know how to do is hang out with good people—keep on being as non-villainous as I can.

In the end, Pork Pie got to slash Cooper, and Cooper got . . . a scar.

A scar that he thinks is "cool" and that he loves to show off at the beach, but a scar all the same.

That's the truth. Pork Pie got away with it.

But Cooper got . . . me.

A willing, adoring, and wildly enthusiastic me. A me who's as heart-meltingly dedicated to Cooper's happiness as he is to mine.

In case you needed proof that it's better to be the good guy.

AND SO, IN the end, my problem set of love . . . got solved.

After I spent endless years working the puzzle, the pieces finally clicked into place.

It took me so long to see the pattern. The irrational series of interactions with Cooper that formed a continuous line: He had always loved me. And I had always loved him back.

Suddenly, now, in the wake of it all, I could see the elegance of it—the artistry under all the human chaos. Love turned out to be math, after all—complex, and hidden, and so hard to unearth, but there. Most of us never get fluent enough in the language of math to see its beauty. Maybe that's true of love, as well. But the beauty is there, all the same. Quietly there, and undiscovered—until it isn't.

Seeing all these deep patterns between Cooper and me probably made me a better person. But I know for sure it made me better at math.

After letting myself fall in love with him, for the first time in my life, I understood how love is not just an underlying structure holding our human universe together, but also a glimpse of something divine. Something awe-inspiring and infinite. Not the kind of infinite that's *out there far away*, like the stars, but the kind of infinite that's embedded in us—and between us. A pattern we follow, yes, but a pattern we also create. An emotional structure built out of the mathematical principles of who we are.

I think about how sculptors sometimes describe the chiseling process as discovering the art inside the marble. Or the poet who said, "Our real poems are already in us, and all we can do is dig." That's math, too: As much discovery as creation. Learning to see beauty that's already there.

It's life, and it's math, and it's art, and it's love—all different and the same, all chaos and patterns, all unknowable but known.

When I was first learning math, I had to visualize its concepts to find answers. But the more fluent I got, the more the answers became things I had to feel.

And isn't that what all the searching we do is for, in the end?

Not just to see our lives, but to feel them.

It was a conjecture I was happy to spend the rest of my life trying to prove: that the pattern of Cooper and me . . . would turn out to be infinite.

Acknowledgments

First of all, I need to thank my family—hubby, kids, and mom—for being hilarious and delightful, and talking through structure, and punching up comedy, and reading drafts of this story . . . but most of all for *taking an actual cruise* with me for research. I'm not sure it was on anybody's bucket list to spend Thanksgiving of 2019 chugging around the Gulf of Mexico on an ocean liner, but I begged them all to come with me, and—bless them—they did.

Up to that point, I had not been on a cruise ship since the age of thirteen—a ten-day cruise where I had my first kiss. Or second. Depending on how you define "first kiss."

A heck of a trip, for sure. And I've always wanted to write about it. And now here we are. Though this story bears almost no resemblance to the real trip my family took back then. Other than just the general cruise vibes.

And, yes: I did say 2019. This story was supposed to be the one I wrote during 2020. I had an outline, and I was well on my way to getting started writing . . . and then 2020 happened. I'm not sure if you remember 2020 at all, but it was not a great time for cruise ships. News story after news story highlighted whole ships felled by infections—from Covid to rotaviruses—culminating in an unforgettable moment in history when a passenger on the unfortunately nicknamed "Poop Cruise" got photographed holding a HELP sign up to his cabin window.

So I called my editor and said, "I think I can't write this story. Nobody's ever going to take another cruise."

She agreed, and so we tabled it.

I wrote *The Bodyguard* that year, instead.

And I'm so glad I did.

And then I wrote *Hello Stranger*, and *The Rom-Commers*, and *The Love Haters*.

I wasn't sure if I'd ever come back to this story, honestly. But then one day I went to Atlanta to speak at a library, and I wound up chatting with Bookstagrammer Ashlee Hunter, and I must have posted something about the story at some point, because she said, "When are you going to write your cruise ship book?"

And I was like, "I think maybe the pandemic killed it."

But she shook her head and said, "Cruise ships are back."

And that was that.

Before I knew it, this story was taking over my brain. It must've been just marinating in there for five-plus years, because when I actually sat down to start writing, I already knew these characters and this setting so well . . . and the whole story just *wrote itself.*

It's the most fun I've ever had writing a story.

So thank you, Ashlee!

And thank you to the legendary Judy Blume for being at her store, Books & Books in Key West, on the day our cruise ship docked there—and so graciously visiting with me and giving me a copy of *Are You There God? It's Me, Margaret.*

I also need to thank my friends Audrey Fersten, a devoted cruiser, for consulting with me on cruise life, and Cristi Connor for taking me for a ride in her open-top Jeep. Thanks to my real-life friends Tracy Pesikoff and Evelyn Cantorna for letting me borrow their last names.

Thanks also to my childhood neighborhood gang of kids in Afton Oaks—who I really did ride bikes and catch tadpoles and peel grapes to make eyeballs with—for providing inspiration for the neighbors in this story. Love you, Hamels, Segers, Tycers, Caughlins, and Tellepsens! I'm so grateful to for our fun childhood on Shetland Lane.

Honestly, everything about writing this story was easy for me . . . except for one thing: making JoJo a math person.

I'm *not* a math person. I struggled in math the whole way through school.

I never finished memorizing my multiplication tables. I applied early to Vassar College because there was no math requirement. When I applied to creative writing grad school, I filled in geometric designs on the math portion of the GRE.

But guess who is a math person?

My brilliant, mathy daughter—Anna.

My mom's a math person, too, actually.

I love math people! And I admire them. I wanted to make JoJo a math person, but I wasn't sure if I could write a character like her from the inside out, if that makes sense. But then my daughter kindly sat me down and talked to me about math in a way that an English major could understand. And she did such a fantastic job that I got it. I still can't *do* it. But she explained what math means to her so poetically that now I can see a version of it in my head that's almost like an invisible constellation.

Anna's dear friend John Moon Black, a mathematician, was a great resource to me writing this story—and inspired one of my favorite lines in the book (a thing Cooper says that starts with: "There is no universe . . ."). I also owe many thanks to Anna's mathematics professor at Carleton College, Claudio Gómez-Gonzáles, who introduced her to knot theory and inspired her real-life presentation on the mathematical principles of knitting knots (which I fully borrowed for JoJo). I also loved the book *The Mathematics of Love* by Hannah Fry, and I can heartily recommend these books about math from Anna's collection: *Math Art: Truth, Beauty, and Equations* by Stephen Ornes; *Do Not*

Erase: Mathematicians and Their Chalkboards by Jessica Wynne; and *Beautiful Symmetry: A Coloring Book About Math* by Alex Berke.

Before I go, let me thank my agent, Helen Breitweiser; my editor, Jen Enderlin; and all the good people at St. Martin's Press, Macmillan Audio, and Macmillan Speakers Bureau for everything they do year in and year out to help me connect with readers in ways big and small. Huge thanks, too, to Patti Murin for bringing this book (and so many of my others) to life so brilliantly on audio. I'm also massively grateful to the other writers, the booksellers, and the fantastic readers who help spread the word about my books.

Thank you. I'm so grateful to you.

You make it all possible—but more than that, you make it a joy.

About the Author

Chandra Wicke Photography

BookPage calls **Katherine Center** the "reigning queen of comfort reads." She's the *New York Times* bestselling author of thirteen novels, including *The Bodyguard*, *The Rom-Commers*, and *The Love Haters*. Katherine writes "deep rom-coms"—laugh-and-cry books about how life knocks us down, and how we get back up. The movie adaptation of Katherine's novel *The Lost Husband* hit #1 on Netflix, and *Happiness for Beginners* is a Netflix original movie starring Ellie Kemper. Katherine lives in her hometown of Houston, Texas, with her husband and their fluffy-but-fierce dog. Join her mailing list at KatherineCenter.com!